PRINCE OF THE ATLANTIC

- The War -

AN EPIC NOVEL BASED ON THE TRUE EXPLOITS OF
CAPTAIN LUKE RYAN
IRISH SWASHBUCKLER & AMERICAN PATRIOT
- BENJAMIN FRANKLIN'S MOST DANGEROUS PRIVATEER -

Mark M. McMillin

Hephaestus Publishing

PRINCE OF THE ATLANTIC
Based on the True Exploits of Captain Luke Ryan - A Trilogy
Book Two: *The War*

Copyright © Mark M. McMillin, 2000 - 2012; Original U.S. Copyright Office Registration Number/Date: TXu000909136/1999-06-10; Reform 2018

Author's website: www.PrivateerLukeRyan.com

ISBN-13: 978-0-9838179-6-3
ISBN-10 09838179-6-0

Hephaestus Publishing/www.hephaestuspublishing.com

Congress's Code of Conduct for American Privateers
IN CONGRESS,
WEDNESDAY, APRIL 3, 1776.

INSTRUCTIONS *to the* COMMANDERS *of Private Ships or Veſſels of War, which shall have commiſſins or Letters Of Marque and Repriſal, authoriſing them to make Captures of British Veſſels and Cargoes.*

I.

YOU may, by Force of Arms, attack, ſubdue, and take all Ships and other Veſſels belonging to the Inhabitants of Great Britain, on the High Seas, or between high-water and low-water Marks, except Ships and Veſſels bringing Perſons who intend to ſettle and reſide in the United Colonies, or bringing Arms, Ammunition or Warlike Stores to the ſaid Colonies, for the Uſe of ſuch Inhabitants thereof as are friends of the American Cauſe, which you ſhall ſuffer to paſs unmolested, the Commanders thereof permitting a peaceable Search, and giving ſatisfactory Information of the Contents of the Lading, and Deſtinations of the Voyages.

II.

You may, by Force of Arms, attack, ſubdue, and take all Ships and other Veſſels whatſorever carrying Soldiers, Arms, Gun powder, Ammunition, Proviſions, or any other contraband Goods, to any of the British Armies or Ships of War employed againſt theſe Colonies.

III.

You ſhall bring ſuch Ships and Veſſels as you ſhall take, with their Guns, Rigging, Tackle, Apparel, Furniture and Ladings; to ſome convenient Port or Ports of the United Colonies, that Proceedings may thereupon be had in due Form before the Courts which are or ſhall be here appointed to hear and determine Cau∫es civil and maritime.

IV.

Your or one of your Chief Officers ∫hall bring or ∫end the Ma∫ter and Pilot and one or more principal Per∫on or Per∫ons of the Company of every Ship or Ve∫∫el by you taken, as ∫oon after the Capture as may be, to the Judge or Judges of ∫uch Court as afore∫aid, to be examined upon Oath, and make An∫wer to the Interrogatories which many be propounded touching the Intere∫t or Property of the Ship or Ve∫∫el, and her Lading; and at the ∫ame Time you ∫hall deliver or cau∫e to be delivered to the Judge or Judges, all Pa∫∫es, Sea Briefs, Charter Parties, Bills of Lading, Cockets Letters, and other Documents and Writings found on board, proving the ∫aid Papers by the Affidavit of your∫elf, or of ∫ome other Per∫on pre∫ent at the Capture, to be produced as they were received, without Fraud, Additions, Subduction, or Embezzlement.

V.

You ∫hall keep and pre∫erve every Ship or Ve∫∫el and Cargo by you taken, until they ∫hall by Sentence of a Court of properly authori∫ied be adjudged lawful Prize, not ∫elling, ∫poiling, wa∫ting, or dimini∫hing the ∫ame or breaking the Bulk thereof, nor ∫uffereing any ∫uch Thing to be done.

VI.

If you, or any of your Officers or Crew ∫hall, in cold Blood, kill or maim, or, by Torture or otherwi∫e, cruelly, inhumanly, and contrary to common U∫age and the practice of civilized Nations in War, treat any Per∫on or Per∫ons ∫urpirzed in the Ship or Ve∫∫el you ∫hall take, the Offender ∫hall be ∫everly puni∫hed.

VII.

You shall, by all convenient opportunities, send to Congress written Accounts of the Captures you shall make, with the Number and Names of the Captives, Copies of your Journal from Time to Time, and Intelligence of what may occur or be discovered concerning the Designs of the Enemy, and the Destinations, Motions, and Operations of their Fleets and Armies.

VIII.

One Third, at the least, of your whole Company shall be Land Men.

IX.

You shall not ransome any Prisoners or Captives, but shall dispose of them in such Manner as the Congress, or if that be not fitting in the Colony whither they shall be brought, as the General Assembly, Convention, or Council or Committee of Safety of such Colony shall direct.

X.

You shall observe all such further Instructions as Congress shall hereafter give in the Premises, when you shall have notice thereof.

XI.

If you shall do any Thing contrary to these Instructions, or to others hereafter to be given, or willingly suffer such Thing to be done, you shall not only forfeit your Commission, and be liable to an Action for Breach of the Condition of your Bond, but be responible to the Party grieved for Damages sustained by such Mal-versation.

By Order of CONGRESS,
JOHN HANCOCK, *President.*

Table of Contents

Map of the British Isles 1772

Other Works by the Author:

Gather the Shadowmen (The Lords of the Ocean)
Napoleon's Gold
The Butcher's Daughter
Blood for Blood

Introduction

Prince of the Atlantic is one of three books (*Gather the Shadowmen (The Lords of the Ocean)* and *Napoleon's Gold* being the other two) based on the true, but little known exploits, of the extraordinary Captain Luke Ryan and his courageous Irishmen during the American War of Independence. While *Prince of the Atlantic* is technically the second book in the series, the books may be read in or out of sequence.

Our story begins in France where Ryan and his men are converting their swift smuggler into a well-armed warship after escaping from a Dublin jail. Fate has introduced the young outlaw to America's ambassador to France, the great Doctor Benjamin Franklin, and this unremarkable meeting will set into motion a series of events that will have a remarkable impact on the war that neither man could have predicted. Armed with an American commission and three powerful, very swift raiders, Ryan sets out against the British with a vengeance.

Roughly 55,000 seamen served aboard 1,700 American privateers during the war at one time or another and took or destroyed 2,283 enemy vessels (compared to the Continental navy, which took or destroyed 196 enemy ships). But no one man caused more damage to British maritime interests than this relatively unknown 25-year-old Irishman named Luke Ryan.

A quick note on style: this story is more about people and the extraordinary events that changed their lives than it is about the technical aspects of sailing a warship or of military tactics. Still, the author has attempted to balance matters by sprinkling enough nautical and military terms throughout the book for the sake of authenticity (for you enthusiasts of authenticity) against adding too much technical jargon that might otherwise bog the flow of the story down (for those who find technical *stuff* tedious). There is a simple Glossary in *Napoleon's Gold* to help the reader to at least distinguish port from starboard and bow from aft and, for the purists among you, at the end of each book there is a section entitled "Separating Fact from Fiction."

Please note that you will find certain grammatical errors, or what we would consider grammatical errors today, in much the correspondence but the material quoted is authentic (or, in the case of fictional letters, an imitation). Otherwise, any errors or mistakes in the book are mine.

Our story continues...

Prologue
The Tale Grows Bolder

he old man grunted. "Ah, the young Mr. Charles Crook, good to see you again," he said in his thick Irish brogue. The old man had shaved off his grey whiskers and looked younger.

Crook smiled, removed his coat and plopped down in a chair next to the fireplace. He held his hands close to the flames and rubbed the chill out of his fingers as the wood hissed and crackled.

"Good to see you again, Mr. Trevett. I wasn't sure you'd make it in this storm."

As before, John Trevett kept his coat on despite the warmth of the fire. Crook then noticed Trevett's eyes. He had somehow missed the magnetic pull of the old man's eyes during their last meeting in the dark. Trevett's eyes, bright blue and alert, had power.

"I've seen worse," offered Trevett with indifference. "Still, must be two foot of snow out there and some of 'em drifts - whew! How are yer fingers?"

"My fingers? Oh, yes, of course. They are fine thank you. I am used to writing for long stretches at a time. That's what newspapermen do. Much the same I suppose as you are used to tying knots over and over again in a cold wind."

"Ah, huh. Well, I see you brought yer writing things again with you - and yer purse. Yer a glutton for punishment to be sure."

"The other night you said you were about to ship-out soon again."

"Aye."

"What ship?"

"Oh, don't know yet. Thar are several to pick from. Harbor's still frozen over tho'. Might be a while yet. *Gawd* only knows why I'm here in Newport in winter. If I had any brains I'd be sittin' on the beach on one of them low latitude islands right now with a warm sun, a cool breeze and a bottle of rum in my hand. But I thought you wanted to know about the war?"

Crook meticulously set out his papers, pens and an ink jar on the table and nodded eagerly. "Indeed I do!"

Trevett smiled, raised his pewter tankard. "Well, thar servin' a fine turkey pot pie for supper and this here grog tastes especially mellow tonight. Good food, good, strong spirits - always puts me in the proper frame of mind. What in particular would you care to know?"

"Turkey pot pie it is then," Crook agreed and tossed a full purse on the table. "We left off with Ryan's escape from Dublin and his plan to seek Franklin's help. I want to know the rest, of course. I want to know everything. How did Ryan manage to get a commission from Franklin? When did he sail? Where did he sail and what battles did he fight? What treachery finally did him in?"

"Bless me. You have a lot of questions. So be it then. Aye. Let me think now. The Black Dog. The summer of '79. Dunkirk. The war..."

Like a quiet mist rolling in from the ocean on a still summer night, a calm spread across the small tavern. Sailors stopped their aimless banter and heads tilted towards Trevett, straining to catch his soft words. There was no denying the old mariner could weave a good tale...

One
Cruising the Oceans of the Great Mistress

France, June 1779

I t is with promises of glittering gold and everlasting glory that the god of war, that trickster, that gruesome scourge whose thirst for blood and gore is never sated, goads men on. He fills men's hearts with greed and violence, banishes any peacemaker. Each nation proclaims God as its mighty ally. Under rousing pageantry (to shore up faltering courage), fleets sail off and battalions march out to *Slaughter*. Red is the war god's color and the world is soon awash in blood, again, no end. Peace? Ha! Peace, friend, is but an illusion...

The roar of the sea seductively whispered his name, called to him, beckoned him to come and join her. The mariner had been away from her charms for too long. He quickly dressed, left his hotel room and hurried down to the docks on foot.

Swarms of sawyers, carpenters and finish carpenters, dubbers, planking gangs, ironsmiths, painters, rope, and sail specialists - Dunkirk's best and master craftsman all - had been crawling over every inch of the handsome, two-masted merchantman for several weeks, practically gutting her. Any wood, iron fitting or line showing the slightest wear and tear was replaced. And the ship's owner, a young Irishman with French roots, had not been shy about lavishing substantial sums of money on the refitting.

Carpenters had started their work by reinforcing the framework underneath the main deck with thick timber braces to support the new heavy guns, parked in neat rows along the wharf and waiting to be hoisted on board. And then they double planked over the bulwarks for extra strength using rare African Blackwood, hard wood to shape but strong. Square gun ports were cut into the wood and stocks were attached to the rails for the swivels. The ship's two great masts, and all her spars, had been removed and sold off as scrap and under the watchful eye of one of France's most promising young naval architects, a man who loved to make things go faster, the sawyers had traveled up into the far woods north of Dunkirk to cut down and debark a half dozen prime trees. After pickling the raw wood in the brine of a nearby tidal creek, the new masts and spars were transported by barge down to the dry dock and once the ship's crew had set the great sticks in place and raised the new spars and booms, the riggers went to work replacing all the stays, shrouds, halliards, lifts and braces. Then the sailmakers, using a tough, new linen material called Oznabrig, imported from Oznaburg, Germany, stitched together new sails and, on the owner's instructions, dyed the bright material in splotches charcoal gray and streaks of reddish brown before setting the sails to the spars.

And as the sailmakers and riggers busied themselves topside the carpenters went below. One team, using the latest in fireproof materials, went to work completing the construction of a powder magazine in the ship's belly to store the kegs of gunpowder that would be needed to feed the heavy guns. The others started planking over the ship's cargo holds to create more room to accommodate a larger crew. Even the captain's great cabin and the officers' quarters were partitioned-off into tiny cubbyholes to squeeze out every inch of usable space on board.

Satisfied with the progress and quality of the shipwrights' work, the mariner - and the *Black Prince's* true master - left the ship and braved a fine drizzle to go back into town. He needed to recruit more men.

Luke Ryan's own Irish veterans, grizzled, tough and loyal, men who had served with him during their smuggling days, were far too few in number to handle a warship on their own. With French press gangs scouring the taverns and whorehouses up and down the coast to satisfy the needs of the French navy, finding good, dependable sailors, even in a major seaport like Dunkirk, had become increasingly difficult for most ship captains. But Ryan knew he would have no trouble finding more men, mostly good, stout Irishmen too. Despite his youth, from Brest to Dunkirk, his reputation for shrewdness, luck, civility and generosity towards his men was well known. And with the lure of prize money, it did not take the mariner long to secure a crew of over 70 officers and men.

And while Ryan scoured the taverns, gambling dens and whorehouses along Dunkirk's rough waterfront, Patrick James Dowlin - in build and beauty a match for any of the deathless gods - cheerfully took charge overseeing the last touches to the ship, down to the smallest detail. The big, fiery Irishman had been with Ryan since the beginning and at getting the best out of both ship and crew there was none better than Dowlin. And when the conversion of the *Prince* from a smuggler to a warship was finally completed, her deck bristling with heavy cannon, Dowlin had four small rowboats brought on board and stacked two-by-two over the main hatch for, he told Ryan obliquely, some entertainment later.

After the men of the *Prince* stowed on board enough provisions for a three-month cruise, the principal owner, a Flemish businessman named John Torris, came aboard with 20,000 *livres* to pay the crew an advance against their share of any future prize money. This was the custom, the financial arrangement, common between an investor and his privateers.

It was a pretty, peaceful morning. The air was still delightfully crisp and fresh. Summer's hand had not yet touched the northern shores of

France. And on board the *Prince*, as she gently rocked back and forth against her moorings, all was calm.

Ryan and the two Kelly giants, Christopher and his brother John, were standing against the rail relaxing, waiting for the ship's two new American officers to arrive when Ryan spotted Dowlin marching down the wharf towards them with six new recruits in tow. Blustery winds racing down the Channel whipped the big Irishman's long mane of red hair into a wild, tangled mess.

As he led the new men across the gangplank, Dowlin looked up at Ryan and gave him a devilish grin. "Detail halt!" he ordered gruffly. "Right turn! Yer other *right* thar, Portuguese! Now stand fast lads."

With the new men stretched out across the main deck, all in a line, Dowlin made his way towards the stern with powerful, fluid strides. He was all muscle and grace.

The Kellys greeted him with smiles. Ryan somehow managed to keep a straight face.

Dowlin snapped crisply to attention, saluted. "Cap... Beg pardon, sir, I mean Mr. Ryan, sir, may I present to you our six newest enlistees?"

Ryan, happy to play the straight man in Dowlin's bit of theater, returned Dowlin's salute, trying hard not to grin. "Indeed you may, Lieutenant Dowlin. Please, proceed."

Dowlin, intent on making the right impression, led Ryan towards the *raw recruits*, wearing his sternest expression.

Ryan walked down the line, pausing briefly to look each man in the eye. They were a rag-tag lot. The men stared sheepishly back at him with grimy faces covered in soot. Clothing was soiled and tattered. None of them looked anything like a sailor and one was a mere boy.

Ryan returned to the center of the line and cleared his throat. "You new men," he began, speaking in the polished tones of an English gentleman, "welcome aboard. My name is Luke Ryan. I am the owner of this vessel, or one of them at least. If any of you are subjects of Great Britain I am compelled to tell you that you risk being charged with piracy and hanged if you are caught sailing with me. You others, if caught, would be made prisoners of war and the British don't treat American prisoners with much benevolence or charity, or so I hear."

He smiled softly and paused for a moment to consider, as was his way, each new face. "Of course," he continued, exchanging his English accent for an Irish brogue, "it is my intention, with a little luck, that none of you will ever see the inside of a British gaol. You're on board the *Black Prince*. She's an American warship, a raider, a *privateer*."

He paused again to let them absorb his words. And then he turned English once more. "Captain Marchant, who is expected to arrive shortly, is the master whom we serve. The *Prince* has been properly commissioned by his Excellency, Doctor Ben Franklin, the United States' Minister Penitentiary to the Court of Versailles. Each of you will be given the opportunity to inspect that commission to verify its authenticity for yourself. If you cannot read it, it shall be read to you. I also have in my cabin a copy of a proclamation dated April 3, 1776 issued by the American Congress. This proclamation authorizes privateers like the *Prince* and any man who wishes to read it is welcome to see me later. The proclamation, in conjunction with our commission, makes our actions at sea against British interests legal. Now, if we are successful, the crew will be paid from prize money, in shares according to each man's rank. How much is that to you? Well, that I cannot say yet. It all depends you see on how many ships we bring in and how much is fetched at auction. Chances are good tho' that you'll all make more with me than you would on most other ships, certainly more than you can in Dunkirk. I intend to keep our cruises short and you'll find the victuals on board wholesome and plentiful. As for discipline, well, Mr. Dowlin here shall explain the finer points to you later. Questions?"

Dowlin, standing behind Ryan, glared at the new men, daring any man to open his mouth. No one spoke.

"No?" Ryan asked gamely, still trying to suppress a smile. "No questions? Hm, I thought not. Well, gentlemen, it is an honor to serve with you. Mr. Dowlin, see to the care of these men - make me sailors, more important than spit and polish - teach them the warriors' code!"

Ryan turned to Dowlin, leaned close to his ear and whispered, "Not exactly a prime lot here, Pat".

"True, Luke, true. We're definitely scrapping the bottom of the barrel with this sorry lookin' bunch. With old King Louis's press gangs workin' the docks, scooping up poor souls for his own ships, thar's not much left for us to pick over. Damn sight better than nothin' tho'."

"Aye. Who's the boy?"

"Street urchin. I took pity on him when he came up to me beggin' for some scrap of bread. He's got no family, no home. I must be gettin' soft, didn't have the heart to turn him away. That coulda been me ten years or so ago. But you happened along and here I be..."

Ryan looked at the boy. "*Garcon*, what is your name?"

The boy shrugged.

"Your name lad?" he repeated in French.

"*Rue Rongeur...*"

"*Rue Rongeur?*" Ryan asked and turned to Dowlin. "Street Rat, or Street Rodent?"

Dowlin shrugged. "I've been called far worse."

Ryan looked back down at the boy. "Well now, lad, that name will never do on board a ship. Hm. Let me think on it a bit. Ha! I know. By the powers vested in me, under the international laws of the sea, I hereby promote you to Cook's Mate and name you: Jean Bart."

The boy recognized the name at once and beamed.

"You've got a good heart there, Patrick Dowlin," Ryan said, patting Dowlin on the shoulder. "Don't worry. It'll be just our dirty, little secret. Let's get these lads all cleaned up and fed, hey? Best start teaching the boy the King's English too..."

"Straight away, Luke!" Dowlin replied and gave Ryan a crisp salute.

Ryan nodded and cracked a smile. He knew Dowlin would keep things entertaining and their cruise, if nothing else, promised to be interesting...

"We ready to sail, Luke?" Dowlin asked.

"Not quite. Marchant and Arnold are the only loose ends..."

"Now how come that don't surprise me?" Dowlin offered with a chuckle.

Dowlin took the new men to the head pump where they were ordered to strip and given and bucket of warm water and soap and told to wash. Then each man was rinsed down with cold seawater. Dowlin led them, naked, down to the galley where they found fresh clothes and a hot meal waiting for them. He told them to relax and rest because soon, he explained, the long and tiresome drills at sea would begin...

As the sun began rising over the rooftops of the two and three-story redbrick buildings facing the waterfront, Ryan stood at the helm with his officers, waiting. They could not sail without Marchant.

"We'll lose the tide soon," the feisty, black-bearded Edward Macatter, a man who claimed to be from Boston but whose accent said County Cork, offered out loud to no one in particular.

"We have some time yet, Ed," Ryan replied flatly, but annoyed at the tardiness of the two Americans. "Why not assemble the lads for me. I had intended to say a few words to them prior to Capt'n Marchant's coming aboard anyway."

"Very well, sir. Mr. Weldin, have all hands called on deck."

Alexander Weldin saluted crisply and barked out orders to the petty officers, who in turn smartly formed up their divisions. Weldin was a soldier now. Dowlin had taught him well since their escape from Poolbeg.

Ryan, as was his custom, took a moment to take in the face of each man before speaking as they assembled on deck. His spine tingled. *God, how I love this so...*

He stood before them wearing a new, double-breasted jacket, a dark-gray piece with brass buttons, and a silk shirt, white, with ruffled cuffs that he had purchased just for the occasion. In place of his usual cravat, he wore a black bow tie and had traded in his French cocked hat for a gentleman's wide-brimmed fedora, complete with an ostrich feather.

He looked like money. He looked like a ship's owner.

"Thank you, Lieutenant Macatter." Ryan could feel the power in him rising. Only a few weeks before, he was nothing but a young Irish ruffian, a punk smuggler and fugitive from British law. Now he was the master of an American warship - and he was in his glory.

"Lads, good mornin' to you! Fine *Irish* weather we're having here today! Lovely day for a sail, hey? For you graybeards, 'tis good to see your ugly mugs again! Hope you didn't break the hearts of too many of France's daughters while on liberty!"

Ryan's Irishmen, his veterans, laughed. The new men fidgeted and looked nervously about. Serving a master with easy-going ways was something new. Ryan could see the confusion in their faces and gave them all a reassuring smile.

"For you new men, some of you I've spoken to already and some of you I haven't. Welcome aboard to all of you! I'm Luke Ryan and you're on the American raider *Black Prince*. Now, this ship is owned by multiple investors and I am one of them. Your captain is Stephan Marchant. Captain Marchant calls Boston, Massachusetts his home and our good captain and his first officer, Jonathan Arnold, also an American, are on their way and should be on board very soon. Now, I'm not going to make any speeches today -"

"Thank God," interrupted Christopher Hoar, one of Ryan's Irish veterans, one of the Shadowmen. "Thank God for small favors!"

The Irish veterans again broke out into fits of laughter and stomped their feet. A few of the new men, feeling more at ease now, joined them.

"Pipe down thar!" Dowlin ordered crossly, unamused.

Ryan gave Dowlin a nod, his smile vanished. "You new lads will learn soon enough from those who have sailed with me before what I expect from each of you. The important thing to bear in mind - always - is we serve a *ship-of-war*. We shall train and work towards that single purpose. This is no pleasure craft. We're American privateers so if your heart is with the British, well, you're on the wrong ship. While our duty to our country is to injure British interests, we're going to try and make some money for ourselves too. Once he is onboard, Captain Marchant will administer an oath of allegiance to each of you before we sail and read the terms of your enlistment. Any man who cannot take this oath in good conscience, or believes he cannot honor the terms of his enlistment, will be paid whatever is owed him and released before we sail - no questions asked. Mr. Dowlin, for those brave enough who decide to take the oath and sail with us, what follows?"

"What follows then, sir," he snarled, "is that thar hearts and balls belong to me..."

Ryan laughed and put his hands on his hips. "Ah, there you have it then, lads! Mr. Dowlin is not one to mince his words. Now, you are standing on the deck of the fastest ship in the Atlantic - I kid you not - and, in time, with proper training, my officers will turn you into the finest, fighting sailors anywhere. They are warriors tried and true and I implore you to trust them and learn well. With this ship and your training, we should be a match for any trouble that comes our way. We sail with the tide. We'll be out for several weeks - or several months - depending upon circumstances. I intend to do some damage to English property in English waters. Any questions?"

There were no questions. Ryan grinned and removed his pocket watch, the one he had given to himself when he had made lieutenant in the British navy, and popped open its gilt metal outer case, covered in dark shagreen, and noted the time.

"*Excellent!* Any of you lads care to join me for a hunt?"

His Irish veterans, hearts filled with joy, were the first to break out into wild cheers and shouts. The new men soon followed. Someone proposed a cheer and the men gave a rousing *huzzah, huzzah, huzzah!*

Ryan nodded back his thanks. "Mr. Macatter, you may dismiss the ship's company and, if you please, I'll have the ship made ready to sail, to catch the outgoing tide."

Macatter saluted crisply, started barking out orders when a carriage pulled up alongside the ship and disgorged two passengers. Ryan, to Dowlin's chagrin, gave the order to pipe Marchant aboard with all the military pomp and circumstance accorded to a captain of a warship. The boatswains' mate's shrill whistle twittered and the men of the American cruiser *Black Prince* quickly fell back into neat rank and file formation again and snapped to attention as the big, lumbering American strutted confidently across the gangplank.

Marchant, never more than the master of a small freighter until now, was unfamiliar with the grand, martial pageantry of a warship. But he was most impressed by the regal welcome and smiled broadly.

"Captain Marchant," Ryan called out in a friendly voice. "Welcome aboard, sir. May I present the ship's officers to you?"

"Indeed, sir," replied an ebullient Marchant, still basking in the pomp and circumstance of it all.

"Captain Marchant, although you have been introduced to these gentlemen socially, I would like to now, formally, present the officers of *Black Prince* to you. This gentleman, with the impressive black beard, is First Lieutenant Edward Macatter, your second officer. And here we have First Lieutenant Alexander Weldin, the ship's master. Mr. Patrick Dowlin, whom you've met on several occasions of course, holds the rank of Second Lieutenant. And that Goliath standing behind him is Second Lieutenant Christopher Kelly and next to him is his brother, Petty Officer and Master-At-Arms, John Kelly."

Marchant nodded and shook each man's hand in turn as Ryan introduced them. "Excellent. Gentlemen, I am delighted to make each of your acquaintances and I trust we all shall get along splendidly together. This is Mr. Jonathan, ah, I mean, Lieutenant Jonathan Arnold, *my* first officer."

"Beg pardon, sir," interrupted Macatter, still anxious to get underway. "I fear the tide and wind won't favor us much longer. May I give the order to take her out?"

Ryan nodded. "Quite so, Mr. Macatter, thank you. Captain Marchant, I see that your baggage has been brought aboard. First things first though. You must administer the oath to the men. Every hand must put his mark to the agreement after it is read. We don't want to give our enemies any reason to someday challenge the legality of our actions. Then we sail."

"But of course, Mr. Ryan," Marchant replied, hurriedly scanned the two documents Ryan handed him and grunted. He read the oath of allegiance first - his deep voice rumbling across the deck like rolling thunder - and no man could rightfully claim he had not heard Marchant's words.

"Raise your right hand and repeat after me: I, do," he began and then paused for the crew to repeat the words back to him in unison, "swear allegiance to the United States of America... and each of its thirteen member states... and vow that I owe no obedience to King George... and swear that I will, to the utmost of my power, support, maintain and defend... the said United States against the said King... and his heirs and successors and his and their abettors, assistants and adherents... *so help me God!*"

Every man gave his oath.

With the oath completed, Marchant, without any sense of urgency, focused on the second piece of paper, taking time to scan its contents for himself.

Ryan began pacing back and forth impatiently.

"Ahem. Very good, men. Now, I am required to read to you the terms of your engagement with this command. I will then have the oath, along with this contract I am about to read to you, posted to the mainmast. Every man must sign his name to both these documents before we sail. Ahem. Very well, pay attention. I'll only read this once. The contract reads as follows:

'ARTICLES OF AGREEMENT

Made and agreed upon between Captain Stephen Marchant, Commander of the privateer Black Prince, mounting sixteen carriage guns, and company.

Article I
The ship's owners shall provide sufficient arms, ammunition and provisions for a cruise extending not more than three months. In return, they shall receive one third of all prizes taken.

Article II
The captain must, to the best of his ability, carry out these instructions.

Article III
The officers and crew must report for duty when so ordered by the captain, they must perform their duties to the best of their

skill and ability.

Article IV
Rewards and Punishments
Any of the company losing an arm or leg in an engagement, or is otherwise disabled and unable to earn his bread, shall receive one thousand pounds from the first prize taken. Whoever first discovers a sail that proves to be a prize, shall receive one hundred pounds as a reward for his vigilance. Whoever enters an enemy ship after boarding orders are issued, shall receive three hundred pounds for his valor. Whoever is guilty of gaming or quarreling shall suffer such punishment as the captain and officers see fit. Any man, absent from the ship for twenty-four hours without leave, shall be guilty of disobedience, any man guilty of cowardice, mutiny, theft, pilfering, embezzlement, concealment of goods belonging to the ship or her company, striking or threatening any man or behaving indecently to a woman, shall lose his shares and receive such other punishment as the crime deserves and such forfeited shares shall be distributed to the remaining ship's company. Seven Dead Shares shall be set aside and divided by the captain and officers among those who behave best and do the most for the interest and service of the cruise. When a prize is taken and sent into port, the prize master and the men aboard are responsible for watching and unloading the prize, if any negligence results in damage, their shares will be held accountable. If the commander is disabled, the next highest officer will strictly comply with the rules, orders, restrictions and agreements between the owners of the privateer and the commander.

Shares shall be proportioned as follows:

Captain's Shares   8   *Steward's Shares*   2

First Lieutenant	4	Sailmaker	2
Second Lieutenant	4	Gunner's Mate	1 ½
Master	4	Boatswain's Mate	1 ½
Surgeon	4	Carpenter's Mate	1 ½
Lt. of Marines	2	Cooper	1 ½
Prize Master	2	Surgeon's Mate	1 ½
Carpenter	2	Armorer	2
Gunner	2	Sergeant-Marines	2
Boatswain	2	Cook	2
Master's Mate	2	Gentlemen Vols.	1
Captain's Clerk	2	Boys under 16	½

If any officer or any of the company be taken prisoner aboard a captured prize vessel, he shall receive a share in all prizes taken during the remainder of the privateer's cruise in the same manner as he would if actually aboard. However, he must obtain his liberty before the end of the cruise or make every effort to join the privateer, or else his prize money shall be forfeited to the owners and the ship's company. The captain shall have full power to displace any officer who may be found unfit for the post. The captain and his principal officers shall have the full power to appoint an agent for the ship's company. The captain, lieutenants, master, surgeon and officer of the marines shall not be entitled to any part of the Dead Shares.'"

Marchant paused to look up at the crew. "All right then, that's all of it. Any questions? No. Any objections to these terms? No? Very well, form a single line at the mainmast and sign your name or make your mark. If there any man here who does not so agree, stand forward and be recognized so you can collect your belongings and be released from any further obligations to this ship."

No man moved.

"No one? Very well then, carry on."

Ryan stopped pacing. "Captain Marchant, if you please, we should make haste. I don't want to lose the tide. We should depart, now. The ship is yours, sir..."

Marchant nodded, turned to look at Macatter. "Aye. Thank you, Mr. Ryan. Mr. Macatter, let loose her cables, bowlines first. Mr. Arnold, you have the first watch, take her out gingerly. I think tops'ls only until we clear the bay."

The young Arnold, an awkward, buck-toothed Yankee from Connecticut, looked nervously around. He understood his orders well enough but didn't know who to relay them to. The fool had never bothered to spend any time on board the ship to get to know her or her crew.

Kelly, tough like iron but softhearted too, and always looking out for seamen and officers alike, saw the confusion in Arnold's eyes and his hesitation to ask any questions. "I'll see to it for you, Mr. Arnold," he offered and bellowed out in his powerful voice: "you lads thar! First division, tops'ls only! Second division to the braces. You men at the prow, let go the cables. And you men thar, aye, you men standin' around dawdlin' - see to them stern lines! Go easy thar! I'll hang the hide of any tar from the masthead who scratches my ship against the dock..."

With cables cast off and her topsails set, *Black Prince* eased her way out of the harbor, negotiating the maze of ships lazily riding anchor. A flock of seagulls circling overhead formed an honor guard for the cutter, following her out of the bay for a ways until the she entered the wine-dark waters of a rolling sea where the Irishmen pointed their ship's nose west, towards England. The mysterious vessel, nearly all black, hull, masts and darkened sails, flew no flag even though she was well stocked with them. Tucked away inside her lockers were flags for America, Britain, France, Holland, Spain, Portugal and even Russia.

Like a wild stallion charging across an open field, free from any reins to hold back its great strength, the *Prince*, with all her canvas set, and a good flowing wind to push her - a parting gift from gentle East Wind - sliced through the rolling waves of the boundless sea with ease. Ryan tossed aside his new hat to feel the sea spray caress his face, to let the wind rustle through his hair, and then resumed his pacing back and forth while he kept a wary eye on the men, new and veterans alike, as they tended to their duties.

Pride filled his heart. It was a disciplined crew. And the *Prince*, decks straining with heavy cannon, a powerful sloop-of-war now, was still as fast as she ever was. And then, unexpectedly, her shining face came to him, a vision of his woman with the long, blond braids. She was smiling at him. How proud she would be of him now and how he wished Shannon could share this moment with him. He was where he was because of her. Exhilaration seized him and he caught himself, as Dowlin was fond of saying, riding the *Wave*. And while he was riding the *Wave* he could do no wrong. For a fleeting moment the world seemed a perfect place.

With clear skies overhead and a hard Channel wind to drive them, the men of the *Black Prince* sailed with high spirits. Dowlin, Weldin and Kelly busied themselves overseeing the work of the crew, paying particular attention to the new men. Arnold kept to himself near the helm while Captain Marchant retired to his cabin, for what reason he did not say.

"Mr. Dowlin, a moment of your time," Ryan called out, pointing to the rowboats. "I've been meanin' to ask you, why the boats sitting over the main hatch there? You afraid the English are going to sink us the first time out?"

Dowlin craned his neck around to look at the four white rowboats stacked neatly upside down, two-by-two, and lashed securely over the main grate. He turned and grinned at Ryan, like some schoolboy who had just pulled off a first-rate prank.

He removed his tri-corner hat and used a sleeve to wipe away the sweat from his brow. "Well, now, sir, I'll give you the long and the short of it. Them thar boats, once we get out to sea a-ways, will be sacrificed to old Poseidon. That is, of course, if my gunners can hit the bloody things and sink 'em durin' target practice. Otherwise, the sea will eventually claim 'em. Should be most entertainin' either way."

Ryan rubbed his chin and smiled. "Hm. I should have known. Very well. I shall enjoy watching that spectacle."

"Aye," Dowlin said smiling, rocking back and forth on his heels.

"So will I, so will I."

"You best save some of that shot and powder for the British my eager friend."

"No worries, Luke. I had extra stowed aboard for my own purposes..."

Separating Dover from Calais - and England from Europe - is a narrow stretch of sea, carved out by a great flood before the memory of men, known as the English Channel to the English, or *La Manche*, the sleeve, to the French. Every day the Calais-Dover ferries plied these waters carrying passengers and mail between England and France. Despite the war, France and England found it convenient to keep a line of communication open between them and these packet ships, as they were called, were free to come and go unmolested.

Ryan figured the British packets would be easy pickings and decided to try their luck there first. But Good Fortune, always keen to protect the Irishmen, intervened, preventing the good *Prince* from intercepting any packet ships. In the mist, the Irishmen missed them all.

The arming of the American cruiser *Prince*, her commissioning and hasty departure from Dunkirk, had not gone unnoticed by French intelligence. Its agents were everywhere and well informed. They were the best in the world. The service even knew of Ryan's plan to attack the Calais-Dover packets and had passed this information on to their chief, on to Count Antoine Raymond Jean Gaulbert Gabriel de Sartine, France's Minister of Marine, David Sartine's uncle.

The Minister was hardly pleased when he heard the news and promptly wrote to Franklin, politely asked Franklin to forbid the captain of the *Black Prince* from attacking any British packet ships. Such a *request*, coming from the powerful Minister of Marine, was equivalent to a command, one that Franklin dared not ignore. And so Franklin in turn had immediately sent off a warning to Marchant. But his letter failed to reach the *Prince* before she sailed.

That is when Good Fortune intervened, sparing the Irishmen from embarrassment and Franklin from a potentially disastrous diplomatic incident, an incident that would have put a quick end to Ryan's marauding ways. Though they did not know it, by missing the packets, the Irishmen had been lucky...

Ryan, Marchant and Macatter huddled close together near the helm and looked down on a small, rectangular wood chest bolted down to the deck. The chest was similar to a chest-of-drawers but held various sea charts and had a nifty folding table attached to it with brass hinges. Ryan unfolded the table and spread a chart of the English Channel across it. With no packet ships in sight, Ryan intended to sail further west, to sail into deeper, more dangerous waters.

Ryan needed no chart for the waters off northern France. He had sailed over these same waters many times before back when he was a smuggler. But now he asked for Marchant's assistance in determining the ship's position, course and speed, feigning ignorance to determine for himself the extent of Marchant's own.

As Marchant poured over the chart, young Tim Kelly, Christopher Kelly's son and perched high up in the ship's masthead, standing watch as lookout, was the first to spot a prize.

"*Sail ho!*" he cried out like a grizzled veteran, his hands cupped over his mouth. "*Starboard side, dead amidships!*"

The boy could hardly believe his good luck! Ryan had promised a gold piece - in addition to the award of 100 pounds under the Articles of Agreement - to the first man to spot a legal prize. Kelly, standing near the bow, looked up at his son and smiled proudly. Tim was born for the sea.

Startled, the three officers whipped their glasses out and searched the horizon until they found a ship exactly where young Tim had said. She was a fine looking merchantman, a brig, and Marchant gave the order for the helmsman to come about while Arnold sent the topmen aloft to let all the ship's canvas out, to give the *Prince* her speed.

But while Marchant was setting a course to intercept the target, Ryan and Macatter traded doubtful looks. Ryan cleared his throat and Macatter took the cue, he understood.

"Excuse me, Capt'n Marchant," interrupted Macatter.

"Yes, Mr. Macatter?"

"Beg pardon, sir, shall I give the order to clear the deck? Might need the guns. Might not. Hard tellin' until we get close up."

"Oh, ahem, yes, of course, by all means Mr. Macatter. See to it at once."

"Aye, sir," Macatter replied, turned and rolled his eyes. And then, like some broad shouldered bull, snorting threats, front leg pawing at the dirt, longing to charge, he strutted down the deck, bellowing out commands to ready the ship for action. And no man failed to heed his words, ringing with power as they did.

And while gunners opened gun ports and rolled out the heavy guns the *Prince*, her dark sails billowing full, overtook the brig with ease. Once the two ships were within hailing distance, Dowlin shouted over to the brig's crew and ordered them to shorten sail.

Not knowing the nationality or intentions of the sleek, black cutter bearing down on them, but seeing the raw power of her heavy cannon, crewed by men who seemed to know their work, the brig's master obeyed and heaved to. The two ships soon came to rest on the sea's gentle waves barely 100 yards apart.

Marchant sent Arnold and six men over in the ship's long boat with orders to inspect the brig's papers. Arnold was to check her ownership, registry and cargo.

It did not take Arnold long to return to the *Prince*, and with a smile on his face. "She's of Portuguese registry," he reported excitedly. "And she's bound for home, loaded down with finished goods made in England."

The men of the *Prince*, lined up against the rails to watch the brig, strained to hear what their officers were discussing up on the quarterdeck. Was the brig or was she not, they wondered, a prize? Portugal was a neutral country.

Marchant nodded. "English goods, you say?" he asked, absently stroking the stubble on his chin. "The vessel may be registered to neutral Portugal but her cargo sounds like contraband to me. Mr. Macatter, pick me a prize crew to sail the brig and her crew back to Dunkirk. You may have the honor, sail her back as prize master."

"Ahem," interrupted Ryan, unable to play the part of the passive observer any longer. "Forgive me Captain, but might it not be best to send the brig directly into Calais? 'Tis a bit closer. Let the French Admiralty Court there decide whether the brig is a legitimate prize or not. And sir, I suggest that someone other than Mr. Macatter take her in as prize master. He is your second officer after all and we may have need of his skills later. Why deprive yourself of a good officer so early on in our cruise? Calais is but 25 leagues off. A child could take her in from here."

Marchant gave Ryan a quizzical look and shrugged. He was not accustomed to having his orders challenged. *Ryan may prove meddlesome* he thought and grunted. *What does it matter who takes her in? But, no harm in indulging this young buck a bit.*

"Very well, Mr. Ryan. As you wish. Mr. Macatter, would you see to it then? Assign a prize master of your choosing. Run the brig into Calais."

Macatter, amused by the exchange between Ryan and Marchant, smiled to himself. He was beginning to suspect that Ryan would need all of his considerable charm and patience during their voyage to keep the American from making a fool of himself. He wouldn't bet against Ryan, but he wasn't sure whether even Ryan could save Marchant from Marchant.

Macatter touched the brim of his hat respectfully and quickly picked out a prize crew for the brig. Within the hour, men on the *Prince* were watching the Portuguese ship turn and head in towards Calais under half sail and spirits soared. There was talk of easy money ahead.

And Good Fortune did not desert the Irishmen either, or so it seemed. Later that afternoon the *Prince* intercepted a second vessel, an unarmed Danish brig, carrying lumber and bound for Dublin. One shot across her bow produced the desired effect. Her master, an enlightened man, gave the order to shorten sail and surrendered his ship without a fight.

Leery of reducing their own numbers even more to muster another prize crew so early in their cruise, and being so close to shore, the

Irishmen decided to simply tow the Danish brig in to Calais. Before nightfall the two ships entered Calais's small harbor where the Irishmen spotted their Portuguese prize and dropped anchor next to her.

In the morning, Ryan and Marchant went ashore to find the French Admiralty Court. The place was not hard to locate. Ryan filed two petitions with the clerk of the court, asking the court to condemn the Portuguese and Danish ships sitting in Calais's harbor, and their cargos too, as war prizes. For a small gratuity, the clerk agreed to add Ryan's petitions to the court's docket that very day.

Ryan and Marchant were waiting patiently in a hallway when the court *baillie* called their names just before noon. The *baillie* led the Americans into a small, dusty room where they saw a bored judge sitting at a crude table with Ryan's petitions in hand. The small room, serving as a temporary courtroom while the courthouse underwent renovations, was otherwise empty. Ryan and Marchant took seats on a front bench and watched the judge shuffle through their claims.

Without comment, the judge took his pen, dipped it in the ink jar and, using bold strokes, scribbled a brief notation across both petitions and then handed the papers back to the *Baillie*. The *baillie* in turn handed the papers over to Ryan, told him that the court was now in recess and that he and Marchant were free to go. Ryan stared down at the judge's decision, dumbfounded. The judge had dismissed the petitions outright and ordered the immediate release of both ships and their crews, holding that the seizures were illegal under maritime international law.

After Ryan shared the judge's decision with Marchant, the big American snorted and jumped to his feet. Red-faced, he started towards the judge and began loudly protesting the ruling. But Ryan, cool tactician, and blessed with more common sense than most, could see the hostility in the judge's eyes, grabbed Marchant by the arm, and forcibly hustled him out of the courtroom. No point, Ryan explained to Marchant outside in the hallway, in alienating an admiralty judge so early on in their new career, a judge whom they might need as a friend later someday.

Back on board the cutter, Ryan reconsidered their actions. He quickly realized that the judge had acted correctly. A French judge had no reason to condemn a war prize under French law in favor of an Irishman who claimed to be working for the Americans. Ryan suddenly felt very foolish. He knew very little about maritime law and knew nothing about the formalities of court. He had acted like an amateur. Next time, he told his officers, they would all keep their noses out of it and let Torris and his French agents handle any condemnation proceedings.

Before departing Calais, Ryan sent a letter off to Torris informing him of their false start, and then instructed Marchant to set out again with the next tide and head west, towards Dover. He had expected some grumbling from the crew about the loss of their two prizes. But he shouldn't have. His men took the news in stride and spirits remained high. The sea, after all, was teeming with hundreds of ships of all shapes and sizes.

Once the high cliffs of Dover came in view, the privateers swung south and turned again, heading southwest. The Irishmen sailed for hours on an empty sea, chased a huge, red sun until it sank beneath the waves, and then set the night watch as blackness closed in around them. And then, just as Ryan laid his head down on his pillow, Arnold, the officer of the watch, sounded the alarm. *A ship!*

Ryan raced up the companionway, stepped out into the cool night air and quickly spotted lanterns dancing on the water less than a league or so away. He could barely make out the dark silhouette of a ship, but it was there. Dowlin, dressed only in his nightshirt, fell in behind him and followed Ryan to the quarterdeck, hopping, barefoot, across the deck while he struggled to slip one trouser leg on.

"Ship off the port bow, sir," Arnold, reported excitedly and pointed to the other ship - as if Ryan might not know which direction port bow was. "She's a very large fish."

"This better be worth gettin' up for," Dowlin told Arnold coldly, with a look that said: *one more word from you and...* Dowlin had taken an instant dislike to both Marchant and Arnold. Two days at sea with the Americans had not improved his opinion any.

The poor Mr. Arnold did not quite grasp Dowlin's dislike of him, nor understand that Dowlin's dislike of him was irreversible. Arnold considered Dowlin's expression and decided it best to say no more, uncertain whether the fiery, red-haired Irishman's thinly veiled threat was serious or a just a poor joke.

Dowlin sensed the man's uncertainty but offered nothing to clear the air. *I'll let the dolt twist in the wind for a bit* he told himself, wondering if everyone from the land called Connecticut was a jackass like Arnold. He hoped not. It would be a shame to waste his talents on a country populated only by men like Marchant and Arnold.

"Should I order the men to the guns, Mr. Ryan?" Arnold asked with a silly grin.

"No, Mr. Arnold, I think not," Ryan answered in a quiet, sober voice.

Dowlin started grinning too, but for an altogether different reason. He knew that tone of voice well. Ryan was not pleased.

"See her flag there?" Ryan asked, pointing, for Arnold's benefit, to a large pennant flying off the other ship's driver boom. "She's a Dutch West Indiaman. Holland is a neutral country. But more importantly, if you'll take note, see there, along her bulwarks? She's carrying enough guns to blow us to kingdom come!"

Arnold's grin instantly vanished.

Ryan cupped his hands over his mouth. "Aboard there! What ship are you?"

"This ship is the *Njörðr*, we're Dutch and bound for Amsterdam," a faceless sailor replied nonchalantly in good English.

"We're off to Portsmouth ourselves," Ryan answered back and waved. "All is well?"

"All is well."

"Good night then and Godspeed to you, sir."

"And to you, English."

As the Dutchman pulled away, Ryan turned to face the unfortunate Mr. Arnold. "Mr. Arnold, *kindly* resume your previous heading and in the future, should you see any more ships, I suggest you determine whether she has more guns than we do before you maneuver us towards her with hostile intent."

Dowlin cringed at the *word*. Ryan always used the word *kindly* as a warning, used it sparingly when his blood was at the boil.

"Aye, sir, very well," the buck-toothed Arnold answered with his foolish grin again, oblivious to Ryan's rebuke.

"I take it, Captain Marchant is still sleeping?" asked Ryan.

"Suppose so, sir, he sleeps like the dead, he does. Should I send a hand to fetch him for you, sir?"

Ryan glanced sideways over at Dowlin. "No. No. That will not be necessary, Mr. Arnold. Best not to disturb the dead when no good will come of it. Let him sleep."

Dowlin shook his head in disgust. "Not much of interest goin' on here," he said and yawned. "Suppose I'll turn in for the evening, again. Good night, Mr. Ryan."

"I think I'll remain on deck for a bit, take in the fresh air. Good night to you as well, Mr. Dowlin."

"Good night, Mr. Dowlin," Arnold called after the big Irishman as he stepped down the companionway - a peace offering.

Dowlin turned and answered Arnold with the same hostile glare as before. And Arnold knew enough, at least, to stop grinning.

For the next several days, the privateers found little but empty sea with only an occasional neutral ship here and there to wave at. Frustrated, Ryan had Marchant head north to try their luck closer in to the English coast and, on the very next morning, just as the cutter rounded Denge Ness and men began to pour into the galley for a leisurely breakfast, the lookout cried out his shrill warning.

"Where away?" Macatter shouted up to the masthead.

The lookout pointed out over the port bow and Macatter was just barely able to make out the top of a mast and furled topgallant sail. And then he saw the furled topgallants of a second ship and then of a third...

Ryan was eating breakfast with Marchant in Marchant's small cabin when the ship's bell suddenly started ringing, the alarm to clear the deck for action. He bolted from the table and scrambled up the companionway with Marchant clumsily chasing after him.

Dowlin, already at the helm, greeted Ryan with a smile and sniffed the air. "Smells like dead fish," he said coldly. "Aye, no mistakin' that smell. We must be near England, Luke."

"Why the fuss?"

Macatter handed his spyglass over to Ryan. "Look over thar, sir!" he said excitedly and pointed. "Six fat little piglets just sittin' in the water waitin' to be led to slaughter."

As Ryan scanned the waters with Macatter's glass, the corners of his mouth curled into a slight grin. *Glory be! We've struck gold!*

Macatter was right. Six British merchantmen were riding anchor in a small bay with a faint, thumbnail sliver of moon sitting over them and not one armed escort to protect them. The crescent moon, waning with the morning, was a good omen thought Ryan. He suddenly felt the warm rush of adrenaline. *An ideal tactical situation. Excellent. Go and finish your breakfast my fine English friends. Pay our little ship charging towards you no mind...*

"I want as much canvas as she'll take hung out, Mr. Macatter!" Ryan ordered eagerly, ignoring both Marchant and Arnold. "Every stitch I say! No need to hold her back now."

"Aye, sir!" Macatter roared back, every bit as eager as Ryan to get into a brawl. "You topmen! Shake a leg there! Full sail, every square inch of it! I'll have the stuns'l booms run out too and set the studding sails! Look lively now! Let her fly!"

Kelly and his men scrambled up into the cutter's two great raked masts, slid out over the yardarms along the foot stirrups and began letting out as much canvas as the spars could hold. With outstretched wings, and a good flowing wind abeam, the cutter sliced her way through the waves with exhilarating speed.

Ryan knew English lookouts would see soon enough the unfamiliar vessel bearing down on them under full sail - a provocative move that any prudent captain would think hostile. Still, the English might hesitate just long enough, might be caught off-guard by the terrific pace of the sleek, black cutter, giving the Irishmen just enough time to close. Ryan's plan was simple. Nothing fancy was needed. Charge in headfirst.

The commander of the small English fleet was no slouch. When he saw the handsome, black cutter racing towards them under full sail, blue water bubbling up around her sharp, curved bow, and flying no flag, he instantly decided not to tarry and signaled his ships to flee for the open sea in haste.

"*By God!*" Macatter exclaimed gleefully, watching the slow, cumbersome merchantmen getting under way and laughed. "Luke, look - they want to make a race of it! They're in a hurry too. They've gone and cut thar cables!"

With spyglass in hand, Dowlin climbed half way up the ratlines to mainmast to get a better view. "I see five good size brigs and a worthless dogger," he called down excitedly, the wind toying with his long, red hair. "Oh, ho! Macatter's little piglets have stingers. Thar armed, gents. Looks like the brigs are carryin' four guns apiece. Two or three-pounders by the look of it. Nothin' larger. They're goin' to make some sport of it sure enough and are headin' north! Leave it to an Englishman to go the wrong way! Ah, ha! *The wind's with us lads!*"

With the wind in her favor, the *Prince* closed with its prey at lightning speed. The privateers easily overtook the small, slow dogger first, punching through the water like some dumb, fat, cow. But Ryan advised Marchant to ignore her. They were after richer prizes.

As the *Prince* passed the dogger by, the Irishmen lined themselves up against the rails, smiled down at her crew and waved. The Englishmen answered the Irishmen with open mouths and stunned faces.

"Don't be insulted!" cried out Hoar, standing out on the bowsprit. "We'll be back for yer little guppy later! Be patient."

The five English brigs, a league or two ahead, were well under way now but slow. Even with canvas stretched taut across every boom and spar, the ships in the small merchant fleet were rapidly losing distance to their pursuer. The cutter's speed was shocking.

Ryan watched the fleeing ships through his spyglass and smiled as they continued sailing in formation. Foolish he thought. *Better to scatter and lose one or two ships and save the rest.*

"Look thar!" Macatter gleefully shouted over to Ryan. "They're turnin', sir. Breakin' for shore towards that bay beyond 'em chalk cliffs! Seems a might reckless. We'll have the bloody buggers trapped in thar."

Marchant gave the order for the helmsman to port his helm to follow the fleet into the bay. But then the *voice*, always gentle and never wrong, began whispering in Ryan's ear and urged caution. Ryan quickly grabbed a chart, unrolled it across the chart table, and began studying it carefully. The fleet's turn into the bay made no sense to him.

"They're making for Beachy Head or Eastbourne," Ryan said out loud to no one in particular. He absently tapped out a random cadence with his right shoe against the deck as he scrutinized the chart. "Curious. Seems a foolish thing to do..."

"I know that look, Luke, what's troublin' you?" Dowlin asked. "We've got 'em corned, we've got 'em dead to rights."

"Captain Marchant," Ryan said, ignoring Dowlin for the moment. "I'm uneasy about sailing into that bay. This is all rather odd. Something is amiss."

"Mr. Ryan, I see easy prize money ahead of us," Marchant replied simply.

"Put a good man in the chains with the lead, sir?" Dowlin asked, assuming Ryan was just nervous about heading into shallow water.

"Aye," replied Ryan cautiously. "Make it so and send a second pair of eyes up to the masthead, Mr. Dowlin."

Dowlin moved out smartly to do Ryan's bidding. He sent Hoar out onto the chains, the man had a strong arm, and sent young Tim up the ratlines to take the masthead. Tim had the best eyes of any man on board.

Coiled over Hoar's shoulder, as he stepped over the rail, was a length of rope, knotted at one-fathom intervals and weighted at the end. A ship always risked running aground when nearing land in unfamiliar waters and the only way to know for certain how much water was underneath her keel was to measure it with a rope.

Hoar sat himself down inside the chains of the mainmast with his feet dangling over the channel and cast the lead line out as far ahead of the ship as he could, as if he was fishing, and pulled the line back in as the ship passed by. He began counting the number of knots and chanted out the soundings.

"By the mark eight... And a half nine... By the deep ten..."

The cutter could safely negotiate waters as shallow as three fathoms, no less. Running aground on English soil meant surrender and disgrace.

As Hoar kept track of the water's depth, the American privateer rounded a small headland and entered a bay in hot pursuit of her quarry, oblivious to any danger. Then, puffs of smoke, like cotton balls floating on air, magically appeared over a hill, followed seconds later by the crack of heavy cannon.

BOOM! BOOM! BOOM!

"What in blazes?" Marchant blurted out, stunned. "My *God*, we're being fired on!"

"Well now, Capt'n," Dowlin asked calmly, amused, "you didn't think we was goin' on a picnic now did ya?"

Marchant ignored the obnoxious Irishman and kept his eyes fixed on the shore batteries. The big Irishman was becoming more insubordinate with each new day. *Too cocky by half that one.*

Plumes of white water shot up several hundred yards in front of the cutter. The *Prince* was still well out of range. The British gunners were sending the privateer a message: *turn tail and run or come dance - a death dance - whatever warms your heart.*

Ryan poured over the chart again, muttering a curse under his breath. How could he have missed the fort? *The mistake of an inexperienced midshipman, an amateur - or a fool.*

But he was being unduly harsh with himself. The fort was not depicted anywhere on the chart and the chart was new. He had made no mistake. The English must have only recently placed their batteries on the bluffs overlooking the bay.

Hoar continued with his chanting. *Six fathoms... Five fathoms... Four fathoms...*

And then the crew heard Tim cry out: "*Sail ho! Yer port stern. Many sails!*"

Every man - save Ryan - snapped his head around to see the new ships. Ryan hardly needed to look. With an enemy fort in front of them and ships, maybe warships, maybe not, but certainly British, behind them and with the water under their keel quickly disappearing, he did not like the tactical situation, not one bit. *This is a fine mess I've gotten us into. Easy lad. Think it through. No good will come from panic.*

They needed to get back out into the open sea. They needed room to maneuver, room to cut away and run or to regroup and renew their assault if they had the odds - and the weather gauge. Either way, they needed time to sort things out and Ryan wasn't about to wait for Marchant. Not for one moment would he wait on that slow-wit.

"You there helmsman, look sharp now!" he called out roughly. "Be prepared to bring her around, hard over to our starboard! Lieutenant Kelly! Man your braces there - we're comin' about! No time to dawdle. And once we're through our turn, squeeze every knot you can get out of her. Set the yards well. We need speed. Every bit you can muster I say!"

The hulking giant bellowed out orders to his topmen. And like some charioteer holding on to the reins of a team of wild horses, Kelly, his feet planted firmly on the deck, took hold of two of the lines himself with his great, brawny arms and leaned back to help trim the mainsail. He saw the concern in Ryan's eyes. Something had spooked Ryan and Ryan, Kelly knew, was not a man who spooked easily.

"Now helmsman, hard to starboard!" Ryan ordered.

The helmsman pulled hard on the tiller, brought it over as far as it would go and held it there with all his might. Kelly barked out fresh orders to his topmen to match the helmsman's turn and the ship came around sharply with her starboard rail dipping low, nearly touching water. Caught off-guard by the violent, sudden turn, men lost their footing and went tumbling.

"We're goin' to turn and run?" asked Arnold. "What about our prizes?"

Ryan and Dowlin both ignored Arnold's stupidity. Even Marchant shook his head in disbelief at his own man.

But Macatter felt some pity for the inexperienced American and saw no harm in explaining things. "Thar's no money in it for us trading shots with a fort, lad. Or in runnin' aground on enemy shores."

"No, no, of course not, Mr. Macatter," Arnold answered awkwardly.

After the *Black Prince* completed her 180-degree turn, she sailed out of the small bay as quickly as she had sailed into it. And none too soon.

Dowlin had scrambled up the mainmast himself to get a better look at things and now reported seeing a number of coasters in tight formation - with five heavily armed British schooners circling around the herd to provide protection. Then the schooner closest to the *Prince* took an interest in her, suddenly peeled off from the convoy and sailed straight for the privateers.

Had the Irishmen tarried in the bay just a little bit longer, debating among themselves which way seemed best, they would have been cut off from their safe haven, the sea. Ryan's quick wits had saved them all from certain disaster.

But they were not clear yet. The British schooner, some ways off yet but coming on fast, fired a warning shot across *Prince's* bow. A small geyser of water shot up into the air less than 100 yards away. One lucky shot, one disabled mast, and the Irishmen were finished.

Ryan advised Marchant to ignore the schooner. Make for open sea, their good ally. That was the plan that seemed best to him. *Fly good Prince. Fly now! All speed!*

The hunter was now being hunted. The king's ship was fast too - but she was not fast enough. Clear of the bay, the *Prince's* dark sails caught a fresh sea wind, held the gift jealously to her bosom, and quickly managed to put more and more water between herself and her pursuer. But then, just as the crew let out a collective sigh of relief and the race seemed all but over - disaster...

How the fearsome god of war, shameless, capricious in his ways, loves to switch allegiances in the struggles of mortal men for no better reason than to suit his own amusement. One day he favors some champion, showers the warrior with triumph, only to send the poor fool plunging headlong down to the House of Death the very next to hand some upstart a taste of glory. And so it goes, around and around without end, and it is we mortals who must pay the awful price for the god's twisted pleasures.

A hideous crack, like the snap of a man's bone, a sickening sound, reverberated through the ship. Every man heard it. looked up at the mainmast with no joy in his eyes.

For no good earthly reason, except, perhaps, for the evil luck that plagues all mariners from time to time, the topmast irons suddenly gave way. The main topsail spar fell halfway down the mast before entangling itself in a mass of rigging, caught like a fly in a web. An awful mess. The *Prince* lost her precious speed.

The king's vessel, looming in the distance, but with no split topmast irons to slow her down, now quickly began closing the distance with the crippled cutter. Her captain and crew, elated by their luck, and smelling blood, drove their ship hard on.

Dowlin jumped back down on deck and stood, rock solid, at Ryan's side, waiting for his orders. He had no worries. *Luke will know what to do.*

Ryan clasped his hands firmly behind his back and silently watched the British schooner's graceful charge at them, unfazed. If their change in fortunes had rattled him any - he wasn't showing it.

"Looks like they're fixin' to have a round with us, Luke," Dowlin finally offered, trying to get a fix on Ryan's thoughts.

Ryan removed his hat, ran his fingers through his wind-blown hair, sweeping the black waves off his brow, and winked at Dowlin. "Aye, Patrick. Appears we'll soon see if your gun crews learned anything from all those drills of yours."

Dowlin grinned. Those were the words he longed to hear. He could feel his warrior's blood begin to stir. "I shouldn't worry about that, Luke!" he promised, as cocky as ever. "Why 'tis those feeble-minded Englishmen overhaulin' us who should worry. They'll soon be pissin' in thar pants - I swear it!"

Ryan offered no reply. He quietly hoped Dowlin was right.

Marchant, no slouch this time around, overheard Ryan's fighting words and ordered the ship cleared for action. Dowlin took command of the starboard batteries, Weldin took the portside batteries. Men scrambled to bring up the thirty swivels from the storage bunkers below and soon were mounting them to the rails. They unloosed the lashings around the crates - used to hide away the cutter's 16 four-pounders - and removed them, but left the gun ports closed. The *Prince* bristled with deadly iron now.

Smelling easy prize money, the king's captain plunged his ship headlong at the mysterious black cutter.

Marchant gave the order to fire the cutter's two stern chasers. Ryan thought it a waste of shot and powder but didn't want to keep too tight a leash on Marchant lest he offend the man and lose his American captain - along with Franklin's commission too - and so held his peace. The two light guns fired away with no effect, except to sooth Marchant's own raw nerves.

And when the two ships drew close enough, Marchant ordered Dowlin to roll out the *Prince's* guns. But Dowlin hesitated and looked to Ryan for his orders.

"Ahem, Captain Marchant, sir," Ryan said politely. "Beg pardon, a good command - but you may wish to belay that order, just for a moment. You see the king's ship?"

"Aye," Marchant said, looking over at the British ship, now less than 1,000 yards away. "Of course I do."

"Well, I can see her guns. Can you?"

"Of course. They're all run out. I count, ah, twelve small carriage guns and a total of eight swivels. No bow or stern guns."

"Just so, Captain. You're quite right. Except for our swivels, she doesn't know our strength yet and our swivels will not concern her master any unless we close to within two hundred and fifty yards or less. And for some odd reason her lookouts have climbed down from the masthead. Maybe your stern guns scared them down. A piece of luck for us. If she knew what else we had, I doubt her capt'n would be so reckless in his approach. Her twelve three-pounders to our sixteen four-pounders. Not bad odds wouldn't you agree? She should stand off a bit to get a gauge of our muscle before taking us head on. Her master's rash, seems to think we're just an ignorant gang of pirates. Why not let her come abreast of us and then run the guns out? Give her a bit of a surprise, if you catch my meaning. She'll feel our sting soon enough."

"Aye! I see. May I say, clever work indeed, Mr. Ryan."

When the king's heavy schooner drew close enough, her gunners poured several broadsides into the sleek, black cutter and the English were fair marksmen too. Shot after shot hit the *Prince* square. But the small caliber balls caused no real damage against her heavy, ironbark planks, layered over with tough, African Blackwood by skilled master craftsmen. The schooner's shots ricocheted off *Prince's* hull. More deadly iron flew overhead but splashed into the waves beyond, leaving behind harmless plumes of white spray. The British maneuvered their schooner closer still to give their solid shot more punch. They came in on black cutter's starboard side where Dowlin stood waiting. And when the ships were close enough, the crews began hurtling taunts and insults across the waves at one another.

Marchant looked anxiously over at Ryan. He had never been shot at before.

Ryan offered him a reassuring smile - and then the nod - and that was all the anxious American needed.

"Mr. Dowlin, sir, you may roll out your guns!"

With a gleam in his eye, Dowlin barked out orders to his gun crews and men jumped smartly. They cast-off the lashings securing the guns against the bulwarks first, then pulled on the training tackle to haul the 1200-pound monsters backwards. Gunners removed the tampions from the muzzles and raised the gun ports while the ammo bearers scurried below to bring up more shot and powder from the storage lockers, then stacked the powder cartridges carefully on the windward side of each gun. The gun captains lit their linstocks next, holding them, always, to the leeward side of their guns. And after each gun had been primed and loaded, the deck vibrated underneath the weight of the heavy bronze as men pushed the noses of their guns out through the gun ports.

Dowlin watched his men with grudging admiration. Each man had accomplished his task flawlessly. Dowlin had spent long, tedious hours training them, practicing hard for this very day. And then he felt the terrible power welling up inside him, the power of death. The sensation was intoxicating, addictive. He was not, he knew, a malevolent man but he was a warrior through and through and felt no shame for who he was. The prospect of combat, inexplicably, had always stirred his blood and killing those who needed killing had never troubled him.

"All right lads," Dowlin cried out. "I keep hearin' what big, bad Irishmen you are - now is yer chance to show me - better yet, show 'em English shits what yer made of! Make yer mothers proud!" Then he roared with ugly laughter. "Ha! Ha! Ha! If any of you sorry slackers even have any mothers! Take your aim now! Watch yer linstocks. Steady. Wait. Wait for it; wait for my command... Ready... Almost... *FIRE!*"

Cannon thundered.

BOOM... BOOM! BA-BA-BOOM! BOOM! BOOM!

The deck shook.

"Stop yer vents now!" Dowlin bellowed. "Roll 'em in lads. Reload. That's the way! Move! Move! Move!"

The gun crews rushed to pull in their guns. First the swabbers took their sponges and swabbed the muzzles down to extinguish any burning powder residue while each loader calmly slit open a paper cartridge, poured the black powder down the muzzle of his gun, folded the paper into a wad and rammed the charge home with his flexible rammer. Then the ammo bearers, having returned from the ammo lockers with two or three shots in hand, the roundest ones they could find, rammed one shot down on the loader's paper wad as the gun captains ripped open a second cartridge to prime the his gun's breech.

With all the guns primed and loaded, the crews, working as one mind, ran their guns out again in near faultless harmony. Each gun captain took his iron handspike, eased his gun's muzzle around until the aim was true, and then waited for the order to fire.

Dowlin squinted, looking through the smoke to see whether his guns had wrecked any damage on the enemy vessel. "Not a scratch on her, damn my soul!" he shouted over to Ryan with a look of disappointment.

Ryan scanned the vessel with his spyglass and turned to Marchant. "If only we had something heavier, nine-pounders or better, that ship would be on her way to the bottom this very moment."

"What'll we do now then?" Marchant asked with a hint of a sneer, suddenly feeling worn and very tired. "Try and run again?"

"With only four-pounders to work with, Capt'n Marchant," Ryan replied callously, ignoring Marchant's reluctance to fight, "we'll simply have to work harder at it. That's all."

"Mr. Dowlin," Ryan shouted down the deck, "another round if you please - and you may fire at will after that."

"Aye, sir - wish I had a nine-pounder or two!" Dowlin shouted back, his thoughts matching Ryan's own, and turned his attention back to his gun crews. "Take yer aim, lads! Steady now! Watch for the swell. As yer guns bear... Make ready... *FIRE!*"

As each gun captain caressed his slow match against his gun's touchhole, the guns erupted in rapid succession: *BOOM! BOOM! BOOM! BA-BA-BA-BOOM!* Fire, smoke, and crackling thunder. The guns recoiled backwards, caught from running amuck by breeching rope and tackle, as clouds of acrid fumes blew back into the sweaty faces of the men.

"Stop your vents thar!" Dowlin growled. "Alrighty then. Yer free to fire at will, lads! Aim low now! As yer guns bear. Send 'em bloody bastards to hell!"

The Irishmen worked their barrels of death like seasoned veterans. British gunners did the same and the two ships sailed side-by-side trading shots. But neither ship did much damage to the other. With the *Prince's* topsail gone, Ryan could not employ any fancy maneuvers and the master of the British warship, with his convoy nearly out of sight, seemed content to simply sail toe-to-toe with the cutter and slug it out under a broiling sun.

But after an hour or two had passed, the superior skills of Dowlin's gunners began to show. His men were relentless, worked their guns like demons. More than one British gunner had fallen, killed or wounded. And then one of the heavy schooner's guns fell silent, followed quickly by a another. British jeers and taunts stopped too, replaced by the pitiful cries and groans of wounded men. Any thoughts of easy prize money were forgotten now, thoughts instead turned to just surviving the day.

Marchant, unaccustomed to the bloody grind of war, paced about the deck with nerves of pudding. He flinched at every boom and choked on the acrid smoke that burned his lungs. The gunpowder's harsh smell filling his nostrils turned his stomach sour. No matter where he stood, he could not escape the noise, the nauseating fumes. He was doing his best not to heave.

Ryan was pacing up and down the deck as well. But his tempo was more like that of some sharp-toothed panther stalking its prey, unflinching, watching, waiting for some advantage to exploit. He kept his eyes fixed on his opponent. The same smoke filled his lungs and he savored it. Like Dowlin, he loved the smell, loved the taste of battle, and breathed deeply.

As the sun began to settle on the water, and seeing his poor ship being mauled, and all unfairly too, the master of the British schooner finally had had enough and reluctantly gave the order to break off the engagement. The mystery battle cruiser and her crew had simply outclassed his own.

Suddenly the British warship sheared off and turned north, her crew hoping to find their convoy.

"Thar! Thar she goes lads with her tail between her legs, off to lick her wounds and bury her dead!" Dowlin proclaimed boldly, gloating for all the world to see.

The Irishmen, hearts bursting with pride, with one might voice raised a wild victory cheer. They had beaten a ship of the Royal Navy and not one of *Prince's* men had been killed or wounded.

Marchant's mood instantly improved. He began grinning like some silly schoolboy, obviously quite pleased. "Not bad for an old merchant sailor, hey?" he asked Ryan, intent on taking all the glory for himself.

Ryan forced a weak smile, his thoughts turned briefly to his former captain, Bartholomew Langley Hughes. "No, sir, not bad at all. My compliments..."

He let Marchant believe what he would. It was of course Dowlin and his gunners who had won the day. Marchant did no more than give permission to fire. Such things do not go unnoticed for long by sailors and, to Ryan's displeasure, there had already been grumbling, talk among the crew against their captain. Ryan had hoped that, with time and experience, Marchant might grow into his position. They were, after all, only on their first cruise. But Ryan's hopes were fading and fading fast.

Exuberance stiffened Marchant's backbone now. He gave the order to turn *his* ship about to pursue the fleeing schooner while Arnold, having made himself useful for once, had climbed up into the rigging as soon as the shelling stopped and was nearly finished fixing the topsail's iron braces. The *Prince* would soon have her awesome speed back. That was her power.

Ryan doubted the wisdom of Marchant's order, but said nothing. While taking on and beating a British warship offered a certain professional satisfaction, it was risky, made no money for the privateers, and captured no prisoners for Franklin. Then again, they had seen a large group of coasters in the convoy. Perhaps, Ryan thought, they could follow the schooner to the convoy and pick off a straggler or two.

But just as Arnold finished his work, Marchant had a change of heart, decided to turn south before nightfall and gave the order for the men to stand down - and none too soon. Weldin was the first to spot the new threat. With her square rigging and distinctive yellow and black checkered stripe running parallel to her gunwale - there was no mistaking her. A frigate, the bane of every privateer, was speeding towards the *Prince* now and the *Prince* was no match against a heavy battle cruiser. Doom was the only reward for falling under the spell of a frigate's big guns. She was still some distance off, probably looking for the convoy, but her crew had seen the duel between the heavy schooner and the black cutter and now she was sailing at the privateers with gun ports flung wide open.

Marchant, suddenly possessed with prudence in abundance, ordered the helmsman to turn away from trouble. The frigate gave a spirited chase. But night overtook them first, covering the retreat of the Irishmen into the vast and rolling sea.

After the Irishmen were certain they had eluded the deadly frigate, Marchant set the night watch and, at Ryan's suggestion, changed course again, heading due west. Despite their failure to take even one prize, the mood of the crew was good, even jubilant. The day had been filled with excitement. They had given a British warship a good pummeling after all and for most, that was a good enough start.

But to be successful the Irishmen needed to take prizes. And so Ryan gathered his officers that night in Marchant's cramped quarters and held his first counsel of war.

"Gentlemen, this has been a fun day," Ryan began with a weary voice. "But it was a dangerous day too and, for all our skill and bravery, we have nothing to show for it."

"Not hard to see now, Luke," Dowlin said, "how so many privateers get themselves caught or sent to the bottom."

"Just so, Pat. It is a dangerous business. And there's no profit for us in trading cannon shot with a British warship. So, no more. From now on, we turn tail and run at the first sign of any trouble. 'Tis damn foolishness for any man to pull on a lion's tail. And we were lucky today no one was hurt or killed. We are after easy game. All agreed?"

There were nods of approval all around.

"Good. Now, I propose we head for the waters off of Land's End next to look for unarmed merchantmen there. We'll run across more revenue cutters around those waters, true, but the *Prince* can deal with revenue cutters, we're faster and better armed. It's the Royal Navy's heavy schooners and frigates we must avoid. All agreed? Good. Finally gentlemen, my compliments to each of you. Fine work today. And I'm most pleased by the professionalism and enthusiasm of this crew. We can all take pride and comfort in what we did today. I did, however, notice that it was not always clear who was in command. You are Captain Marchant, of course, this ship's master. But, here forward, should we get ourselves into a brawl again, I intend to assume temporary command of the ship. I mean no insult, sir - I simply have more experience in these matters than you. Understood?"

Marchant did not care for that idea at all. Captains did not abdicate their power to anyone while at sea. A captain's authority was supreme. Still, he had to admit, Ryan seemed to have an uncanny understanding of British naval tactics and the young Irishman had been one cold fish earlier when cannon shots had been whizzing by over their heads. Marchant was grateful he had not soiled his trousers. No matter, he decided. One or two more engagements under *his* belt he figured and then he would be in a position to set Ryan straight. He bit his lip, would bide his time, and nodded reluctantly.

"Thank you, gentlemen. We are in agreement then. You may return to your duties now."

As the officers started filing out of Marchant's cabin, Ryan caught Dowlin's arm.

"Aye, sir?"

"Walk with me."

"Of course, Luke."

"Fine work out there today, Pat," Ryan said as they went topside and took a leisurely stroll around the deck, pausing to watch a brilliant shooting star zip by overhead. "Would you pass the word on to the lads, all the lads, how proud I am of each man? Lesser men, especially inexperienced men, would have panicked at the first sign of trouble today, especially when the tops'l brace gave way. Every man on board acquitted himself like a veteran today. I suppose every man is a veteran now. I'd like the lads to know, especially the new lads."

Dowlin smiled warmly and patted Ryan on the shoulder. "Thank'ee kindly, Luke. It'll be my pleasure to pass the word down. Truth be told tho', a lesser capt'n would have gotten us all killed or captured today. You haven't lost yer touch from the old days. You kept yer wits about you and saved us all from disaster. Shame we couldn't have finished the job and sunk that schooner tho'."

"We'll get our chance soon enough I suspect. Another day, Pat, another day..."

"No doubt, no doubt. You look tired Luke. You best get some rest. I'll go check on things for a bit before I turn in myself."

Ryan chuckled. "Don't you ever trust anything or anyone?"

Dowlin stopped walking, turned and flashed his brilliant smile. "Well, now, let me see. I trust liquor to get me drunk. I trust a good woman with a generous bosom to always make me smile, even when she parts me from my silver. I trust our own lads certainly. And, of course, I trust you, Luke - I trust you with my very life. And when the day comes for me to give up the ghost, I trust that old St. Patrick will whisper a few kind words into the Lord's ear for me - if only because we're both Irishmen and share the same given name. As for all the rest, well..."

The next day, as the privateers continued sailing west, hugging the south coast of England off Dorsetshire, the specter of disaster raised its ugly head yet again. They were moving through a thick fog when suddenly, as the morning sun burned through, as the mist lifted, the Irishmen found themselves heading straight for the middle of the British Grand Fleet making its way down Channel under full sail!

Ryan and his men lined up along the rails and watched the British juggernaut in awe. The sight was breathtaking - and sobering.

The Irishmen quickly changed course to steer well clear of the danger. And Good Fortune was still with them. The Grand Fleet took no interest in one small vessel and sailed on.

Marchant let out a sigh of relief. "That was close. Don't fancy seeing myself inside the walls of a British prison again."

"Aye, Capt'n Marchant," Ryan replied with a nervous chuckle. "That was close indeed. I don't know whose lucky star to thank this time around, yours or mine?"

"Get no complaints from me," Dowlin added, "if we just get through one day with a wee bit less excitement."

Ryan nodded. "Why don't we swing south Captain Marchant, take the long way around to Land's End? Less traffic out that way."

Marchant took Ryan's advice gladly and for several days the cutter cruised along England's southern shores before Good Fortune, fickle as the changing winds, saw fit to embrace the privateers again. Off Land's End, a single, large brig sailed straight for them, blissfully ignorant of any danger. She was English, unquestionably a legitimate prize, and ripe for the plucking.

One well-placed warning shot fired across her bow quickly convinced the brig's master to heave to. This time the honor of leading the boarding party went to Dowlin.

"What's the meaning of this outrage?" demanded the brig's master as Dowlin and ten men stormed aboard his vessel with muskets and swords at the ready.

"Outrage is it now?" Dowlin asked gamely.

"Aye, outrage! Clearly yer not the king's revenue agents. You, sir, from the ship flying no ensign and firin' on an unarmed merchantman. What are you, pirates? If so, yer a fool to attack one of the king's ships right in his own front yard. You'll hang sure enough for it."

"Fool is it? What ship is this?"

"This be the good ship *Blessing*."

Dowlin cocked his pistol's hammer back. "Well bless this, fool. I'll have yer papers, NOW if you don't mind! I'm in a bit of a hurry."

The brig's master considered Dowlin and his armed brigands for a moment and then went to his cabin, leaving his crew and the Irishmen staring uneasily at one another on deck. He returned soon enough with his ship's registry, his logbook, a crew list, a cargo inventory and all the bills of lading. Dowlin read through each document carefully. The brig was on her way back to Wales, her homeport, but unfortunately had already offloaded her cargo in Portsmouth and was sailing home in ballast.

Dowlin neatly folded the papers and handed them back to *Blessing's* master. "I'm no pirate, sir. I'm Lieutenant Dowlin of the American raider *Black Prince* and you, yer crew and yer ship are this day captured. *Blessing* is now the property of the government of the United States, to be condemned and sold at auction. You and yer men are prisoners of war."

The *Blessing's* master shook his head. "You must indeed take me for a fool, Mr. Dowlin. Yer no more American than I am. Yer goddamn *Irish*! No American ship would venture into these waters unless she were lost, exceptin' for Capt'n Jones p'haps, and you an't Capt'n Jones."

The Englishman smiled smugly. "Do you know what is just over the horizon there?" he asked, raising his arm and pointed east. "Why the whole British fleet, Mr. Dowlin! P'haps you ought to think on that before you go stealin' me ship!"

Dowlin laughed out loud. "Yer a feisty one - I'll give you that! Capt'n, believe whatever you like. But you and yer crew *will* come with me - on yer own two legs or I'll have you bound, gagged and carried over.

Makes no difference to me." Then he paused to look out over an empty sea. "You say the British fleet is over there somewhere? The whole fleet? Bit out of range aren't they, even with them big, bad 24-pounders?"

Realizing that his position was hopeless, the blustery brig's master surrendered his ship. Dowlin left six men on board the *Blessing* with orders to sail the brig back to Morlaix, a fine little seaport on the north side of France's Brittany Coast and a shorter sail to safety than Dunkirk. Even without any cargo, the brig was still a good prize and the privateers saw her fetching a handsome price at auction. Dowlin took *Blessing's* crew back to the *Prince* with him and had them locked up in one of the holds below.

And as soon as *Blessing* disappeared over the horizon, sailing towards France, the privateers, in rapid succession, intercepted six more ships off Land's End. They seized the small brig *Liberty* first, sailing in ballast out of Devon, and then took the sloop *Sally*, loaded down with Welsh coal. After *Sally*, they overtook another brig, the *Hampton*, sailing to London with coal and earthenware and then snared the sloop *Elizabeth*, heading for Falmouth with a cargo of coal, oats and butter. And then the privateers overtook the *Three Sisters*, returning in ballast from Devon, followed a day later by the *Orange Tree*, bound for Cork with a load of the king's peas.

The Irishmen put prize crews on board all five vessels and sent the vessels back to France, except for the *Three Sisters*, which they decided to take in tow. She was a very large and valuable brig. She was the choicest prize.

"You see the problem, sir?" Marchant asked Ryan as the two men paced up and down the deck, passing by two wandering British seamen.

The *Black Prince* had taken 35 prisoners, with no place to hold them all, and so the Irishmen allowed them to roam about the ship freely. And to complicate matters, the *Prince* had lost 21 men to the prize crews and was down to only 50 men.

"Aye, Mr. Marchant, your point is well taken," Ryan replied. "We don't have enough men to guard the prisoners and work the ship and God help us if we are forced into another duel. I hate to return to port so early, but it appears we are a victim of our own success and have no choice."

"That's how I see it."

Ryan scratched his head. "Then again, why not ransom *Three Sisters* and parole some of the prisoners?"

"Parole?"

"Aye. We release some prisoners on their oath that they will return to England and present themselves to the authorities, who are then obligated to release the same number of American prisoners in a fair exchange. We'll put them on board *Three Sisters* and send her on her way - to make whatever port they desire. It is, I've heard, not an uncommon practice. Even the American navy observes the custom and paroles British prisoners at sea."

Marchant nodded. "Yes, why not? That would solve our problem certainly, Mr. Ryan."

"Fine. I'll prepare the ransom bill. You see to transferring twenty or so prisoners over to *Three Sisters*. I doubt you'll have any lack of volunteers."

Ryan went to his cabin to draft a ransom bill, setting the ransom price at 73 pounds for the *Three Sisters*. He knew the ship was worth far more but if the *Sisters'* master refused the price, Ryan would be forced to sink the brig. If the *Sisters'* master agreed to the ransom then he was obligated to present the ransom bill to the ship's owners once he was back in England who, in turn, were obliged to pay the ransom money "to the Order of Mr. John Torris Merchant in Dunkirk, or to his Order in London." By paying a ransom, the owner kept his investment and avoided the higher cost of having to replace it. The privateers profited too as they were paid without the risk of having to sail their prize all the way back to France. It was all a very civilized, tidy way to wage war.

The master of the *Three Sisters* understood the arrangement and signed Ryan's ransom bill without debate. After twenty British seamen gave their oral paroles, the Irishmen rowed them over to *Three Sisters* and set them free. The *Sisters'* master was not among them though. He was forced to remain behind as a hostage to secure payment of the ransom bill.

As *Sisters* sailed off, Macatter whistled loudly and pointed over the bow. A very large brig, flying English colors, was just emerging from a fog bank and within easy cannon shot.

"Now thar's a beauty!" he cried out excitedly.

Dowlin nodded. "Puts to shame those seven other guppies we caught."

"Aye," replied Macatter, "this one vessel is worth all the rest and will fetch us a tidy sum indeed!"

Marchant sent Macatter over this time with a boarding party. The ship was the very large brig *Goodwill* from London and bound for Waterford. Macatter and his men found her holds crammed full with a rich cargo of pottery, iron and assorted dry goods. Macatter took the *Goodwill's* master back with him over to the *Prince* and, none too gently, prodded him up the Jacob's ladder. The unhappy Englishman had been screaming obscenities at Macatter the whole row over.

"Now, now," Marchant said as the unwilling master and Macatter stepped on board, "what is all of this about, hey?"

"You the captain of this ship of brigands?" asked the *Goodwill's* master calmly.

"Indeed I am. And who might you be?"

The Englishman's voice rose to a hysterical pitch. "I am the master of the *Goodwill* damn you! Crammer is the name. You tricked us into shortening sail by waving the king's colors at us and then you fired on an unarmed ship! And you *dare* ask me what this is all about? I demand you release my ship and crew at once!"

Marchant looked up into the rigging. "I see no flag flapping in the breeze, British or otherwise, do you Mr. Dowlin?"

Dowlin looked up at the spar and smiled. "No, sir, don't see no flag." The Union Jack Dowlin had run up earlier had been hauled down and stowed away below.

Nostrils flaring, eyes smoldering, the English master glared at Marchant and looked like he might burst a gut at any moment. He started to open his mouth but Marchant held up a hand and cut him off.

"You are a prisoner of war, sir. You'll control that temper of yours or I'll have the master-at-arms lock you up for the rest of our cruise. Mr. Kelly! Be good enough to show our guest the hold and if he opens his mouth again - clap the irons on him and gag him!"

The colossal Kelly, a terror to behold, casually walked over to the *Goodwill's* master, peered down on him, grabbed him roughly by the collar and led the Englishman away. The man had no more talk left in him after that and went quietly.

"Mr. Marchant, are you," Ryan asked, "thinking what I'm thinking?"

"Time to return to France?"

"Aye, were shorthanded as it is and this prize is too valuable to risk losing. Mr. Macatter is quite right: this one ship is worth all the others. Let's put our own lads aboard the brig and take her in."

"Very well, Mr. Ryan. I'll see to a prize crew straight away. And you there helmsman, as soon as the boat is away, fix your course south by south-east."

"Aye, aye, sir. South by south-east."

And so, under a cloudless, azure blue sky, the swift and nimble *Prince*, a joy to her Irishmen, a growing menace to her enemies, headed back towards France with the handsome brig *Goodwill* in tow. After a rocky start, events had turned out well for the newly minted privateers after all - or so things seemed - and the Irishmen enthusiastically slapped each other on the back and took turns congratulating themselves on a most successful first cruise. Pledging allegiance to the new United States was proving to be most profitable. But what the Irishmen did not know, what they could not know, was that Good Fortune - that two-faced bitch - had already fled their side, had shamelessly deserted them...

Two

Foolish Doubts or a Doubting Fool?

And there on the rolling waves of a vast and hostile sea, the men of the *Black Prince*, veterans all of hard, cruel combat and now flush with easy victory - their first cruise a wild success - pointed their ship's nose east and charted a course for home. Having nearly sailed into the middle of the whole Grand Fleet off the coast of Dorsetshire early in their voyage, and having no idea where England's mighty armada might now be, the Irishmen wisely paid that monster their respect by sailing far south, down and around the Isles of Scilly. Even so, they sighted many an enemy frigate, thick as flees in places, patrolling the treacherous waters off England's south coast. Zigzagging their way safely through cost the Irishmen another two days of sailing. But then, when the Irishmen rounded the Isle of Bas, so very close to the sanctuary of Morlaix, trouble found them.

Startled out of a sound sleep by the loud clanging of the ship's bell, used only in an emergency and never to count time, the mariner grabbed two pistols off the shelf above his head, always loaded, and tumbled out of his hammock. He bolted up to the deck wearing only trousers.

"Thar, sir!" Macatter cried out and pointed. "*Frigate*! And she's got herself a sloop in tow. She was standin' leeward off of Bas, lurkin' thar as if she was waitin' for somethin'. If you look through the glass, Luke, looks to me like the sloop she has in tow is our poor *Elizabeth*."

Ryan grabbed Macatter's spyglass, anxiously scanned the waves until he found two dark silhouettes in the distance. Macatter was right. The larger vessel was a frigate class warship, flying the French *fleur de lys*. But that didn't fool the mariner any. Hard to fool a fox with his own tricks.

"Aye, Edward," Ryan said with a sigh. "I agree with you. That frigate was lying in wait sure enough and I have no doubt this is the ship she was waiting for..."

Dowlin straddled up next to Ryan, rubbing the sleep out of his eyes. "You figurin' on firin' at that frigate with them two *pistolas* of yers Luke?"

he asked, grinning at the two pistol butts sticking out of Ryan's trousers.

Before Ryan could answer the French boy Jean scurried by on some errand. Dowlin caught the boy by the back of his shirt and yanked him off his feet. The boy frantically kicked the air, trying to wriggle free, trying hard not to laugh. He had no fear of the big Irishman.

"Where you goin' thar boy in such a hurry? Never you mind, be a good lad, go below and fetch Mr. Ryan his boots and a shirt, hey? He remembered to bring his pistols to this here fight but not his clothes. Skedaddle on with you now."

The boy looked up at Dowlin with big, brown eyes and smiled. "*Oui, Monsieur Doolin.*"

"*Oui, Monsieur Doolin?*" Dowlin said playfully and released the boy. "Son, I'm goin' to knock all that Frenchy talk out of you yet! Now shake a leg lad before I find some truly nasty, stinkin' chore for you to do!"

The boy scampered off like a demon, giggling, eager to please Dowlin.

Then Marchant and Arnold strolled on deck and joined Ryan, Macatter and Dowlin at the ship's rail. All eyes were fixed on the frigate.

"What do you think, Mr. Ryan," asked Marchant. "Friend or foe?"

"She's flying French colors sure enough and she's awfully close to the French coast. But as the French would say, 'tis a *ruse de guerre*, and not a particularly clever one at that. For one thing, she's of English design. See her sails, see there, not cut square like what the French use. Note her canvas. See the rounder, softer angles? That's an English cut."

Ryan paused, took another look through the spyglass. "She could be an English ship captured by the French of course but, look close, you can just make out the short, blue coats and striped trousers of British seaman running around her decks. And, besides, why would a French frigate have *Elizabeth* in tow? No gentlemen, that ship is British and I fear the *Elizabeth* has been retaken."

"Doesn't bode well for our lads," Dowlin added sadly.

Ryan collapsed the telescope hard and handed it back to Macatter. "Aye. We best not think on that now Pat and look to our own situation."

Arnold started to say something but one scathing look from Dowlin convinced the young Connecticut man to reconsider. He closed his mouth.

"Well," said Dowlin calmly, taking another look at the frigate through his glass, "no surprise, but she's wearin' around and coming straight for us. I suspect they want to invite us back to England..."

Ryan could feel his stomach churn and turn sour. Two of man's most useless emotions - panic and heartsick - reached out for him. If the British frigate had intercepted one of their prize ships, it was a good bet she had intercepted some of the others too, maybe all six. Each prize crew would have sailed past Bas on their way to Morlaix with little concern for enemy frigates so close to home.

The English captain must have received word somehow that an American raider was on the loose and had laid a perfect trap. Ryan, grudgingly, had to admire the Englishman's cleverness and daring.

He thought back to the day, just three weeks before, when they had set all out from Dunkirk with eager hearts and brimming with confidence. And until a just a moment ago, they all thought they were returning home with gold and glory.

But Ryan could see things more clearly now. The frigate said it all. He suddenly knew in his heart that the English had retaken all their prizes. An embarrassed Franklin would have no choice but to withdraw his commission and, with no money to repay Torris and his other investors in Dunkirk, his ship would be forfeited. His men would abandon him. He would be ridiculed everywhere.

Ryan made a 360-degree sweep of the ocean and sighed. There we no friendly ships in sight. They were on their own. *After this fiasco, I'll be lucky to get a job as a cook on a small dogger somewhere in the Mediterranean. My God - how could things have gone so wrong? What a fool I've been to think that I could pull this off...*

And then his thoughts turned to Shannon. *Shannon!* How he ached for her now, longed to feel her soft flesh against his own. She would know how to heal his wounded pride and, pure of heart, she would stand by him too. Of that much at least he was certain. He could feel her warm breath against his face, could feel her long fingers caressing his hair, her eyes seductively inviting him to take her. He could hear her voice, whispering to him in loving, reassuring tones: *all shall be well my dear heart, have faith in yourself my fine, good man...*

Young Jean interrupted Ryan's lovely vision with a smile, and a pair boots, stockings and a shirt for him to wear. Ryan suddenly felt the early morning's chill and was grateful to have his shirt. He rubbed the boy's hair to thank him and quickly dressed while trying to think things through. It wasn't his fault that the Grand Fleet had decided to park itself between his ship and France - or so he told himself. *Bad luck that is, Luke.* He could face combat with an honest indifference to danger but, humiliation, that was something else again. These were the thoughts, like green-eyed offspring, vying for his attention.

No man knew Ryan's moods better than Dowlin. Sensing his friend's troubled heart, his dark emotions, Dowlin rested a reassuring hand on Ryan's shoulder.

"It's not over by a long shot, Luke. Let's give these slimy bastards a lesson in sailin', hey? We still got the brig and she's a fine prize, worth all the rest. Lots of fight left in our lads too. We'll put some distance between us and that frigate, make port and put out to sea straight away again to take new prizes. You know how fickle the wind can be. Against you one day, favors you the next. Same with a man's fortune. This day belongs to the English. Better luck for us tomorrow. I can feel it."

Ryan looked down the cutter's long, narrow deck, sanded down smooth by men who loved their swift, trim ships, and took in the anxious faces of his crew. Every man had seen the frigate. He turned to face Dowlin. Dowlin was right, of course. He could hang his head low and wallow in self-pity later, to his heart's content, if it so pleased him. But now his men needed him. Now they needed every bit of his cunning and skill to get them out of this jam. That was why they sailed with him. They believed in him. They trusted him. He straightened his shoulders back, took a deep breath and, for the moment at least, shook off all despair.

"Thank you, Patrick. I'm grateful to you, old friend."

Dowlin shrugged. "'Tis nothing. Tomorrow, we'll be sipping whisky together on French soil, I swear it. What are yer orders, Luke?"

Ryan turned to find Marchant. The captain had moved over towards the helm and was standing next to Arnold, looking rather pale. The Americans didn't seem to have a clue what to do.

Marchant could see Ryan walking towards him, but was preoccupied with his own thoughts of life in a British jail. He had been there once before. A shudder ran down his spine as he relived the unpleasantness. *These Irish are a curse! I wish to God I had taken Franklin's money, bought my passage home.*

"Mr. Marchant, Mr. Marchant, Mr. *Marchant!*" Ryan repeated, finally able to startle the man out of his own private world. "The frigate, sir, she is coming downwind on us. She has the weather gauge. I suggest we not waste another minute. We must cut *Goodwill* loose and send her into Morlaix on her own. Now."

Marchant looked at Ryan, confused.

"With haste, Mr. Marchant, we must move with haste."

"But the frigate's got our sloop *Elizabeth!*" Marchant blurted out irrationally.

"Aye," Ryan replied sadly. "Nothing to be done about that now. Let's hope the other lads made it safely back to port."

"But won't she take the brig too if we cut her loose?"

"That's a fair possibility. But that frigate can only take one of us if we part ways. *Goodwill* is slowing us down. I'll wager the master of that British frigate will ignore *Goodwill*, let her go scot-free, and give us chase. We're the choicest prize. That's what I would do. Captain Marchant, it's time to declare ourselves. It is time to hoist our true colors - I'll have the American stars and stripes raised if you please!"

Dowlin nodded his approval. "With a fair breeze, and on a good tack, she'd have no chance catchin' us," he offered, pausing to look up at the sky. And then he baited Ryan. "But winds been fluky, Luke. She's got the wind on us as you say. Hard tellin' who'll win this race."

"Aye, Pat, 'tis a gamble true enough," Ryan answered. "But what choice do we have?"

He turned to face Marchant again. "Mr. Marchant, spread out every stitch of canvas on her! Every stitch I say! I'll have the ship cleared for action too if you please! And we need wind - let's turn us about and head for open sea."

Marchant relayed Ryan's orders to the crew with conspicuous indifference, miffed at the manner in which the ship's arrogant purser had so rudely usurped his authority once again. He was the captain, not some junior officer, after all. Well, after they were caught and thrown into prison, he and Arnold could at least hope to be exchanged sometime down the road. After that he would return home, maybe try his hand at farming. Ryan and his band of Irish marauders would face the hangman's noose though. Bad luck for him that was - but Marchant felt an odd sense of satisfaction at the prospect.

Macatter, mimicking Dowlin, showed no panic, no concern. Not a hint of it. "Well," Macatter said with a grin, stroking his well-trimmed beard, "if you want to be runnin' around with the *big dogs*, you can't be pissin' like a *puppy*."

Dowlin slapped his knee and howled. Even Ryan cracked a smile.

The boatswains' mate blew his whistle and men scrambled to their stations. No man needed to be told what the plan was. The plan was simple: out-sail the frigate or face the gallows.

Macatter looked over at the *Goodwill*, cupped his hands and bellowed: "we're cuttin' you loose, lads! Make for Morlaix and you best skim the waves like a bat out of hell lest you want to eat your next meal in iron shackles! We'll keep the British busy for you as best we can! Godspeed!"

John Kelly, the *Goodwill's* prize master, acknowledged Macatter's order with a wave and had his men cast off the tow cable. John Kelly had his first command. The *Goodwill's* helmsman ported the ship's wheel hard over and the brig headed in towards the friendly shores of France, an easy half day's sail away.

On board the cutter, the Irishmen made all their guns ready and for the first time raised the American colors. Ryan felt an odd twinge of pride as he watched the flag unfurl in the light breeze. That surprised him. It was, with its circle of thirteen stars on a field of blue and red and white stripes, a handsome, balanced flag he thought. He hadn't paid the American cause much heed before. And then it struck him that, perhaps, he should. Risking your life - and the lives of your men - for only money seemed an empty pursuit.

Ryan then gave the order to fire the stern chasers, just to make a statement. He wanted to make sure the British understood which ship to pursue. He knew the British would have interrogated *Elizabeth's* prize crew, would have accused his men of piracy to try and unnerve them. But he knew his men. They would only have said enough to try and dispel that onerous charge and no more. Even so, the frigate's captain would know at least that an American raider was on the prowl and catching her would be his first priority. That is how Ryan knew the *Goodwill* would make Morlaix safely.

The British captain did not disappoint Ryan. The frigate's men ignored the unarmed brig and tore after the heavily armed cutter flying the stars and stripes instead. The race was on...

The *Prince* couldn't trade shots with a British frigate, not for very long. The frigate's guns were bigger - nine-pounders or heavier - and she had more of them. The *Prince* had mostly four-pounders and swivels. The only hope the Irishmen had was to outrun the frigate or, failing that, beach their handsome cutter against the craggy French coast and swim for safety.

Dowlin decided to go up the mainmast to double check Arnold's earlier handiwork repairing the main topsail's braces, damaged in the fight off Beachy Head. Best to check all the other braces and fittings too he figured as the loss of a spar or torn sail now would mean the end.

Macatter, watching Dowlin climb up into the rigging, turned to look at Marchant. "Fair warnin' Capt'n," he said with a mischievous grin, "if yer Mr. Arnold did a poor job of it, I'd be lookin' out for squalls if I was you..."

Marchant bit his lip and turned his back on Macatter. No, he really didn't like Irishmen very much.

The normal cruising speed for England's smaller, faster frigates was between four to six knots. Under the very best of conditions, and with a hard driver, they could manage up to 11 knots or so. When smuggling goods between Dunkirk and Dublin the *Prince*, then the *Friendship*, had hit close to 14 knots when Ryan pushed her and he was certain he could still wrestle one or two more knots out of her. if he really tried. But speed wasn't everything. Many a faster ship had been run down by a British frigate simply through better seamanship, or bad luck.

In a good wind, the frigate wouldn't stand a chance of catching the Irishmen's swift cutter. But now the wind was little more than a breeze, shifting back and forth erratically, and the frigate was handling the tricky conditions well. And it was a down Channel wind, making any quick dash to the French coast nearly impossible. This day would belong to the master who made the fewest mistakes tacking.

All through the long afternoon the frigate, like some hound trained for the hunt, sleek, relentless, pursued the cutter. Ryan put the gifted Michael Morgan at the helm, a man who could talk to ships and coax the very best out of them, while he took command of the ship himself, marshaling every one of his sailor's skills, employing every trick. No need to hold back now. No false modesty either. It was all or nothing.

And the British captain proved a worthy opponent, matching Ryan move for move as if they were playing a friendly game of chess or tennis. Move and countermove. At times the frigate even managed to close the distance with the *Prince* - only to fall behind again after some twist or turn by Ryan.

The giant Kelly kept his topmen hard at work at the braces and up in the rigging. The rest of the crew, with little to do, stood idly by their guns and watched with anxious hearts.

And then blissful night, stalwart friend to the Irish, always, closed in around the privateers and men found reason to hope again. They lit no lanterns, they cooked no food, they made no sound and men slept next to their guns through the night. After midnight, the winds freshened and shifted, from north to south to west to east, a *French Wind*, and Ryan gave the order to come about and head in towards land. And with a lively wind abeam of her, her sails billowing full, the American cutter bolted towards western Brittany with tremendous speed.

As the first hint of light broke over the land the *Prince*, her spars all draped in dark gray canvas and the stars and stripes still flying off the halliards, gracefully glided under the big guns at Fort Morlaix with no British frigate in sight. Ryan stood at the stern rail, scanning the empty sea behind them, quietly hoping that, if nothing else, perhaps he had at least sunk the career of one British naval officer for failing to intercept one small enemy raider.

"Mr. Dowlin, if you please," Ryan called out, "a salute to our allies."

Dowlin had the starboard bow chaser run out and fired a single shot. Standing on the fort's ramparts, French soldiers, smartly dressed in blue and white, raised their shakos, waved and shouted cheers at the *American* cutter in return. The Irishmen waved back, grateful for the warm welcome. With the smell of rain in the air, they shortened sail and pointed their ship up river, towards the town of Morlaix.

And when they rounded the river's bend and Morlaix came into view, the privateers found the impressive brig *Goodwill* resting peacefully against the wharfs. Good Fortune hadn't abandoned the Irishmen altogether. The *Prince's* men, in a heavy downpour now, eased their sleek, black cutter up alongside the larger ship, furled all sail and dropped anchor.

"Good to see you lads safe and sound!" Ryan called over to the *Goodwill's* prize crew.

"And you too, Luke!" John Kelly replied joyfully. "We all knew you'd make fools out of 'em British whimpers!"

"Any word on the others, John?"

"Aye, bad news, Capt'n. All six prizes were taken or so we've heard. We were making ready to weigh anchor and go out lookin' for you lads..."

Ryan let out a long sigh and stared down at his boots - 21 men, lost.

"What tomfoolery is this I hear about weighing anchor to come lookin' for us, big John?" Dowlin asked with an impish grin. "What the devil were you goin' to do, blow 'em British rascals big, sloppy kisses with that ugly mug of yers?"

"Whatever we would have done, Mr. Dowlin," replied John Kelly, set on a bit of horseplay, "rest assured it would have put the fear of God into 'em bloody bastards!"

"Ha! Ha! Ha! Brother John, yer all talk," the older and larger of the two Goliaths shouted, relieved to see his brother safe.

"That so, dear brother?" John Kelly answered smartly. "Seems our dear mum bore herself only one son with any wits between his ears! See that French man-o-war sittin' over thar? I had her capt'n and crew sold on the idea of sailin' out this mornin' with us to help you lads out - in exchange for this brig and her cargo."

Kelly slapped his big hand against the ship's rail. "Now yer tellin' tall tales little brother. No damn Frog would sail out against a British frigate with only a man-o-war!"

"*Frigate*? Who said anythin' about a frigate, dear brother?" asked John Kelly, his eyes filled with mischief. "Thought you lads was up against only an armed sloop - *honest*, I did!"

On both ships the crews roared with laughter. Even Ryan, distracted by his melancholy, but still listening to the friendly jousting between two brothers, cracked a smile - and was impressed with his prize master's resourcefulness. John Kelly had kept his wits and used his head and Ryan, never one to waste good talent, tucked that gem of knowledge away for another day.

The Irishmen would later learn from the London *Chronicle* that it had been His Majesty's frigate *Quebec*, under the command of Captain George Farmer, which had retaken the *Black Prince's* prizes and captured all 21 of their friends. The paper also reported that Captain Farmer had given a spirited chase to a new American privateer and had just missed snagging her.

Ryan knew Farmer by reputation. The Englishman enjoyed a good one. They had all been very lucky to escape his grasp.

After reprovisioning the *Prince* with the non-perishables, Ryan gave the crew their liberty and then faced the hard task of reporting his failures to Franklin and Torris. He dictated the letters to young Tim, Kelly's fine son and, among the Irish, the best man with a pen. Ryan recounted each day of their first cruise out and closed his letter to

Franklin by imploring the ambassador to secure the release of his 21 men by offering to exchange them for the 35 British sailors the Irishmen captured, some in custody and some paroled. Marchant, still the unwitting dupe, signed Franklin's letter as the *Prince's* captain, *de jure*.

And with his crew ashore, seeking those elusive pleasures sought by mariners since the days when great Egyptian war galleys roamed the Mediterranean, Ryan stayed on board the cutter, kept to himself and brooded, waiting, anxiously, for the recriminations that were sure to follow. During the day he lost himself in work. Sanding, painting, scrubbing and cleaning, doing any menial task he could find to take his mind off matters. One afternoon he took his knife and passed the time carving the word "fool" into the ship's rail. *I saw myself a champion, a winner*, he thought to himself, *more the fool, as useless as a piece of flotsam floundering on a sea of rejection, I'm finished.*

Not even Dowlin could reach him. But deciphering what is real and what is not is often a tricky business and as matters turned out, Ryan's despair, his fear of humiliation, had all been wasted energy.

When Torris read Ryan's report the Flemish businessman was ecstatic, not the least bit disappointed, and boasted to his colleagues that the capture of the *Goodwill* alone had made the whole investment a tremendous financial success! Once the large brig and her cargo were condemned as legitimate war prizes, Torris was confident that the ship and cargo would fetch them a minimum of £5,000 Sterling at auction. A handsome sum indeed. Torris viewed the loss of Ryan's 21 men as simply an unfortunate cost of doing business. Torris immediately dispatched one of his agents off to Morlaix to handle the disposition of the *Goodwill* and to deliver his warmest congratulations to Ryan!

The American Plenipotentiary to the Court of Versailles was no less pleased. The capture of 35 British seamen was an impressive feat, though Franklin was annoyed that Marchant had decided to ransom most of them away, dubious the British government would honor any oral paroles. As for the six ships retaken by the *Quebec*, Franklin didn't care about the loss, not at all, and informed Marchant that the United States had no interest in prizes or in any prize money. Franklin wanted, needed, prisoners.

"I see," Franklin wrote to Marchant, "you have been both diligent and successful. The misfortune of having several of your prizes retaken was what you could not help." Regarding the 21 captured Irishmen, Franklin promised "...in the general Exchange that is going on your men will be discharged in their Turn..." He also informed Marchant that a second British cartel ship, returning 100 American prisoners, was expected in Nantes any day and that "...you will be at liberty to take as many of them as you may want to make up for your Loss and as shall be willing to go with you."

Franklin implored Marchant not to release any future prisoners though as "...they serve to relieve so many of our Countrymen from their Captivity in England..." but, if "...again you should be obliged to dismiss some, take their Engagements in writing to procure the Discharge of an equal Number from the Prisoners in England."

Ryan, sitting in his cabin with Dowlin and Macatter peering over his shoulder, read Franklin's letter out loud first and then read Torris's letter. Far from rebuking him, his political and financial benefactors were congratulating him on his success and urging him to put to sea again without delay! He brushed aside a tear, astonished. Like a soldier weary from hard, cruel combat, he unbuckles his bloody gear, a heavy burden, and lets it slip from his shoulders after the duel is finished, Ryan, weary from hard, cruel doubt, unbuckled his anxiety, his painful doubt, a heavy burden, and let it slip from his shoulders after reading Franklin's praise. The world seemed good once more.

Dowlin and Macatter saw the instant change in him and traded knowing smiles. All was well again. They took turns giving Ryan vigorous pats on the back and congratulated him.

"Apparently," Dowlin observed dryly, as he produced a bottle of whiskey and begin pouring the liquor into three glasses, "not all Americans are blithering fools. This fellow Franklin must be a man of good, clear sense."

"We're back in business, Luke!" added Macatter, grinning. "What are yer orders, sir?"

Ryan nodded, took a sip of whiskey and shook his head in disbelief.

"It does appear indeed we have done all right... Incredible... I expected, well, I expected something altogether different. Ah well now my friends, I suppose it's time to go into town, start gathering the lads."

"Good *Gawd*, Luke," Dowlin said sharply and shook his head. "Yer a queer one at times. No one, and I mean no one - except you of course - ever doubted our success!"

Macatter nodded silently in agreement.

Ryan bowed his head and nodded. "I certainly have my flaws, no question about that. And I'll try not to repeat my mistakes. Gentleman, I feel grand! I intend to set out again as soon as we can assemble the men and reprovision the ship. May I count on both of you to join me?"

"It would be an honor, sir," replied the serious-minded Macatter.

"I'll be just as honored as Ed here, Luke," Dowlin chimed in and drained his glass. "But only after I go into town first and drink the place dry, maybe *liaise* with a saucy French beauty or two. You know where to find me when yer ready to sail out again..."

Three
The Committee

Where away, where away my strapping, young lad?
I pray you're not without compass, bly me that would be bad.
And should the waves claim your body, oh, your poor Mum, childless, would be left terrible sad.
Still, we trust in the Lord's blessings and are every day glad.
But upon your return, you best visit your home lest you make this ill-tempered, cantankerous, cold Irishman mad.
Aye, an ocean away no doubt you be, but write to us my good boy and God speed to thee.
Forever and always, always and forever, your loving, dear, old Dad...

It was late and Captain Henry Ward Patterson was exhausted. He had felt woozy all day and retired to his hammock early, his body not yet having adjusted to the lack of nourishment. Blissful sleep had just touched his eyes when a strong hand shook him on the shoulder.

"Capt'n, I've been ordered to rouse you. Apologies. If you'll be so good as to follow me, sir..."

Patterson opened his eyes to find the face, a face like chiseled granite, of Petty Officer Jeremiah Simmons staring down at him. He slipped on his shoes, grabbed his hat and followed Simmons past the rows of snoring men. With no windows the air inside the barracks was damp and chilly. Even during the summer months Long House, the building used to house all American prisoners at Old Mill Prison, was perpetually cold and dark and reeked of mildew.

Simmons led Patterson to the northeast corner of the barracks, to a small area partitioned off with blankets hung over the ceiling rafters. A line of men stood quietly outside the makeshift room, waiting to enter.

Patterson could barely make out their faces in the darkness.

Simmons gruffly ordered the men to make way, walked past them. No one complained. The privileges of rank. Simmons parted the blankets and slipped inside with Patterson following close behind.

The makeshift room was lit by a single, half-melted candle sitting in the center of a small, crude table. The power of the candle against the gloom was pathetic. Behind the table sat three officers whose features, in the flickering candlelight, could only be described as ghoulish.

"Good evenin' to you, Mr. Patterson," offered the officer seated in the middle and pointed to an empty chair in front of the table. "Please, sir, do sit down."

Patterson removed his hat and did as he was instructed. Simmons remained inside, standing behind him.

"Thank you, sir. Is there some problem, sir?" Patterson asked uneasily.

He could feel the sweat beginning to trickle down his armpits. He cocked his head around slowly, half expecting to find Simmons holding a club, or length of rope to hold him down. He had been told that justice inside Long House was swift. He racked his brain, trying to think of what offense he might have given, what rule he might have inadvertently broken.

"Problem? Why, no problem. None at all Capt'n Patterson. You are Capt'n Patterson, Capt'n Henry Patterson?"

"Aye, sir, I am."

"I'm Capt'n Gustavus Conyngham. We met briefly in the yard not long ago."

"Yes, sir, I recall."

"This gentleman sitting to my left is Capt'n Morgan and to my right is Capt'n Slater."

"Pleased to meet you gentlemen."

"As we are equally pleased to make your acquaintance, Capt'n Patterson. Now, to get to the heart of matters, we are the *Committee*."

"The Committee, sir?" Patterson asked a bit confused. He had heard of the Committee but didn't understand why the Committee would summon him in the middle of the night.

"Aye," answered Conyngham. "I do apologize. I had forgotten how new you are to Old Mill. Mr. Simmons has not explained the Committee to you yet?"

"No, sir," Simmons interjected. "Thought it best to wait, sir, Mr. Patterson bein' an officer and all. Didn't want to step out of place."

Conyngham nodded approvingly. You could always depend on Simmons to show exceptional judgment. And thank God for good, dependable petty officers. The navy would implode without them.

"Quite right, Mr. Simmons, quite right. Mr. Patterson, you have no doubt heard of the British Commission for Sick & Hurt Seamen?"

"Aye, sir."

"A worthless assortment of bureaucrats if ever there was one. In theory, they are the governing body that runs the gaols. But it is we prisoners who run the gaols and it is we three officers, being the most senior ranking officers among the Americans, who constitute the Committee. We establish the rules for all prisoners, a code of conduct if you like. We judge prisoners for any infractions of those rules and decide upon the proper punishment if the accused is found guilty. We hear prisoner grievances too and do what we can where and when we can. When appropriate, we lodge, or try to lodge, formal petitions of protest with the British government. We decide many things dealing with the day-to-day affairs of the men. We also, and this is why you are here, plan and oversee all attempts at escape. We determine the means, the methods, the timing and select the men for each enterprise."

Patterson stared at Conyngham and raised an eyebrow. "Then it is true, men have escaped from this place, sir?"

"Indeed they have!" Conyngham replied with pride. "Quite a few actually. Of course, more of our brothers escape from Forton Gaol outside of Portsmouth. Before the war, Forton was a hospital you see and is less secure than Old Mill. Mill was planned and built specifically as a prison. Of course, many of our lads get caught again through bad luck, stupidity or treachery. They pay the awful price if they do. Enlisted men who make it safely out of England are free to return home and are discharged from service or, if they are so inclined, they are welcome to re-enlist and find another ship. On the other hand, we officers are expected to sign on with a new ship as soon as an opportunity presents itself."

"I see," answered Patterson. "I hesitate to say this, sir. I want to do whatever it is I can do of course. I want to do my duty. But I doubt I have any talents to assist you in such endeavors. I know how to drive ships, gentlemen. That is what I do, that is the extent of my expertise."

"Oh pish-posh, Captain Patterson," Slater interjected in a friendly tone. "I suspect you are being a bit too modest. But not to worry, yours is precisely the talent we are seeking."

"What can I possibly do, sirs?"

"Ah, an excellent question," Conyngham continued cheerfully. "You are a Connecticut man I'm told - you folks get right to the crux of any matter, hey? Don't let my Irish manner of speaking fool you. I'm from Pennsylvania myself. We didn't approach you until now because our British keepers have been known to plant agents inside these walls from time to time. Occasionally they'll find some weak-minded prisoner, usually someone who was born in England or Scotland, a man with divided loyalties, to use against us. Turncoats. We must be careful. Concerning yer loyalties, we are satisfied that you are a patriot."

"Thank you, sir."

"We have a major enterprise planned for the near future. Because of your rank and your skills, you have been chosen to go with this next group. If for some ungodly reason you would prefer to stay here, well, you have that choice of course. Your participation is strictly voluntary. There is one condition for officers as I have said, but I am compelled to remind you of it again now so that we are clear: if you make good your escape, you are obliged to find another warship to sail with as soon as you are able, as captain or in some lesser capacity. If you cannot agree to this condition, your name will be added to the roster and you can wait your turn like everyone else. Men are ordinarily selected based on the length of time they've served here. Being a newcomer your name would, of course, go to the bottom of that list. Any questions? Do you need time to think the matter over?"

"No, sir. I think I understand you clearly, point-by-point. I can, happily, agree this very instant to your terms, gentlemen. What is there to think about? This is a most dreadful place. I long to be on the open sea again. And I pledge to you this night, gentlemen - and do so gladly - should I succeed in escaping from this place I shall take up arms once more and fight for liberty, fight to free our country from British tyranny. When do we go?"

A smile touched Conyngham's face, an austere schoolmaster's face. "Wonderful! Well said, Capt'n Patterson, well said! I knew we could count on you. Mr. Simmons will explain the details to you later and we shall leave you in his capable hands. Pay close attention to Mr. Simmons, there is none better. Now I bid you a good night, sir."

Patterson stood, saluted and followed Simmons back through the blankets, past the line of men still waiting patiently, quietly, outside the room. After a restless sleep and breakfast of tasteless, boiled oats, Patterson put on his coat and hat and began his usual stroll around the prison yard.

When Simmons spotted Patterson talking his daily walk, the petty officer was quick to join him.

"Good morning," Patterson offered with forced cheerfulness as he watched the leaves tumble across the grass, one chasing after the other. Fall was coming early.

"And a good morning to you, sir."

"Last night was quite something I must say, Mr. Simmons. Rather eerie."

"Indeed, sir. Bit spooky in there. Like meetin' the Grand Inquisitors or somethin'."

"Your thoughts match my own. What happens next? How do we get out?"

"Well, sir, it's like this. There are many ways out of here. Men have actually walked out the front gate after bribing a guard or two if you can believe that. With a mass escape, it's always by tunnel."

"Tunnel? Honestly? How so?"

"Oh the tunnelin' part is easy. Hiddin' all that dirt, well, that's the tricky part. We make picks and shovels out of discarded scraps of metal and planks of wood. The dirt is packed into canvas bags and hidden inside hammocks with dirty clothes thrown over them, dumped under the floorboards or stuffed into the chimneys until we can move it outside at a later time. Only a few of the fireplaces actually work as you've noticed. The space underneath the floorboards has become a tad full tho'. The boys on the tunnel details work from ten o'clock at night until four o'clock in the mornin' in three, two hour shifts - every day. We dig strait down, fifteen feet, and then cut across the yard under the outside double walls. English soil is soft here. Nothin' to it."

"Don't the guards ever catch on?"

"Aye. Sometimes. Then we fill in that tunnel and start all over with a new one."

"I see."

Simmons stopped to chuckle. "One time, forgive me, sir, we filled in a tunnel discovered by the redcoats using the dirt from a new tunnel. Those fellers never were the wiser. Guards hardly ever step inside Long House and when they do it is never at night so we're left pretty much undisturbed."

"What do you do once you're outside the walls? Last time I looked at a map, Mr. Simmons, England was an island. How does one, well, get off it?"

"You might recall, sir, I mentioned to you there's a kind of an underground river that flows from here to France. It works like so. You'll have to memorize the names and addresses later sir, but, for now, you can just listen. Before we leave, you'll be supplied money and with forged identification papers, maybe a disguise too. You'll be given a name and an address to make for. There are many good English folk who sympathize with our cause or who are sorely troubled by the poor conditions here. Follow so far, sir?"

"Yes, indeed. Do continue, Mr. Simmons."

"Once we're through the tunnel and outside the prison walls we'll separate into small groups of three or four men and scatter in different directions. Any larger group than that would attract too much attention. If the guards spot us they'll shoot, but their aim is a might poor and I shouldn't worry about that too much. Just keep runnin'. Aren't enough guards at Old Mill to go chasin' after us so that's not the worry. The bounty hunters - that's the worry. Most men get caught by them rascals."

"Bounty hunters?"

"Aye, sir. Many poor folks live in and around Hampshire. King pays anyone who catches an escaped prisoner five pounds. Tidy sum of money to many in these parts. The bounty hunters patrol the countryside with ill-tempered dogs and carry large, heavy clubs. And they're just itchin' to catch themselves an American and they're pretty good at it too. If you're not caught by one of them bastards, then you head for one of the safe houses until arrangements can be made to get you out of England. Or, you can proceed directly on to London if you have the stomach for it. Once in London you're fairly safe. Big city. No language problem. No one will bother you there until you can make arrangements to catch a packet ship for France or Holland, exceptin' that is for the king's press gangs. They're always on the prowl, roamin' the streets lookin' for fresh meat. You get snatched up by one of them gangs and you'll wake up next mornin' on one of the king's ships with a split skull."

"Is there anyone in London who we can count on? I believe you said that there are many in England who are sympathetic to our cause."

"Aye, if you run into trouble, or if you can't make it directly to London, there are a number of English gentlemen who can be trusted to help you with money, shelter, food, clothes and even travel arrangements. Some are sympathizers as I said and some are agents for Ben Franklin. There's a Presbyterian Minister, Thomas Wren of High Street Chapel in Portsmouth, who's a wonder I hear and another fellow, a Mr. Phillip Hancock, residing in Portsmouth. In London there's a Marylander named Thomas Digges. He lives on Villars Street but I've heard some troubling rumors about his true sympathies. And then there's a Dr. Griffith Williams there in London and one Captain Tristram Barnard too. I've heard tell that Barnard was a Nantucket whaler before the war. Dover's almost as good as London, smaller town but easier passage to France from there. I only know of one man in Dover and that's the Reverend Thomas Denward."

Patterson made a soft whistle. "This is all most impressive, Mr. Simmons."

"Aye, sir. Long time in the makin'."

"You are well versed in all of it."

Simmons smiled. "Aye. I've escaped before. Made it all the way to

London too and was about to board ship until one of the prison guards right here from Old Mill recognized me! The damn fool, beg pardon, sir, was on home leave! Foul luck for me that was. This will be my second, well, I suppose third try."

"Third?"

"Aye, the last time doesn't count as I came back on my own."

"What on earth for?"

"The Committee sent me 'outside' to right a wrong. We were betrayed."

"Oh? And you were sent, outside, to discover who had betrayed you?"

"Oh, we knew the 'who' of it."

"And so the matter has been fixed?"

"Fixed? Aye, in a manner of speaking the matter has been fixed. The lady in question will do no more harm to any one, ever."

"Dear God... Well, I, ahem. What happens if you're caught?"

Simmons looked down at the ground and kicked a lump of clay with the toe of his boot. "Nothin' good I'm afraid, Capt'n. You'll be brought back here of course. And then it's the black hole and half rations."

"Yes, the black hole. I've heard of it already."

"It's a small room underneath the barracks, a ditch really. No light, no hammock or mattress. Have to sleep on a cold, stone floor. Worst of it is, mind you, is that damned floor. It's often covered in water and filth. Hard to sleep in cold water. Knew a man once who was thrown into the hole for six weeks. He survived the hole but was never quite the same after that - touched in the head. Another poor soul came out alive but feverish and died a week later from exposure I suspect."

"And should one succeed in making it out of England to France, then what happens?"

"Ah, Capt'n Patterson, that's the easy part. If you get that far, then you only have to get yourself to a French Commissary or French Admiralty officer. They'll lend you a hand to reach Franklin. Better yet, if you find yourself in Oostend or Dunkirk you can contact Franklin's agent, let's see now, what's that gent's name, aye, Coffyn; Francis Coffyn is your man. He'll help you with money, clothes and food and get you aboard an American vessel, either a Continental ship with John Paul Jones or with one of the privateers."

"All sounds simple enough."

Simmons narrowed his eyes, gave Patterson a sly smile. "Aye, always sounds simple don't it now, sir?"

Four
Irish Rogues & American Patriots · Brothers-In-Arms

e spurred the beast on, wildly racing down a hill. But Shannon was an exceptional rider and her horse was fast, very fast. She outpaced him with ease before vanishing into the mist.

He pressed on until he came upon her horse tethered to an old barn, built of stone and thatch and neglected for many years. He found her inside, waiting for him, naked, lying across her horse's blanket spread over a pile of straw.

Her firm breasts rose and fell with each breath and seized with a reckless yearning for him, no inhibitions, her green eyes inviting, no, begging him to take her with all his raw, savage lust. She unlocked her legs and summoned him with a curl of her finger to join her. Longing to please her, he frantically stripped, slid on top of her and indulged her every craving - holding nothing back. She giggled, cooed with delight and called out his name - all to urge him on - until she arched her back and screamed. And then the lovers, intertwined as one and spent, savoring passion's afterglow, rested and dozed to the muffled rumblings of distant thunder.

No, not thunder... Ryan heard an annoying rapping at his cabin door. He struggled for a moment, unsure of where he was. The dream had been so real.

"Beg pardon, sir. 'Tis time."

"Aye, I'm awake blast it, Hoar. Enter!"

"A bit grumpy today aren't we?" Hoar asked as he poked his head inside Ryan's cabin. "Ship's officers are all assembled as *you* ordered. I'm just the good messenger..."

"Yeah, yeah. My apologies."

"You look a bit flushed, Luke - you feelin' all right?"

"I feel grand, just a bit stuffy in here. Very well then, I'm on my way. Have the lads meet me in the crew's quarters."

One-by-one Ryan's officers, Marchant and his man Arnold,

Macatter and Weldin, who had sailed a rumrunner together before the British caught them, Dowlin and Kelly, and Kelly's brother John, who Ryan had promoted to chief petty officer for his recent good work, filed into the ship's *wardroom*, which was nothing more than a small table and some chairs set up in the crew's quarters. Ryan cheerfully greeted each man with a glass of Madeira. The men stood behind their chairs and waited until Ryan, according to proper military etiquette, took his seat first.

Ryan raised his glass. "Gentlemen, thank you all for joining me. Not the best Madeira, I'm afraid, but tolerable. I liberated these bottles from the *Goodwill's* stores. To your health, gentlemen."

His officers raised their glasses and in one voice replied, "Here, here."

"Except for the watch, Mr. Ryan, I don't see any of the hands on board," Marchant commented curiously. "Thought you summoned us aboard so we could put to sea on the next tide. We're as ready as we'll ever be I suspect, unless Franklin's cartel ship arrives soon with more Americans released from England. Some of those lads might wish to sign on with us seeing how were short-handed now."

"Ah," Ryan began, pausing to help himself to more wine. "We won't be putting to sea yet, tho' I have no intention of sitting idly in port waiting on a cartel ship. I agree the *Prince* is ready enough, but we shall stay put right here in Morlaix until we receive word on the whereabouts of the Grand Fleet. No sense in taking on that monster again or any of its tentacles."

A few days earlier Ryan had sent a letter off to his friend David Sartine in Paris, asking for information on the position of the Grand Fleet. Sartine's uncle, the Minister of Marine, was always kept well informed about the English fleet's whereabouts by his vast network of spies and Ryan hoped Sartine would have no reason not to pass such information on to him.

"I am convening this counsel of war to discuss the particulars of our next cruise, whenever that might be. I have my own thoughts about what our next moves should be but I am always open to alternate points of view."

"We'll not sail any time soon then?" asked Marchant.

"Not today, Capt'n," Ryan answered evasively. "Gentlemen. I propose we return to the waters off Land's End when we're ready. We did some good hunting there and, except for an exceptional prize like *Goodwill*, from here forward I say we ransom or sink every ship we take. Sending prizes back to France was a disaster for us. P'haps *Quebec's* good luck was a fluke, p'haps not. But peeling off a prize crew for every ship we take is too risky and impractical. We simply don't have enough men. Fool me once and shame on you, fool me twice and shame on me or so the Scotsman says. We made a mistake, let's not repeat the error."

"So far," Dowlin said, "I like the part about sinking things, Luke."

"I knew you would, Patrick! Gentlemen, now here's the bad news - as *Goodwill* has not yet been auctioned off, there is no money to pay you or the lads and, regrettably, I cannot cover all these obligations out of my own pocket. Most of what money I had went to buy the bulk of our provisions and I was able to purchase the rest on credit. I can and will, however, pay any man who does not wish to sail with us whatever wages are due him and then release that man from any further service to this ship. Does any man here disagree with anything I have said or have a different view?"

Each of Ryan's officers saw the wisdom of his plan. Every man shook his head no.

"Very well. Then we are all agreed gentlemen and the matter is settled?"

Everyone quietly nodded his approval.

"Good. I'll not sail out blind again. Once we know where the Grand Fleet is stationed, then we sail. I thank each of you for your indulgence and I would be honored if you would all join me later tonight for supper as my guests at *Marie's*. She is expecting us and has promised to cook us a splendid feast."

"Ah, well now thar, Mr. Ryan, sir," Dowlin began, a twinkle in his eye, "I regret that a fair young lass has asked me to give her lessons tonight in how to speak the King's English. It would be a shame to disappoint her."

Marchant sneered at Dowlin. "Mr. Dowlin," he said indignantly, "you forget yourself, sir! Mr. Ryan is your superior and has graciously invited you to dine with him. It is not a request. It is a command. And it is certainly more important than tutoring some young tart!"

Macatter leaned close to Weldin, smoothed down the whiskers around his chin and mouth, trying to hide a smile. "I'm goin' to enjoy this," he whispered into Weldin's ear.

Dowlin narrowed his eyes, considered how best to respond to the overbearing, tactless American. Offer a sheepish snicker and ignore the idiot or berate the man now, in front of everybody, and finally have it out? He liked the second way far better. *Maybe I'll get lucky and the fool will challenge me to a duel. Now that would be sweet.* When it came to fools and idiots, Dowlin had no patience.

Macatter could see what was brewing in Dowlin's heart, thought it best to try and defuse a time bomb. "Pat, you learned your English mostly in taverns and whorehouses! Except for ship talk, what English do you know other than words like swive, jape and sard? Poor girl is in for a bawdy education!"

Except for Marchant, everyone started laughing. Even Arnold cracked a smile.

Dowlin decided to let the matter go. Macatter's words had soothed away his anger, had won him over.

"Not to worry thar, Mr. Marchant, *sir*," he said with a touch of disdain in his voice. "I'll be at supper tonight. Thar'll be time enough afterwards to teach the young lass the few words I do know - before I bed her down!"

"I do apologize, Mr. Ryan," offered Marchant for what he considered to be Dowlin's disrespect and vulgarity. "As master of this good ship I do apologize if you feel slighted in any way, though, I must hasten to add that it was you who brought Mr. Dowlin on board, not I."

Ryan bowed his head. "Just so, Captain Marchant. No blame to you. I'll deal with Mr. Dowlin later in my own fashion. No need for you to concern yourself. We Irish know how to *bloody our own*."

Marchant nodded with satisfaction. The impertinent Mr. Dowlin would finally get his comeuppance.

After some chitchat and more wine, Ryan dismissed all his officers, except for Dowlin. Marchant had the ship's boat made ready and led the others back to shore.

"Time for a dose of my discipline is it, Luke?" Dowlin asked with an impish grin.

"I don't believe," Ryan replied, smiling in return, "that our good Capt'n appreciates your humor much, Patrick. Don't think he likes you very much at all truth be known."

"Feelin's mutual," Dowlin answered smugly. "Be glad when we part ways."

"Aye, but for now keep a cool head, hey? We need the good Capt'n. Without him, we have no commission. Without a commission we have no work. And without work we have no money, no protection from English law..."

"Without that buffoon and his simpleton from Connecticut, Arnold," Dowlin grunted, "the Americans just might win their bloody war..."

Ryan reached down under the table, produced a bottle of whiskey and set it on the table.

Dowlin whistled and smiled. "Ahhh, St Magdalene single malt, scotch whiskey. You are resourceful. I'm partial to Bushmills or Jameson as you know but this will do just fine. Never look a gift horse in the mouth, eh? You know *Gawd* gave us Irish whiskey for fear that, sober, we'd rule the world..."

"Aye," replied Ryan smiling back. "And He saddled me with you I suspect as my penance for past misdeeds!"

Ryan filled their glasses and the two friends from boyhood sat back and spent a lazy afternoon drinking and reminiscing about old times.

The next day a horseman, wearing the light blue jacket of one of the King's Royal Hussars, arrived in Morlaix from Paris bearing dispatches.

He had explicit instructions to deliver the letter tucked inside his saddlebag personally to Luke Ryan and to no one else. He had been given a good description of the Irishman and found Ryan standing outside a hotel flipping through the pages of an English newspaper.

"Pardon, are you *Capitaine* Luke Ryan, *Monsieur?*" he asked in French as he dismounted from his horse.

Ryan looked up from his paper to find a young second lieutenant, covered from head to toe in dust, looking down at him with serious, determined eyes. "*Oui, mon Lieutenant.*"

The young officer snapped to attention, removed a dirty-white gauntlet and saluted. "First Lieutenant Marc O'Henry Gerard of His Majesty's Royal Hussars, Eleventh Regiment, at your service, sir! *Capitaine* Sartine sends you his compliments and I am to deliver this sealed dispatch to you personally. I have also been instructed by *Capitaine* Sartine to tell you this, word-for-word: you are a rogue and a pirate and he will drink a toast to the devil when the British finally snag and hang you."

Ryan smiled as the lieutenant handed him an envelope. "Is that so? Hm. O'Henry - some Irish blood, hey?"

"My mother's maiden name," the lieutenant answered flatly.

"Nothin' to be ashamed of, lad. O'Henry is a good name, fine stock. Those are second lieutenant insignias on your epaulettes are they not?"

A bare hint of a smile touched the serious-minded young man's lips. "Correct, sir. I was promoted recently but have not yet had time to sew on my first lieutenant pins."

"Ah, well then, congratulations are in order First Lieutenant Gerard. I see you have ridden hard, and all the way from Paris. May I offer you something to eat, something to drink? This hotel has a decent cook. You are most welcome to join me for breakfast."

The lieutenant bowed. "Regrettably no, sir. I am expected back in Paris without delay. Those are my orders."

"Very well then, Lieutenant. I shall not detain you from you mission. You will see Captain Sartine again?"

"*Certainement.*"

"Good. Then please give Captain Sartine my compliments when you see him. And you may tell him for me," Ryan paused, and then continued with a wry smile, "from this Irish pirate, that he can drink himself into oblivion for all I care. He is a menace to the civilized world. Inform the good captain that when next we meet I shall demand satisfaction. He may choose the place and time."

The lieutenant gave Ryan a puzzled look. He had his orders though and it mattered not at all whether he understood them.

"*Oui, Monsieur,*" he simply replied and saluted smartly.

Ryan returned the salute and watched the lieutenant gallop back towards Paris in a swirl of dust. He knew the man would deliver his simple message to Sartine, or die in the attempt. The few cavalrymen he had known were all like that. They lived by a simple all-or-nothing code: glory or death.

Ryan broke the official seal of the office of the Minister of Marine and removed a single sheet of paper, penned by his friend. It read simply, "*The fat goose sits at Tor Bay.*"

So, thought Ryan, the Grand Fleet has sailed back up the Channel and no longer posed a threat to his ship. He looked down the road leading to the river which led to the sea and, beyond that, to a world of possibilities. *Now is the time to strike!*

Ryan immediately recalled his crew. Before the next high tide, the ship was revictualized with hogsheads of bullock, pig, salt, potatoes, rice, fish, peas, lime juice, ship's bread, flour to make biscuits and hard tack, 100 pounds of coffee, 50 pounds of tobacco and several crates of fresh fruits and vegetables.

Then, on a glorious early July morning, the *Prince* ventured out into the boundless blue waters of the wild Atlantic once again with a mixed crew of Irish, English, Spanish, Portuguese, French - and the Americans. And though they numbered less than 70 in number, every heart was confident, every spirit soared.

Only 50 leagues of open water separates Morlaix from Land's End. The *Prince* covered that distance, against a prevailing west wind, in a respectable 24 hours. After rounding Land's End, and without encountering one British warship, the helmsman pointed the cutter's nose north and headed for the Cornish coast under brilliant, blue skies and with an invigorating breeze. Mariners accept such weather gladly and, even in enemy waters, hearts were light.

And then, trolling the waters off Cape Cornwall, the privateers sighted their first ship, a small collier named *Lucy*. She was coming down from the Welsh coalmines near Swansea and heading for St. Ives.

The honors went to Macatter this time but the usually serious-minded Irishman was in a playful mood. The occasion called for a bit of *panache*, he told Ryan and, by God, he decided, he was going to have some fun!

The men of the *Lucy* watched the black-bearded, little man with curiosity as he moved a crate to the middle of the deck and then rolled a barrel next to it. Stone-faced, Macatter took a seat on the barrel, produced a bottle of rum from his coat pocket and placed it on the crate. Then he removed a sheaf of paper from his other pocket and slipped the papers under the bottle, using the bottle as a paperweight against the breezes.

"Well now, lads," he said smiling up at his captive audience. "We're open for business. Gather around. Here's the long and the short of it: yer ship is mine and you are mine. Yer prisoners of war and thar's two ways to go. You can return with me now over to that handsome, American raider sitting across the water as my prisoners, the fortunes of war I'm afraid, or you can sign these here paroles and sail on yer merry way, free as seabirds."

"You would," asked one of the English sailors with surprise, "cross the Atlantic to America just to put us in gaol?"

"No. Not America, son, France. You'll be treated fairly while in my custody but, as soon as we put into a French port, you'll be handed over to the Frogs and thrown into a shit-hole of a French gaol. Not very cheery places or so I've heard. And thar you'll stay and rot until yer king has a mind to exchange you for some poor American prisoner down the road."

"And the parole, sir, how does that work?" the same man asked.

"If you sign a parole, I'll set you free today - on yer own personal recognizance, on yer oath, that you'll present yer name to the British Admiralty as a paroled prisoner of war upon yer return to England. That means yer king will need to release one American prisoner for each one of you I parole here today. Should yer king choose not honor yer parole, then, on yer oath, you'll be expected to surrender yerselves later to us. That's what these papers sittin' underneath this here bottle say. And, beware, I'll hold you to that oath and things will go much worse for you if you break yer word to me and I catch you a second time around."

"And what about my ship?" asked the *Lucy's* master.

"Well, Capt'n, we can tow her back to France as a prize and sell her at auction or we can burn her right here and now or - if you and me can agree on a fair price for her, a ransom price - then I'll spare yer good ship. Of course, you'll need to sign the ransom bill, a promissory note, before I can release yer ship back into yer hands. Well, that's the gist of it. Any more questions lads?"

"That looks like rum, sir," commented another sailor who had been eyeing the bottle ever since Macatter had set it down and smacked his lips.

"Aye, 'tis indeed rum, how observant you are, lad," Macatter answered with a broad smile. "And I've got more. For later p'haps. Business first..."

The *Lucy's* master and his men huddled at the stern to consider Macatter's words point-by-point. It all seemed so unfair, true, but war is unfair and they quickly agreed to accept their misfortune but keep their freedom.

They quickly formed a line in front of Macatter's crate and after each man signed his name or made his mark on a parole, Macatter thanked him and handed him a glass of rum - *to seal the bargain*, or so he said - and took one sip from the bottle himself each time. Then, after some haggling, Macatter and the English master settled on a price of 70 guineas for *Lucy*, as she was a small vessel, and the master signed the ransom bill. With written paroles, and the ransom bill in hand, Macatter bid the *Lucy's* master a safe passage home and returned to the cutter with his men. Once back in France, Ryan would send the paroles on to Franklin to use in his prisoner exchanges and send the ransom bill to Torris who, in turn, would present the bill to the *Lucy's* owner, demanding payment.

Leaving Basset's Cove with a cargo of copper and oil, the large sloop *John* was on her way to Bristol when a sleek, black cutter flying no flag closed on her and fired a warning shot across her bow. And though *John* carried an impressive array of guns, her master quickly realized his ship was outgunned and outclassed and gave the order to shorten sail.

The Englishmen watched as a tall, powerfully built man with long, flowing red hair stepped on board their sloop with six brigands, armed with muskets and cutlasses, behind him. The big man stepped aboard with swagger, and with two pistols tucked inside his belt.

Dowlin demanded to see the ship's papers and then, amused by how Macatter had done things on board the *Lucy*, he did much the same with crate and barrel and rum. As the sloop was worth substantially more than the *Lucy*, Dowlin negotiated a ransom price of 300 guineas with her master for her. And after the ransom bill was signed, each crewman signed his name to a parole, preferring parole to being taken back to France in chains, and joined Dowlin in a drink. The *John* and her crew were then allowed to proceed on to Bristol unharmed and the Irishmen disappeared, as if the whole unpleasantness had never happened.

The brig *Ann*, coming from Bideford carrying beef for Plymouth, was intercepted next. Ryan decided it was his turn for some fun and led the boarding party over.

"Luke, Luke Ryan is that you?" asked a man with an Irishman's brogue as Ryan climbed up the ship's rope ladder.

Ryan looked up surprised. "Why, William Thompson!" he exclaimed, laughing as he jumped down onto the brig's cluttered deck. "What brings you into these waters you *old pirate*!"

"Shhh!" the ship's master smiled slyly and put a finger to his lips.

He took a step closer to Ryan. "*Pirate* indeed!" he said, dropping his voice to a whisper. "Look whose talkin' about pirates! I'm an honest man now, runnin' ships for the Baileys between Bideford and Plymouth. Not a bad life, less money than smugglin' mind ye, but the misses worries less about me this way."

"Well, now you're my prisoner Will and Mrs. Thompson will just have to worry that much more!" Ryan replied laughing and gave Thompson a hardy slap on the back. "'Tis good to see you, Will. It has been a while hasn't it? We had some rollicking good times together and made some money too. Truth be told, I'm an honest man myself now."

Now it was Thompson's turn to laugh. "Ha, ha! Thar's nothin' honest about you, Luke Ryan! Tell me lad, what's this all about now, firin' a shot across me bow, comin' on board me ship with armed men at yer back? Yer comin' to steal our ship I says to me lads - turned from smuggler to pirate after all have ye?"

Thompson had no fear of Ryan. He had worked for O'Keeffe too. He was a Rushman, one of the *clan*.

"No, not pirates, Will, privateers," Ryan explained and pointed over to his cutter sitting a 100 yards away with all her guns run out. "I serve aboard the *Black Prince*. She's an American warship, Will!"

Thompson doubled over with laughter. "No! Yer pullin' me leg, friend - American is it? Seems I've seen that handsome ship in these waters before. Aye, no mistaken her graceful lines. She was a rumrunner named *Friendship* last time I seen her, back in the good ole days. Fastest ship I ever laid eyes on. Don't recall seein' her loaded down with so much heavy bronze before tho'! Her master was some English *gentleman* who went by the name of Luke Ryan. Finest smuggler in all of Europe and he was my friend. Liked to dress well too as I recall."

Thompson reached over and ran his fingers over the lapels of Ryan's coat to feel the fine material.

Still smiling, Ryan put a finger to his lips. "Shhh! Looks like we both have our secrets, Will."

"Pat Dowlin, and that giant tree of a man, what was his name... Kelly? They still with you?"

"Aye," replied Ryan, "like my right and left arm they go wherever I go. Old Callahan, he still with you?"

"No, may the Saints keep his soul. He died of the fever last spring. Good man, he was. Well, now Mr. American, dressed so fine, I see you still have a weakness for good tailorin'. Seems to me I've heard about some sleek, black corsair cruisin' the Irish Sea and taken prizes for the Americans. What do you aim to do with us? Rob us and toss us overboard for the sharks? Burn the ship and all that?"

"Noooo," Ryan replied with a chuckle. "Not today. You go along your way, William Thompson. You have a free pass! I'll catch you again in better times."

"You and yer lads caused quite a stir last spring in Poolbeg..."

"The English shouldn't have touched my ship, Will! They only have themselves to blame for this mischief! You give my best to your misses now. She always set a fine, generous table. No man ever lacked his fair share of good food or strong drink in your home!"

"God bless ya, Luke. Take care. You've always had the Devil's own luck but keep a wary eye out for 'em British - don't let 'em run you down. I doubt they'll see much difference between raidin' and piratin' no matter what flag you sail under. You'll always be Irish in thar eyes. Can't hide it."

"I appreciate your concern."

"Say thar, Luke, I almost forgot," Thompson said, pausing to give Ryan a wink, "how's that fiery, young daughter of O'Keeffe's? Heard you two made quite a handsome pair."

Ryan blushed. "She's fine, last time I saw her. How did you know about that, Will?"

"Ha! Ha! Ha! For such a smart fella you can be a bit thick at times. You think you can court O'Keeffe's daughter and keep it a secret? Ireland's a small place, Luke."

Ryan laughed too. "Aye, I suppose it is."

"Well, lad, take it from an old sea dog that knows a trick or two, you don't keep somethin' that lovely waitin' for ya too long. She's a fine prize for the man who can tame her!"

The two men shook hands with *Ann's* crew looking on, amused, and

Ryan returned to his ship with no paroles or ransom bill in hand. His men understood. The *Prince* and *Ann* dropped sail and headed out in opposite directions.

No one on either ship realized that they were being watched. True, the Fates were there, the triplets, Clotho the spinner, Lachesis the measurer and Atropos the shearer, always are and beamed with delight at Ryan's sense of chivalry and fair play and sent word on high to the gods who forever crave entertainment. But men were watching too.

The *Prince* had been very close to shore when she had fired on the *Lucy*, *John* and *Ann*. The crack of cannon was heard for miles around, bringing dozens of people out along the bluffs to catch a glimpse of any action. Someone in the crowd claimed to have seen the *pirates* kill a man and toss his lifeless body over the side and others were soon whispering that they had seen it too - among mortals, nothing carries news faster than cursed Rumor.

Rumor, that rabble-rouser, how she delights in breathing life into words with reckless disregard for what is true and what is not. She weaves strands of fact and fiction into whole cloth until one strand is indistinguishable from the other and then dresses her half-sisters Rout and Panic in her handiwork and sets them loose on the world!

Rumor, her winged words travelling fast, remade the *Prince* into something larger and more menacing. People up and down England's western shores traded stories about a black pirate ship terrorizing the coast. And by the time the news reached London, the *Prince* was a frigate class warship leading a whole pack of pirate ships.

Panic saw an opportunity in Rumor's good work and raced up and down the coast, filling the weak-minded with lies. Reports of murder, rape and pillaging by the pirates - none of it true - quickly spread from town to town. And wherever Panic chooses to strike, her twin sister Rout is never far behind. Militias were put on high alert and people near the sea lived in constant fear, some prepared to move.

The privateers, oblivious to the trouble they had stirred up on land, and not satisfied with 370 guineas, continued scouring English waters, looking for fresh victims. And the sea gave up her bounty. The fortunes of the privateers soared after Ryan released the *Ann*.

In rapid succession, the *Prince* quickly overtook three valuable sloops plying the Celtic Sea. The ships were ransomed for good prices and written paroles were taken. Then the Irishmen overtook a large brig, the *Union*, carrying oats from Padstow to Bristol. Ryan set the ransom price for both brig and cargo at £200 and sent Weldin over to close the bargain. But the *Union's* master, a man named John Trick, obstinately refused to sign the ransom bill and forbid his men from signing any paroles. Flustered, Weldin returned to the cutter empty-handed but with the disagreeable Mr. Trick in custody.

Standing toe-to-toe with Trick, Ryan laid it all out for him point-by-point and clearly too. No need to mince any words with the enemy. But Weldin was right; the *Union's* master, like some immovable rock, refused to budge.

Trick defiantly folded his arms and ignored Ryan, and then looked over at Marchant, who he took to be the cutter's captain. "Yer a damned fool, sir!" Trick declared bitterly. "Yer less than twenty-five leagues from the fleet in Plymouth."

"I may be damned, sir, but I'm no fool," Marchant replied in his deep voice, then added, sounding and acting for once to all the world like a *captain*, "you're the one who's lost his ship and crew, not me, and would now let his ship burn and see his men tossed into jail rather than be reasonable. So I ask you my good man - who's the fool?"

The big American did not intimidate Trick though. The Englishman was not only stubborn, he was ignorant of his own precarious situation.

"The king's men," he said coldly, "will run you down like dogs soon enough!"

"Gentlemen, gentlemen," Ryan interrupted, "Captain Trick, shall we go below and discuss business?"

"Thar be nothin' in the way of business to talk about," Trick replied scornfully.

"I beg to differ, sir," Ryan said, smiling agreeably. He nodded to Marchant and Marchant led Trick below to his quarters and had him take a chair at his small table. Ryan poured a glass of sherry and placed the glass in front of Trick. No good ever comes from inhospitality.

But Trick took the glass and slowly poured the red liquor on the floor.

Ryan pretended not to notice the man's rudeness. "Now, turning to the subject of business, Mr. Trick, I must humbly disagree with you, sir, we do have something to discuss. There is the matter of price. You have, I take it, some objection to the quote given to you by Lieutenant Weldin?"

"Lieutenant Weldin? Didn't know pirates had officers."

"Precisely," replied Ryan, "but privateers do."

"Ha!" scoffed *Union's* hardheaded master. "And you want to talk about price?"

"Aye," said Marchant. "We've set a value of two hundred pounds on your ship and cargo."

"Two hundred pounds! Outrageous! Who's got two hundred pounds just layin' about waitin' for the likes of you bastards to come along to pick it up without so much as a by yer leave, eh? Besides, I'll not buy me own ship back. You can kiss my backside..."

"Well, sir, it so happens I know your vessel," Ryan said, his patience nearly spent but managing to keep a cool demeanor. "She belongs to that old rogue Kingdon, who I know is well able to pay the ransom amount."

Trick's eyes narrowed as he studied Ryan's face more carefully. "You know a lot about me ship, I see mister."

"I know Kingdon," Ryan replied evasively.

"We're wastin' time," Marchant interjected and slid a piece of paper across the table to Trick. "I've prepared a ransom bill for your ship. You want to make your mark on the bill or not?"

"I'll see you in hell first!" replied Trick obstinately and folded his arms again to show his stubbornness. "Now, piss off..."

Ryan looked up at the cabin door where he had Tim standing by. "Tim, fetch Mr. Dowlin at once for me if you please."

"Aye, aye, sir!" the boy answered and hurried up the companionway.

Dowlin appeared a few moments later, poked his head through the door. "You asked for me, sir?"

"Aye, Mr. Dowlin," answered Ryan. "Appears we've got ourselves a bit of a problem here."

"Oh? You be needin' a fire boat then, sir?"

"If you please, Mr. Dowlin."

"*Dowlin*, that be a Patrick Dowlin from Rush, I'll wager!" Trick exclaimed as he swung around to see Dowlin's face. "Ah, I knows you. You traded shots of whiskey with old Trick here in some Dublin hole not long ago. I see you've fallen in with the wrong sort. By God, you'll hang with the rest of 'em, mark my words, Mr. Dowlin."

Dowlin looked down at Trick and grinned, not a friendly grin either, forcing Trick to look away. "I'll make ready that boat for you, sir."

"Mr. Trick, please accompany us on deck and we'll show you how it's done," Ryan said smugly and paused to look down at Trick's empty glass, "and by all means take your sherry with you. 'Tis rather good."

"I knows how it's done," Trick shot back indignantly. "Dowlin... Dowlin... I remember that name from somewheres else! He sailed with an Irish smuggler by the name of... *Ryan*. One of you fine *gentleman* is him no doubt! Well if you are, too bad for you. Stealin' one of the king's ships at Poolbeg and pitchin' the king's men into the sea with weights tied around their ankles has sealed yer doom - you've all got the halter about yer necks you do. Grisly work. Won't be long 'til they execute you. Yer necks will stretch a good long way and then snap like dry twigs. Well, I've said my peace. I see yer desperate rogues and not bluffin' about settin' poor old *Union* on fire. I'll sign yer ransom note for two hundred pounds. I'd gladly pay that price just to see you hang!"

Ryan's playful mood vanished with Trick's ugly accusations. He jumped to his feet, knocking his chair over and placed his hands on the table, leaning close to Trick until he was nose-to-nose with him.

His voice took on a tone that surprised even him. "*Aye - you'll sign sure enough!* So will every other ship's master we catch. And by all means tell the king's men what has happened here today - tell them anything you want when you put into port. You can save your empty threats with me tho'. We killed no revenue agents at Poolbeg. No one was drowned at sea. But given time, I swear by God, I'll sink or ransom every vessel between here and Liverpool! Now sign the bloody ransom bill or we'll go topside to watch her burn. Then it's off to a French prison for you where you can catch the leprosy and rot for all I care. You've become a bore, Mr. Trick. No more talk!"

The younger man, Trick realized, was clearly more dangerous than the cutter's captain. Rattled, he took the ransom bill in his hands, pretended to read it, but couldn't focus, and promptly signed.

"Pleasure doing business with you," Marchant offered sarcastically and led Trick back up on deck.

With the cutter's crew watching him, Trick stepped over the side and started down the rope ladder for the boat. He turned to look at Ryan and smiled. "I'll be seein' you soon..."

"That is a very fine hat," Ryan said and snatched it off Trick's head. He tossed the hat in the sea. "Something to remember me by and thank whatever god you pray to that your head is still not inside your hat..."

The privateers seized the *Sea Nymph* next. She was loaded down with dry goods for Devon and a good catch. After ransoming the *Sea Nymph* and taking paroles from her crew, the Irishmen sailed west to try their luck in Irish waters and came across a small sloop armed with heavy cannon off Wexford.

With her sails all slack, she was bobbing up and down on the water, adrift, with not one soul in sight, not even at the helm. She appeared to be abandoned.

"Boat in the water - on the far side!" the *Prince's* lookout cried out as the privateers closed in. "On yer port beam, their makin' for shore! Eleven men, ten at the oars and one has the tiller."

"What do you make of that, Capt'n Marchant?" Ryan asked.

"Don't rightly know, Mr. Ryan. Queer that is."

Dowlin looked up at the cutter's mainmast and pointed to the ensign fluttering in the breeze.

"Gentlemen, we're flyin' the Union Jack this time around. Looks like the crew decided to abandonin' ship thinkin' we're one of the king's revenue ships. They must have contraband on board. Why, now, that's the perfect crime an't it? We seize thar ship and illegal cargo and they have no one to complain to!"

Ryan nodded in agreement. "Could be Patrick, but the interesting question is why? Why try to escape in the ship's long boat? Smugglers, maybe. But they must know we can still run them down well before they reach shore. They could have tried to beach their ship and then fled on foot, given themselves a better chance. Someone panicked. Let's have ourselves a look."

Ryan led Macatter, Dowlin and 12-armed men over to the sloop. She was in a terrible state of disrepair. Her sails were tattered, her rigging was a mess and she was filthy. Debris and discarded food littered the deck. Both rough weather and careless men had abused the poor ship badly.

Dowlin removed the main hatch grate, made his way below and was met with a foul stench filling his nostrils. He had to put a handkerchief to his face. Then he saw why the crew had abandoned their ship in haste. The ship's cargo was flesh and blood.

"*Luke!*" Dowlin called up to the deck loudly. "You better come down here and have a look at this yerself!"

A shaft of sunlight settled on Ryan's face and shoulders as he stood in the center of the hold next to Dowlin, staring into the black abyss, horrified. Chained to the bulkhead and lying in their own filth were scores of naked men and women. The Africans stared back at the Irishmen in silence. The overpowering smell of sweat, urine and excrement saturated the warm, humid air and Ryan started feeling nauseous.

"Sweet *Jesus*, Luke," whispered Dowlin. "She's a slaver!"

"Aye, but in these waters? Never heard of such a thing."

Dowlin shook his head. "Nope. She musta been blown off course coming out of West Africa. Probably on her way to the West Indies or Cuba. From the mess I seen on deck, the crew weren't especially gifted sailors. More like amateurs and pigs, I'd say."

"Your attention please," Ryan called out. "Do any of you speak English?"

No one stirred. No one spoke.

"The crew of this ship, they're gone," Ryan said. "They've run off, fled in the ship's long boat. No need to fear them any longer. They won't be back, I promise, and we are not here to harm you. You have my word on that. Please, do not be frightened. Speak up if you understand me."

"I speak the English," volunteered a voice from the darkness, ringing with power.

"Where you from lad?" Dowlin asked and took a step closer.

"I am a Berber. Others here come from other nations."

"Tripoli?" Ryan asked.

"Not Tripoli. Further west."

"Ah, ha, I see... Well then, how long have you been at sea?"

The African stood. His chains scraped against the bulkhead as he held up his hands and flashed his fingers three times.

"Thirty days?" asked Ryan.

The African ignored Ryan and sat back down.

"Don't think he understood you, Luke."

But the African pulled hard on his chains. "Jumbaaliyia understand the English very well."

"Aye, easy lad," Ryan responded carefully. "We're not English. We're near a place called Ireland. Slavery is frowned upon in Ireland and the men who did this to you have run off. Do you understand?"

The African did not reply.

"Patrick, get some of the lads down here straight away and cut the chains off these poor wretches. We need to find them some clothes or something they can cover themselves with. God, I've never seen anything like this before and I pray I never do again."

"Straight away, Luke. But what do you intend to do with these poor bastards? We can't just leave 'em here. They hardly look like they can handle this ship and we can't take 'em with us..."

"No. We'll put them ashore."

"Aye, but I am not certain anything good will happen to them in Ireland."

"No. But what choice do we have? See if you can find papers for this, this *cargo* and destroy them. Without papers, these people just might have a fighting chance to be returned home. Let the English courts sort the bloody matter out."

Ryan's men began freeing the Africans from their chains and led them up on deck, out into the sunlight, where they were handed dirty rags and pieces of sailcloth to cover their nakedness. That was all the Irishmen could find.

The slaver rocked gently back and forth in the calm swells. The Irishmen and Africans stared uneasily at each other under a hot sun. Ryan set a bucket of fresh water out and handed the closest African, a young woman, a ladle. She took a sip and passed the ladle on. Then Morgan came up the companionway with loaves of bread and a pot of porridge from the galley. The Africans attacked the bread.

Ryan approached the African who had spoken English. He often liked to joke, that if he ever gave up life at sea, he would turn to boxing and unleash the giant Kelly on the world. Kelly was by far the biggest, strongest man he had ever laid eyes on - until now. The huge African peered down on him with hollow eyes. Like the others, he was very thin but, unlike the others, there was nothing frail about him. His flesh still carried the shadow of powerful muscles that had once wrapped themselves around his great frame. Even half-starved, his massive hands looked capable of crushing a man's skull with ease.

Ryan pointed to the coast. "See there? That's Ireland. King George's land. You and your kin will be safe there. Ireland does not have slaves and the English frown upon the practice." Ryan then turned and pointed to the cutter. "And that ship there, she's mine. My people make war against King George so I cannot put you ashore on King George's land. But I'll run you in as close as I can and put you in the boats. From there it will be an easy row to shore and then English soldiers can help you. You will be safe. Understand?"

The African stared down at Ryan. His eyes were filled with power.

"Jumbaaliyia understands. But safe is not free. Why does the master of the great ship make war on good King George?"

"To free my people."

A knowing smile touched the African's lips. It was his first smile in many months. He liked the Irishman straight off.

"I can work ships," the African proclaimed boldly. "I can work the white man's great ships. See these hands?" he asked, holding out his palms, covered thick in calluses. "Yes, I know ships. Send these people to King George. They are strangers to me. They are not my people. I, Jumbaaliyia, will go with the master of the great ship."

Ryan looked over to Dowlin for help. But Dowlin answered him with only the hint of a chuckle and rolled his eyes, still trying to decide whether the African was asking or commanding Ryan to take him along.

Ryan turned back to the African, shook his head. "I don't think that is a good idea, ah, J-a-u-m-b-a-l-a, you say?"

"*Jum-bow-lie-e-ya.*"

"Yes, well, my ship is a warship and my men are soldiers. You will be much safer on land. And Mr. Dowlin here found the ship's papers. The crew in their haste forgot them and we will destroy them. Without these papers no one will be able to prove who owns you or even that any of you are slaves."

"The power is strong in me," the African replied defiantly, wide-eyed. "I know about your great ships, with sticks as big as trees that catch the wind and armed with cannon made of bronze. I know war. I was a great warrior to my people. I do not go with these people to King George's land."

"I see," Ryan said and began tapping his foot against the deck, for once unsure of what to do.

Dowlin leaned close to his ear. "Looks like you've got yerself a new friend, Luke," he whispered. "He seems to like his chances better with us. Can't blame him. We can always use another hand."

Dowlin had, of course never, laid eyes on the African giant but he felt something, something unmistakably familiar about the man and the feeling was strangely comforting. Even standing nearly naked, sweating in the sun, his hair and beard matted down with filth, the African had a certain quality about him, a regal bearing, something *exceptional. This man was a prince of king in some other world,* thought Dowlin. *Luke sees it too.*

"True enough, Pat. But I don't know what the crew will make of having a Blackamoor on board. We could be asking for big trouble."

"Never know," replied Dowlin. "I've heard told the Americans have 'em aboard thar ships. Never heard a contrary word about it. French use ‘em too. I only know, Capt'n, that if I was standin' where that man is standin' now, I sure would be prayin' to *Gawd* above for a second chance in life. He wants the same thing we do - his freedom. Once we put some meat on his bones, he looks like he'll be fit enough to me.”

“Patrick makes a fair point, Luke,” Macatter added. “Other crews have Africans. And we're shorthanded as it is. Worst that happens is we put the man ashore sometime down the road and say good riddance to him. But, if he's worth his salt, he looks the equal of half a dozen men.”

Ryan had his doubts. Still, if Dowlin and Macatter had no problem with it, perhaps the rest of the crew wouldn't either.

“Hm. Very well gentleman. Let me think on it a bit. Mr. Dowlin, if you please, let's transfer these folks over to the ship and then deliver them to Wexford Harbor. Take those two skiffs along. We'll need them for the Blackamoors.”

“Aye, Capt'n. What about the sloop? She's well built. Spruce her up some and she might fetch a pretty penny for us.”

Ryan looked down the sloop's deck and shook his head in disgust. “Burn her, Pat! Burn this evil, her papers and everything else on board too! We'll take nothing but the Africans and the skiffs.”

“Aye, sir...”

After torching the slaver, the Irishmen sailed into Wexford Harbor under a white flag and set some 60 lost souls adrift in the slaver's boats with a letter explaining the circumstances under which the Irishmen had found them. The cutter fired off one salvo and stayed with the boats until one of the king's ships raised sail and ventured out into the bay to investigate the commotion.

“Mr. Kelly,” Ryan called out, “a moment of your time if you please.”

“Aye, sir.”

Ryan pointed to Jumbaaliyia. The African hadn't moved from the rail since coming aboard the cutter. “That Blackamoor over there.”

“Aye. Big rascal an't he, sir?”

“Indeed. Never in my life did I expect to see a man as big as you, Chris. But there he stands. We're going to see if he's a sailor. Don't know how the lads will take to that. His English is decent. The man pretty much refused to go with the others. I'm not sure why. Keep an eye

92

on him for me. Clean him up, find him some fresh clothes and feed him. See if there's anything he can do on board. And make certain the lads don't abuse him. If there's any trouble let me know. Can I count on you, Chris?"

Kelly glanced over at the big African. He wasn't sure what to make of the man. "Don't know anythin' about Ethiopians. But I'll give it a go if that's yer pleasure, sir. My God, I think he might be as big as me!"

"He's bigger, Chris," said Dowlin with a grin. "But you smell worse!"

"His name, Chris," interjected Ryan, "is Jumbaaliyia."

"*Jambell* what, sir?"

"Don't worry about it for now. Just call him mister."

Kelly nodded and walked over to the African. Dowlin's first point was on the mark, the man was taller than him by an inch. And for the first time in his adult life, Kelly had to look up at another man while standing toe to toe.

"I'm Lieutenant Kelly. What's yer name, lad?"

"Jumbaaliyia."

"*Jam* what?"

"*Jum-bow-lie-e-ya.*"

"*Jum-bell-eye-a,*" Kelly tried again pronouncing the name slowly.

"*Jum-bow-lie-e-ya.*"

"Ah, forget it, lad. For now yer Jumbo. Aye, that's it, Jumbo. That suits such a big man such as yerself just fine. Come along with me, lad. We'll get you cleaned up and fed. Then we'll see if a sailor's life agrees with ya."

"*Jumbo* is not my name," the African replied indignantly.

"No need to take offense thar, son. My name, my Christian name, is Christopher, but the lads all call me Chris. Well sometimes, they call me far worse. But Chris is just short for Christopher. Makes things easy, that's all. Catch my meanin'?"

The African nodded.

"Good," replied Kelly and then saw the power in the African's eyes. "You look like a man who was important back home."

"I was a prince among my people," the African answered casually.

Kelly didn't know whether to believe the man or not. It really didn't matter. Sailors were well acquainted with the art of spinning out tall tales.

"So you'll go back home then, to yer kingdom?"

"No. I have no home. I was a poor prince, a brutish man and an abomination in the eyes of the one living Allah. My people spared my life, sold me to the slavers. I say this with no bitterness. I was judged fairly. Now, I would be a good man. I prepare for the day when I meet the Father, the Father who rules us all, in the next world. I wish to meet Him only as a good man."

"Sort of like lookin' for redemption, hey?" Kelly asked a bit awkwardly and looking puzzled.

The African shrugged as if he didn't understand Kelly's question.

Kelly considered the man's broad chest and his long arms, arms that not too long ago Kelly judged, had been wrapped in rippling muscle.

"Have you ever done any wrestlin' lad?"

"*Wrestlin'*?"

"Aye," Kelly said with a mischievous grin. "Wrestlin'. 'Tis an old-fashioned contest to test strength against strength and a favorite sport on board this ship. Ah, never you mind, we'll get some meat on those bones of yers first then we'll see about the other!"

"If he's smart enough," Marchant offered, joining Ryan and Dowlin at the helm as they watched the exchange between Kelly and the African, "he'll do admirably well I suspect."

"You sail with any Blackamoors before, Capt'n Marchant?" asked Dowlin.

"Indeed I have. The Negroes I knew were damn fine sailors too. Hard working. I regret to say, our countrymen in the South use them as slaves. Dreadful business. It will all end very badly for us one day, I fear. The states are divided on this issue. Except for the color of their skin, they're no different from you or me, Mr. Dowlin."

"Let's hope," offered Ryan as the three men watched the two giants disappear below, "that the lads see it that way."

Dowlin shook his head and laughed. "Well, now, we already have every sort of riff-raff aboard this here ship of ours and now, by *Jesus*, we've got ourselves a king too! My *Gawd*, Luke, life with you just gets more and more interestin' with each passing day."

Ryan stood at the rail of his good ship, alone, as Ageless Dawn, matchless in her beauty, and obedient to the sacred rites, mounted her golden chariot and soared into the heavens once more to join her lordly lover, the Sun where, locked in love's embrace, they set the sky on fire with pink, turquoise, and saffron hues and chased the night away. And then Hephaestus, Zeus's master craftsman, skilled in fire and metal and laboring tirelessly at his great anvil to fashion objects of rare and exquisite beauty to please all the deathless gods, poured a lip of fine gold around the edge of every purple cloud, imbuing each with regal splendor. It must have been Hephaestus, or his ghost, or so Ryan reasoned, for who but an immortal could create such breathtaking, perfect beauty?

Ryan relished his bit of stolen solitude. And then Morgan, always thoughtful, came up from the galley with a mug of hot coffee and a hunk of fresh bread for him. Ryan accepted the offerings gladly, nodding his appreciation for the small kindness. Morgan then went to relieve the night helmsman, took the tiller. No better man was there than Morgan at driving ships at sea. He handled the helm with fine instincts and liked to boast that when he talked to ships, which was not infrequent, they answered him, as if they were living creatures. With his extraordinary gifts at seamanship beyond dispute, no one dared challenge him.

The cutter was standing off Lundy Island, a small rock just outside of the Bristol Channel, and in a good position to spy on ships sailing in or out of the major English seaport when Ryan, savoring his coffee in the early morning chill, caught a bit of movement on the waves out of the corner of his eye, no more than a shadow. The eye always senses movement first.

And then moments later the ship's lookout, perched high up in the masthead, raised the alarm, cried out his warning. He saw sails. That stirred the privateers from their slumber.

"She's a large brig by the cut of her sail!" the lookout called down to the deck.

Ryan looked over at the officer of the watch and found Weldin, quiet, competent always, standing near the helm. "I'll have the ship cleared for action if you please, Mr. Weldin," he ordered in a soft voice so as not to disturb the morning's serenity.

Weldin, a veteran now, knew the drill and knew it well. He cleared his throat and in a deep voice barked out his master's orders. The ship's sleepy crew sprang to life, adrenaline pumping hard, answering his call-to-arms. Men brought up the 30 swivels but did not mount them in the pedestals, not yet. Others brought up powder and shot from the storage lockers. The gunners kept the ship's 16 four-pounders housed inside their crates and the gun ports closed, patiently waiting for the order to prime, load and run out the guns.

Then Weldin, knowing Ryan's mind, ordered Morgan and the men at the braces to come about and bring the *Prince* on a course that would intercept the brig sailing past them and ignorant of any trouble. Morgan hardly needed to be told what to do. He was one of the grizzled veterans. He was one the *Shadowmen* from the old days, but he stayed his hand until the order came. The men of the *Black Prince* went about their tasks in almost perfect harmony. Dowlin, Kelly and Weldin had seen to that, had worked the men hard in monotonous, daily drills. They were all soldiers now and good ones too.

Marchant, Arnold, Macatter and Dowlin, they all tumbled out of their hammocks and rushed to join Ryan at the helm with spyglasses in hand while the Kelly brothers, sired by giants, raced forward to the foremast to direct the topmen. Ryan allowed the hint of a smile, impressed, even proud, of his crew's efficiency.

The two ships closed quickly. Marchant assumed command, as was his right, and gave the order to fire one warning shot. He had learned to do that much at least.

With a gleam in his eye, the gunner blew on his linstock, raised a spark and touched it to a swivel gun he had mounted on the ship's prow. Designated as the number one gun, the weapon exploded with fire and smoke and a loud *BOOM!* - rudely shattering the day's quiet. After hearing the *Prince's* war cry, and defenseless, the brig's men obediently shortened sail. The Irishmen did the same and Morgan maneuvered the *Prince* close in until the two ships came to rest peacefully on the gentle swells.

The honor of leading the boarding party belonged to the bumbling Mr. Arnold this time around. He boarded the brig with enthusiasm, demanded and received the ship's papers and quickly discovered that the brig was Spanish and carrying a full and valuable cargo of wine, cochineal, and indigo - a small fortune.

A rotund, bald man dressed in a priest's habit, a plain brown robe and sandals, studied Arnold as he shifted through the ship's papers. The priest then decided to approach Arnold and tapped him on the shoulder.

"Excuse me thar," the priest asked in an Irish brogue, "are ye Irish lad or do you hail from other parts?"

"Why I'm an American, father," answered Arnold with a broad grin, exposing his buckteeth. "Some of my boys here are Irish. You Irish, father?"

An odd question thought the priest to himself. With his thick, Irish brogue and round Irish face, there was no mistaking his heritage.

"Aye me boy, Father Bryan Murphy at yer service. You've come to rescue us I gather?"

Arnold blinked, gave the priest a dumbfounded stare. "Rescue you, father? I don't follow."

The priest had watched the boarding party carefully, and he was no fool. He had sized Arnold up quickly - and fairly well.

"Oh, forgive me, lad, yer here for somethin' else I suspect," he said and pointed at a group of sailors standing near the main hatch. "See those seven lads standin' over there? They're British navy my good man. No doubt they're all still armed. This ship is the *San Joseph* from Cádiz. We was headed for Dublin when, let's see, four days ago, aye four days ago it was, we were seized by the English warship *Epervier*. Them seven good lookin' fellas over there are the prize crew and charged with taken us into Bristol."

"Oh, ho!" replied Arnold and looked over at the seven Englishmen. "I say there! You men. You're my prisoners! I am Lieutenant Jonathan Arnold of the American ship *Black Prince*. You'll surrender your arms at once to my gunner's mate here or we'll spill your guts!"

Startled by their lieutenant's sudden, rash revelation, given with no forewarning, his men lowered their muskets and braced themselves for a firefight.

"And those men and the women over there?" Arnold asked Father Murphy.

"That small fellow is Guerre, the ship's master," the priest answered, barely able to conceal his amusement. "The others are his crew and the two men and the lady huddled together over there are passengers like myself."

Upon hearing his name mentioned, the brig's master politely bowed to Arnold.

"You father, and Guerre there, will accompany me back to my ship along with the ship's papers here. The rest of you will remain here under guard. Mr. Hoar, see to it that those Englishmen are disarmed."

Hoar nodded and quickly removed several pistols and knives from the English sailors without any trouble. Arnold then rowed back to the cutter with the priest, the captain and the ship's papers. Marchant brought them to his quarters, poured each man a glass of wine, and then studied the ship's papers while Father Murphy repeated his story. Ryan, sitting in the corner under the shadows, with Dowlin standing at his side, listened quietly.

"Well," said Marchant stroking his chin, handing the papers over to Ryan, "she was Spanish sure enough, no prize there. But now she's English and that makes her fair game, a legitimate war prize, and a fat one at that."

"What, sir, will become of us?" asked Father Murphy.

"You're free, father," Ryan answered softly for Marchant as he reviewed the papers, "so is the Spaniard here and his crew and the rest of the passengers. The English, I'm afraid, shall not fare quite so well. As Captain Marchant just observed, the brig is a war prize. She was an English prize. Now she is an American prize. The shifting fortunes of war, I'm afraid father. I trust that *Señor* Guerre will understand."

"Bless you, lad."

Guerre understood enough to know that he was free. He started speaking excitedly to Ryan in Castellan and Ryan looked over at Father Murphy for help.

"He thanks you and wishes you continued good luck against the English, the common enemy of all God fearing people."

Ryan smiled at the Spaniard and cleared his throat. "Thank him for me, father, if you will. Explain to him that, in the name of the United States of America, his ship is confiscated. He may not like that, seeing how France and Spain are allies. But the ship was English when she fell into our hands. He can petition the French Admiralty upon his return should he hold a different point of view."

Father Murphy made the translation and Guerre offered no protest.

Marchant and Ryan both agreed the brig was worth risking a prize crew for. Marchant decided to send the brig back to France with Arnold as her prize master. Ryan had mixed feelings about sending Arnold. Any one of his own officers would have stood a better chance of safely reaching France. But he decided to hold his peace and let Marchant play the part of captain.

The English sailors were transported over to the *Prince* as prisoners of war and Arnold, standing on *San Joseph's* quarterdeck and giddy with excitement, waved goodbye to his brothers-in-arms on the *Prince* as his own men unfurled sail.

Ryan and Dowlin, leaning against the rail, watched the impressive brig fade slowly over the horizon.

"Last, I suspect, we'll ever see of poor Mr. Arnold," Dowlin offered with disdain. "That simpleton couldn't stumble into a clear thought on his best day. He'll sink his ship or get himself hopelessly lost for sure. No doubt about it."

"Now, Pat, have some faith," Ryan replied with a thin smile. "After all, he's got himself a priest on board!"

"Well," answered Dowlin wryly, "assumin' father has the ear of the Almighty, p'haps He will show some mercy and see the brig and our lads safely back to France. But I for one hope to never see that fool again..."

Off Caldy Island, the sloop *Two Sisters*, a handsome prize, fell into the hands of the privateers next and Marchant removed her crew and took the ship in tow. And then the Irishmen caught the *Dublin Trader* off Milford Haven after her skillful master tried to make a run for it. The cutter's Union jack had not fooled the brig's master any. But the large brig was no match for the *Prince's* awesome speed, even with *Two Sisters* in tow.

Armed with a full bottle of rum tucked inside his coat pocket, Macatter went aboard the *Dublin Trader* to inspect her papers and cargo. The procedure had now become all so routine.

Macatter found 17 English passengers on their way to Dublin on board and a rich English cargo of oil, copper, tin and dry goods. Marchant wanted to put another prize crew on board and send her into France but Ryan, still feeling uneasy about the *San Joseph*, convinced Marchant to transfer the brig's 17 passengers over to the *Two Sisters* and set her free and take the *Dublin Trader* in tow instead. She was the richer prize, too good to risk losing. After some thought, Ryan's *suggestion* did seem best to Marchant and he agreed.

The master of the *Two Sisters* had been allowed to roam the *Prince's* deck freely to stretch his legs and was standing at the cutter's rail when the *Dublin Trader* came into view. He had watched, with grudging admiration, how the skillful Irishmen had run the *Dublin* down. *Left unchecked*, the Englishman muttered to himself, *these Irishmen will do great damage to English shipping. Where in God's name is the Royal Navy?*

With the *Prince* and her two prizes sitting in a circle, he strained to hear what the Irishmen were discussing up on the quarterdeck. He had all but given up hope of ever getting back his sloop. But then Ryan approached him, offered to release his ship in exchange for a ransom bill of only 50 pounds. The sum seemed reasonable enough and so he agreed, and agreed as well to take the *Dublin's* passengers with him, a burden to the privateers. The *Dublin's* crew and two men from *Two Sisters* stayed with the privateers as hostages, to secure payment of the ransom bills.

After setting *Two Sisters* free, and with the *Dublin Trader* in tow, the *Prince* cruised casually up and down Milford Haven and took two more vessels in a single day - the *Charlotte*, a large sloop from Cork, and the small brig *Monmouth*, from Lancaster. With 22 prisoners on board, and 29 paroles taken, Marchant and Ryan agreed that it was time to return to France. And so the *Prince* headed due east for home, leaving fear and chaos in her wake...

One by one the *Prince's* victims returned to different ports across the Empire with new stories about Irish pirates masquerading as American marauders, causing an even greater uproar than before all along England's west coast. The new stories about the Irishmen spread from tavern to tavern and from town to town until the news reached the very halls of power in London. Some even said the pirate ship was the same vessel that had been captured off Dublin earlier that spring and retaken at Poolbeg by her murderous crew who now roamed the seas looking for bloody revenge. The escape of the *Prince's* men from the Black Dog and Poolbeg were well known by the public. The major London papers, the *Chronicle*, the *Courant*, the *Evening Post* and the *Public Advertiser* had all carried articles about the cutter and the daring escape of her Irish crew.

In Padstow, 16 gentlemen of substance, including the collector of taxes, the harbor master, a notary, a vicar and one of His Majesty's justices of the peace, sent off a signed petition to Admiral Molyneux Shuldham, the commander of the British fleet lying at anchor in Plymouth, informing the admiral that the stories were largely true, that a "...privateer of 14 Guns besides Swivells called the Black Prince and painted black appeared off this Harbor & in the course of 24 Hours took 13 Vessels of different Burdens." The gentlemen of Padstow pleaded for protection. Fearing the admiral might underestimate the threat and ignore them, these same gentlemen sent a letter to the First Secretary of the Admiralty in London too, complaining bitterly that "...this Coast is totally defenseless there not being one King's Ship

Stationed between Bristol and Lands End to our Knowledge."

True, the inhabitants in the coastal towns along western England and Wales could be faulted for some exaggeration here and there. But they had not missed the mark by all that much. The western shores of Great Britain were in fact under attack and largely unprotected. Not even English sea power could dominate all the oceans of the world at once.

Sir Philip Stephens sat at his desk and removed a pair of waterlogged shoes. It was another dreary day, a rainy, depressing day. His office, with its dark mahogany paneling and dingy brown drapes, plagued by a lingering, musty smell, did nothing to improve his mood. He longed to leave the misery that was London, to spend some time in the country, but it had been an impossibly hectic summer.

The First Secretary's thoughts momentarily strayed, turned to matters of the heart. *What is that fetching young maiden's name anyway? Full bosom, small waist, a fetching smile. So lovely and lithe...*

He shook his head and scolded himself. Time to focus on his duties. The American rebellion consumed most of his attention these days. He massaged his toes through his wet stockings and considered the overwhelming amount of work sprawled out across his desk. He was normally a compulsively, neat man but his desk was now a shambles. Mason, his faithful secretary, had suddenly taken ill and stacks of papers, reports and files had been piled high on top of his desk like little immovable mountains.

His mind began to wonder again. *Catherine! Yes! No, no... Ah, Katelyn! Yes, that was her name. My, my, a lovely girl...*

In the middle of his desk, he saw a plain folder with red ribbon wrapped around it, tied off in a neat bow and Mason had scribbled the words: "*Letters from Sundrys giving informn of the piratical Vessel Black Prince*" across the folder's outside jacket. Stephens decided to tackle this chore first and proceeded to rummage through the bundle of newspaper clippings, letters from panicked citizens, dispatches from coastal militia officers and pleas for help from town mayors stuffed inside the folder in no particular order. One military report, from a Captain George Farmer of His Majesty's Frigate *Quebec*, caught his eye. He had a good opinion of *Quebec's* captain and began reading Farmer's report first and then recalled hearing about Farmer's good work off the Isle of Bas.

To the First Secretary's great annoyance, the Admiralty's file on *Black Prince* seemed to be growing thicker by the day. He had better things to do than worry about one, lone rogue ship. *Well,* he thought, *this Black Prince will be like all the others, a flash in the pan. Wickes has come and gone. The Dunkirk Pirate is tucked away inside Mill Gaol. Ha! I'll wager he's feeling a bit blue in that hellhole. Jones - what a nuisance that man has been, but even he hasn't caused much trouble since taking the Drake off the coast of Ireland last year.*

The Secretary's thoughts were suddenly interrupted by four Royal Navy officers as they filed into his office with hats in hand. Admiral Molyneux Shuldham and three subordinate officers, two captains and one young lieutenant, snapped to attention in front of the Secretary's cluttered desk and stood quietly while King George peered down on them from an unflattering oil portrait hanging on the wall behind the First Secretary.

Stephens did not invite the officers to sit nor did he offer any refreshments. He was in no mood for pleasantries.

"I have summoned you Admiral because this," he began with an angry tone and slapped his hand on top of the red-ribbon folder, "is an outrage to the Crown, intolerable. Ahem, by *this*, I am of course referring to the rogue pirate ship named, rather curiously, *Black Prince* and her crew of Irish hoodlums. Some pompous Irishman named Reilly, Regan, Ryan or something of the sort, leads these outlaws, these ruffians. Fancies himself an English gentleman too say some and owns the fastest ship on the sea or so say others. She cruises our waters *disguised* as an American privateer. But she is nothing of the sort. This vessel, I have it on good authority, is the same smuggler that broke free from Poolbeg in April. *Scandalous!* You Admiral are, of course, familiar with all of these reports?"

"Aye, my Lord Secretary. Ryan, Ryan is indeed the man's name."

"What?"

"The man's name, sir, it's -"

"Blast it, man!" Stephens thundered and began coughing. For a week, he had suffered from the ill effects of a nasty summer cold, which had done nothing to improve his temperament. "Ahem. I know the man's name! What do you propose to do about him? Is the British Empire - or is it not - the undisputed sovereign of the seas? This ship of brigands insults us in our own backwaters for God's sake! And this Ryan fellow has humbugged you all! Absurd situation. A puny vessel running amuck, sailing circles around the Grand Fleet! What do you suppose my response should be to His Majesty's inquiries on the matter? Would you have me say to the King that his fleet officers are all knaves, fools and incompetents? Or perhaps I should throw my hands up in the air and say: 'oh your Highness, though we outnumber the enemy one hundred to one, your fleet officers all urge caution and there is nothing to be done.' Well?"

Admiral Shuldham stiffened while his three subordinates, unaccustomed to being dressed down so, remained rigidly at attention and silent.

"The reports from America are distressing enough. The King has no use for excuses. I have no use for excuses. I want this sordid business brought to an end! And damn my eyes sir if I do not have my way! Are we clear?"

"My Lord Secretary," the admiral pleaded uneasily, "the reports are much exaggerated. This is a small cutter moderately armed and manned by Irish scallywags, common criminals, as you so correctly have stated, my lord. They pose no real threat to the realm. She has captured a few merchant ships and a handful of seamen, all expendable and easily replaced. These losses are insignificant. This ship is like a gnat buzzing about the ear of a great elephant. She is a nuisance, nothing more."

"Well, then by thunder!" roared Stephens, red-faced and leaning menacingly over his desk, "you certainly have been given abundant resources Admiral to *crush one gnat!*"

"My Lord Stephens," interrupted the shorter of the two captains. He absently took his hand and, with a certain smug indifference common among minor nobility, brushed the hair back off his ears. "The home fleet is stretched rather thin. Why, with the French fleet at Brest and the Spanish fleet at Ferrol, our enemies are poised to strike us hard at the first opportune moment. Our agents have reported that Captain Jones is organizing a number of American ships at L'Orient. He has proven to be a dangerous man with one ship - soon he'll have a squadron of warships at his disposal. Once he sails, a British force of at least equal strength must sail out to intercept and destroy him. And of course, my lord, Vice Admiral Byron cannot spare any ships from America. His priority must be to neutralize Admiral Comte de Grasse's fleet in the West Indies. We could, of course, release a few additional frigates to patrol the west coast, but it is a large ocean and, notwithstanding the *Quebec's* good fortune, it would only be a matter of pure luck for a frigate to actually run afoul of the American raider. This captain of the *Prince*, whomever he is, has shown remarkable resourcefulness, skill and daring for a common smuggler."

Stephens looked hard at the captain with ice-cold eyes. Though still on the pudgy side, the man had lost weight since the last he had seen him. Normally Stephens would have lashed out at such impertinence from a lowly captain. Officers below the rank of admiral addressed him only when spoken to. But this man was the son of a powerful and wealthy lord of Parliament.

"Hughes, isn't it?"

"Aye, your grace, Captain Bartholomew Langley Hughes."

Stephens nodded. *Best*, he thought, *not to offend the man, dress him down for his arrogance in front of his fellow officers and peers - but I can still ignore him.*

Stephens turned his attention back to the admiral, a man whom he considered an utter fool. *How did such a timid officer ever make admiral?*

"So, Admiral," Stephens began in a softer voice, "England, the most powerful nation on this earth, is powerless to hunt down and destroy this one tiny, inconsequential *gnat*? Is that what you would have me tell his Majesty?"

"Certainly not, my lord," answered the admiral cautiously. "But it will not be easy. As Captain Hughes observed, this privateer, small though she may be, is ably commanded. Her captain has been most shrewd and, I would hasten to add, remarkably lucky so far."

Stephens removed his spectacles, used the lace on his shirt cuff to polish the lenses, and then carefully pushed the wire loops back through his powdered wig and over his ears. It was going to be a long and fruitless day. Britain's naval achievements were always a source of amazement to him. So many of her senior officers were hopeless bunglers. That, he realized, did not speak well for their counterparts in the French and Spanish navies.

"Well, gentlemen, we do not serve the Crown to oversee simple tasks nor are we here to fix problems that any shopkeeper could do. If all Crown matters were so plain the King, I assure you, would be better served by employing simpletons who ask for little in return. He has instead chosen to employ us, at great expense I might add, and we dare not just sit by on our rumps twiddling our thumbs. These Irish outlaws have made us look like fools already. The public is clamoring for protection and Parliament is making noises. And then there are the papers and their outrageous stories to contend with too! How we ever allowed such damn, irresponsible men the right to fill the heads of ignorant and gullible common folk with such nonsense is beyond me! What a sham these newspapers are! No way to run an empire let me tell you. But alas, gentlemen, we must deal with them. They will not be kind to us if we cannot keep secure our own shores. Let me warn you too: Lord North is not pleased, and I can assure each of you, if the public is persuaded to lay blame at *our* doorstep, Lord North shall not look upon us with any charity in his heart. Recriminations will certainly follow and, I fear, if this rogue warship is allowed to continue on with her rampaging she shall encourage other rascals to do the same. We must nip this problem in the bud before those dowdy, sniveling men writing for the papers romanticize the whole affair and make these Irish thugs heroes!"

"We could, sir," offered the admiral carefully, not wishing to be the target of another outburst, "spare say, four, perhaps as many as six frigates, to hunt these rogues down. Station a picket line perhaps outside of Morlaix and Dunkirk. Our spies have reported this raider operates primarily out of those two ports. We should be able to intercept this supposedly clever captain as he returns home."

"Four or six frigates you say?" asked Stephens, tapping his fingers on the desk.

"Aye, my lord. At present, we have about two hundred and seventy warships of all types in service. Admiral Howe in the Atlantic and Admiral Byron in the West Indies have..."

"Admiral," Stephens interrupted in a testy tone again. "I am well acquainted with the number and disposition of our ships." Whatever point the admiral was attempting to make was lost on him.

"If I may, my lord, and with your indulgence, Admiral," interjected Captain Hughes, "*Quebec* also captured twenty-one prisoners from the *Prince*. These men are presently being held on Guernsey Island and are to be transferred over to Penzance within the week."

"So?" asked the admiral.

The captain casually picked up a crystal paperweight off Stephens's desk, took a moment to absently admire the crystal's quality. "Well, don't you see, sir, they're all Irishmen, subjects of the Crown. Why not try them for piracy? Let's see how many fellows this Ryan scoundrel is able to recruit once word travels through the taverns and whorehouses of Dunkirk that sailing with him will only get you your neck snapped at the end of the gallows' rope."

The admiral shook his head. "Captain, I rather think that is a poor -
"

But Stephens was quick to cut the admiral off again. "Yes," he said, scrutinizing the captain more closely. "Yes, indeed, Captain. An excellent suggestion actually. Most astute really. See to it." *This young buck of a captain shows promise. Finally, an officer with some advice that might actually prove useful...*

"Do you think Parliament will go along with this, your grace?" the admiral asked in a hopeless attempt to save face.

"Hm," began Stephens pausing to think. The admiral had made a fair point. Many in Parliament might be squeamish, even outright opposed, to such harsh tactics. "Well, as I see things, it doesn't really matter. We do not actually need to initiate formal legal proceedings against these traitors. No, not yet. We simply need to let the world think that we intend to try and hang them for piracy. That should have the desired effect for now and then, after the rebellion is finally put down, we can hang them all without any political consequences."

"Perhaps some word, some hint, to the papers?" offered Hughes. "A sop?"

Stephens allowed himself a brief feeling of satisfaction. "Perfect, Captain. Perhaps we can use the papers to our advantage for once. You will attend to the details personally."

The captain, pleased his advice had been well received, bowed, set the paperweight back down and smiled to himself.

Stephens stood. "Very well, gentlemen. This meeting is adjourned. Admiral, see to your plans to intercept this pirate ship at once. I want the ship destroyed and these men caught, tried and hanged before Parliament asks for my neck."

"As you wish, sir."

Stephens looked away and stared absently at the wall. "There may be another way to approach this matter. Actually, there may be two possibilities. I have it on good authority that this Ryan fellow was once in the employ of Daniel O'Keeffe, a black market man in Dublin. He still visits O'Keeffe's daughter from time to time in Ireland. I will have the house watched."

"Won't that require keeping a company of militia on standby - maybe for months?"

"No. I have something else in mind."

"Ah, ha. And the other option, sir?"

"Even across the havoc of war, I have some influence at Versailles. If we cannot ambush Ryan on land, or should your plan fail, Admiral, I may need to avail myself of that influence. But such things do not come without cost and I would prefer to handle this untidy, little matter in our own way. Do I make myself understood?"

"Abundantly clear, sir," answered the admiral, flustered.

"Good. That is all gentlemen. Oh, and Admiral, let me be crystal clear on one final point: I shall have this pirate's head on a plate, or I shall have *yours*...

Five

A Second Raider Puts to Sea

nder a fine drizzle the *Dublin Trader* fell in close behind the *Prince* as the two ships entered the mouth of Morlaix River. Flanked on both sides by wooded banks, the ships meandered lazily upriver as the tide began retreating towards the sea. The river's living waters diminished quickly and the *Prince* stirred up swirls of brown muck as her keel scraped against the riverbed's gravel bottom here and there. But there was water enough to navigate by still and her crew pressed on without worry.

At low tide the river shriveled to little more than a creek, exposing hundreds of small keys, and for this reason the port of Morlaix was a popular destination for ships of 300 tons or less. Crews could safely beach their vessels and grave the bottoms of their ships, cleaning off all the sea crustaceans that can slow even the swiftest ship down, and save the ship's owner the expense of dry-docking. And then at high tide the sea surges inland again, replenishing the river's waters, and gently lifts the ships up with plenty of draft for them to float back out to sea.

After the Irishmen had secured their vessels to the wharfs, they walked into town. The drizzle soon turned into a steady rain and then into a downpour. Once in town, Ryan and his men learned that the British had retaken the *San Joseph* and had captured the unfortunate Mr. Arnold. No one was surprised.

Arnold had somehow strayed off course the locals told the Irishmen and sailed straight into enemy waters near Padstow. Suspicious, British warships were dispatched to investigate and easily intercepted the *San Joseph* and Arnold and his men were immediately interrogated. The English interrogated them separately and when their stories failed to match, the English promptly arrested all of them. Arnold had thoughtlessly claimed that he was the master of the *San Joseph* and that they were fleeing from an American warship. Not a bad story but, unfortunately for Arnold, his name didn't appear on any of the ship's papers, which he had neglected to destroy. Threatened with torture, Arnold quickly confessed his sins. His English captors were thrilled to learn that they had snagged a prize crew from the dreaded *Black Prince*. Arnold and his four men were taken to Portsmouth, shackled for the amusement of the angry crowds, and marched 38 miles to Old Mill prison under an escort of 24 British soldiers.

Ryan caught the next available coach to Dunkirk, bringing Dowlin and Macatter with him. Marchant stayed with the cutter to keep an eye on some minor repairs and Kelly stayed behind to keep an eye on Marchant.

As the coach bounced along a rutted road heading north to Dunkirk, the three Irishmen took turns reading articles in several English newspapers describing their exploits. A kindly innkeeper of the small hotel where Ryan and his officers stayed while in Morlaix had saved the papers for the Irishmen - they always paid him on time and in full for their room and board.

Ryan was surprised by all the publicity his small ship had stirred up and dismayed by how much the British knew about the *Black Prince* and her crew.

"Sweet *Jesus*," Dowlin said. "Damn English press. See here, they got yers and Edward's name in thar. Bloody bastards even mention Marchant. *Marchant* for the love of Christ! Don't see my name anywheres. I'll need to remedy that oversight. Pompous idiots wouldn't now truth from fiction even if it bit one of him hard in his fat, old arse."

Ryan looked over at his friend and smiled. Macatter had fallen asleep and was snoring loudly.

"I'm not sure I'd be wanting all this notoriety if I was you, Pat. When musket balls start flying what's the first thing you do? You duck and keep your head down that's what. They're calling us pirates. I suspect there are prices on our heads and that may complicate matters for us."

Dowlin scoffed. "Aw, I shouldn't worry about that none if I was you. Yer the best thar is Luke. And that's a fact. Maybe the best thar ever was. Look at all you've accomplished. Macatter here has proven his mettle and I'm hardly some toothless guppy. Man for man, sail for sail, gun for gun, I'd put our crew and ship up against anythin' the English can scrape together. They haven't found a ship yet that can out sail us and I'll wager all I have they won't any time soon. English never have had much imagination."

Ryan nodded. *It is indeed a fine ship and I have the best crew a man could ask for.* "Your praise of me is a might thick, my friend. We do indeed have ourselves a fine ship and crew. None better. I agree with you there. But we're only one small ship, Pat and if we're not careful, or if our luck runs out, the English lion will rip us apart."

"You worry too much, Luke. Let's go find that Irish priest, Murphy, and sign him aboard. His prayers couldn't save poor, old Arnold. Nothin' could have helped that blithering idiot from himself - sailin' straight into Padstow. *Jesus Christ!*"

"A good priest couldn't hurt."

Dowlin shook his head in disgust. "How the devil do you do that, sail into an English port? We coulda put young Jean in charge of *Joseph* and he woulda had enough sense to steer clear of Padstow! Murphy's prayers saved himself and Captain Guerre from the jail keeper tho'. Says so here in this paper that they were set free. Father Murphy must have the Lord's ear. Yep, I think we need a ship's priest for the *Prince*."

Ryan chuckled and turned to look out the window. They were traveling through rich farmland, across soft rolling hills where an army of women dressed in black dresses and white aprons, oblivious to the steady rain, toiled in the fields planting crops or tending to the many vineyards that lined the way. The land was green and lush. Pretty country and not much different from Ireland Ryan thought to himself, though the colors seemed to him less vibrant, more muted perhaps. But despite this tranquility, the stain of war had marked the land. Ryan saw precious few men in the fields or in the towns and those he did see were mostly old or crippled. Like a scythe mowing down wheat at harvest time, the press gangs of the French military - a ruthless, efficient machine with an insatiable appetite for new blood - had passed through the land to harvest fresh, young men.

He turned to say something to Dowlin, but found his friend fast asleep and so settled back on the cushions to do the same. His last thoughts, before gentle sleep took him, were of Shannon, his Irish woman with the long, blond braids. He would need to replace his losses and decided a visit to Rush to recruit more men on their next voyage out was not a bad idea. And Kenmure was only 20 miles south of Rush, an easy ride away...

Torris, delighted to find the three Irishmen at his front door, greeted each man with a kiss on the cheek. The Irishmen looked worn and tired from the long ride up from Morlaix and he quickly brought them in out of the drizzle. The rains hadn't stopped falling over northern France since the cutter had dropped anchor in Morlaix.

Torris led them into his study and produced several bottles of wine, the best he had, and stoked the embers in the fireplace. The day was raw and cold, a day more like early March than late July.

Moments later Torris's wife appeared with platters of meats, fruits and cheeses. She was a petite, quiet woman with a pleasant smile - the kind of sweet smile that said: *all will be well in the end.* A mother's smile. But there were no children in the Torris home for her to smile at.

Ryan stood next to the fire, warming himself, while Macatter and Dowlin wasted no time helping themselves to the food. They filled their bellies gladly and washed it all down with generous amounts of wine.

"It is good to see you, Luke. And you, Edward and Patrick, it is an honor to have you here in my home again. Your home... Good, please, eat, eat! *Bon appetite!*"

"Likewise for us, John," offered Ryan. "You and your misses are well?"

"*Oui*, excellent as always, God is good," he chuckled and plopped down behind his desk, an ornate, highly polished piece of furniture. He patted his stomach and smiled. "Please! Do not keep me in suspense any longer. What news? I am certain you are the bearers of good tidings. Ah, but of course you are! I have read the accounts of your triumphs from the English papers. You are famous! *Magnifique mon ami!*"

Macatter and Dowlin broke out into wide grins, raised their wine glasses and clinked them together in a silent toast.

Ryan smiled despite himself. Torris, with his simple charm and quaint accent, was a likeable fellow though Ryan sometimes wondered how loyal a friend he would be if the *Black Prince* turned into a financial loss.

"I wish we could have stayed out longer, John. But the trick is to go in and out quickly, keep the cruises short and not get caught. Hit and run, hit and run. Sound tactics when you go up against a giant. The ship is in excellent condition and the spirits of the lads are good. We can sail out again on a moment's notice. It does appear we've stirred up quite a hornet's nest across the Channel."

"Indeed! Indeed you have!" answered Torris enthusiastically and clapped his hands, rubbing them together. "You've managed to capture a number of good prizes and bagged a good many prisoners too. And, I am informed," Torris added with a broad smile, "you returned to Morlaix with the *Dublin Trader, oui?*"

"Aye," answered Dowlin. "That we did. News travels fast in this country."

"Yes, yes. My agent, John Diot, sent a dispatch to me immediately upon your safe return. The *Dublin Trader* and her cargo will fetch at least one hundred fifty thousand *livres* I am told. And eleven other ships ransomed! Not a bad piece of business! Not bad at all! People are talking. There is excitement about the daring feats of you and your crew. And our good Doctor Franklin should be pleased with the prisoner count."

"I trust the good doctor will be most satisfied," replied Ryan, returning to his chair. "The *Goodwill*, how did that go? We saw her still moored at the docks. It appears the French have her impounded."

Torris's smile vanished. "She has been condemned in Admiralty Court, but not yet released to us to be sold at auction. I understand that most of her cargo were perishables. I fear they have rotted by now. Lost. Ah... shameful waste. Still, the ship herself is a splendid catch. I am confident the authorities in Morlaix will release her to us soon. Bureaucrats will be the ruin of me! The wheels of the French government turn painfully slow but we must have confidence, yes? We can only hope that the Admiralty Court moves with more alacrity in condemning *Dublin Trader*. I have also attempted to redeem the ransom note on the *Three Sisters* for the agreed ransom price of seventy-three pounds sterling. But her owner refuses to pay. He claims the *Black Prince* is a pirate vessel, not a legitimate privateer, and believes that this allows him to void the entire transaction. I shall prevail upon Franklin to assist us in this matter and will suggest to him that he produce a copy of your ship's American commission for the owner's inspection."

Torris paused to take a sip of wine. "There is another matter. Distressing news I fear, Luke. I, um, I hesitate to tell you."

"Go on," Ryan insisted with a hint of impatience.

"Luke, your twenty-one men held on Guernsey Island, they have been moved to Penzance. The British intend to - try them."

"Try them?"

"Yes, try them for piracy. And the English have promised a public hanging. They want to make a spectacle of you, of your Irishmen, I think."

"The bloody hell they will!" cursed the usually affable Dowlin. His eyes suddenly began smoldering with dark hate. His mood turned ugly, predator like.

Ryan caught the sudden transformation. It had been some time since he had seen Dowlin display such raw fury.

Macatter, always sober, subdued, sat impassively and said nothing. But despite his seeming indifference, he was no less dangerous than Dowlin.

Dowlin, his face flushed, twisted uncomfortably in his chair. "They can't do that!" he growled. "We've got our bloody American commission. We took the oath! We're American subjects!"

"Even so Patrick," replied Torris uncomfortably, "the English seem to think they can do it." He watched Dowlin move to the edge of his chair with his hands coiled tightly around the armrests, as if he were some wild beast ready to spring. Torris kept his voice level. He liked

Dowlin, but always suspected the fiery Irishman to be the hotheaded one of the group - and unpredictable.

"Whether they will carry out their threat or not is another matter. Possibly, it is meant as a warning only, a message to you and nothing more."

"That would be my guess too, John," offered Ryan calmly and stood. "But British justice is often erratic." He walked behind Dowlin and placed his hands on his friend's shoulders. "We dare not take this threat lightly. We mustn't assume it is a bluff. But I for one won't be blackmailed. The *Prince* will sail again - threats or no. We have British prisoners in our custody too and I swear by God, for every Irishman the British hang, we'll hang two Englishmen in turn. That should make those fools in London reconsider."

Torris shook his head in disagreement. "That could create a very complex situation for Paris, and for Franklin. Such actions might prove - unwise - even cause unintended consequences."

Ryan thought on that for a moment. He had meant what he said about a life for a life but was perhaps wrong to confide such things in Torris. "You're right of course my friend," agreed Ryan reassuringly. "I was speaking out of frustration. Forgive my rashness."

Torris's counsel for caution had little effect on Dowlin. "Things," Dowlin said grimly, "often happen at sea, nasty things."

"Aye," Macatter added, nodding his head in agreement. "Many a score has been settled at sea, Mr. Torris, with no one the wiser."

"No, doubt, no doubt," Torris replied. "I sympathize, truly. But how would retribution in secret, without publicity, help your *frères d'armes?*"

Dowlin and Macatter exchanged glances. Neither man had an answer.

Ryan walked over to the fire, taking his wine with him, and stared out the window, a window that faced west, a window that faced England. He listened to the winds whipping around outside. The winds seemed to be taunting him, the winds that blew from England.

Watching him with admiration, Torris would have gladly commissioned an artist on the spot to paint a portrait of the handsome, young Irishman. Ryan had presence and it all came naturally to him, nothing false or pompous, no pretense. Torris liked doing business with people far more than he liked the people he did business with. Ryan was the exception. Suddenly a thought struck him and a shiver ran down his spine, forcing him to look away. *The British will need to crush this Irishman if they catch him. They will make an example of the young man and will hang him; they must, they will have no choice and the English always win in the end, always.*

"Well, we need not take any action on this yet," Ryan said after a moment's reflection. "Perhaps Franklin can provide us with some guidance. I have heard of his profound intellectual gifts. Regardless tho' of what his Excellency can or cannot do on our behalf, British threats - and I believe I speak for my whole crew - won't stop us from sailing."

"Damn sure won't - not by a long shot!" Dowlin pledged boastfully in a calmer voice.

Ryan returned to his chair. "John, the reason we came to Dunkirk is to discuss another matter with you. I'll get straight to the heart it. We want a second ship, another cutter. Even have a name ready for her: the *Black Princess*. Fitting, yes? Two privateers sailing in tandem would create many interesting, and profitable, possibilities. We could have caused a great deal more damage to British shipping and prestige with two ships working as a pair. Perhaps sending out a second raider could even serve as *our* response to the British."

"I see..." offered Torris, somewhat relieved. Torris wasn't sure why his Irish captain had found the need to travel all the way from Morlaix to Dunkirk to see him personally. He had some fear that Ryan had come to discuss money, to ask for his share of the prize money, money he didn't yet have because of the complexities encountered with the sale of the *Goodwill*. He had been prepared for a heated discussion. But he should have known better. Torris had come to understand that money held little power over Ryan. Torris wasn't quite sure what motivated Ryan, but it wasn't money. Ryan was a romantic and from the tone and substance of Ryan's letters to himself and to Franklin, written with great passion, Torris suspected that the young Irishman was getting himself caught up in, was being seduced by, America's ideals of equality and liberty.

"May we know your thoughts on the matter, John?" asked Ryan.

"You have commented on this possibility before, Luke. When you speak as a seafarer and soldier, I have no doubts about the wisdom of what you say. You possess, may I observe in all candor, remarkable skills. The exploits of your ship and crew have captured the imagination of the people! You have taken enemy ships right under the nose of the great British fleet. You have chased ships into shore under fire from a harbor's fortress guns. A larger enemy warship attacks your crippled ship and you fight her off, killing and wounding a good number of her crew with not one loss among your own men. Then a British frigate, lying in wait, pounces on your prizes and takes all save one and comes at you. She hunts you relentlessly during the night, but the fearless men of the *Black Prince* elude her. Wonderful! Exceptional feats of skill and bravery! A *second* ship though? Ah, it would demand substantial amounts of money. Money I do not have. I do not know my friend, I do not know."

Torris paused to rock back and forth in his chair, mulling Ryan's suggestion over. He absently rubbed his ear lobe between two fingers. *Two ships. That could be most profitable.*

"There must be a way," Ryan said and drained his glass.

"Hm. On the other hand, there is plenty of investment money in France if you know who to approach. Would you have any objection to bringing in additional partners? And who would be her captain?"

"Additional partners," answered Ryan, "are fine by me. Command would go to Edward here. During all my years at sea, I have only known one officer as competent and as skilled as Edward and that's Patrick. The nod goes to Edward only because he's the senior officer."

Macatter, who had too much wine and was slouched down in his chair, suddenly bolted straight up, looked at Ryan in stunned silence. Ryan's promotion of him to captain had caught him off guard.

"And a crew? Your own ship is undermanned as it is, no? Where will you find men to sail her?"

"Plenty of Irish lads right here in Dunkirk," Dowlin answered.

"Yes, that is true, Patrick. And as your successes multiply, a legend grows. Many Irish have flocked to Dunkirk hoping to sail with you. A few weeks ago, those men would have joined you with enthusiasm. But now, with British threats of execution hanging over your men like some dark cloud, their ardor I suspect may have cooled. There is fear, Patrick. Who can blame them? Many have families here in Dunkirk or back in Ireland to support and they have no political motivations to inspire them, none leastwise to make them want to risk their lives for the Americans."

"A second cartel ship with American prisoners was due to arrive in France, has it?" asked Ryan.

"*Oui*, it arrived at Nantes during your voyage," replied Torris but shook his head. "But you can dismiss that notion. Most have already signed on with Captain Jones. Jones they say will soon sail from L'Orient, if he has not already, with a powerful American squadron. The rest I hear have returned to America."

"Then," Ryan replied unperturbed, "we shall simply have to persuade our own countrymen and, perhaps, some of yours as well. We shall need Franklin's help to protect our lads at Penzance from being tried for treason. I won't let good men like that hang, not on trumped-up charges. I'll storm Penzance if I have to. John, I want that second ship - and an American commission for her. Make it so. I know you can. We'll find her a crew. Have no worries there. And we'll provision her ourselves if we must."

"How so? Sartine?"

"No. I cannot ask him for any more help tho' I suspect he would gladly give it. He has been too generous as it is and I do not wish to impose upon our friendship or compromise him in any way." Ryan paused with a wry smile. "And besides, the enemy has plenty. We'll take whatever stores we need from the English if we must."

Torris smiled at his young captain. Ryan was a man who always spoke from the heart - and with passion.

"My, but I just now had a thought, a deliciously wicked thought, my friends. Sends goose pimples down my arms. How grand it would be Luke to see you and Captain Jones sail together - what a fighting pair of wolves you would make! Frightening prospect. Oh, pardon me Edward, Patrick... I meant no disrespect to you. You are all to be commended for your exemplary work."

"None taken," replied Macatter still basking in the glow of his new promotion and drained his glass. "Luke deserves the credit true enough."

"Jones is a Scotsman I hear," Dowlin chuckled. "That's almost as good as bein' Irish. *Gawd* created the Scots as a special favor to us Irish don't you know - to give the English someone else to kick the snot out of once in a while and give us Irish a breather. They make damn good scotch too..."

The Irishmen left Torris's home with full bellies and high hopes. Macatter went on to visit his wife, who had come from Ireland to make a home for them in Dunkirk while Dowlin went on to visit the local taverns, to hone his rusty social skills to a keen edge. Ryan began his search in Dunkirk Harbor, looking for a suitable, new raider. He would have a second ship, he had told Dowlin and Macatter, *even if I have to build it with my own hands.*

But finding a second ship would prove far easier than finding the men to sail her, Ryan would soon learn. Torris's warning was true - there was fear among the Irish. Few men were willing to risk being hanged for piracy or treason for fighting for the Americans.

Unable to find a suitable ship or the men to sail her, and anxious to put to sea again, Ryan returned to Morlaix with Dowlin two weeks later. Macatter stayed behind in Dunkirk to tend to his wife, who had taken ill, and would to continue Ryan's search for a new ship and crew.

Warming to the idea of operating two raiders, Torris wasted no time in sharing Ryan's proposal with Coffyn and Coffyn promptly wrote to Franklin. Coffyn informed Franklin that Torris and Marchant intended to "...fitt out another Cutter of 60 feet keel & 20 feet beam mounting 16 three pounders 24 swivels & Small arms with sixty-five men all Americans & Irish under the command of Capn. Edward Macartor of Boston; this Cutter will be called the black Princess, and is intended to cruise in Company with the black Prince. The owners have again apply'd to me, to request your Excellency thinks proper to comply with this request, I shall conform to your Excellency's orders and intentions, respecting the instructions and oaths of allegiance to the united states to be taken by Captn. Macartor his officers & Crew... if these two privateers cruize together as intended, I hope they'll be able to keep all their prisoners on board, which the former did not do on account of the smallness of his vessell."

Torris sent a separate letter to Franklin, appealing to Franklin to do whatever he could do to save Ryan's men at Penzance from the gallows. "Humanity & Friendship," he wrote, "make me Shake for these Poor People & I hasten to Communicate your Excellency these advices, that you might Take quickly, the measures your Prudence & Wisdom will direct, to put these Prisoners of War, Sworn subjects to the united states out of the reach of malice & furour of the British Court - The 25 and 30 English Prisoners taken by the Black Prince & landed at Morlaix, will doubtless be awfull to the Ennemy, as they might Justly be made fearful of reprisails on them."

Under a blistering August sun the Irishmen, men who loved their swift, trim ships, confidently sailed their black cutter out into the rolling waves of a wine-dark sea - eager to win new glory. They made their way to the southwest tip of England first where two prominent headlands - known by all as Lizard Point and Land's End - jutted far out into the boiling sea like the pincers of a stubby claw. And trolling the waters inside Mount's Bay for ships leaving Plymouth, the privateers pounced on three rich trophies in rapid succession. The whaler *Reward*, the brig *Diligence* and the sloop *Friend's Adventure* all surrendered to the Irishmen without a fight. And after each ship's master had signed a ransom note for his vessel and cargo - and surrendered a hostage or two to guarantee payment - and after every crewman gave his written parole, the ships were set free. This was how the Irishmen liked to do their raiding.

And then the master tactician, still hungry, cunning, plotting always, considered matters through and through. Continue to cruise the fertile waters around Land's End, the Isles of Scilly and Wolf's Rock where they had taken so many fat prizes, or slip back into the vast stretches of the windswept sea to look for fresh game in new waters?

When Ryan finally decided to move on, Marchant protested loudly. You don't, Marchant argued, leave waters with holds half-empty when the fishing is good. But fishermen, Ryan shot back, do not need to concern themselves with hostile warships on the prowl. *We hit and run...* These were the sound tactics that had favored the side with inferior numbers down through the ages. The two men exchanged heated words, tempers flared, but Ryan decided to go further out, to head west for Ireland, and told Marchant the matter was closed. But first, before sailing into the Celtic Sea, he set a course north, cutting across Bristol Channel, and pointed his ship towards Pembroke.

Macatter found Ryan at the binnacle, hunched over the table studying a chart while Dowlin held a lantern over his shoulder. "Luke, Pat, evenin'. Lovely night. I see lights to our larboard. Pembroke?"

"Good evening to you Ed, aye, Pembroke," Ryan answered.

"What's in Pembroke?" asked Macatter, rubbing the sleep from his eyes.

"A castle," Dowlin replied.

"Oh? We goin' to lay siege to it?" Macatter asked in jest.

"No," replied Ryan with a smile. "I had in mind to deliver a warning to the British tho'."

"Luke has," interjected Dowlin, "an inspired thought. We bombard the castle and leave a calling card on shore, threatin' more direct strikes against English cities if they try and hang our lads imprisoned at Guernsey or at Penzance."

"Ah. I see the poetry in it. The Brits hold prisoners of war at Pembroke Castle and if we can attack them there with impunity..."

"Precisely," interrupted Ryan. "Then we show them we can attack English soil at any time we please and they dare not mess with our lads. That was the plan anyway. But while you were snoozing, we hit a snag. Regrettably, there's a small frigate anchored in the harbor."

"Ah. And now the two of you are lookin' for an alternate target?"

"Quite so."

Macatter leaned over the map and tapped his finger on a place called Fishguard, just on the other side of the Pembrokeshire headland and an easy sail away. "Been here before. Not far. Small, pretty little town at the mouth of the Gwaun River with a good harbor. No defenses."

"You want to shell defenseless civilians?" Dowlin asked with surprise. He had taken a liking to Macatter from the start and thought he knew the man fairly well. There had never been any hint of cruelty or barbarism in the fellow before. "Tad cold-bloodied isn't it?"

Macatter scratched his beard and grinned, a reassuring grin to show Dowlin that he hadn't lost his mind. "It's night. Folks are in bed. There's a church near the water and it will be empty at this hour. We could lob a few balls into it."

"Shell a church you say?" asked Dowlin incredulously. "And accomplish what?"

"Seems to me it's the same as striking at Pembroke except it's less dangerous for us. We send the English the same message: *we can attack your island when and where we like and come off safely.* Maybe it's a better message. We remind the English just how naked they are up and down their shores. Not even King George has enough frigates to guard every town and harbor."

"Ed," Dowlin said smiling, "that you never served in the army or navy is of no great moment. Always knew you had it in you - you are a very dangerous man."

Ryan nodded his approval and went to take the tiller himself while Dowlin quietly disappeared below to wake up his gunners. Macatter went to rally the rest of the crew.

After easing into Fishguard's quiet harbor in the dead of night, the *Prince's* men obliterated serenity, obliterated Fishguard's small, clapboard church too after firing off several broadsides. And the town folk - unaccustomed to the ways of war and fearing at first that perhaps an angry God had come to smite them - all turned out of their beds, panic-stricken, to find their poor church ablaze and in shambles. The attackers slipped away into the blackness before anyone could catch a glimpse of them. But in the morning the town's reverend, while inspecting the damage to his church, found a sword stuck in a piling at the water's edge. Attached to the sword he found a note, a warning, that read: An *Eye for an Eye* and signed *The Prince's Men*. The king's good subjects, frightened and confused, sent the sword and note on to London, along with an urgent plea for help.

After leaving the ungodly work in Fishguard behind them, the Irishmen sailed west and cruised around the waters off Waterford for several lazy days until their audacity was rewarded. On the third day the privateers snagged four worthy ships in a row. In the morning they took the brig *Blossom* sailing in ballast followed by two sloops: the *Resolution* and the *Matthew & Sally*. Both sloops were colliers loaded down with coal and destined for Cork. And then in the afternoon a very large sloop, the *Betsey*, carrying pork from Bideford to Youghal, fell under the spell of the Irishmen's heavy cannon.

And after Ryan's privateers had finished ravaging each victim, helping themselves to anything of value and taking paroles, ransom notes and hostages, the vessels, one-by-one, fled into Waterford where their unhappy crews spread the dire warnings. The men of the black *pirate* ship had returned, intent on plunder.

Rout is never so far away that she cannot hear the sounds of wailing men. She heard the pitiful cries rising up in Waterford now and decided to see for herself what all the fuss was about down on the rolling waves below. Under her dark shadow Waterford's entire fishing fleet fled, scrambled back to port with word that a black warship, like some killer shark lurking off shore, had attacked them too. And with the sound of booming cannon, Rout's sister Panic hurried to reach her side, to find some opportunity for herself. With Panic close at hand, no ship's master dared to put to sea again.

But an Irishman's luck never lasts for long. It changes with the wind.

As Ryan and his men were terrorizing Waterford's commercial fleet, the British warship *Spry*, a tender for the fleet, happened to be sitting in Waterford's harbor taking on provisions. The *Spry*, at 130 feet and carrying 18 carriage guns, was a large brig, a fine warship, with a crew of well over 200 fighting men. Her captain, a seasoned master named Woolsey, soon received word that the *Black Prince* was only several leagues away. The Englishman was no coward - but he was no fool either. The pirate ship, or so he had heard, was well armed and often sailed with escorts. Woolsey would have preferred to sail out against the enemy with a frigate under his feet, or at least with an escort of his own. But the *Spry* was the only warship in Waterford and Woolsey knew his duty.

The order went out. The *Spry's* men were soon casting off warps, dropping sails and pointing their ship's nose out to sea, eager for a fight. The smell of easy prize money hung heavy in the air. Privateers fared well enough against helpless merchantmen, but rarely did these civilian mercenaries perform well against fully armed warships manned by professional soldiers. Everyone knew that privateers had no stomach for a real fight, preferring to spend some time in jail to being killed or wounded. Most surrendered without a shot. That was the way of the privateer. But the trick in capturing privateers had always been in finding them.

Woolsey quickly went to his cabin to change into his best uniform, taking a moment to admire himself in the mirror. He was a fine figure of a man. Tall and handsome despite middle age, he still wore the uniform well. *Black Prince you have been found! By God, they'll give me command of a frigate when I bring you in! Glorious day!*

And while the *Spry's* master readied himself and his ship for battle, Ryan and his men were scanning the horizon looking for fresh victims, unaware of the violence approaching them. It was not long until *Prince's* lookout reported spotting more sails. Prize number five! It was turning into a very profitable day indeed.

"Where away?" Dowlin shouted up to the lookout, annoyed that he even had to ask.

"She's broad on the larboard bow, Lieutenant."

The sailor at the masthead was a new man and didn't think to give the ship's type, course or speed.

"What kind of vessel, damnit man?" Dowlin called up to sailor, flustered. But the lookout didn't answer.

"Damn yer eyes, Fulton!" Dowlin cursed. "Don't make me come up thar!"

But in the rough winds knocking the ship about - the last remnants of a fearsome clash between the titans West Wind and East Wind in a dispute over territory the night before - Fulton couldn't hear Dowlin. Blustery gusts whistled through the rigging, playing an eerie melody, and set the blocks to clattering.

Ryan started to climb up the shrouds to get a better look at things for himself until Dowlin grabbed him by his boot and pulled him down.

"That'll be my job as officer of the watch if you don't mind, sir," Dowlin said bluntly. "No sense in you riskin' yer neck, Luke."

Ryan nodded, obediently dropped back down. Dowlin, like Kelly, was always overly protective of him. Sometimes he resented it but he couldn't argue with his friend's logic now.

Dowlin grinned, as if he had just managed to pull off some mischievous schoolboy prank, and raced up the ratlines with ease. But the ship he saw was too far off, probably heading to Dublin, and seemed small so the Irishmen decided to ignore her. But then a second set of sails appeared, a vessel leaving Waterford and heading towards them.

"We've got ourselves a Royal Navy ship, an eighteen gunner with two bow and two stern chasers!" Dowlin excitedly cried out. "And she's comin' in close hauled, comin' in fast and, by *Jesus*, she's spoilin' for a fight! Got her guns run out already!"

The boatswain's mate blew his bo'sun's pipe for all he was worth and the men of the *Prince* scrambled to their positions. Every sailor knew his place. Even Jumbaaliyia, still learning, but showing the skills of a sailor far beyond those of some raw recruit, rushed to take his post at the foremast braces.

Word quickly spread up and down the deck that this was no toothless, fat cow, no fishing trawler or cargo ship, coming their way this time around. One of the king's warships was closing with them! Men soused the deck with water and then sprinkled sand. Gunners primed and loaded their heavy guns. Topmen manned the braces or scrambled up into the rigging. Bulkheads were knocked away and fires extinguished. The younger, quicker lads brought up extra shot and powder from the magazine lockers below, usually a job for boys, but *Black Prince* carried no boys - save one: the former Dunkirk street urchin named Jean and he claimed to be a man despite his tender years. And once the men of the *Prince* had their ship in fighting trim, the officers assembled quickly at the helm to receive their orders.

As officer of the watch, Dowlin made his report directly to the captain just as he had been trained to do by the finest navy in the world. "Sir, ship cleared for action, six minutes, twelve seconds!"

Marchant nodded. Dowlin's military professionalism was lost on him. Who cared, he wondered, how long it took the men to ready the ship for action so long as it was done before the enemy was near? The British warship was still well out of range.

"Very well, Mr. Dowlin. We'll port her helm and swing south-west. Wind favors us in that direction. We'll lose 'em soon enough. Helmsman, be alert there! You men at the braces, look lively now! Stand by to port your helm hard, set your course south by south-west."

Now Marchant's order - by previous agreement of all - would ordinarily have been the proper one. The Irishmen were at sea to prey on easy, helpless victims, to make some money for themselves and to take prisoners for Franklin. There was no need to get themselves bloodied in a fight with a British warship. Turning tail and running was the prudent thing to do.

But Ryan was under a strange spell that day and would have none of it. In later years, not even he could say what it was that had roused his fighting fury. Perhaps it was because the fate of his men imprisoned at Penzance weighed heavily on his mind. He had toyed with the idea of landing at Penzance to break his lads out, but dismissed the scheme as too risky. Perhaps he wanted to show the British, to prove to them, that *Black Prince* was a legitimate warship sailing under an enemy flag. Who can say what is in a man's heart, what leads him on, when he doesn't know himself?

"Belay that order, Mr. Marchant!" Ryan commanded sternly with a fire in his eyes.

Dowlin and Kelly snapped their heads around to look at Ryan. His words had caught them both off-guard. They knew their friend, knew him well, and at once understood Ryan's hostile tone, his intent. Their master wasn't going to run. No. Not this time. Ryan was in the mood to fight.

There were murmurs among the crew. They were going to take on the British! Every heart was filled with joy and anxiety mixed. With long, hard hours of training day after day, and a few old scores to settle, many liked to boast about what damage they would wreak on the British if only given the chance. Bold talk. Or empty words born of tavern gibberish? Now it seemed they would all get their chance, the chance to prove their mettle. Not one among them had any second thoughts.

Marchant looked about apprehensively. He did not share the *reckless* enthusiasm of these Irish. And with Arnold gone, his only colleague, his only friend on board, he felt alone, isolated, and was becoming more and more frustrated each day. And he resented what he saw as Ryan's nagging, growing interference with the command of *his* ship. He, after all, was the captain of the *Black Prince* by the unanimous agreement of all her owners and by the law of the sea. His powers on board ship were absolute. Ryan was merely an owner, one of several at that, and on board at Marchant's pleasure - or so Marchant thought.

And in return, the crew had come to resent him. Just hours before Weldin and John Kelly had approached Ryan to make their case against Marchant.

"Sir, I hope you'll forgive my boldness," Weldin had said, a bit hesitantly as he and Kelly stood shoulder-to-shoulder in Ryan's cabin, still smarting over some insulting remark made to him by Marchant, "but I can't kiss the back of that fool's trousers much longer."

John Kelly nodded in agreement. "The lads are gettin' a wee bit touchy about it, sir. The man is his own worst enemy. I won't mince words. He don't know his arse from his elbow. And he had the gall to rebuke some poor sailor earlier for a job that was done proper, just to stoke his own ego! You know how well run this ship is. We hardly need the likes of him lecturin' us. An unplucked tavern wench has more damn sense."

"Marchant?"

"Aye, Marchant," replied John Kelly.

Ryan had listened sympathetically to his two officers' complaints. But he still needed Marchant and had told them so.

Now Marchant, standing near the helm at the spot where captains stand, felt slighted at Ryan's last order. With wounded pride, his temper began to boil. *By God, it is time to show this young upstart what it means to be master!*

"Mr. Ryan," Marchant said, "my plan, according to your own wishes, is to avoid reckless combat."

"Quite right, Captain. I find no fault with your order, but..."

Marchant cut him off. "Mr. Ryan, beg pardon, but nothing. If you want to teach this British dog a lesson, fine by me. But allow me to do the job you're paying me to do - allow me to command my ship *properly*."

Ryan, never petty, ignored Marchant's last remark, an implied insult. *The American can think whatever he likes.*

"Very well, Captain Marchant, the ship is yours. You have my consent to engage the enemy."

Ryan had no misgivings about entrusting the ship to Marchant, or about the man's false bravado. None at all. He would, if he had to, override any of Marchant's orders without hesitation. And, if the man gave him any trouble about it, he would have Marchant clapped in irons.

With the young owner put in his place, Marchant, oblivious to his own precarious position, gave the order to close with the enemy warship. The crew eagerly ran up the stars and stripes and rolled out the four-pounders.

You can sense fear in others. You can smell it, see it, taste it. Fear is not something one can hide for very long. One can only hope to control it.

Marchant had spent enough years at sea to know when a man, or a whole crew, was in Panic's iron grip. He found no hint of it aboard the *Prince* now and that puzzled him.

Studying the enemy vessel more closely through his spyglass, Dowlin reported the brig's main armament included deadly nine-pounders, 14 of them. If the enemy's heavy weapons concerned him any, he didn't show it. But how he wished he had some nine-pounders to play with!

The winds, more brisk now, whipped the sea into a frenzy of whitecaps. And like two angry eagles, wings outstretched, spoiling for a fight over some prey or meager strip of ground, the two ships charged at one another through the choppy waves under full sail, top speed.

"Mr. Dowlin, Mr. Weldin," Marchant shouted down the deck, "prepare your guns for a full broadside and wait for my command."

Dowlin and Weldin saluted and looked to their gun crews.

On board the *Spry*, Woolsey gave the same order.

Men scrambled. Hearts pounded against ribs and the lust for blood, never sated, rose to a fever pitch.

And when the ships came within shouting distance Dowlin, like some maniac, stepped up on the rail and led his men in a blood-curdling yell, rattling the nerves of even the stoutest English heart. Then he looked back at Ryan and winked.

Ryan answered him with a smile, whispered to himself: *Patrick Dowlin, lord of the Irish war cry!*

"Take yer aim, lads!" Dowlin shouted, giddy with excitement. How he loved the cut and thrust of battle - and it mattered not at all to him that some blood might be spilt for his own amusement, English blood at least.

"Check yer windage an elevation. Steady now. Watch yer linstocks thar! Steady lads, wait for my word. Wait for the rise of the swell. Steady. Steady. Make ready. Wait. Wait for it..."

Marchant looked over at Ryan for guidance. He had that much sense at least. Ryan gave the nod.

"*FIRE!*" Marchant thundered with his magnificent preacher's voice.

"*FIRE!*" Dowlin repeated.

BOOM! BOOM! BA-BA-BA-BOOM! BOOM! BOOM! BOOM!

Eight heavy guns belched out deadly iron in flawless unison. The deck rumbled as the black monsters recoiled. Five shots, flying true, smashed into the British brig raising a cry of jubilation among the Irish.

But the *Lord of the Irish War Cry* was hardly content. No, never, not until his foe lay bloodied and vanquished. He urged his men on.

"Well done, lads! Stop yer vents thar! Sponges. Reload. Faster! Faster! Faster! That's it. Quickly now! Make ready to fire as yer guns bare! Move! Move! Move! Remember to wait for the swell…"

His gunners, obedient to their sacred cause, methodically, efficiently, began swabbing down the bore of their guns with wet sponges to extinguish any burning residue and then, using the flexible rammers, rammed down powder and ball. They primed their guns with more powder next and pulled on the side tackles to roll the monsters out through the gun ports. Then they set the elevation using iron hand spikes and adjusted the windage by pulling on the training tackles. And finally, the gun captains, each with his burning linstock in hand, prepared to fire his gun at his own discretion.

Ryan ordered the swivels brought up and loaded - but did not want them mounted to the rails, not yet. Dowlin's men quickly went about placing the swivels, all 30 of them and wrapped in burlap bags, against the bulwarks, hidden away from prying English eyes.

The British, unimpressed with the Irishmen's feeble first volley, unleashed their own fury at the cutter, fired off their starboard guns, sending seven deadly nine-pound balls at the *Prince*. The Irishmen braced themselves for pain. Two shots punched holes through *Prince's* main sail. The rest flew harmlessly overhead and splashed into the empty sea beyond. British petty officers, brutish men, shouted at the ratings, spurring them on to work their guns more quickly.

Woolsey now realized he faced only four-pounders and gave the order, his voice surging with confidence, to close with the enemy. He had the advantage in heavy guns and would use his nine-pounders close in to bludgeon the privateer. Simple, brutal work. And well he knew that, if they were really lucky, they might even be able to pull up alongside the cutter and board her - keeping any damage to his new prize to a minimum. He had more than enough men to handle the grisly, close-up work.

Woolsey kept his eye on the heavy sloop-of-war through his spyglass, puzzled. "Odd that she makes no attempt to flee," he told his number two. "She is outclassed and in unfriendly waters!"

"Perhaps, sir, her captain is a fool," replied his number two. "My, she is a handsome craft tho' and should fetch a goodly price, a fortune! What luck, sir!"

"What luck indeed, Lieutenant..."

The men of the *Black Prince* were too busy with their labors to notice the slight smile on Ryan's lips. The master tactician saw the British captain's plan, saw it clearly, and felt no concern. None at all. Ryan had been counting on the English captain's use of simple logic. *Patrick was right, the British have no imagination.*

The two winged warriors, trading shot for shot, moved in closer for the kill while men, seized with blood lust, traded taunts and insults.

Yearning to have some fun, Dowlin climbed up the mainmast shrouds.

A British gunner saw him, called out to him: "Hey, Irish! Here's some English iron for you! Hold still now so I can put a quick end to yer miserable, fookin' life. *To hell you go!*"

BOOM!

The English gunner was good. Dowlin felt the rush of hot air rip past his head as a cannon ball whizzed by. But he did not flinch. He did not cower. Not that proud man, never. '*Tis the bold man who comes off best* he told himself and moved on. The near miss had roused his fighting fury even more.

"To hell you say?" he shouted boldly across the waves, a grim smile on his lips. "You first, my fine, *English bitch!* What do you know of misery my friend? I'll show you misery. Have a taste of American iron, set in the muzzle just for you with my own Irish hands! Embrace it - like a lover - then we'll see how well you boast after yer cut in two, you spineless coward!"

He looked down at the gun below his feet. Tim, the first among the Irishmen to win a gold sovereign for spotting a prize, was holding a linstock firmly in his hand, taking care that the yarn wrapped around the stick still smoldered.

"Tim! Ready?"

"Aye, sir!"

"Wait for it, ready, wait, almost - *FIRE!*"

BOOM!

After spitting out its ruthless iron on a tongue of orange flame, Tim's gun recoiled violently back across the deck. His gun crew sprang into action to reload.

Dowlin could feel the heat of the muzzle flash below his feet, was enveloped in a cloud of white smoke and couldn't see. But he heard Tim's shot smash into the brig's wood hull with a loud crack, a solid hit! And then he heard the sounds of wounded men, he heard the groans from splinter wounds. But live, English oak stands up well against four-pound iron and when the smoke cleared Dowlin could see that Tim's shot inflicted no real damage.

"You squawk like a woman, Irish!" a second English gunner angrily cried out and - *BOOM!*

A solid shot slammed into the *Prince* with a dull thud. No miss this time! The two ships were too close. But the cutter's master craftsmen had built a warhorse using the choicest hardwood planking, triple thick in places, and she shook the hit off with ease and sailed on.

Dowlin, his face covered in black soot, his eyes smoldering, smiled, a sardonic smile, yes, a smile to freeze the blood of any champion. "That the best you can do, English? Come now and die! No need to fret about it. We mortals must all depart this world one day or the next and yer time has come, my friend! I'm the better man by far in strength and wit and beyond compare in the ways of combat! And after I lay you low, I'll be coming' for yer mates, send them all to fiery hell just to keep you company..."

Tim needed no instruction this time. He wiped the sweat off his brow, carefully rechecked his gun, waited for the rise of the ship on the swell and, when the brig crossed his sight, he dropped his burning linstock near the touch ring's base, taking care not to actually touch the metal lest the flames and hot gases shooting up doused his slow match. He knew the drill and knew it well...

BOOM!

Whether young Tim hit their English taunter or not, no Irishman could say for certain. But after Tim's shot hit home, no more was heard from the boastful Englishman on that pretty, August day.

Dowlin's insane antics had escaped Ryan's notice at first. But when Ryan caught Dowlin standing up in the shrouds, flaunting his power, flaunting his own invincibility as if he was Achilles, his face turned bright red. For the first time that any Irishman could recall, Ryan lost his composure for all to see. He charged straight at Dowlin, seething, ignoring the havoc around him.

"*Patrick James Dowlin!*" he yelled through clenched teeth, pointing an accusing finger at him, "you'll *kindly* remove yourself from my shrouds and return to the deck now mister or I'll save the British the trouble of shooting you and do it myself! Get down, NOW!"

Dowlin at once realized he had gone too far. But he was having so much *fun*. He casually smiled back at Ryan and nodded, to let Ryan know that all was well. He had had his bit of play.

He leapt off the shrouds. But he did not jump quite fast enough.

Click-boom! He never heard it coming. But before his feet touched the deck, an errant musket ball drilled a hole through his soft flesh. Some English sharpshooter, hiding in the shadows, had shot well - or was lucky.

Ryan watched him stagger back and forth, like some drunkard, and then saw the red spot spreading across the back of his linen shirt. Ryan looked at Dowlin, his blackened face streaked with sweat, in horror.

Dowlin felt something pinch him, glanced down at the blood oozing from a hole in his shirt with disbelief. At first he laughed. But then he couldn't feel his legs. *Strange...*

"Bare a hand there, lads!" Ryan ordered. Hoar and Tim were nearest and caught Dowlin just as his legs began to buckle. They helped Ryan carry him below to the French surgeon who had yet to earn his keep. The three men gently laid Dowlin down across a galley table.

As the doctor gave him a spoonful of laudanum, Dowlin looked up at Ryan and forced a faint smile. "Sorry, Luke. Got carried away a bit. Brazen son-of-a-bitches aren't they? Won't happen again. Promise."

Ryan patted his friend, his brother, lightly on the arm and gave him a reassuring smile too. "Rest easy, Pat. You've always excelled most others before at good, clear sense. Helluva-way to show it now. As soon as you're well, you can taunt the English to your heart's content my friend - just don't give the bastards such an easy target next time, hey? You certainly let loose with your banter there. You're the brazen son-of-a-bitch, I'd say. But, truth be told, you carried it off with style, lad! *Dowlin the Magnificent! Ireland's own Achilles! Lord of the Irish war cry!* That's what they'll be calling you back home."

"Oh? More like Dublin's idiot son. Sorry, Luke."

"Rest easy now," Ryan offered softly, took Dowlin's hand and squeezed it. "And sleep. I'll be needin' you again, full strength, soon enough."

"Let death take me if it is my time but promise me, Luke, don't let me wake up in a British jail."

"You have my word on it. Rest now."

Dowlin surrendered himself to gentle sleep but it was not his day to die. The Fates, not men, decide such things. No mortal wound, the ball had passed clean through his upper shoulder, tearing flesh but missing bone and lung.

The surgeon cut away Dowlin's shirt and began cleaning the wound with an ointment made of wax, turpentine and oil of hypericum, and then applied a compress. Once the surgeon was satisfied that Dowlin was in no immediate danger, Ryan returned to the hot action back on deck.

Brig and cutter continued trading iron. Relentless hate.

The air turned hazy with smoke and like two ravenous wolves, both intent on bringing the other down, the ships circled around each other in a death dance, each fighter probing the other for some weakness to exploit, searching, testing strength against strength - waiting for the right moment to lunge for the kill. Both captains showed skill and patience, each one biding his time for the right moment to close and strike. On several passes the brig's men attempted to move in close enough to throw out grappling hooks to snag the cutter, but the cutter's master was too cagey. Ryan could see that the British outnumbered his crew by three to one. He would not let them board and maneuvered his ship away each time.

And then Ryan saw his opportunity. The brig was trying yet again to close in for the kill, this time coming at the *Prince* head-on. But Ryan had the wind and could afford to let the brig come in closer before he would need to give the order to sheer- off, to turn to their starboard away from the brig. He gave the order to Weldin - Marchant was too engrossed in watching the battle - to mount the swivels. The range was a bit far he figured, over 200 yards, but they were close enough and he didn't wish to risk getting any closer.

The gunners took fifteen swivels, already loaded with canister shot, small bags filled with tiny mini-balls or razor-sharp bits of metal, chain or nails, and mounted them on the starboard rail with one elegant, concerted action. The precision of the movement would have made the most demanding British officer proud.

"*FIRE!*" Weldin cried out.

The *Spry's* young captain saw the swivels too late to give the order to turn. Woolsey barely had time enough to duck as a hailstorm of countless bits of jagged metal shredded sails, shredded rigging and flesh. *Spry's* mainsail went slack and she suddenly lost speed. The Irishmen raised a victory cheer.

"That-a-way lads!" Weldin cried out excitedly. "Let's give 'em another taste of it! For Patrick! Aim well. Fire when ready!"

But just then the winds shifted without warning and the cutter, inexplicably, started sailing like some drunken sailor, weaving to and fro. Ryan glanced back at the helmsman. It was Mulvany, not the best man at the tiller. Morgan or Knight had the better skills. But he could find no fault with Mulvany. He checked the masts and saw nothing wrong and then looked down the length of the deck, looking at the bow. And there he saw the problem: someone had left the storm jib up from the previous night's gale. Not Mulvany's fault. Marchant was to blame. But Mulvany should have known better and spoken up. After today, Ryan told himself, either Morgan or Knight would always take the helm whenever they came to blows.

"Capt'n Marchant," Ryan called out, "I hope you will take no offense, sir. Well I see you are occupied. But may I suggest we break off the engagement for a bit and reset the jib sail? Give us better sailing.

She's too sluggish in these winds with that infernal storm jib up."

"Oh?" Marchant replied and turned to look at the jib. "Why yes, of course! You there helmsman, hard to starboard. Mr. Kelly, we'll sheer off - see to the storm jib once we're clear. Understood?"

Kelly understood all too well. He had heard Ryan's *suggestion* to Marchant. The giant simply touched his hat with two fingers and gave the American a flattering smile. Then he made his way forward towards the bow, cursing Marchant under his breath and barking out orders to his men at the braces as he passed them by.

"Damn fool Marchant!" he muttered to himself out loud. "Well, to be fair about it, I shoulda noticed that damn jib myself..."

The *Prince* suddenly peeled away from the *Spry* and the British brig took the opportunity to change course too - but she did not turn with the American.

The *Spry's* captain counted the growing number of dead, dying and wounded huddled in small groups against the masts. The deck was slick with blood and gore. The dead were still, no complaints. Never again would they feel the sun's warmth against their skin. Never again would they feel a mother's loving embrace or feel the soft caresses of a lover's touch. The wounded, sprawled out across the deck and moaning, felt all too much. Woolsey couldn't have been more heartsick.

Next, he surveyed the damage to his ship. Several of the *Spry's* guns were out of action, a great deal of rigging had been shot away and half her sails were badly torn. The main sail was completely useless.

To continue the contest meant risking the loss of his ship. They had simply been outfought. *Enough slaughter,* Woolsey thought soberly to himself. *I have done my duty, time to return to port and lick our wounds. Save this ship to fight another battle. This day is yours Irish - but our day will come, I swear it...*

Woolsey reluctantly gave the order to break off the engagement. With heavy hearts, his men obeyed. They turned their battered ship around and headed for the safety of Waterford under as much sail as her split spars and shredded rigging could carry. Let the Irish rove the open seas for now. The filth and gore splattered across their poor brig's deck had dampened their lust for blood and glory.

A different mood settled over *Prince's* men. The Irishmen cheered wildly at the sight of the British warship turning tail and running - and after Kelly and his small detail finished resetting the jib - Ryan gave the order to come about and his men cheered again when they realized they were going to pursue the fleeing brig. The British might be through with the Irish, but the Irish were not through with them. Spirits soared. There were heady notions of taking a British warship as a prize. What a coup that would be!

"We're overhaulin' 'em fast, Capt'n!" observed Morgan, who had quietly relieved Mulvany at the helm.

"Aye," answered Marchant - not realizing that Morgan was addressing Ryan, not him.

Ryan quietly, coolly, paced back and forth like some lion on the prowl, his mind churning. How best to intercept and take the brig before she reached Waterford's safety?

Marchant glanced sideways at Morgan with a stern eye. "Aren't enough wind for her to escape us!" he snorted. "Steer small blast you! I don't want to lose her over a helmsman's laxness."

No better man was there than Morgan at guiding the sharp-prowed cutter across the waves.

Ryan overheard the petty, hurtful remark and glanced over at Morgan. Morgan had done no wrong. Morgan frowned but held his peace out of respect for his master. That earned him Ryan's gratitude. Ryan nodded silently at Morgan. Morgan understood.

On board the *Spry*, the crew looked back and watched the American raider racing towards them in awe. She sliced through the waves with tremendous speed.

"My God!" Woolsey whispered to no one in particular. He stood next to the wheel, studied the privateer through his spyglass.

The *Spry* had taken a good lead, had every stitch of canvas spread out, as much as the spars and gaffs could carry, but it was not enough. The black cutter, like an angel of death, was tearing down on his poor ship, on his abused men, at frightening speed. And he could see the angry faces of her men, men bent on killing.

When the *Prince* came up alongside the *Spry*, the two warships resumed trading deadly iron. The range was close and hits were easy. But then, with most of her powder nearly spent, and more men falling, the brig's fire began to taper off. One-by-one, her guns fell silent. British sailors mumbled the unthinkable: *surrender*.

A wave of excitement, like wildfire, swept over the privateers. A British warship was theirs!

But then, both ships entered Waterford's harbor nose-to-nose. The Fates, to please the fickle gods, chose not to completely desert the *Spry* that day.

Ryan urged his Irishmen on. His gunners kept up their hot work, relentlessly pounding the brig. Wood splintered, canvas split and lines snapped. But the Irishmen could not deliver a deathblow.

In desperation the Irishmen trained their guns on the *Spry's* great mainmast, a difficult target on a rolling sea, and give the tall wood their close attention. If only they could disable *Spry*... But no man could hit the target and *Spry* kept plodding forward.

And then the shore batteries sitting on top of Tower Hook came into view. The Irishmen were out of time.

The garrison at Tower Hook could hardly believe their eyes. Sailing into their harbor, and within fair range of their big guns, was a single American warship trying to run the *Spry* down! Unbelievable audacity or a fool's arrogance the marines asked one another. The drummers beat to action and the battery crews quickly trained their cannon on the black cutter, opening fire with 12-pound balls. They would force the Americans to retreat or sink their ship.

When the shore batteries fired off the first salvo, the men of the *Spry* raised a weary cheer. Relief filled every heart. The *Spry* had narrowly escaped capture... Or had she?

Geysers of white water shot up all around the privateer - but she did not turn and run. Her Irishmen did not flinch. English sailors watched in stunned silence as the privateers ignored the shelling, slowed their ship down to cut across *Spry's* stern, and then eased their warship up on

Spry's port side. The Irishmen now had the *Spry* between themselves and Tower Hook now, using the British warship as cover! The shore batteries fell silent.

Woolsey shook his head in disbelief - and grudging admiration. "My God!" he said to his circle of officers on the quarterdeck, "the audacity of these rebels. They still mean to disable us right in our own harbor! I should like to meet the master of that cutter and shake his hand. Wonderful bravery! Fine piece of seamanship!"

The Irishmen kept firing, round after round, and *Spry* took a frightful beating. A spar split in two, more rigging snapped and *Spry* lost more speed. Like a sea hawk with a broken wing, she was nearly helpless. But then, just as Ryan was about to give the order to move in for the kill - every Irishmen heard it, the sickening sound of cracking wood. The cutter's bowsprit cap had split in two without warning. No enemy ball had struck it - the wood had just given way from stress. The bowsprit wobbled, threatened to collapse entirely. A line holding the forward jib sail snapped and the canvas floated gently down to the deck. Hobbled, the cutter lost precious speed and the lucky brig slowly began to pull ahead.

Ryan couldn't believe their luck and shook his head in disgust. A British warship, only yards away and his for the taking, was slipping away because of a broken piece of wood! And with a clear target, the shore batteries on Tower Hook resumed lobbying 12-pound balls at the Irishmen.

Ryan gave the nod to Marchant, who in turn gave the order to come about. They had no choice. *Prince* swung around sharply and headed for the open sea as quick as she was able.

The *Spry* limped back into port, bruised and battered. Her poor captain would, at least, face a board of inquiry to explain his failure.

Once they had cleared the bay, and after the cannons at Tower Hook fell silent, Kelly crawled out on the bowsprit to inspect the damage. The bowsprit, he soon reported, was finished, probably weakened from the previous night's storm and there was not enough lumber on board to fashion a new one. And so the Irishmen reluctantly headed back for France with Dowlin and the bowsprit the only casualties. Off Hook Head though, Good Fortune gave the Irishmen a consolation gift, sent the large brig *Southam* their way. The Irishmen gladly seized her as a prize. And then they sailed for Brest, the closest friendly port.

News of the sea battle between the *Prince* and the *Spry* spread quickly up and down the Ireland's east coast, and then traveled across the water over to England. On September 14, 1779, the London Chronicle reported that the "American privateer the Black Prince is put into Brest to replace her bowsprit which was broken in an engagement. In the space of three months and 11 days, this privateer, mounting 16 guns, and commanded by Capt. Marchant, has made 27 prizes, 12 of which she ransomed."

Within the span of three short months, *Black Prince* had blossomed from a minor nuisance into a dangerous menace. Across the world's mightiest empire, she was causing quite a stir - and attracting the attention of London's most powerful.

With the ship safely anchored in Brest, and the *Southam* in the hands of Torris's agent, Ryan sent Macatter on to Dunkirk to again look after his ailing wife and put Marchant in charge of overseeing the repairs to the *Prince*. Obtaining spare parts from the docks was the one talent Marchant actually excelled at. The man had a gift of making friends with just the right person, usually a quartermaster or some foremen in one of the king's shipyards, and had a knack for *liberating* things. The *Spry's* nine-pounders had inflicted no real damage and within a week the cutter had a new bowsprit, was fully re-rigged, repaired and ready to sail.

Dowlin kept to his hammock for several days suffering bouts of intermittent fever. The wound was clean and the loss of blood had been stopped in time and so the only real worry was gangrene. The ship's French surgeon had done his job well though and except for some laudable pus, the kind all doctors like to see, the wound began healing nicely. It didn't take Dowlin long to leave his bed, to sample the livelier taverns in Brest, and he took great pleasure in showing off his scar, his *badge of honor*, to any pretty woman who would indulge him.

With repairs to the ship well in hand, and Dowlin on the mend, Ryan took some cheese, some bread and two bottles and walked down to the water's edge to spend a lazy afternoon basking in the sun. Striping down to his trousers, he ambled along the sandy shore, alone, reflecting on matters past and plotting future actions. The success of his privateers - the taste of hot action against the *Spry* - now stirred his imagination. He burned with a desire to cause the British even more woe. It was as if some unearthly wind had swept him up, some inexplicable force greater than his own will, exceeding his own ambitions, carrying him to where he knew not, but carrying him off nonetheless.

Marchant and his incompetent Lieutenant Arnold had gained no favor among his harden Irish veterans and yet, the two Americans had *something*, possessed a quality - something rare and fine - they all envied. Americans by the thousands were leaving their families and property behind to risk everything, even death, to take up arms against a far stronger opponent, to fight for a cause they called liberty. Ryan saw a spirit in the Americans that refused to yield, a spirit that would not break or rest, ever, until their land, their country, was free.

As the day wore on, after walking for miles along the shore and with most of the liquor gone, a thought, an epiphany really, and wholly unexpected, struck him hard. Money no longer mattered, no longer held any allure for him. He suddenly realized that he had not written to Torris, not once, to inquire about the monies owed to him or his crew and that surprised him. What then, he wondered, was he fighting for? Why had he risked his ship, his life and the lives of his men in deadly combat with the *Spry*, a ship that far outclassed his own? A tingle raced up his spine when the truth embraced him. America's fight for her freedom was becoming his own fight too.

As the sun laid down its golden crown, he sat down on the beach and finished off the last of the rum. And as he stared out across the deep and boundless sea, his thoughts turned to Captain Jones. He wondered where the Scotsman might be now with his powerful squadron. Jones had set out from L'Orient with the battleship *Bon Homme Richard* and a small flotilla only a few days earlier. Ryan had wanted to introduce himself to the great American hero but had just missed him. *Now there's a man who will make the British sorry*, he mused. *If only I had such ships!*

And when the darkness closed in around the mariner, and a chill touched the evening air, he dressed, wrapped a cloak around his broad shoulders and made his way back to his ship - his head buzzing with new plans, his heart eager to win new glory.

Six

Ryan Takes Command

⚓

September 1779

He found a newspaper in his cabin with a note from Dowlin scribbled across the top of it, telling him to read the article he had circled. The pirate ship *Black Prince*, the paper reported, had attacked Fishguard, known as Abergwaun by the locals, and inflicted extensive damage on St. Mary's church, a small, Catholic church with ninety sittings, and minor damage to several other nearby buildings. While no one had been harmed in the attack, other than some frayed nerves, the army was sending in its engineers and soldiers to fortify the town anyway. No mention was made of the sword with its warning of course.

But, for the price of a few iron balls and some gunpowder, the Irishmen had forced the British Admiralty to garrison troops and spend precious resources on a remote military installation at a place where Ryan would likely never visit again. Not a bad trade Ryan thought and smiled.

And then a small package from Torris, containing his letters, caught his eye. He quickly tore the wrapping open and recognized Shannon's handwriting on one of the envelopes. She did not enjoy writing and her letters were nearly always short. That she wrote to him at all was proof enough to Ryan of her enduring love for him. He lit a lantern and settled back on his bunk.

🖋

Luke, My Dearest Love:
My father passed away in his sleep last night. It was his wish that I not mourn him. Why weep for one, he would ask, who is joyously celebrating his new Life in a New World, a world

of love and perfection, a place beyond human understanding? I believe in his words, truly I do. And yet, is it not our way, for the living to miss the dead whom we loved so well? I feel alone, so alone and cold. I do weep for him.

My heart aches for you. My dear, precious Luke, my gallant warrior. They say you are the Breaker of English ships, the Raider of English cities...

There is much talk about you and your ship, proud talk too. We have all read about your deeds at sea in the papers. What a fuss you have made! Naughty lad! I can see you standing before me now, a wondrous sight! So Proud and Strong and Handsome too you are. And elegant, yes. And you have the Soul of a gentle Man. I stain the paper with my tears as I write these words. Tears of Joy, Luke! The vision of you is so clear in my mind's eye. I must be going mad. My good Prince, fly to me when you are able. My heart yearns for you. My heart is yours, forever. God bless thee and keep thee and speed thee safely home to me...

Eternal Love,

Shannon

He set the letter down and brushed away a tear. Ryan would miss the old man. O'Keeffe had been very good to him, almost like a father, and had been his silent partner when he had been smuggling goods between France and Ireland. O'Keeffe had openly encouraged Ryan to pursue his affections for Shannon, O'Keeffe's only child.

What had Shannon called him though? *Breaker of English ships; raider of English cities...* That brought a smile. He reached for paper and pen and, having little more patience for writing letters than Shannon, scribbled out a short reply.

Dearest, Lovely Shannon:

I received the terible news about your father with sorrow and regrett. He was a good man and certainly most generous to me. Let us know that he is in a better place. Many shal miss him. I apologize for not being there to comfort you. I shal be with You soon enough my good angel. Look for me before the next full moon.

Had I a whole kingdom, I would gladly trade it all away for one brief kiss from your sweet lips this very moment. To hold you in my arms now would be worth all the treasure in the world to me. You are my joy, my life. At times, I wonder - can a man love a woman too much? I would not pretend to know the answer. Such questions are best left to the poets and priests to ponder.

This much I know: My soul is yours and I shall Love you forever. I pray you are well. And, take this to heart, I urge you, you are not alone my dearest Shannon. No, never. Not even as I sail across the cold and boundless sea are you alone, for you are in my heart, always.

The ship is near ready to set out again and my crew is eager. I intend to cause a bit more mischief.

Soon, soon I will be with you, hold and comfort you, kiss your eyes, pay amorous attention to you.

With all my heart & with deep Affection, Love, Luke

He held her letter up to the dim glow of the lantern and reread her words. He longed to hold her, to feel the touch of her soft skin against his own. It had been nearly two months since he had kissed her last. They had met in London, a secret rendezvous, and had stolen a few days and nights together. Rush was an easy sail away...

Several days later, Ryan gathered his men and sailed *Black Prince* out of Brest and into the wild Atlantic once again. The early autumn winds blew fair, the Channel's usually choppy waters rolled along with a tender, easy grace.

Marchant, thinking he was in command, decided to return to the quiet waters off Land's End. He had in mind to do some leisurely trolling for fresh victims there for a week or two, maybe three, avoid any more battles, and then return to France to sit out the cold winter. But Ryan had something altogether different in mind and, with Franklin's commission due to expire at the end of the month, he had precious little time to do it.

Satisfied that the night watch was in place, and that his orders were understood, Marchant retired to his cabin. After all this time, the big American still did not understand who the *Prince's* true master was. That evening the uneasy truce between Marchant and Ryan began to crack.

Early in the day, Marchant had overheard a sailor's unkind remark about him. He took great offense. Without consulting Ryan, he summoned John Kelly, the ship's master-at-arms, to his cabin and called for the whip. The crew was to assemble in the morning to witness punishment and a dozen lashes were to be laid across the insolent sailor's bare back.

Ryan was in his quarters reading when Dowlin rushed in to tell him about Marchant's orders. Ryan angrily threw his book aside and barged into Marchant's cabin with barely a knock. With forced politeness, Ryan explained to Marchant that he had a longstanding covenant with his men regarding punishment, about what was acceptable and what was not, and that whippings had been altogether banned.

Marchant, in his nightshirt and lying in his bunk, looked up at Ryan with disdain. "Suit yourself, Mr. Ryan. No lashing. Understood. But without a firm hand, mark my words well, these rascals will someday mutiny and cut your throat whenever it so pleases them."

"That is my concern, not yours," Ryan replied with no charity in his tone. He left Marchant's cabin with an uneasy tension in the air.

The next day, only the second day into their cruise, the fragile truce between the two men finally, irreparably, shattered.

Weldin was the officer of the morning watch and as the *Prince* neared Land's End, Ryan gave him new orders to turn north and head for Rush without consulting Marchant. And then he told Weldin to report to his cabin where Weldin found Dowlin and the Kelly brothers already waiting. Ryan was not sure why, but he did not invite Marchant even though he knew the slight would send Marchant over the edge.

"Alex tells me, Luke," Dowlin started, greeting Ryan with a smile. "We're on our way to Rush and that Marchant doesn't know?"

"That is true," replied Ryan as he entered his cabin carrying a pitcher of coffee and a loaf of hot bread. He poured each man a coffee and passed the bread around. "Gentlemen, we're undermanned and our commission expires in three weeks so there wasn't any time to return to Morlaix or Dunkirk. Before we sailed I received a letter from Shannon. She said we've captured the imagination of many a young man. There is talk in Ireland, proud talk, about an American privateer with an Irish crew raiding up and down the English coast at will. So, to my mind we have two objectives. One is to recruit more lads. We've always had good luck in Rush and so we'll put in there first. Then, it is most important we return to France with another successful cruise to persuade Franklin to renew our commission. And, to that end, I have a new plan."

Dowlin howled. "So now yer concocting war plans from love letters! Not so long ago you used yer brain for thinkin', not yer cock."

There were smiles all around.

"Might we know the plan, sir?" asked Weldin.

"I thought we could visit Scotland..."

"Scotland?" asked Dowlin.

Ryan's thoughts turned to Shannon. What had she called him? The *breaker of English ships*, the *raider of English cities*... The Irishmen had not raided any English cities. Silly rumors. But Shannon's words had inspired him. Perhaps, he thought, it was high time someone took the war to Great Britain.

"Aye, Scotland!" Ryan answered enthusiastically. "We've been too predictable and that's dangerous. If we're to survive this war, we must learn the art of unpredictability. 'Tis a fool's game to keep sailing the same waters over and over again."

Every man saw the wisdom in Ryan's bold plan to strike north and bowed his head, giving his assent, and gladly too.

And after breakfast, when Marchant came up to the quarterdeck and realized the ship's course had been changed - without his approval - he ordered Hoar, standing at the tiller, to come about and make for Land's End. And when Hoar refused without confirming matters with *Captain* Ryan first, Marchant exploded in a fit of rage. He dressed Hoar down with curses and stormed off to find Ryan, bent on putting the arrogant meddler finally in his place. Hoar blew Marchant a kiss after the American turned his back to leave.

John Kelly walked over to Hoar to see what all the fuss was about.

"Storm's brewin'," Hoar offered curtly.

Kelly nodded with a roguish smile. "I couldn't make out all of it but I heard enough. I think our good Capt'n Marchant is about to go a step too far. He's goin' to get his ears boxed."

"About time says I."

Marchant, red-faced, nostrils flaring, burst into Ryan's cabin without knocking. "Mr. Ryan! I've suffered quite enough of your impertinence and your interference, sir! You've made the situation on board this ship quite intolerable. A ship can only have one captain and on this ship, I tell you plainly, sir, I am that captain! Have you never read the scriptures? A man cannot serve two masters. A house divided against itself cannot stand!"

"I have read the scriptures," Ryan answered in careful, measured tones.

"Good! Now, sir, you'll not change another one of my orders again. Do you understand? You are the ship's owner. I respect that. But at sea, as captain, I am the supreme authority on board this vessel and any challenge to that authority is mutiny - nothing less! And let me assure you sir: the American Navy is no less harsh in disciplining mutineers than the British. Now, I am agreeable to defer to you on all matters pertaining to the ship's safety, to oversee your investment. But *I command* this ship. Do I make myself clear? I swear I'll put you ashore and continue this cruise without you if you cannot understand this simple truth!"

Dowlin and Weldin, sharing a cubby hole of a space next to Ryan's quarters, overheard Marchant's outburst. Like two school boys smelling trouble, and anxious not to miss out on any fun, jumped down from their hammocks and stood outside Ryan's door.

Dowlin couldn't help himself and burst out laughing. Weldin joined him.

Marchant spun around with a scowl on his face. "Damn you, sirs! I would know at once what it is you find so damn amusing!"

"Are all Americans," Dowlin replied with a broad grin, "as thick as you and yer poor, old Mr. Arnold? *Gawd* I pray not or yer country has no chance, no chance in hell, against the English colossus in this little tiff between you!"

"Damn your insolent eyes, sir!" Marchant said through clenched teeth, spit flying from his mouth. "You, you whoremonger! You drunkard!"

Ryan saw Marchant balling his hand into a fist, ready to strike Dowlin. Taking a swing at Dowlin would have been the American's last act on earth.

"*Captain Marchant!*" Ryan commanded sternly.

Marchant spun around.

Ryan, not wishing to provoke Marchant further, remained sitting on the edge of his bunk and tried to appear calm. But there was no need to mince words with Marchant any longer.

"Mr. Marchant, from what I've seen these past months since I've known you, sir, you are a man of few admirable qualities. How you ever attained the rank of ship's master is beyond my comprehension. No matter. It is time you understood things plainly. Your position as captain on board this ship has never been anything more than a charade, sir. We needed an American to get a commission from Franklin. We stumbled on you. Had you proven yourself worthy, a competent seaman, a *fighter*, I would have interfered less with your authority. In time, *you* could have been the *Prince's* true master. Regrettably, these things did not come to pass and I am compelled to relieve you of your command - an unfortunate circumstance for us both."

Marchant stared at Ryan, dumbfounded. His hands began to shake and he had a sudden urge to pee. The whole world was unexpectedly crashing down around his head. No one had ever insulted him so. He tried to offer some reply, but couldn't get his lips to move so narrowed his eyes instead. *No matter Mr. Ryan, Franklin will hear of this outrage. You shall all rue the day you crossed this old sailor...*

Ryan took no pleasure in humiliating Marchant, in stripping away the American's pride. But the time had come to set matters straight and he wanted to be absolutely clear.

"Now, sir," Ryan continued, confident that he had Marchant's full attention. "From this moment forward, I shall dictate all tactical operations of this ship. As the commission remains in your name, for now, you may continue to sign the ship's log, any letters approved by me and the ransom notes. And that sir, is the extent of your authority on board this ship. When we return to France I shall inform Doctor Franklin of this change in command and you may collect the monies owed you from Mr. Torris and do as you will. That shall be all, sir."

Marchant knew he was finished. He would find no support among the crew. He bit his lip, slowly turned and slipped past Dowlin and Weldin without looking at either man. He went back to his cabin and bolted the door.

Scudding across a diamond-studded sea, with the British Union Jack fluttering in the wind, the privateers happened upon a heavily armed Danish brig. The Irishmen ordered her Viking crew to shorten sail, for inspection or so they said, but the proud Danes were not easily fooled. Danish gunners flung open gun ports, ran out their guns and answered the Irishmen with ruthless, deadly iron. But the Danes show of teeth made no impression on the privateers. The stout Irish veterans made short work of the brig's brave gunners. The *Prince* far outclassed the brig in firepower and speed.

The Danes could have saved themselves the trouble of a fight. Neither the old brig nor her cargo had much value. Ryan's men removed what little they found of interest and then debated what to do with ship and crew. Dowlin and Weldin wanted to put the crew in boats and burn the brig. But the fighting Danes had earned themselves Ryan's admiration. After all, they had done no more than what he would have had done. Being in a charitable mood, he decided to let the Danes go their way and even saluted their gallantry by requiring no ransom.

The next day they came upon the English brig *Hopewell*. With holds jammed full with iron, tar and timber, she made a handsome trophy. Ryan saw the greed in his men's eyes, though they were too disciplined to grumble. They were eager to share in some prize money - and rightly so - they had yet to see one penny from any prizes taken.

Reluctantly, Ryan put a prize crew aboard the *Hopewell* and sent the fat goose back to France even though this left the *Prince* short-handed. He waved his men off with an uneasy feeling. The brig was very cumbersome and slow. With light hearts, the brig's new crew unfurled sail and headed east, sailing towards treacherous waters teaming with swift, British interceptors.

As *Hopewell* slowly slipped over one horizon, two new ships appeared over the other. The first was a small coaster racing towards shore. The other, a large, well-armed schooner, was giving the smaller vessel a spirited chase.

"Luke, do you see what I see?" Dowlin asked wide-eyed.

"Aye! Looks like we've got ourselves a British revenue ship trying to run down an Irish smuggler..."

"Yep. Look'ee thar, the coaster is fleein' towards shallow water. But that heavy schooner looks too fast. Our brothers will never make it."

"Hm - are you thinking what I'm thinking, Pat?"

Dowlin flashed his brilliant smile. "A chance to settle an old grudge or two? How sweet that would be."

Ryan raised his voice for all to hear. "Are you lads up for another scrap?"

His men answered him at once with a rousing cheer.

Beaming, Dowlin squandered no time. He issued fresh orders to the helmsman to steer towards the racing ships with all speed. And while the helmsman adjusted the ship's course, the topmen eagerly scrambled up into the rigging to work the sail-draped spars. But not even the swift *Prince* was speedy enough to close the distance in time for the privateers to help their fellow Irishmen. Ryan's men could only line the rails and watch helplessly, with sad hearts, as the British warship opened fire on the smugglers.

Outgunned and cornered, geysers of white sea foam shooting up all around them, the smugglers made a desperate run for shore. And then, disaster. Their ship shuddered violently after plowing nose first into hidden sandbar. The violence of the impact sent men flying and shattered the coaster's keel. She settled on the water, and died. Her crew had no time to launch the boats. Those who could swim jumped into the cold currents and tried to swim to shore while comrades left behind scrambled up into the rigging, afraid to touch a cruel and hungry sea.

Ryan and his men were not the only spectators. Not far off, the double-headed twins Death and Destruction circled overhead - always eager to cause men woe, always eager to wet their talons in blood and gruesome gore. A horror even to their mother, Gorgon, their nauseating stink filled the air. But the twins had no interest in one small coaster. Their lust-filled eyes were fixed on something far more worthy...

The British raised a great victory cheer after the coaster floated off the sandbar, capsized and slipped beneath the waves, taking the poor souls left behind with her. And then a very handsome cutter sailing towards them with no flag, dark, elegant, a marvel to behold, caught their eye.

British sailors were already tallying up their share of prize money as they realigned their spars and sails and headed, top speed, out into deeper water to intercept the black ship. Greed blinded them. No one gave thought to what might lay ahead.

"Luke, she's wearin' around and comin' for us fast!" Weldin exclaimed excitedly, keeping the schooner centered in his spyglass.

"Aye, Luke," added Dowlin with no emotion. "Under full sail and with a good wind abeam of her, she looks a might faster than anythin' we've seen before. And I count twenty-one guns lashed to her bulwarks. She's better armed than *Spry*."

"Indeed," Ryan said flatly. "From your observations then, gentlemen, I take it the two of you want to turn tail and run?"

Weldin and Dowlin traded grins.

"Not on yer life, Luke," replied Weldin.

"You know my thoughts, Luke," added Dowlin.

"Hm. I am not so sure, gentlemen. That vessel looks like a hefty challenge. In any case, I'll have the ship made ready..."

While Dowlin bellowed out orders to the petty officers to ready the ship for action, Ryan ordered the helmsman and Kelly's topmen to turn the ship *away* from the British schooner. Men scrambled but, as they carried out their orders, they whispered among themselves: had their captain decided to turn and run? Sound tactics and the crew understood. This British speedster looked like trouble.

But the master tactician had no thoughts of running.

At the twitter of the boatswain mate's whistle, the Irishmen, all veterans now of grim, brutal combat, and full of fight, cleared the cutter's trim deck for battle. Faithful, dependable Morgan, the man who could talk to ships, rushed back to the quarterdeck to take the helm. Ryan told him to steer poorly. Morgan gave him a puzzled look but acknowledged his instructions with a nod and did as he was told. His captain, always, knew what he was doing.

The British master smiled to himself. He was certain the ship fleeing from them was another Irish smuggler. *Two victories in one day! What good fortune!*

The Irishmen watched on anxiously as the British heavy schooner closed with them. Hearts pounded against ribs. What was Ryan up to? Hadn't he given the order to flee? As fast as the schooner was, the *Prince* was faster still and could easily out-race her pursuer, but Morgan was steering sloppy, handling the helm like some drunken sot. Not that the deadly schooner speeding towards them intimidated any man. No. To a man, the Irishmen were eager to give the British another good walloping, to fill English hearts with woe. Revenge for the coaster just run aground, maybe with friends or family aboard, was on the mind of many too.

The gun crews primed and loaded every gun. But, just as they had done with the *Spry*, they did not remove the crates - not yet - and kept the swivels hidden and out-of-sight, lying against the bulwarks and wrapped in burlap rags.

The British drew nearer, not realizing they were headed for a fight. The helmsman steered their impressive schooner in close as the gun crews ran their heavy guns out smartly. Ammunition bearers brought up shot and powder from the ship's magazine and stacked the balls in nice, neat pyramids next to each gun. Other sailors filled water pails and sprinkled sand across the deck. Then Royal Marines raced up the forward and aft companionways to the rat-a-tat-tat of a drum and took up their positions amidships with parade-like precision. These were first-rate professionals, through-and-through.

But then the British gunners, prideful, arrogant, ignorant, stood by their weapons with a lazy indifference, saw no need to prime and load them - unsuspecting fools.

It was plain for to all to see what poor sailors manned this new smuggler trying to run away from them. The English thought they were coming up on another gang of thugs. Easy pickings for seasoned veterans. But the smuggler herself, well, the black cutter was a beauty!

The king's men casually pulled up alongside their new prize - where Weldin and his platoon stood waiting. The schooner's master, in full dress uniform, complete with sword and tassels, and holding a brass trumpet in his hand, not the kind used to hail ships, but a musical instrument, nimbly scampered up the ratlines. The king's good servant must have thought he was on review - or on some gentlemen's hunt. He made a grand appearance. His mother had raised herself a fool...

He looked down on the smuggler with an air of contempt, saw the crates sitting on her deck, and took in the hardscrabble men dressed in shabby clothes awkwardly standing around. He thought the sight a bit peculiar. But he gave the matter no importance. The cutter was plainly loaded down with goods - or so he imagined - and he smiled broadly. *Sailing poorly and trying to flee with all those crates crowded on her deck... She's a smuggler all right and laden down with rich cargo!*

The cutter's crew, swarthy, disciplined Irishmen - but dumbfounded too - watched the Englishman climb up the ratlines with a gold trumpet in his hand. Dowlin stifled a chuckle as Ryan raised his arm. That was Weldin's signal and he knew what to do. They had all rehearsed it so many times before.

The Englishman put the trumpet to his lips to sound a tune, a call to attack or a call for surrender no one knew. But then he hesitated. He saw Ryan drop his arm. He could see the cutter's men springing into action. *What?*

"Knock down 'em crates, roll out yer guns!" Weldin bellowed. "Mount yer swivels! *Move! Quick! Quick! Quick!*"

The Irishmen, of one mind, moved with fluid motion - like a troupe of superbly trained dancers in an exquisitely choreographed ballet - men tossed over the flimsy, false crates, pitched them into the sea, while their mates pulled open the gun ports for the four-pounders and mounted the swivels to the rails. Not one man stumbled. Weldin watched *his* men with awe, proud of their deadly efficiency.

The schooner's master lowered his trumpet, watching the feverish activity on board the *smuggler* with fascination. At first, he thought her crew was dumping their contraband overboard. But then he saw men opening up *gun ports* and running out the black, stubby noses of *cannon*. Horror gripped him. He glanced down at the deck below his feet and considered jumping, but he was too high up and so covered his face instead.

"Ready there!" Weldin commanded. "*FIRE!*"

Weldin's words were the last the English captain ever heard.

BOOM! BOOM! BOOM! BA-BA-BA-BOOOOOOOOOOOOM!

Fire and smoke enveloped the British schooner. Too close to miss, every shot hit its mark. The trumpeter, his elegant uniform shredded and splattered in red, went limp and death closed in around his eyes. He let his trumpet slip from his fingers. It disappeared into the sea. Then his lifeless body fell from the rigging, hit the deck with a hideous thump and bounced.

Ryan and Dowlin exchanged silent glances. The blood of one of His Majesty's officers was now on their hands. Ryan, taking no pleasure from it, looked away with sadness. Dowlin smiled grimly, elated with the kill.

On paper, it seemed hardly a fair match. The *Prince* was undermanned and outgunned. She could bring to bare only 16 four-pounders and 30 swivels - useless at long range - against a British heavy schooner armed with a mix of 21 heavier six and nine-pounders. And the British crew outnumbered the Irishmen by two-to-one or more. Any captain of a privateer would have been toasted by his fellow mariners back in port for his prudence in turning away and running - if he was even lucky enough to escape the odds against him.

Not Ryan. His mind turned with thoughts of winning new glory, the same thoughts that had fired his imagination during his stroll along the sandy beach not so long ago. He had supreme confidence in himself, in his crew and in his ship. And his Irish veterans were of like mind. They knew the bloody grind of war, knew it well, and were all with him.

Ryan gave the order to run up the American stars and stripes as he studied the chaos unfolding on board the schooner. The first broadside had done little physical damage to the ship, a few cut lines and a hull peppered with iron. But, psychologically a hard blow had been landed, creating confusion among British ranks. Caught off-guard, and with no captain to lead them, the stunned Englishmen wavered and in the confusion their guns stayed silent.

"Damn my eyes!" Dowlin cursed, scanning the British ship through his spyglass. "Here we go again Luke, barely a scratch on her! But I see a number of fallen English sailors."

"Aye, same as *Spry*, Pat," Ryan observed matter-of-factly. "That may have been our best chance to disable her. Now we're in it. If only we had something heavier - nine-pounders or better. By God, we'd win this day for certain!"

BOOM-BA-BA-BA-BOOOOOOOOOOOM!

Weldin's gunners fired off a second broadside.

"How true, Luke, how true. I'd take even a dozen or so six-pounders right about now!"

"Well, what do you think, Pat? With her captain down, the crew in disarray, will she strike her colors or turn and run or - will she fight?"

"Hard tellin'," Dowlin answered with a sly smirk. "All depends on the mettle of their number two man don't it now?"

The English soon answered.

BOOM! BOOM! BOOM!

The *Prince* shuttered from the iron slamming into her side. One ball imbedded itself in a plank just below Ryan's feet. A foot higher Ryan realized, and...

The schooner's first officer had rallied his men, vowed to make short work out of the smaller vessel. English hearts, filled with rage at American skullduggery, at the loss of their poor master and their mates, reloaded and fired off another volley. The Irish did the same.

The ships circled around each other, like two wary prizefighters, trading blow after glancing blow. Dueling gun crews stripped down to their britches and labored under a merciless, sizzling sun.

"At my command, another broadside lads!" shouted Weldin to his men, just as Dowlin had taught him. "Go for thar guns... Take yer aim! Watch yer linstocks now! Steady. Steady now lads. Wait for the command... Ready... FIRE!"

BA-BA-BA-BOOOOOOM!

"Stop yer vents thar! Alrighty, lads... Reload... Quickly now! Move smartly there! Faster! *Move! Move! Move!* When I give the word, fire as yer guns bear. But first one more broadside... Wait for the swell... *FIRE!*

BA-BA-BOOOOOOOOOOOOOOOM!

"Good, good! Now - fire at will!"

Tim took his handspike and adjusted his gun around. The boy had a keen eye and had been promoted to gun captain. Just as Dowlin had taught him, he calmly waited for a target to cross his sight, then touched his slow match to the muzzle.

BOOM!

Exhilarating fun. He had practiced for long hours under Dowlin's watchful eye. Well he knew the drill now, the bloody grind of war. No raw recruit worked his gun! Then one of *his* men swabbed the muzzle down with water and while Jumbaaliyia took his flexible rammer and rammed another shot home. The day Dowlin had yanked him out of the way of a gun's nasty recoil seemed like a lifetime ago. He took careful aim and fired off another round, choking on the white, hot smoke blowing back in his face.

Dowlin saw Tim's shot. The boy's aim was true! His ball had hit a spar and shattered it. A portion of the schooner's mainsail tore away and fell into the sea. Not a mortal blow perhaps, but the damage would slow the enemy down a bit and give Tim bragging rights at supper later. Dowlin's heart swelled with pride as he looked back at Tim, his face and bare chest stained in black powder and streaked in sweat.

Dowlin removed his hat and slapped it against his thigh. "That'll show 'em, Tim! *Gawd* blast 'em, that'll show 'em! Fine work thar, Mr. Timothy Kelly! Now don't be spoilin' it by standin' around admirin' yer own handiwork. Shake a leg, son! Give 'em another round!"

The other gunners, his *mates*, urged Tim on with cheers and shouts. Tim and his gunners quickly repeated the whole routine again, eager to win more praise, maybe even new glory.

Then Ryan offered a challenge. "Five pounds sterling and a keg of ale lads to Tim for that remarkable shot - ten pounds and two kegs more to the man who does him better!"

The gunners roared their approval, resumed their hot work with new energy. Heavy cannon cracked the air like angry thunder.

On board the heavy schooner the British first officer, a flat-nosed, muscular man with a pugnacious temperament to match, proved more prudent than his dead master. He maneuvered his ship out of the range of the privateer's swivels first. And then, standing off at a safer distance, he let his gun crews pound the black ship with their heavier iron. But the cutter, fitted with thick, hardwood timber, seasoned for strength by master craftsmen, warded off each blow with ease. After trading shots for a long hours, and with nothing to show for it, the young officer, smart but eager and impatient, decided on a different tactic. English topmen realigned the sails and spars and the British warship ominously rushed in towards the privateer. Curiously, all her guns, even her bow chasers, fell silent.

Kelly, who had been directing his men from the mainmast, raced back to the helm to get his orders. It was his job to muster whatever spare men he could find to repel boarders if the need arose.

"She's wearin' around and movin' in, sir, lookin' to board us, I'd say," Kelly observed coolly, no emotion. "Idiots must think we're beat. You want armed men in the riggin' Capt'n, or lined up along the bulwarks? 'Fraid we don't have enough lads to do both."

Ryan took his time to answer, his mind toying with different thoughts. Dowlin watched him, curious to see what his friend would do. Better than any man, Dowlin understood and appreciated Ryan's gift for waging cruel, hard war.

Ryan put his spyglass to his eye, examined the enemy schooner from stem to stern. *Damn!* There was so much more he could do if only he had a larger ship or heavier guns. They were always fighting under some handicap. The thought of men locked in brutal hand-to-hand combat - men mad to kill pitted against men mad to live, a tangled mess of flesh - brought him no joy. Grisly work. His Irishmen were brave. He knew they could hold their own and they would fight to the last. But they were too few in number. And he had eight Englishmen on board, men whom Marchant had liberated from a prison back in Morlaix to augment the crew, men with questionable loyalties. Ryan did not like the odds. A larger ship carried booms and nets to stave off boarders, but the *Prince* was too small for such luxuries. It was her speed that gave her her power.

Ryan considered the winds and currents. "Better keep your lads at the bulwarks, Chris. When it comes to muskets, we don't have many a good marksman on board, none leastwise I've seen. She's fast, that schooner. And her new master is handling her well. But I don't think he'll be able to board us if that's his purpose. If I'm wrong - send our English friends below and lock the hatch down. I don't trust any of them in a pinch. If you have a lad or two who's any good with a musket, send them aloft into the rigging, see what mischief they can make as sharpshooters."

"Aye, Capt'n. No worries, sir. They'll be mighty sorry if they mean to board us. That much I can promise you! Anythin' else I was to say," Kelly paused, with an evil look in his eye and trying to reassure Ryan, "would be shameless boastin' and unworthy of an *Irishman!*"

"You just keep that big head of yours low, Chris."

Kelly made a knuckle and worked his way down the gauntlet of booming cannon, past swarms of sweaty, bare-chested men, stalwart men who loved their deadly guns. Dowlin started after him.

"Where you headed, Pat?" Ryan called after him, afraid Dowlin might be tempted to repeat his show of bravado with the *Spry.*

Dowlin spun around and offered Ryan one of his impish grins, "Not to worry, Luke. I'll be gettin' us a couple extra pistols - just in case..."

Ryan could see the anticipation in Dowlin's eyes. The big, fiery Irishman was actually looking forward to close-up fighting. The man had no fear.

The privateers kept up their steady barrage of deadly iron, splintering wood, snapping rigging and ripping the enemy's sails to shreds. But the British warship ignored these barbs and like some mindless beast kept charging straight at them. Ryan climbed half way up the mainmast rigging to get a better view, to see for himself what was happening on board the enemy cruiser. She was less than 200 yards away now and Weldin had the swivels back in action. It was time to decide whether to turn and run or stay the course. Ryan expected to see heavily armed British sailors and marines massed along the schooner's bulwarks, preparing to storm over the side, but there were none. *Curious.*

And then... Too late before he realized...

"*Christ! Everyone, get down!*" he screamed for all he was worth.

Too far up in the shrouds to jump, to reach the safety of the deck, and with nowhere to hide, Ryan leapt off the ropes and plunged feet first towards the water. He tried desperately, with arms flailing, to grab a loose line before he hit the water. Certain he was about to die, he closed his eyes, bid Shannon a quick farewell and made the Sign of the Cross.

BA-BOOOOOM!

British smoke and fire filled the air. Now it was the cocky Irishmen who had been caught off-guard. The English had mounted their own swivels and fired. A few nails and bits of chain - but mostly pieces of broken glass - homemade grape shot, went slicing through the air. Thousands of tiny, deadly missiles indiscriminately punctured wood, canvas and flesh...

Weldin was the first Irishman to fall. Cut down in his prime, the Fates, those twisted, merciless crones who even the gods hate, had marked him from birth for an early death that day. Dowlin saw his friend falling just as he was coming up the hatch with a handful of loaded pistols. He dropped the small arms to rush to Weldin's side. But there was nothing anyone could do for poor Weldin now. Dowlin held his friend's lifeless body, a headless torso, in his arms, unable to stop the warm spray of blood. Then, vaguely, he heard cheers. *How odd the lads are cheerin'* he thought to himself, unable to focus. But then he understood - these were British cheers.

Young Tim had heard Ryan's warning, was quick to duck behind the bulwark and was only a foot away from Dowlin. "Good God, Mr. Dowlin. 'Em bastards knocked poor Mr. Weldin's head clean off. How dretful he looks."

"Aye, Tim," Dowlin answered grimly, added in a low voice, "turn away now. See to yer gun thar boy." Then a shudder ran down his spine when he saw Tim's chest splattered with blood and gore and bits of brain. "Are *you* hurt lad?"

The boy looked down at himself and answered with an unsteady voice. "No, sir. I went down to me knees when Mr. Ryan shouted out. Sorry, Mr. Dowlin, sir, this must be Mr. Weldin's blood."

Warm, live tears started streaming down the boy's sooty cheeks.

Dowlin looked up to find Hoar standing over him and cocked his head towards Tim. Hoar understood and gently pulled the boy away.

Then Dowlin looked back down at Weldin's headless corpse and wished his spirit well, hoping his friend was soaring towards a better world. He swallowed hard and tried to clear his mind. There was work to be done.

"You thar, lads," he called to several crewmen still in shock. "Stop yer gawking and give us a hand here. Let's get this poor wretch out of the way!"

Then he heard whimpering. *Jean.* The boy had seen Weldin die and was crouching low, down behind a barrel. Dowlin reached over with his free hand and rubbed the young boy's shoulder.

"You get yerself below," he told Jean in a soft voice. "I want you to count the powder bags for me. Every one of 'em. Get on with you now..."

A useless order but Jean didn't know any better. The boy did as he was told and headed for the magazine room down in the ship's belly, sobbing, shaking.

Three more Irishmen had fallen dead to British trickery along with Weldin and a half dozen more took serious wounds. The brutality of war had finally caught up with the Irishmen who had, until this day, roamed the open seas unscathed.

Then Dowlin noticed the jagged shards of glass embedded in the bulwarks and scattered across the deck. He picked one piece up, examined it with a scowl. *Bloody hell!*

Whether it is bits of razor-sharp metal or broken pieces of glass that cuts a man down might seem to some to be a distinction without much difference. But firing shards of glass at your opponent was strictly against the rules of war, a dishonorable thing to do, and made a difference to fighting sailors.

British wickedness now roused Dowlin's fighting spirit to a fever pitch! He whipped the privateers into a bloodlust with words of encouragement and praise and challenged them all to avenge their fallen comrades.

Adrenaline pumping hard, the privateers rallied around Dowlin and resumed their deadly work with newfound strength. The gunners launched withering volley after withering volley of killing iron at the schooner and her crew. But, unlike the men of the *Spry*, these Englishmen had heart. They did not shrink back. They had the same taste, the same craving, for blood the Irish had, and returned each volley, blow-for-blow.

Seething with dark hate, Dowlin stood up on the rail - Ryan could reprimand him to his heart's content if that was his pleasure later - and called out to the schooner's crew. "Hey you dickless, English bastards! Why so quiet now? No more fight left in you or are you all stone dead? Can't hear a fooking word from you! Where's yer pride? Speak out damn your eyes! Don't quit on me now - 'cause I an't through with you! An eye for an eye they say. Time to lay on some pain, lay it on thick - to hell you go..."

Eager to give his words power, he dropped back down on deck and snatched a linstock out of the hands of one of his men, nearly knocking him over, aimed the gun himself and fired.

But Dowlin's vile mocking hardly went unchallenged. English gunners, poised, professional, fired off another broadside with devastating accuracy. The *Prince* shuddered, lines snapped and her forecourse sail went slack.

Kelly and his men quickly went about splicing shredded rope and raised the forecourse back in place while Dowlin and his gunners kept up their own murderous barrage of iron, firing the guns as fast as bone and muscle could move. And even though Irish marksmanship proved far better, the English fought on stubbornly with hearts still set on taking the *Prince* for their own.

But as the wild brawl dragged on, limbs grew heavy and men, exhausted beyond caring, forgot about winning glory or even riches. They turned their thoughts instead to water, rest and living through the day.

Oblivious to Ryan's situation, or his whereabouts, Dowlin fought like a man possessed, like some wild maniac, no let up. He urged his men on with more words of inspiration and with action too. He primed and loaded one of the swivels and took careful aim.

"That the *very best* you can do English?" he cried out with a voice like rolling thunder. "Let me show you how it's done, bitch. When I'm through with you, yer own mothers won't recognize the bloody mess!"

"Do yer worst," an unsteady voice from the schooner bravely shot back, "then I'll lay you low - you foul-mouthed braggart."

Dowlin waited, searching for just the right target, until his patience was rewarded. He saw a head sticking up just a tad too high and fired off a round.

BOOM!

The Englishman was dead before his body collapsed into a bloody heap.

Tenacious British gunners, following British navy doctrine, were aiming low to inflict maximum casualties on the *Prince's* crew, especially on her gunners, and fired off another broadside. But their rounds were having little impact against the *Prince's* hull and ricocheted off over and over again. By contrast, French and Spanish crews were trained to shoot high, aiming for masts and rigging, preferring to disable an enemy ship to killing her crew. They paid an awful price for their tactics. French and Spanish sailors suffered far higher casualties than their British brothers. Dowlin and his men simply shot at anything that moved.

While the *Prince* continued shaking off each British blow with ease, the Irishmen, so far away from any friendly port, knew they were risking real trouble if the British managed to cripple their ship with some lucky hit. And with every smack of solid shot against the cutter's hull, men flinched.

Despite all his bluster, Dowlin was no fool. He could see the weariness in the sweaty faces of his men. And despite the pummeling they had lavished on the British, British guns, except for one or two, continued spewing out their smoke and tongues of flame. The battle's outcome was by no means certain.

"'Tis the crucial moment lads!" Dowlin called out with a challenge, urging hearts on. "The scales can tip either way, for or against us! Summon up yer courage now! We grab the glory for ourselves - or give it to our foe! Again! Another round... *FIRE!*"

BOOM! BOOM! BA-BA-BA-BOOOOOOOM!

The English replied with ugly groans and one more English gun fell silent.

When the hot action had first started, Marchant had chosen to leave his self-imposed exile in his cabin and had reassumed his post on the quarterdeck near the helm. Stripped of command, the only thing Marchant could do was watch the awful spectacle unfold. He had seen Ryan fall into the water, was clueless what to do. Morgan had also seen

Ryan fall, as had Jumbaaliyia and a Portuguese man named Fernando Tavares - a sailor of great skill and one of Ryan's favorites.

Tavares was the first to move and jumped overboard, feet first, with a good-sized length of plank in hand.

Morgan reacted with lightning speed as well. Forearms knotted in thick muscle, he rudely grabbed Marchant by the collar and roughly pulled the big man towards himself. "This is your moment, sir!" he shouted. "Take the tiller - NOW!"

On sheer gut instinct, he had no time to think, Morgan then reached for a line, one with an end already tied around the rail but loose at the other, wrapped it around his waist - he had never learned to swim - and threw himself over the side, nearly landing on top of someone.

Still dazed but relieved to be alive, Ryan shook the salt water off his face from Morgan's splash and grinned at his helmsman.

"Why, Mr. Morgan, odd time for a swim, isn't it?"

"You hurt, sir?" Morgan asked anxiously, handed Ryan a length of rope and started sinking.

Ryan pulled him up. "The body's fine, Michael. Relax, use your arms like so and kick your feet. That's it. No, I am not hurt. Only my pride is wounded. I'm a damn fool. Shoulda seen it coming..."

As the ship dragged Ryan and Morgan through the water, with cannons booming overhead, bubbles suddenly popped up all around them and Tavares's head broke the surface. A moment later Jumbaaliyia joined them.

"Saw you take a spill from the rigging, Mr. Ryan," offered Jumbaaliyia. "Came to lend a hand."

Ryan nodded his appreciation, touched by the bravery of all three men. "Much obliged to you, sir. Good to have you along for the ride, Mr. Jumbaaliyia. And Mr. Tavares, what is your excuse?"

"Ah, *Capitàno*, I needed a bath."

"Ah, huh. I'm swimming in the middle of the ocean with a funnyman. What's the plank for Fernando?"

"Lisbon is my city, my home. First settled by shinning Odysseus - or so the legend goes - after his ship, loaded down with plundered Trojan treasures, was blown-off course. And when he left Lisbon for Ithaca, his home, he lost his ship and all his men to the Charybdis. The only survivor, he drifted on a ship's plank for many long days before washing ashore at Ogygia, the island of the beautiful but dangerous nymph Calypso. The plank saved his life."

"Truly? Well, now, you have enlightened us all with your knowledge of history and with the practical application of history's lessons to the modern world. But Ogygia sounds a bit far for the four of us on that one plank."

Even Morgan smiled, after spitting out a mouthful of brine. "That Odysseus fella, Fernando, sounds damn lucky. Speakin' of luck, my God, Capt'n, I thought we'd lost you fur sure! English almost did to you what we did to their capt'n."

"Aye - I'm damn lucky. I thought I was a dead man for certain. Well lads, if this line snaps, it will be a fair swim to shore. Who's got her helm?"

"Marchant."

Ryan winced and started laughing. "*Jesus Christ*, Almighty! This ship is blessed with two capt'ns but one's a fool treading water amidst a raging battle while the other is a knucklehead and probably sailing around in circles to God knows where. If only the English knew... What do you say, lads, Mr. Morgan, Mr. Jumbaaliyia, Mr. Tavares, shall we put off a visit to Calypso's fair island for better times and hoist ourselves back aboard before Marchant does any real damage?"

"Aye, Capt'n. Right behind ya, sir!" Morgan answered, cracking one of his rare smiles and looked up at the ship. "Hey! Anybody up thar? Give us a hand now! Capt'n's in the water!"

Men came rushing to the rail, grabbed Morgan's line and pulled the swimmers around the stern and over to the ship's portside, away from British guns. And, one-by-one, the four swimmers were helped back up on deck.

Morgan relieved Marchant at the helm. Jumbaaliyia and Tavares rushed to their stations.

Ryan stood quietly for a moment to survey the damage to the ship. He saw the red-stained deck, followed the trail of blood to the mainmast where victims had been stacked, and counted four bodies. He closed his eyes, relieved that Dowlin was not among them but heartsick nonetheless. A sudden, stabbing pain shot through his gut. He felt the urge to cry. *What have you done you arrogant son-of-a-bitch? No - no time to think on it now. Get a grip. Think things through; steady now.*

Then Ryan saw Dowlin directing Weldin's gunners. That meant Weldin was down - dead or wounded. That good man's loss would be a grievous blow! He stripped off his dripping coat and threw it down, disgusted.

Marchant had watched in horror as men dragged off bloody corpses. Fear wrapped its ugly grip around him now. He felt nauseous. His knees began to buckle. Never before had he seen the gruesome face of war up close. Not like this. Shooting at British ships from a distance had been good sport but this was something altogether different. He moved next to Ryan.

"My God, Mr. Ryan, we're done for. We must strike our colors. Seek terms and surrender the ship! Save what lives we can!"

Ryan, his heart grieving for the loss of his men, turned and glared at Marchant. He had known all along that this moment, men dead and dying, would someday steal upon them if they pursued their marauding ways - even if his men had not. They were at war after all, not out in the country on some pleasure hunt through the gentle woods. With all of their easy successes during the summer, and with no serious casualties suffered, it had been all too easy. Men forgot how dangerous their work could be. No more. Cold reality had smacked them all full in the face.

"Surrender? *By God, man,*" Ryan shouted at Marchant through clenched teeth. "You'll get yourself below and out of my sight damn your soul or I'll have the master-at-arms clap you in irons! I swear it! Off my deck with you - now, sir!"

Marchant, taken aback, appalled by Ryan's ranting, summoned up what little courage he had left and willed his legs to move. He made his way down the ladder and returned to his cabin.

Ryan instantly regretted his harsh remarks, felt ashamed. He had not meant to be so cruel. But Marchant was a fool. Still, he knew, he only had himself to blame, not Marchant, for their present circumstances.

He took in the condition of his ship and crew. The *Prince* had suffered plenty of superficial damage, but nothing significant that he could see. His men looked bloodied and bone-weary. He looked over at the British schooner and studied her through his spyglass. Her condition appeared no better or worse but her crew had certainly suffered far more causalities.

The ships continued their vicious dance, their jousting with deadly iron. But neither vessel could gain a decisive edge. Carnage mounted. The sisters Rout and Panic, loveless to the core, heard the cries of angry men locked in grisly combat. They swooped down from the heavens with hopes of stirring up more trouble. And wherever Rout and Panic go, their unholy half-brothers Terror and Doom are never far behind. More men fell.

No matter which way he looked at things, Ryan could find no way to win. His four-pounders simply did not have enough punch and he didn't have the muscle to board the schooner. Continue on with the bloody stalemate or cut and run, those were his sad choices. Something inside him though simply would not allow him to run, not when there might be some chance yet to take the day. And he was certain his men would not forgive him easily if he gave the order to withdraw with dead comrades to avenge. Ryan considered the wind and currents and decided to hold their present course and speed. Patience was needed now. He would wait for some opportunity to show itself while the gunners' grueling work went on.

By late afternoon, roasting under a broiling sun, heat and fatigue made limbs heavy and men began surrendering to exhaustion. By early evening, the pace of the gun crews had slackened-off considerably, to little more than a sporadic exchange of cannon shot here and there.

And then, after all the long hours of maneuver and fire, British guns fell silent. The schooner suddenly sheared off. Her young master and crew had had enough.

Ryan - more relieved than elated at the sight of the fleeing British - hesitated. They had won the day, yes, and another British officer would perhaps face a board of inquiry, even though the Englishman had performed admirably well and Ryan would have gladly testified on the man's behalf - if only such a thing were possible. His men had taken on and bested another British warship, larger and more powerful than their own, a ship from the finest navy in the world. The Irishmen would all have bragging rights back home.

But his weary crew raised only a weak, half-hearted victory cheer as they watched the enemy turn and sail away. The men then turned to look at Ryan. Would their captain give the order to pursue, to hunt the British down, or would he leave well enough alone? Men held their breath, waiting for the captain's pleasure. Half the crew, fuelled by courage or old hatreds, wanted to finish the job they had started and half, exhausted and with no more to give, silently hoped their captain would call it quits, put an end to an ugly day.

Ryan could see it all as he took in their dirty, sweaty faces. He grabbed his spyglass and climbed half way up the mainmast shrouds to study the retreating enemy once more. He saw the dead and wounded piled high around the heavy schooner's masts. A good number of sails were badly torn and her jib sail was down, wrapped around the bowsprit, useless. Many of her lines were cut and one broken spar dangled from the foremast. The Irishmen had inflicted far more damage on the schooner than Ryan had at first realized and the English had just cause to quit the battle after taking such a beating. A few more broadsides perhaps, twenty, thirty minutes more pounding, and the British master, Ryan was certain, would have been forced to strike his colors! Another trophy was slipping through his hands. But more than any glory, he wanted the deaths of his men to have purpose.

Ryan desperately wanted to give chase, to take a British warship. He weighed each possibility, considered the circumstances around them and the odds against them.

But men cannot move day or night. The sun was low on the far horizon and would soon melt into the ocean's depths. The day was nearly done. And his own ship needed repairs. The *Prince* herself was limping along with shredded rigging and tattered sails and deprived of her full speed, in the middle of hostile waters, was asking for big trouble. And the ammunition, Ryan knew, had to be running low. His men, despite their resolve and discipline, had little left to give. They had taken on a British crew over twice their number with heavier guns and had held their own, trading shot for shot for long hours without relief.

Ryan collapsed his spyglass, made his way down the rigging and jumped back on deck. He removed a wet handkerchief from his vest pocket and wiped away the beads of sweat forming on his brow.

Every man could see the disappointment in Ryan's face. There would be no pursuit.

Ryan hesitated for a bit, but then reluctantly gave the order to stand down. His Irishmen, too disciplined to voice a contrary word, did so without one grumble. Not even Dowlin, unstoppable, relentless, covered from head to toe in blood and gore, offered a word of protest. The helmsman pointed their ship's sharp prow northwest and the men quietly dispersed to go about their duties, securing guns, forming repair details and mending painful wounds.

And after the Irishmen had washed away the grime of war and had taken supper, the bodies of fallen comrades were wrapped inside their hammocks, the cloth stitched tight, and gently placed side-by-side on deck. With a solemn nod from Ryan, Dowlin called all hands on deck to witness burial. Each man, with a soldier's discipline, fell somberly into rank and file formation and quietly stared out over the rail, watching the rocky coast of ancient Ireland slip by.

With the last rays of light fading below Ireland's soft hills, faithful Venus climbed into the heavens to assume her brief reign over twilight. The night air turned chilly and men, despite the company of friends, felt vulnerable and alone. A somber, introspective mood settled over the ship.

The ship's officers, less one, gathered near the stern and stood rigidly at attention.

"Division commanders, report!" Dowlin roared.

The petty officers replied in turn.

"Very well," he said, with no joy in his voice. "Men of the *Prince* - doff hats, stand easy thar!" He struggled to keep his emotions in check, choked back a tear and crisply made an about face. "All hands present or accounted for to witness burial, sir!" he reported to Ryan and saluted.

Ryan nodded and took a step forward. "Lads," he began softly, "those of you who have served with me for some time know the gory work of war - you've seen the face of death up close. Nothin' new to you or me. It is something you learn to deal with but never really get accustomed to, not a pious man anyway. For you others, this might be something new for you. It is a hard thing, killing. No shame in being queasy about what happened here today. I want each of you to know - you men of the *Black Prince* - you all acquitted yourselves with valor and great honor here today. I saw in you a courage that I've rarely seen before in other crews. I'm proud - *proud* - to serve with such men of fortitude and bravery. 'Tis no small matter to take on and beat a British warship. Her guns were larger than ours and she had more of them. She had considerably more men too. But we beat her, gave her a good, sound thrashing and her crew will think twice before tangling with us again I'm sure. Something you can all tell your grandchildren about someday with pride. Now, I know many of you wanted to finish the job we started here today, many of you wanted to take that schooner down. I certainly did. I thought long and hard about it too. But, under the circumstances, giving chase seemed a bit reckless to me. The British are hunting us now. Any fool can rush in like a dumb beast and blindly attack whatever comes his way. But we've got to be smart, smarter than the enemy we face and always have a plan. Had another British warship happened upon us this afternoon, we might have been in serious jeopardy. Well, now I'm preaching. Sorry about that. It's been a long day, a hard day, for all of us. I thought you should know my thoughts."

Ryan paused for a moment to collect himself and stared up at the sky, saw lovely Venus, stalwart friend of men who roam the sea, and then looked back at his crew. A tear stained his cheek. He had no power to stop it.

"Men of the *Black Prince*!" he cried out with a shaky voice.

The crew - all at once - snapped proudly to attention. Whenever Ryan invoked the name *Black Prince*, that was their way though no one could quite remember who had started the custom.

The gesture filled Ryan's heart with new courage. He found his voice again.

"My brothers, warriors in a just and noble cause! We lost four men today. Four good men and fine seamen too. And they were our friends. Brave lads all. We shall miss their good company. They died for a purpose. They died for the sake of liberty and I tell you, with all my heart I believe it true, their lives were not wasted. Their deaths were not in vain. We shall not forget their sacrifice. America shall not forget. We are gathered here now to commit their bodies to the deep and we ask God, in the name of our Lord and Savior, Jesus Christ, to keep their souls. May they dwell in the house of the Lord with joy and love and peace forever and ever. Amen."

To help speed the souls of the fallen along death's way, the crew, in one voice, recited the Lord's Prayer together. And when they had finished, Ryan looked to Dowlin and nodded.

Dowlin saw the tears in Ryan's eyes. His own eyes turned misty. He could feel his lower lip quiver. "Commit the bodies!" he bellowed.

Hoar took up his bagpipes and began to play. A sad melody filled the air while men gently lifted the four corpses up over the ship's rail and let the bodies gently slip into the sea.

"On hats!" Dowlin ordered sharply. "Ship's company - dismissed!"

Men dispersed and the night watch took up their positions. The mood throughout the ship was somber.

Dowlin followed Ryan below to his cabin.

"You all right, Luke?"

"Aye. I don't know tho' if I did right here today, Pat. I risked the lives of these good men, risked the ship too. P'haps we should have run at the first sign of trouble. P'haps we should have fled and stayed the hell away from that schooner. A fool's pride kept me from doing so..."

Dowlin pushed his cap back off his forehead. "What nonsense is this slippin' threw yer teeth now, eh? Yer doubtin' yerself again? I don't believe it! Not the Luke Ryan I know. We're at war for the love of Christ! Men die, Luke. Nothin' new to you or me."

"Aye. But I'm not certain any of our men had to die this day. Despite what I said to the lads, that our friends did not die in vain, I pray to God in Heaven above that this is true. I pray that my own pride, my vanity, did not kill those good men."

Dowlin pursed his lips, bowed his head deep in thought for a moment before he spoke again. "Luke, you did what you thought best. We almost took that heavy schooner. Think what that would have meant. I don't mean the money now. We would have really put some fear into the hearts of those fat fools and knaves sittin' on their duffs in London. That's the whole point to all of this, right? We an't no frigate. We have no squadron to play with. Thar's only so much a small ship like ours can do. But, by *Gawd*, Luke, we are doin' it! Look at what we've accomplished so far. We've achieved so much! And let me tell you, take it to heart, I urge you: every man on board - every veteran leastwise - wanted to fight those *fookin'* British to the finish. Pay 'em back in kind for past transgressions. Our lads knew the risks and accepted 'em freely. And I'll tell you this too Luke, and in the light of a new mornin' you'll see that I am right, once we're back in port, not one man will leave this ship because of today. Not one soul because they believe in *you*."

Ryan bit his lip, took the back of his hand and wiped away another tear. He could feel the exhaustion weighing down on him.

"You possess a rare, simple wisdom, Patrick James Dowlin. I shall always be grateful for our friendship and proud to call you brother. Thank you. Thank you, Pat..."

Dowlin tossed aside his sober expression for grin. He had stomached enough sadness for one day. Time to be cheery again. Weldin would have agreed.

He patted Ryan firmly on the shoulder. "Another fine speech thar, Luke," he said in a lighter tone. "Hope you'll give me as good a send-off when my time comes."

"Patrick - you're too damn ornery to get yourself killed by a British ball or blade," Ryan shot back, picking up on Dowlin's lighter mood. "Now, Mr. Dowlin, if you please, sir, be so good as to see to it that our course for Rush is set."

"Aye, sir. Rush it is. Good man, Weldin. I shall sorely miss him."

Ryan looked away. "All good men. Bound to lose some more before we're through I fear."

Dowlin nodded. "Auck - that would mean more of Hoar's bagpipes. What an assault against the senses that infernal instrument is."

"Oh? I rather enjoyed them."

"So much for yer taste in music. Enough about that. Before I bid you good night tho', thar's someone I'd like to introduce to you, Luke."

"What?"

"You mean who?"

"Alright. Who?"

"Anderson."

"The American?"

"Aye. I'll be right back."

"But I know Anderson and -"

"No, no you don't. I'll be right back."

Dowlin soon returned with the American, a quiet, young man with a fresh face who had signed aboard the *Prince* in Brest.

"This is Seaman Anderson, sir."

"Indeed. How are you, lad?"

"Fine, sir," replied the young man, his voice trembling. He had no idea why the captain wanted to see him - but when a captain summons you to his cabin it is rarely for a good reason.

"No wounds I hope?"

Dowlin took the back of his hand and knocked Anderson's hat off his head before he could answer.

Anderson caught it with large hands and turned to Dowlin. "Oh, sorry, sir. Bit nervous, sir."

"No need to be nervous, Anderson," Dowlin offered with a kind smile. "Yer among friends."

"Yes, Mr. Dowlin," the young man replied, still confused and turned to face Ryan again. "No, sir, no wounds."

"Good. That's good. What can I do for you?"

"'Tis not," Dowlin interrupted, answering for the seaman, "what you can do for him, Capt'n. Anderson - I'd like you to tell the Capt'n here why you signed aboard the *Prince*."

"Oh? Well, sir, I mean, sirs, I wanted to fight the British."

"No, lad. Tell the Capt'n what you told the crew at supper a few nights ago. Remember when Hoar asked you the same question? I was there. I remember."

"Oh. You want me to tell the Capt'n what I told Hoar?"

"Aye."

"Well, sirs, it's like this: one of the boys asked me what I intended to do with my share of any prize money once we got back to port. I answered I didn't much care about money and then Mr. Hoar asked me what I did care about. I told him I volunteered to serve aboard the *Prince* to fight the British to be sure. But more than that, I would fight against any foreign country that would use the yoke of tyranny to usurp the natural rights of my kinfolk to live free. And I said once we was back in port, I hoped we didn't dilly-dally there too long as I would be anxious to put to sea again, to do my part to end this terrible struggle. Meanin' no disrespect, Capt'n."

"None taken," Ryan replied softly, smiling. He liked the American.

"How is it you came to France, to the *Prince?*" asked Dowlin. "I mean to say, what happened to yer ship?"

"My ship was taken, Mr. Dowlin, by a British man-o-war. A few of us managed to escape over the side and slipped into the longboat without being noticed, as it was dark with fog. 'Cause of the westerly trade winds and strong currents, we decided to make for Spain, but landed in Portugal instead and from there traveled by land to Dunkirk as we heard there was American ships there. But we couldn't find none. We went our separate ways after that. I walked on to Brest 'cause I heard Capt'n Jones was there. But he had sailed already by the time I got there and then I heard about the *Prince*."

"Lookin' for fame and fortune then, eh?"

"Gosh no, Mr. Dowlin. Wouldn't know what to do with fame. And as I said that night during supper, no amount of money could cause me to go to sea. I was born on a farm in Pennsylvania, near Harrisburg. My ma and pa are plain folk and raised me and my brothers to love the land. I miss tilling the soil, planting, watching things grow, harvest time. I miss feeling dirt under my feet. The sea makes me a wee frightful still, sir."

"You're a long way from home," offered Ryan and took note of the boy's large, strong hands, perfectly made for working the good, rich earth. "Don't you miss your family?"

"Oh, yes, sir! But my brothers enlisted with the army and are with

General Washington, last I heard they were anyways. And I won't let them pull my load. If we are to win our liberty, my country needs every man."

"Why didn't you join the army with your brothers?" asked Ryan.

"When I set out from home, I was on my way to do that very thing, Capt'n. Don't remember much, but I fell asleep in a tavern one night before enlisting and, well, I, I, um, I wasn't accustomed to strong drink and, well, I kinda woke up the next day on board a ship. She was already under sail and headed out to sea."

"Ha! Ha! Ha!" Dowlin roared and slapped the young American on the back. "You an't the first man to mix liquor with saltwater and be worse off for it!"

"You have some mighty noble thoughts rattling around inside that head of yours," observed Ryan. "I admire your spunk. You could have been killed today. And Lord only knows when I can pay you - doesn't any of that trouble you son?"

"Forgive my boldness, Capt'n but, ah, well..."

"Speak freely, sailor."

"Well, sir, you bein' Irish and all I thought you and the men would understand. There are things in this world worth getting bloodied for, worth dying for. My brothers and me didn't leave home for money. We left home to fight - to fight so that when we have families of our own someday our children will be born free and live under just laws made by just men, by men we choose to govern us and not by some king who claims his powers come from God."

"You're a rare breed, Mr. Anderson."

"Beg pardon, Capt'n. I don't mean to be contrary none, but no sir, not really. There are thousands more like me back home willing to fight and die - if needs be - for liberty. We fight for a just cause, a universal cause all men can rejoice in."

"I see. You speak well and do your country great honor. It is good to have you aboard, Mr. Anderson."

"Thank you kindly, Capt'n. Beg pardon, sir. I'm on watch, sir. May I go now?"

"By all means, return to your duties, and - thank you," Ryan said and shook the boy's hand.

"Much obliged, sir."

As the American disappeared, Ryan turned to Dowlin and winked. "Fine lad, I think I understand your point."

"Always glad to lend a helping hand, Luke!" Dowlin replied. "Now if you'll excuse me, I'll try to find my way topside and to the helm to give the night watch their orders."

Later that evening Ryan went on deck to stretch his legs and found Marchant standing alone near the main hatch, amidships, looking out over the water. He walked to Marchant's side but Marchant refused to look at him and said nothing.

"Captain Marchant, a moment of your time, sir. I ask you, most humbly, to accept my apologies for my harsh tone earlier today. My words were, p'haps, more cutting than I had intended. War is not an easy thing, especially when you are so close to it, when you come face-to-face with it. As I have some experience with such matters, I knew p'haps what you did not. I knew we could hold our own against that schooner and had a better than even chance of besting the king's men. It was a calculated risk of course. And, as matters turned out, it was a bit too - *premature* - for us to surrender this ship to the British…"

Marchant merely nodded, bowed his head low. He understood the foolishness of his behavior earlier. But there was nothing he could say and so offered no reply.

Ryan felt pity for the American and was tempted to shake Marchant's hand or pat him on the shoulder as a gesture of good will. But he couldn't bring himself to do so and simply wished Marchant a good night instead. He left Marchant standing in the darkness, alone, with his own thoughts.

As the *Prince* made her way towards Rush, she happened upon the small brig *Penny* in the middle of the night. Neither the brig nor her cargo was very impressive and the Irishmen were in a foul and uncharitable mood over the loss of their friends. There would be no ransom note, no paroles offered. The Irishmen removed the small brig's crew, took them into custody, and then torched the *Penny*. And then in the morning they caught the unlucky sloop *Limont* carrying a cargo of pork from Liverpool. They could take no more prisoners on board so Ryan had to ransom the ship and parole her crew - otherwise he and his men would have burned the *Limont* too.

And in the afternoon, the privateers eased their sleek black cutter into a secluded inlet on the western side of Lambay Island and quietly dropped anchor. After six long months, the Irishmen were finally back in Ireland. They were finally home.

She was reading a book by the fire in the front parlor when she heard the door swing open. Ryan's last letter to her had not yet arrived and she had no idea Ryan was even headed back for Ireland. She was stunned to see him standing in the doorway, his weathered, handsome face smiling at her. Her heart began to flutter. How gallant he appeared in her eyes! She absently let the book slip from her hands and rushed into his arms, pressing her body into his, eager to feel his flesh against her own.

"Luke! Luke!" she cried out, her voice filled with adoration for the mariner. She kissed his eyes, his cheeks, his forehead. "My darlin', why are you here?"

Ryan kissed her on the mouth, could feel her body rise up to meet his. He pulled away briefly to admire her face, her figure, her exquisite beauty. His woman with the long blond braids, radiant, inviting, she brought such joy to his heart.

"Why am I here did you say?" he asked teasingly. "Have I been gone so long that Irish manners are no more? Is that any way to greet your lover? Asking him why he's come home? Hm..."

"My God, Luke, you take my breath away!" she exclaimed, pulling him closer.

She wrapped her arms snugly around his neck. Her heart burned with desire. She slipped her tongue inside his mouth to taste him and felt her knees go soft.

Ryan kissed her back hard, caressed the soft golden strands of her hair. Then he pulled away again.

"I received your letter about your father. I had to come to see you. I am so very sorry. Are you well? His death has been difficult for you hasn't it?"

She glanced away, looked down at the floor. She couldn't stop the tears and wanted to hide her face.

Ryan gently pulled her head against his chest and let her sob. "Shhhhhh..."

"Oh, I am sorry, Luke."

"Hush, my dear girl. 'Tis all right."

"No, no, I need to put this behind me. The dead are gone. My father was old and ill and, towards the end, in pain. 'Tis foolishness to be so saddened by his passing. He is in a better place - I truly believe this - and I don't know why I weep."

"We humans are fragile creatures," replied Ryan in a soft, soothing tone. "Ruled by emotions we often do not, cannot, understand."

"Yes, how very true but, well, it's not just my father's passing, it's, it's *everything!*" she blurted out and began to shake and sob even harder.

Ryan stroked her hair. "What's this now, more tears? What is *everything?* What do you mean?"

She took a few moments to try and calm herself. "Even before my, my, fath, father, father's death, the business was faring poorly. When it was only the British and Americans fighting between themselves business was, was good but, now with the French in the thick of it, the waters are filled with warships and more and more of our smugglers are caught. Now with my father gone, I'm not sure I can handle the business on my own. There's fighting between the bosses too without my father here to keep them in line and men won't deal with me. I'm just a *woman!* They'd rather deal with their own kind - even if it means getting cheated in the bargain. But enough about that my dear, brave Captain. I'll prattle on and on and start talking silly gibberish if you let me."

"I am sorry to hear of your troubles."

"Now there," she said, wiping away her tears with the palm of her hand and forcing a smile. "Let's have a look at you! Oh, you're so fine!

So grand! And now you're a *hero*! How I've missed you, Luke! But tell me, when did you arrive in Ireland? And how?"

"*Hero* did you say?" Ryan asked. He placed his hands on his hips, leaned back and laughed. "I'm no hero, Shannon O'Keeffe. But I'm glad you think me so. As for when I arrived - why just hours ago. We put in at Rush. My ship is hidden away while Dowlin and the lads visit friends and family and look for new men to join us."

Shannon stared at him with disbelief. "Your ship and men, Luke, here? You brought your ship to Ireland?"

"Aye, of course I sailed here," he replied with a grin. "I haven't learned to walk on water just yet. Why all the fuss now?"

She took his hand, led him into the parlor and sat him down. She stood in front of him, her golden braids sparkled in the glow of the soft firelight, but her look was stern.

"And you came here to see me? Are you mad? My dearest Luke, how you fill my heart with joy! But it is much too dangerous for you here! This is folly!"

"What danger, what folly?" scoffed Ryan with a chuckle, assuming Shannon was simply being overly protective. "The roads were clear. Don't go and trouble that pretty head of yours now. Not to worry, the ship is safely tucked away and I'm here with you. *You'll* protect me from any evil!"

But his humor brought no smile to her shining face. She clenched her jaw, cupped his chin in both her hands and held it firmly.

"Foolish man," she scolded, like a mother reprimanding a child. But he looked at her perplexed and then she realized that he really didn't understand the danger. She narrowed her eyes. "Oh... You don't know, do you? No. I see now that you don't."

"Know, know what?" Ryan asked, stifling a yawn.

Shannon sat down on the narrow couch next to him. "The British are looking for *you*! And there is a price on your head."

Ryan smiled at her. "But of course the British are looking for me darlin', and the lads too. Nothing new there. Just means I'm doing my job. And a fine job it is too if you don't mind me saying so!"

Shannon slipped into her brogue, as she liked to do whenever she was dealing with men and needed to sound tough, needed to sound like one of them. "No, Luke. Listen to me. 'Tis more to it than that. British warships are scouring the Irish Sea determined to find you. Word has it that two frigates are trying to hunt you down with a number of small escorts. The *Ulysses* and *Boston* are the names of the frigates I believe. This is no longer some silly game, Luke. The British want you dead..."

The names of the two frigates caught Ryan's attention, cured his drowsiness like some tonic. If Shannon's bit of news caused him any anxiety though, he did not let her see it.

He massaged his chin. "The *Ulysses* and *Boston* you say? Humph! I've earned more respect than that! Fear not my young lady. The *Prince* can out run any frigate. And as for the smaller ships, we came close to sinking one just the other day, a heavy schooner. And then there was a Royal Navy warship, the *Spry*, out of Waterford, a brig, before that a few weeks ago. The schooner was one of the king's revenue ships, I suspect, and well-armed. She made the mistake of tangling with us and we gave her a proper thrashing. We almost took her too. Doubt her crew will sail out against us any time soon, not willingly anyhow. The same is true of the brig out of Waterford we bloodied. Had the cannon overlooking Tower Hook not interfered, we would have taken her as a prize or sunk her."

Shannon reached over to caress his hair. "Aye, the heavy schooner would be the *Townsend* my brave soldier. And so the ship out of Waterford is also some of your fine handiwork? I had my suspicions it might be! You certainly are cocksure of yourself my handsome lad aren't you now? You bloodied both crews on both ships all right. You killed the *Townsend's* captain and a good number of her men. All of Dublin is talkin' about it."

"Aye. The *Spry* suffered killed and wounded too. It is, after all, a war."

"Well, the British will most certainly come at you with no mercy now. Expect no quarter if you're cornered. Expect no fair treatment or leniency if you're nabbed. Luke, London won't be satisfied - until you're *dead."*

Ryan grinned. "I hope they do," he said gritting his teeth. "Try and hunt me down that is. In fact - I'm counting on it. I have one or two nasty unpleasantries in mind for the English, just to make certain they'll not soon forget the name Luke Ryan!"

At first, Shannon thought he was teasing her, that his words were no more than a kind of child's empty boastfulness. Men could be like that she knew and Ryan was no exception. But then she saw the arrogant, defiant look in his eyes. And she felt fear. She reached over, took both his hands inside her own and held them in her lap.

"My darling," she said, looking at him nervously. "They say the *Townsend* took on a pirate ship of thirty-guns and killed a great number of her crew. Over half the pirates were killed or wounded or so the English claim. Is that true, Luke? Were men killed?"

But before Ryan could answer, her eyes filled with tears again. "I was so worried it was your ship they were talkin' about. That you might have been one of those killed..."

Ryan looked away for a moment. "Aye, men were killed. We lost four good lads, including Weldin, I'm sorry to say. He was a fine, fine man. Your father, if he was still alive, God rest his soul, would not look too kindly on me losing Weldin."

Shannon saw the mist in his eyes. She leaned over to hug him, put her cheek next to his to comfort him.

"Oh, I'm sorry, Luke," she whispered softly into his ear as she ran her hands down his shoulders, down the length of his arms to soothe him.

He grimaced at her touch, but didn't think she saw him wince.

She spoke again with the refined, English accent she had learned in school. "My father thought the world of you, Luke. Yes. Like his own son. Alexander Weldin was a dear man. But he was no fool. He knew the danger. He knew the risks of making war against the English."

"Dowlin said something very similar to me about Alex," Ryan replied, almost whispering. "No need to be sorry, Shannon. As you say, we're at war after all. It was bound to happen eventually. And don't believe everything you hear or read in the papers. We're no pirate ship.

We're no thirty-gunner either! The truth of it is we killed or wounded a good many of the *Townsend's* crew. She turned tail and ran before we could finish her off. Her master was the first to fall. She was trying to run down some poor smuggler, a small coaster, when we happened upon her. We were too far away to help the smuggler. The *Townsend* forced her onto the rocks and there she sank with men still on board. One of your father's ships?"

"Aye, possibly. The rumrunner *Night Angel* is missing. I know nothing about ships or battles at sea but, it seems to me, Luke, it is something of a miracle you lost only four men. The talk is that the *Townsend* is no child's toy. She'll be repaired soon enough to rejoin the others to hunt for you again."

Ryan looked away for a moment, deep in thought. "Aye, true enough. She was no toy. Neither was the *Spry...*"

Shannon stroked the back of his neck. "I worry so. About you, about us..."

"Now there, my dear, sweet Shannon, you go too far. Not to worry. You'll be fine; I'll be fine. Look here, not a scratch on me. Ship captains rarely seem to suffer any harm. Oh, like the *Townsend's* poor master, I admit some of the dafter ones manage to get themselves killed one way or the other, but never hurt. It is the rule of the sea. No good will come from worrying about it in any case."

Shannon leaned over to kiss his eyes, then unloosened his cravat and unbuttoned his shirt, pulling it back to see his bare chest. She had seen him wince with pain. His right side was all black and blue. She gave him a dirty look.

"Not a scratch on you, Mr. Ryan?"

Ryan offered a sly smile. "Indeed. Not a scratch on me dear lady. That is a bruise! Happened when I was a bit clumsy going for a swim."

Shannon's lips curled into a pout. She shook her head and wiggled a finger in his face. "Oh - a swim was it? And just who do you think you're foolin' now Capt'n Ryan, some dolt, some tart down at the wharfs?"

"I would *never* think that!"

"A swim indeed!" she said and playfully pushed him away. She decided it was time for her to mask her fear, to summon up her courage. It was hard. But she knew it was the most loving gesture she could give her man at this fragile moment in their lives. Why burden him with her own fears? She kissed his bare chest and smiled up bravely at him.

"That's my girl..."

"There's been so much gossip about you, Luke, and the *Prince*," she said in a happier, carefree voice. "My heart fills with pride for you when I hear of it! God how I've missed you, Luke, my brave and daring Captain!"

She pressed her open mouth against his and the two lovers exchanged a lingering, inviting kiss. Then they stood and held each other quietly for a time, man and woman, both longing to be one.

What more can any of us in this wretched world really desire? To love and to be loved in return, that is the best we mortals, while chained to this Earth, can hope for.

Shannon started to button his shirt back up, was the first to break their silence. "Luke, I've missed you so. And my body aches for you. But you cannot stay here, not now. It's not safe. Especially here. My father's house is often watched. Gather your men and return to your ship, now. Sail her to safer waters. As soon as things settle down a bit, I'll book a passage to France to be with you! Yes. That's exactly what I'll do."

Ryan nodded. There was no denying she was right. *Clever girl.* Despite all his bravado, he knew he needed to hurry back to Rush and warn his men. They were all indeed in serious danger.

"P'haps you're right, my lady. No need to tempt fate. Your father used to say that to me. I had best go, I agree. How grand it would be to see you in France! And you would love France. Ha! Ha! France would love you, my dear lady! But why wait so long? I intend to cruise the waters off of Scotland next and give those haughty Scots a taste of war! No British frigates will be that far north looking for us. After we *capture* Scotland - and all the wild Highlanders there - it should be safe to return to Rush again to try and sign up some new lads. Things should quiet down in a week or two, at least for a bit. Why not take a room in Rush, say in two weeks' time, and wait for me there? Agreed?"

Her eyes sparkled at his winning words. "I shall wait for you with pleasure my dashing, young mariner, my warrior prince!"

"Grand! I'll bring you back a wild Highlander or two for your amusement."

She giggled. "I have no need for any wild Highlanders! You are my one, my only desire."

For an awkward moment, the lovers could say or do no more and simply contented themselves with holding each other. Ryan longed to seize her, to feel her naked skin against his own, to have her soft skin quiver against his touch, to make her shudder with waves of pleasure. But, there was no time.

She sensed his frustration. She too wanted to hold him in her arms, to be held by him, to lose herself in that delirious place of exquisite ecstasy with him. The air turned super-charged with arousal. But she did not take him. No. She gathered all her will power instead, beat down her lust, ignored her body's hot cravings and smiled at him - a soft, loving smile, yes.

He understood and nodded quietly in return. He brushed her cheek with the back of his hand and sighed.

"I best be off then. How I love you so, Shannon. I, I don't know if I say that very well. I stumble over such words sometimes. But 'tis what is in a man's heart that matters most and the love I have for you in my heart overflows."

Her lower lip trembled. "Your words have never failed me. At times, I wonder though. Our love is so rich, so sublime. Do you suppose, Luke...? Well, I fear I will start babbling now but, I, I shudder to think that someone, something, might try to rip away this splendor from us. At times I feel as if our lives are spinning out of control, as if the whole damn world has gone mad with this hideous war."

Ryan pulled her close, kissed her lightly on the forehead. "I shall come back for you, Shannon. That much I promise you. How are your finances? Do you need money?"

"Money? Heavens no!" she replied with a hint of irritation. "I doubt that I can hold on to father's business much longer as I say, but he still left me with the house, enough money and a fair amount of property with business on them, small holdings mind you, but all profitable. I'm in no need of money." She sighed and added whimsically, "How I loved the business though. And I was good at it, Luke, truly I was. Better than most of those numbskulls who claim some higher right over me only because of what dangles between their legs."

"I have no doubt about how shrewd in business you are. Never met a more clever girl. You are, after all, your father's daughter. I wish there was more I could do to help. But I have faith in you. If you have a mind to keep your father's business, well, those numbskulls are in trouble."

Shannon smiled. "Off you go then! *And keep your powder dry!* I'll be seeing you soon enough and I have in mind to make sure all your parts are in working order."

"Oh?"

She laughed and stood and pushed him towards the door.

Ryan paused at the threshold, took her hands into his own and held them firmly. "One last matter, Shannon."

"Yes?"

"I would have preferred to wait for a better time. The winds of change are blowing across Ireland, across Europe, across the whole world I suppose. But I, well, I, I..."

"Luke," Shannon interrupted and gave him a warm smile, "stuttering hardly suits a man like you. Out with it now. Then be on your way!"

He straightened his shoulders back and took a deep breath. "Aye. Just so my lady. Miss Shannon Grace O'Keeffe, if you would have me, I would make you my wife. Will you marry me?"

Her heart fluttered; her lips parted. She fell into his arms, held him close with all her strength and started to sob again.

Ryan kissed her hair, lifted her off her feet and twirled her around in a circle as she looked at him with her green and sparkling eyes, eyes filled with love for him. He saw the warm, live tears too.

"What is this now?" he asked.

"I... I... Oh! Damn, now it is me who stutters! You don't know how much I've longed to hear those words from you, Luke Ryan! But, first, well, I wanted to wait for a better time to tell you. I didn't want to add to your burdens."

"Burdens? Tell me what?"

"Luke, I am with child."

Ryan seized her and held her close.

"You aren't angry?"

He pulled away and smiled. "Angry? What a silly question. Angry. I am overwhelmed with joy. I will be a father! But, why didn't you tell me earlier?"

"You have seventy souls in your care. You carry the weight of command and are at war with the English. I did not want to add to that. And, I did not know if the thought of marriage had crossed your mind - we have not discussed it until now. And, to be honest, I was unsure whether this news would please you..."

Ryan tweaked her nose gently. "You still have much to learn about me my good lady. My love for you is not selfish. I love you with all my heart and I will love our child too. Again, I ask, will you be my wife, Shannon?"

"With all my heart - yes! Yes, I shall be your wife! It hardly seems just, so many poor and broken people in this wretched world and I, I have been blessed with so much..."

"London?" Ryan asked.

Shannon understood his question. "Yes, London," she answered smiling. "But I want our son, or daughter, to be born on free soil not subject to King George's rule."

"America?"

"Yes, why not. America."

Ryan smiled, a proud smile, and the young lovers embraced one last time and exchanged tender kisses. It was hard for either to let go.

Shannon was the first to pry their arms loose. She gently pushed him on the porch.

He stole one last kiss before mounting his horse. "Is your health good? Do you require anything?"

"I have never felt better, Luke. No worries."

"When we are together in France then," he said with a smile, "then I shall make you Mrs. Luke Ryan!"

"I'll hold you to your word, Capt'n Ryan!" she called after him and blew him a kiss. "Have a care with my heart, Luke. Come back to me safe and well..."

As he spurred his horse on he turned and waved at her one last time and then hurried back to Rush. Despite the new danger, he felt oddly confident. *Mrs. Luke Ryan.* That exquisite thought brought a smile. And he was going to be a father - that thought made him scared and he laughed at himself. Then his thoughts turned to other matters. *The Boston and the Ulysses. Aye. My, my, but haven't we made an impression on someone!*

Success never comes without cost. A price must be paid by anyone who would have it. Sometimes the tab is affordable, sometimes not, but, either way, success always brings with it a measure of complexity and, for the men of the *Black Prince*, privateering was becoming an increasingly complex endeavor.

A warm drizzle fell on the small seaside town loved by smugglers. *Good,* Ryan thought. That would keep all but a few hearty souls off of Rush's dark and dreary roads. He found Dowlin and his men already assembled at the waterfront with a dozen new men lined up along the wharf ready to board the cutter's launch. Even in the faint torchlight, Ryan could make out their rough faces and coarse clothes. These were the faces and clothes of sailors. Only time would tell whether they were good sailors but, at least, Dowlin had not rounded up ignorant farm boys.

Dowlin was sorely tempted to laugh when he saw Ryan approaching the wharf on horseback. With a deck under his feet, Ryan had a commanding presence. But on a horse, he made an awkward sight. Only because of the new men did Dowlin decide to check his humor.

Ryan dismounted and took in the new recruits. "Appears you did well, Patrick."

"Well enough for now I suppose. We'll find more willin' souls when we get back from wherever it is you plan on takin' us next. I've passed the word around town. I was just about to take these fine gentlemen over to the *Prince*."

"Good."

He leaned close to Ryan's ear and whispered, "Didn't expect to see you back so soon, Luke. My yer awfully fast an't ya? Women don't like it too fast or so they say..."

"Doesn't anythin' other than liquor, women or the ship ever enter that half-wit brain of yours?" Ryan whispered back.

"Ah, now, let me think on it for a bit. Hm, nope. Never. You've covered all the necessaries."

Then Dowlin lowered his voice even more. "We've got trouble, Luke. Two frigates are out lookin' for us. Squalls on the horizon. Best not to linger here waitin' for it to hit. Rush is an obvious place to come look for us. I planned on sending one of the lads down to Kenmure to fetch yer sorry arse back up here tonight."

"Aye, I know. The *Boston* and the *Ulysses*. We best be on our way. *That's* why I'm back so soon. Shannon warned me."

Ryan turned to face the new men. They looked fit enough.

"Welcome, lads. I know Mr. Dowlin here has already explained things to you so I'll be quick. We're in a bit of a hurry. I'm Luke Ryan, master of the *Black Prince*. The *Prince* is an American privateer under lawful commission by his Excellency, Doctor Ben Franklin. Odds are good we will see some action. I trust none of you lads are gun shy or squeamish. If you are, best we part company here and now. For those stout hearts willing to sail with me, glad to have you with us."

"Yer Luke Ryan?" asked one man.

"Aye, that I am."

"Heard you was, well, sir, beg pardon, heard you was a real big fella."

Ryan roared out loud. "This is all of me," he said and stretched his arms out into the night sky. "Sorry if you're disappointed. Any more questions? As I said before, we're a tad short on time. Any of you lads mind mixing it up with the British? Might be a round or two of fist-a-cuffs or worse..."

A second man removed his hat and stepped forward. "Mr. Dowlin here, sir, told us what to expect. We've all spilt some blood in our day I suspect. Some of theirs, some of ours. If you'll have us, sir, we come aboard yer warship gladly and of our own free will."

"Well said, lad! That's the spirit! You're all very welcome indeed! Mr. Dowlin, shall we?"

"Aye! You heard the man. Let's make haste!"

The men piled into the launch with their ditty bags, took up oars and rowed out to the *Prince*. Once on board, Ryan quickly administered the oath of allegiance to the new recruits and America, 3,000 miles away, suddenly had twelve new citizens, twelve new sons of the *Revolution*, ready to fight for her.

Ryan gave the order to weigh anchor and the deck hands snapped to, quietly straining at the capstan to pull the 1,000-pound anchor in. Topmen unfurled sails and trimmed spars while the helmsmen pointed the *Prince's* nose north where, beyond the sea, stood a rugged, cold land of hills and steep mountains inhabited by a fiercely independent race of rugged men, partial to games of strength, broad swords and fancy, colorful tartans.

Sailing up the Firth of Lorn, where skies are cold and unfriendly and the sea is a lonely place, the Irishmen trolled the waters for many days but caught no fat prizes. Not one sail crossed their path.

Ryan and Dowlin were standing together at the rail, watching the breakers crash against Scotland's rocky shores, when off in the distance a small village came into view. Ryan grabbed his spyglass to get a better look and saw a number of small, well-kept cottages. There were fishing nets spread out along the beach and two large fishing trawlers anchored in the village's small harbor.

"What town is that, Pat?"

Dowlin removed a chart from the binnacle, rolled it out over the rail and traced a squiggly line with his index finger.

"I suspect that be Lismore, Luke."

"Lismore?"

"Aye. Why, you want to stop and get a drink?" Dowlin asked jokingly and quickly added with a grin, "if so, we'll make a toast to your lovely bride-to-be, and, I'll buy..."

"You'll buy?"

"Yep."

"No kidding? You'll buy? Whoa. Generosity has never been your strongest skill. We best move fast then, before you change your mind! Let's do, let's go into town and have ourselves a drink!"

Dowlin looked at Ryan cockeyed, unsure whether Ryan was toying with him or not.

"I'm serious, Pat. Look there, two fat herring boats. Why not go into town, see what we can take? We're just wastin' time out here. Why not invade Scotland, violate the king's sacred lands a little, have a bit of fun!"

Luke Ryan, sacker of cities... Those had been Shannon's words to him.

"Invade Scotland?" Dowlin asked incredulously and rolled his eyes. "I didn't think you were serious about such talk before."

"And why not? It will, if nothing else, give the lads a change of scenery. We could replenish our perishables too."

"Ha! Ha! Yer pissin' in the wind again my friend! Always a sure-fire way to get wet. Been away from Shannon too long maybe, hey, and not thinkin' with yer brain? That's bloody Scotland over there, Luke. Great Britain, the Empire, all that rot. King George's land protected by King George's great army of lobsterbacks, thousands and thousands of redcoats. Remember? With only eighty souls or so on board this here ship, we an't no army my friend!"

Ryan smiled, a broad smile to mimic one of Dowlin's own. "Ah, where's your sense of adventure, man?" he asked and pointed at the shore. "We'll put her in over in that cove there. Take twenty well-armed men with us and make our way into town by land. This is a war we are fighting after all."

"And what about the British army? They've got one, a big one too!"

"Do they now? Do they indeed?" Ryan asked with a shrug.

Word quickly spread among the crew that they were going to land in Scotland! Kelly formed a raiding party with twenty of his best men and they enthusiastically armed themselves with muskets, pistols, cutlasses and knives and decided to take two small swivels loaded with grape shot with them. The Irishmen waited for darkness, and then rowed ashore in three boats. The small band of invaders from the sea, with torches and muskets in hand, picked their way between the rocks and boulders along the shore and then moved inland, through the high-reeds of a dry marsh in single file.

Lismore was a quiet, little town with modest homes made of whitewashed brick and thatch. Ryan and his men found the local magistrate's house first, broke inside and forced him from his supper table. They marched the magistrate through the streets at bayonet point and rounded up any one else they caught loitering outside - which was just about the whole town as people stepped outside to see what all the commotion was about. The Irishmen herded their prisoners into a field of grass, the town square, surrounded by whitewashed rocks and bunches of scraggly thistle, and waited.

The magistrate glared at Dowlin, whom he presumed to be leader of the band of ruffians. "What's the meanin' of this outrage!" he demanded in a Highlander's thick accent.

"Outrage?" Dowlin asked and raised an eyebrow.

"Aye, outrage," the magistrate replied gruffly. "Are you brigands, pirates? This is a poor town, nothin' for you here. And know this: the British Militia is only a mile or two away."

"Oh?"

"That's right," the Scotsman offered boldly. He raised his arm and pointed down the town's main street. "One garrison is at Port Appin and the others at Duart."

Dowlin's eyes casually followed the length of the magistrate's arm. He looked down the dirt road, to the place the magistrate was pointing.

"Ah, I sees that's got yer attention," the magistrate offered smugly.

Dowlin simply shrugged his shoulders and smiled.

Ryan stepped forward and cleared his throat. "My good people of

Lismore. Listen now. No harm will come to anyone here. We're neither brigands nor pirates. We're American privateers and we've come to help ourselves to some of your stores. We've come a long way and we're short on supplies. We need fresh water and will gladly accept some flour to make bread. A slaughtered sheep or two might inspire us to show you our gratitude. Then, by your leave, we'll be on our merry way and depart these shores as quickly as we came."

"Ye'll get nothin' from us, you dirty thieves!" one townsman shouted out.

Ryan searched the faces in the crowd, looking for the man who had uttered the staunch words. "And who do I have the pleasure of addressing, sir?"

"Name's MacDonald. I'm the town's constable and I don't see no Americans here. I sees stinkin' Irishmen and subjects of the Crown just like we be. Deserters maybe? No matter. Be off with you now before I sic me dogs on the lot of you! They have a taste for scoundrels. Word to the wise mister riff-raff: we've already sent runners out to call out the militia. They'll tan your hides but good, laddie. Looks like you've bit off more than you can chew, eh?" MacDonald paused to laugh. "Ha! Ha! Ha! What a sorry lot of fools you be!"

Dowlin, nostrils flaring, stepped nose-to-nose with the constable. "Not very hospitable, are ya?"

But MacDonald was not intimidated. He had faced bigger, stronger men in his day than this *Irishman*. He grinned, an ugly smile, half his teeth were missing. "Don't you worry now, Mr. American with the Irish talk in you. Hee! Hee! Hee! The king's good soldiers will show you some hospitality at the end of some good English rope when they catch you, laddie! And mark my words, they *will* catch thee!"

Dowlin laughed in MacDonald's face. "Ha! Yer threats mean nothin' to me. I've heard it all before my cocksure *friend*. You Scots have been around yer English bitches - the ones you call yer masters - far too long my good man. I see you've taken to makin' idle boasts just like 'em. Didn't use to be that way. Why, I can still remember the days, not so long ago, when a Scotsman's promise - or his threat - used to mean somethin'. No more it seems..."

MacDonald stepped forward, opened his mouth to offer some foul reply but Dowlin had heard enough and cut the Scotsman off.

"Save yer breath, old man," he said and spit at the ground. "Yer words are wasted on me."

And then a grizzled giant, a man colossal in size, walked towards the square with one small boy tucked inside each of his massive arms, both wriggling against his grip like fish caught on a hook. Wasted energy. Ryan had sent Kelly out earlier with two teams of four men on reconnaissance to encircle the town, one party had gone south and the other had gone north to snag any town folk who might try to run for help.

"Beg pardon, sir," interrupted Kelly, looking down on the constable. "These be yer two runners? I suspect yer militia won't be here anytime soon."

Kelly turned to Ryan as he gently let the boys drop to the ground. "Capt'n, I left some of the lads posted at the end of town to watch the roads."

The two boys, wide-eyed, scrambled to their feet and bolted into the crowd, away from the grinning giant.

"Capt'n, we're wastin' time here," Dowlin said with an edge in his voice. Standing on foreign soil with enemy soldiers nearby brought him no joy. "Whatever you intend to do here we should do it and do it quick."

"Well," Ryan began, pausing to look at the huddled, frightened Scots, "since you people aren't disposed to making this easy on yourselves, you leave me with no choice." He smiled, bowed his head and made an exaggerated sweep of his arm through the air, mimicking his friend Sartine. "By your leave, my lords and ladies, I shall take my crew and depart from these inhospitable shores at once. But, first a gift. Something for you to remember us by. A thoughtful guest never continues on his journey without first leaving his generous host a parting gift, a token of his appreciation - something to warm the heart. That is the custom is it not? Mr. Kelly, sir, would you be so kind as to signal the ship, have her pull into the bay."

Kelly grabbed a torch, walked down to the water's edge a short distance away. The people of Lismore watched him as he raised the torch above his head and waved it around in a circle.

"Ha! You got no ship," offered a large woman, her old, shriveled hands holding tightly on to a shawl wrapped around her shoulders to ward off the night's chill. "Yer all bluff, no guts. Yer goin' to steal our fishing boats. Common thieves, you are!" She cleared her throat of phlegm and spit on the ground, on the same spot Dowlin had spit.

Ryan smiled politely at the woman, touching the brim of his hat as he did so. "We shall soon see who's bluffing, mother. I'll be back momentarily to see how you fancy our gift."

Ryan gathered his men and led them down to the dock where they found several small boats and launched them on the water. On board the *Prince*, John Kelly had seen the signal and slowly eased the cutter into the bay. The crew lit all her lanterns to show her off. The bewildered people of Lismore, standing in the square, unguarded, watched with curiosity to see what these strange Irishmen were up to.

"Are you havin' fun, Luke?" Dowlin asked as the men pulled crisply at the oars.

Ryan thought for a moment. "Aye. Aye, as a matter-of-fact, I am. You?"

"I'll be better with a deck under my feet. Yer a pistol Luke... things are always interestin' with you around. I'll grudgingly give you that much. Made me smile when you was pleasant to that old shrew!"

Ryan laughed. "'Tis my nature I suppose. A flaw in my character if you like. I see no gain in being rude."

"No. Suppose not, Luke. What now?"

"The time has come to show our brave Scots that there is a war on."

The captain of the privateers stepped back on board his ship and considered how best to win over the hearts of the stubborn Highlanders. Ryan had in mind to teach the town a lesson. Not too serious a lesson for he had no wish to frighten, much less harm, any woman or child, but a lesson nonetheless - something that would be heard and talked about in London's halls of power and reported about in her newspapers.

The black cutter, nearly invisible in the dark except for the lanterns set along her rails, slipped in between the town's two deserted herring boats. Ryan ordered the heavy guns run out, his gunners opened fire and pulverized both vessels.

The Scots watched in stunned silence as the two vessels erupted into balls of flame, lighting up the night sky. The hot blazes soon softened their cold hearts, melted away any desire to be frugal. Someone even thought to raise a white flag, in any language, the signal for a parlay. The good folks of Lismore were now disposed to show their generosity, to give their guests from the sea a parting gift, something rare and fine to soothe their angry spirits and speed them along their way.

Just as their ancestors had done 1,000 years before to appease heathen Norsemen raiders roving the boundless sea, they gathered a peace offering, a tribute to the god of war. The Lismoreians rounded-up chickens, goats, sheep and even one scrawny heifer, and herded the animals down to the dock. Barrels of fresh water and kegs of whiskey and ale were brought down to the water's edge too. The spoils of war.

The privateers lined the rails and watched the spectacle with amusement.

Dowlin shook his head, was the first to speak out. "Good Lord, Luke. Whatcha goin' to do with all that?"

"Take it with us I suppose," Ryan answered with a shrug.

"Oh? Fine. Just fine. We sailed all this way for this? Now we're a goddamn cattle boat! Not much money in sheep shit and cow pies for us Capt'n. Helluva way to fight a war if you ask me."

"Ah my friend, you miss the point. Tonight we have insulted the very coasts of His Royal Majesty. Now that *is* something. We fight this battle for more than just money. We took the solemn oath, the two of us. Remember? We swore before God to protect and support the American States, to the utmost of our abilities. Those were the words as I recall and I for one intend to honor them. What good is a man who cannot honor his solemn pledge? Now the Admiralty will be forced to send warships far north to look for us, maybe even station another militia nearby too. We, of course, will be hundreds of miles away by then. The English will be on a wild goose chase. It's not much p'haps. We're a small ship with a small crew. But we do what we can, where we can, to support our American brothers. Seems to me, if memory serves, I recall similar words from you after the *Townsend...*"

Dowlin didn't respond at first. He turned to watch the two burning wrecks, hissing at them before they slipped below the water. The night turned pitch black again after the smoldering messes disappeared. He considered Ryan's words with care and finally shook his head.

"You don't," Ryan asked, "agree, old friend?"

"Luke, this damn business has infected us all I suppose. I dare say yer beginnin' to sound like one of 'em American patriots. America has a dream worth fightin' for, p'haps even worth dyin' for. Aye, I do agree. But life was... well, it was simpler when we were plain smugglers. That's all I'm sayin'."

"Life indeed was simpler, Pat."

"Ah, huh. Well, it'll probably all go badly for us in the end. Then again, maybe not. Yer a lucky bastard. Lord only knows why. Sometimes I feel as tho' some great invisible hand has swept us up and we're just ridin' on the wind, no control. Sure, it's been exhilarating, but things are slippin' away fast from us. *Jesus*, Luke, I sound like you! Am I makin' any sense?"

Ryan patted Dowlin on the shoulder and nodded. "Aye, you do make very good sense indeed to me. I've had similar thoughts at times. We've gone and grabbed a tiger by the tail and can't let go. We've gone and got ourselves caught up in something big, bigger than ourselves certainly. And I think, possibly, we are witnessing history in the making and on a scale so grand, so sweeping, it might just obliterate the old world order."

"Aye, Luke, just so. Couldn't have said it better."

"On the contrary, my friend, I believe you already did."

Dowlin stretched his arms and took a moment to bask in Ryan's compliment. He had done enough serious thinking for one day. "*Weeeeell*, Capt'n. We are all well acquainted with yer rules aboard ship. Yer one callous brute to keep a dry ship! But as you said, what good is a man who doesn't keep his word, eh? I'd be much obliged to you now for that drink you promised earlier."

Ryan chuckled. "Aye! So I did! Thought I saw a keg or two left on the dock for us. Let's go collect our gifts and the rest of the men. We can slaughter the meat and sample some of what's in those kegs. One *small* gill for every man can't do any harm on this delightful night."

"*Small* gill?" Dowlin asked mischievously. "A pint is a pint, a quart is a quart and a gill is a gill, Luke..."

"Not the way you pour."

"Ha, a *small* gill it is then!" Dowlin shot back with a twinkle in his eye. "Three gills would suit me better tho', help wash away all that filthy British dust out of my pipes."

Ryan smiled back. "Two now and I'll buy you the third once we're back in Dunkirk."

Dowlin smacked his lips. "So be it. Two for now and a third in Dunkirk. As I said, yer a coldhearted one, Luke Ryan. As a point of honor, I best warn Shannon about yer darker side. Bein' the Irish *gentleman* that I am, I'm obliged to do that much at least..."

Ryan slapped Dowlin on the back. "Ha! You've claimed to be many things Patrick Dowlin. But a lowbred gentleman? I shudder to think of you as such and best perish the thought before I heave up supper!"

Seven

A Friend Crosses Over the Stream

ith their three-month commission from Franklin nearly at an end, the Irishmen needed to return to France again after Lismore. But along the way to Dunkirk was Rush... Ryan went on to the inn where Shannon had agreed to meet him. But she wasn't there. The innkeeper there instead handed him a simple message from her asking him to ride to Kenmure as quickly as he was able, that it was urgent. He borrowed a fast horse and galloped off at once. But as darkness settled over the land, thin wisps of mist rose up from the bogs along the road, reaching out for his horse's legs, trying to slow him down. Ryan charged through it, oblivious to the signs.

The old watchman standing at O'Keeffe's front gate, ever vigilant, lifted his lantern high when he saw Ryan approach and waved him through without a word. Shannon raced out to the porch when she heard the sound of a horse's hooves and smiled when she saw his face. She watched him as he dismounted, rather gracefully for once she thought, and ran out to greet him. With eagerness in their hearts, the lovers held each other tightly and traded long, hard kisses. And then they got the giggles when they realized the old watchman was watching.

Ryan briefly pulled himself away to see her face, never tiring of her beauty. The flame inside her heart - some would say the soul - burned hot wrapped in love's embrace. Her lips were fuller, more sensuous, her green eyes sparkled. Her face was more radiant. Even her hair seemed glossier. Love's magic. Ryan felt overwhelming pride for her and smiled, a loving smile, yes.

"I thought we agreed to meet in Rush, my darling girl?" Ryan asked as they walked inside the house.

She looked at him curiously. "Yes, but your message said for me to wait for you here, Luke."

"Message?" Ryan asked at first perplexed. Then he grabbed Shannon firmly by the shoulders. "What message, Shannon? I sent no message! I came here because of the message you left me at the hotel in Rush! You wrote that it was urgent!"

Shannon put her hand to her mouth and gasped. "No! Oh, no! I sent no message either, Luke!"

Ryan removed the note from his pocket and handed it to her. "You didn't leave this for me?"

"No! No. You must go and go now! Something is very, very wrong with this!"

"Aye... But you're coming with me! It's no longer safe for you here. Can you ride?"

"Of course I can ride."

"Good. Gather up your things Shannon, just what your horse can carry. We'll ride to the ship and sail to France and stay there until we can sort this thing out. Agreed?"

She kissed him hard, gave him a confident smile, and raced upstairs to collect some clothes and money.

And then the old watchman's shrill voice cut through the still, night air. "Riders comin' in fast!" he cried out and grabbed the musket leaning against the fence.

Ryan went to the front window, pulled the curtains back. A dozen or more horsemen with torches in hand were riding up from the Dublin road. They were riding hard. A man named Flanagan, O'Keeffe's foreman, and three of his men came up from their quarters behind the stables and dashed into the house armed with muskets, pistols and swords. Three more followed after them.

Shannon came downstairs with a knapsack in hand and rushed to Ryan's side.

"Do you know these men?" Ryan asked.

"No. I don't know what this is about. Nothing like this has ever happened before. Whatever it is, whoever these men are, it can't be good."

Flanagan stepped into the parlor with his six men. He moved to Shannon's side and waited for his orders.

The riders, a well-armed mobbed, stopped at the gate and surrounded the watchman. One of them reached down and yanked the old man's musket out of his hands. Another pulled his horse behind the old man and struck him down hard with the butt of his musket. The old man sank to his knees and collapsed. Dust swirled around his crumpled body, death closed in around his eyes.

Horrified, Shannon started for the door to run to the old man's side.

Ryan grabbed her arm and pulled her back. "No Shannon! You cannot! I don't know who these men are or what they want. Maybe they're the king's men after me. Maybe they're hoodlums or rivals of your father set on running you out now that he is gone. It makes no difference right now - we must leave. We must reach the ship!"

"But poor, old Murphy's hurt!" she blurted out.

"Mr. Ryan," Flanagan said, "is right ma'am. 'Tis best you and he go now, Ms. Shannon and find a safe place. We're outnumbered here and there's no time to summon more lads up for a fight. We'll fetch a doctor for Murphy when we can."

"Yes, yes, you're both right, of course," replied Shannon. "All right. Mr. Flanagan, you and your men hold these ruffians off for as long as you can. I'll ride out with Mr. Ryan to fetch more lads. Remember father's orders: no killing. No need for anybody to get hurt on either side. Just give us enough time to get a clear of the house and get a good lead on them. Then you and your lads scatter across the fields if you can or surrender if you must - whichever way seems best. If your thrown in jail I'll see to your bail soon enough. Any time behind bars will be rewarded with fat purses."

Flanagan understood his orders, was in no mood to discuss money. The O'Keeffe's had always been generous to the hired hands.

"You handle yourself as well as yer father, God rest his soul, please ma'am!" Flanagan pleaded. "Get yourself outta here, now!"

Flanagan jerked his head, motioning to his men to cover the windows and doors. He took his musket and smashed out a pane of glass. His men scattered throughout the house and did the same.

The riders dismounted and carefully approached the house on foot, fanning out to surround the place. Shannon took Ryan's arm and pulled him towards the cellar door, grabbing a candle off the fireplace mantel along the way.

"No, Shannon," Ryan protested. "Not that way. We'll be trapped down there."

She flashed a smile, a smile he knew well, a smile that said: *I know something you don't.* Ryan sighed and followed her down the cellar's narrow steps. The cellar was musty and pitch-black.

Then they heard musket shots above their heads. The riders were firing at the house.

Shannon went over to a wine rack standing against the cellar's far wall. "Luke, help me pull this down. Come now."

He gave her a puzzled look but helped her topple the wine rack over. Dozens of bottles of wine went tumbling and shattered against the cellar's stone floor.

Behind the rack were wood planks nailed into the brick wall. Shannon pried one of the boards loose. Ryan quickly helped her remove the rest until they had made a hole big enough to squeeze through. Beyond the hole was a dark tunnel.

Shannon stepped inside. "Quickly Luke, through here. It runs over to the stables."

Ryan smiled his approval. "Your father was a careful, clever man, Shannon. I should've known. Go. I'm right behind you."

She kissed him on the cheek. "Yes, and he saw a bit of himself in you. I believe that is why he liked you so."

At the end of the tunnel, they came to ladder leading up to a trap door directly underneath the stable. Ryan brushed away the cobwebs and started up a ladder, slid back a bolt locking the trap door and cautiously lifted himself inside the stable. The air was sweet with the smell of fresh straw. The horses cocked their heads and eyed the intruder suspiciously. Ryan helped Shannon up the ladder and they quickly saddled two horses.

More shots rang out and Shannon went to a window. She gasped. The hoodlums were using their torches to set her house on fire!

She clenched her teeth. "How *dare* they!" she murmured. Blind rage seized her now. Her nostrils flared, her cheeks turned red. She lifted the hem of her skirt and ran to her horse, removed two pistols from her saddlebag and made a dash towards the stable doors. For the first time in her life, she felt the ugly urge to kill.

Ryan grabbed her, pulled her back. "*No Shannon*! I know you're sorely tempted to take on these bastards. But this is a fight we cannot win. Not like this, not now."

He gently spun her around and tapped her on the forehead with his finger. "Use this, my darling girl, not muscle. We're badly outmatched here. To fight would be sheer folly - suicide - and accomplish nothing."

Her lips quivered. Her eyes softened and pooled with tears. "Flanagan and his men! My house, Luke! My home and all my father's things! All will be lost..."

He wrapped his arms around her, held her close and could feel her body tremble.

"I'm so sorry, Shannon, truly. But there be nothing here worth dying for. We must leave now while we still can. You want a chance to avenge this wrong? Follow me, mount up - let's ride!"

"Yes," she said sadly and looked away. "There'll be a reckoning though! On my father's grave - I *swear* it!"

Ryan nodded silently.

She walked towards her horse, but then paused at the trap door.

"Wait, Luke! I must go back, through the tunnel. Just for a moment. I left the business ledgers behind. I must have them."

They heard more shots. One man screamed.

"There is *no time*, Shannon!" he told her sternly. "We ride now or die!"

He gripped her arm firmly and nearly tossed her up into the saddle. She knew he was right and said no more.

Ryan kicked the stable doors open, mounted his horse, and the two riders rushed out into the darkness. But in the yard their horses abruptly stopped in terror at the sight of the raging fire. Ryan dug his heels into his horse's flanks. The animal bolted forward. Shannon did the same. But then her horse suddenly reared up on its hind legs and began neighing wildly.

Three men watching the house burn, with their backs turned to the riders, suddenly spun around at the sound of Shannon's horse. But Ryan had seen them first. His quick wits did not fail him. He whipped his horse around, reached down and snatched the nearest man's musket out of his hands and then charged at the second. The fool went to cock and raise his musket instead of stepping aside. Ryan rammed his horse hard into the man and bowled him over. The man's ankle snapped as he fell and he discharged his musket harmlessly into the dirt.

Shannon had the third man, little more than a boy, covered with her pistol. But then the boy panicked and ran towards the front yard, crying out for help. Ryan drew his pistol and took aim, but he couldn't bring himself to shoot the boy down.

A killing fire, unstoppable, completely engulfed the house now. Greedy flames shot out of windows and began licking their way up to the roof. Ryan did not know whether Flanagan and his men had fled or were still inside. Leaving men behind in trouble was a hard thing to do but he had Shannon, and an unborn child, to protect. He decided there was nothing he could do for O'Keeffe's men even if they were still alive.

Ryan reluctantly spurred his horse on and told Shannon to follow. He raced towards the open fields, towards the safety of the woods beyond with Shannon close behind.

More shots rang out as they galloped through fields of tall wheat. Ryan turned in his saddle, saw Shannon riding well and only a step or two behind him. And then he saw a skirmish line of men, a dozen strong, charging into the fields after them. The shots were meant for them!

"Are you all right?" Ryan shouted back.

Shannon nodded, too weak to speak. Ryan could not see the paleness of her skin, the listlessness in her eyes.

"Let's ride to Macpherson's old barn," he cried out to her. "Then we'll decide how best to make our way to Rush. Agreed?"

She nodded again and spurred her horse on. The mob of men reloaded and fired another volley, cracking the still night air. Ryan felt something pinch his side, as if a sharp stick had poked him. He ignored the pain and dug his heels even harder into his horse's flanks. The beast reared its head, neighing defiantly, and charged forward, chasing after a small pale moon, nearly full, rising over the treetops ahead.

The two desperate riders rode hard for the protection of the trees. Once they were inside the wood line the shooting stopped.

Ryan pulled up on his reigns to slow his horse down, trying to avoid the low branches, and stopped at the stream to catch his breath. He smiled. They were at the very place where his horse had thrown him earlier that spring, the same day the English had taken his ship from him. He could still picture Shannon sitting proudly in her saddle on top of the embankment beyond, waiting for him, watching him with a seductive look in her eyes. How they had laughed when his horse had pitched him into the cold water! Then she had disappeared over the ridge before he could reach her...

"Good horse, good horse," he said, patting the animal's sweaty neck. He felt a certain satisfaction at having ridden so well. "Guess those riding lessons of yours paid off," he shouted back to Shannon and turned around to smile at her.

But she was some distance back, slumped over her saddle. Horror cut into his gut like a knife. Even in the moonlight, he could make out the black stain, like ink from a tipped bottle, soaking across clean paper, spreading across the back of her white blouse. He quickly dismounted but his foot slipped on a small rock, slick with moss, and he stumbled forward, twisting his ankle. A sharp pain shot up his leg. He shook the pain off, lifted himself up and limped back towards Shannon as best he could. He gently lifted her down from her saddle, could feel the warm, sticky blood coating his hands, and carefully laid her on the ground, resting her head on a fallen branch.

"Oh, Shannon, my dear, sweet Shannon!" he whispered, stroking her hair.

She was breathing heavily now, managed a weak smile. She could feel her life slipping away. The wound was mortal. She gripped his wrist as if somehow that might save her.

Ryan's eyes filled with tears. He looked up at the sky and pleaded, "no, no, no, please, God, Noooo!"

She summoned up the last bit of her strength, reached out to touch his face.

"Hush now my man, my dear, sweet man. Death is nothin' to

trouble yourself about, a journey to a foreign place. That's all. '*For I the Lord thy God will hold thy right hand, saying unto thee, Fear not. Fe... Fe... I, I will help thee.*'"

He continued stroking her hair. "Shhh. Don't talk now my love, rest a bit. Save your strength."

"Yes. Fear not for me my darlin' prince. I'm not afraid to die. But oh, oh, of losin' you, Luke... Of that I, I, am afraid..."

"You'll not lose me. Never. Let me go to fetch a doctor and a wagon. I'll be quick about it, I promise."

She gazed into the clear night sky to see the stars, marveled at the mystery of it all. She grabbed his wrist again. "No. No, Luke. Please. Don't leave me. I won't need a doctor. Not now. Just let me rest here a bit. Whew! So tired. The stars, see them? So lovely... God's good work. Luke. Luke..."

And then she closed her eyes.

Ryan found it hard to breathe.

"What god have I offended? What loving God could permit this?"

She forced a smile, a brave smile, yes, and opened her eyes. She reached up to stroke his thick, black hair, wavy like the sea, one last time.

"This... this is not His work, Luke. My dear heart, my fine, young man - we made this world, with our own mortal hands, and we suffer from our own imperfect work. That's why God speaks to us. He calls to us home, to come home to His perfect world. Luke, please, say my name. I love to hear you say my name..."

He held her tightly, whispered her name, repeating it over and over again into her ear. But not even his great strength could keep her soul from fleeing Ireland. She breathed her last breath and her body went limp.

He broke down and sobbed. Anguish glutted his soul, sorrow beyond measure. Then he heard the sound of men, angry voices making their way slowly through the fields, towards the trees. They were close, very close and he knew he had little time. He wavered at first, unsure of what to do. He considered charging at them, killing as many as he could before they cut him down. But the soldier in him would not allow that. The master tactician could not throw his life away without taking all of his enemies with him. And Shannon had promised a reckoning, a blood reckoning. Now the burden fell to him to see her promise fulfilled.

He placed the bulk of his weight on his good leg and lifted Shannon's body up off the cold ground. But he nearly doubled over from a stabbing pain biting into his side. He suddenly felt weak and woozy. The trees began to spin. Confused, he looked down to see blood oozing from a hole in the side of his shirt. Then he understood - the pinch he had felt earlier when they were riding through the fields - he had been hit too. He summoned up the last bit of his strength and swung Shannon's lifeless body over the back of her saddle, as gently as he could, and wedged it against the pummel. Then he mounted her horse too, held on to her, and headed north with only one thought in mind: *Dowlin.*

"Be thar a Patrick Dowlin here?" a stranger called out loud enough to cut through the din. The Royal Oak, a favorite watering hole of Rush's pirate hero Bachelor Jack before his death only seven years earlier, and now a favorite of the Shadowmen, was packed and noisy.

"Who's askin'?" gruffly asked a large man with long, flowing red hair. Dowlin, sitting at a back table near the fire, looked as if he was ready to hit something or someone. He sat alone, working on his sixth pint of ale, and for no particular reason he was in one of his rare, foul moods and had been out of sorts all day. He was doing his best to cure whatever evil vexed his spirit with heavy doses of dark, thick Guinness.

The stranger carefully approached Dowlin and touched his hat.

"Beggin' yer pardon; mean you no 'arm mate. There's a man on a 'orse outside askin' for ya. He looks hurt, hurt bad. Got a young lassie with him too and she looks a might worse."

Dowlin bolted from his chair, toppling it over, and rushed outside where he found Ryan on top of a saddle slumped over Shannon. There was blood everywhere.

Dowlin began to cry. "Ah... *Jesus... Sweet Jesus.* No, *Jesus Christ,* no!

Luke! Luke! Please *Gawd*, let him be alive. Luke, can you hear me?"

Ryan managed to raise his head slightly. "Shootin' at O'Keeffe's place," he said weakly. "Don't know who. Sha - Shannon. She was an innocent, an innocent..."

"Easy thar, lad. Steady, now. We've got to get you off the street. Brace yerself now."

Dowlin gingerly lifted Ryan down from his horse, cradling his friend in his arms, and carried him behind the tavern and up a back stairway to his room on the second floor. After laying Ryan carefully across the bed, he removed a knife tucked inside his boot and cut away Ryan's shirt to inspect the damage. He saw the hole in Ryan's side. The lead ball had punched right through Ryan's thick leather belt and drilled itself into his soft flesh. Dowlin put a compress over the wound to stem the flow of blood and then rushed back downstairs to check on Shannon. He found a small group of men gathered around her horse, staring.

"You men thar!" he growled in a menacing voice, his eyes filled dark with rage. He was ready to take on the whole world. "Clear out now if you know what's good for *you*! Nothin' but trouble waitin' for you here. Now move along!"

The crowd quickly scattered. A Rushman knows the value of minding his own business.

Dowlin gently brushed the hair off Shannon's face and put a finger on her neck, searching for a pulse. He found none and started sobbing again. He had loved her too.

He saw a young boy standing on the tavern's small porch watching him. He tossed a silver coin at the boy, sent him off to fetch a doctor first and then he was to find Kelly and round up the other members of *Prince's* crew. The boy vanished and did as he was told. Dowlin then walked Shannon's horse to a nearby house where he knew one of O'Keeffe's men lived and had the man move Shannon's body and the horse out of sight. Whoever had done the awful deed, Dowlin figured, would still be looking for Ryan and Shannon and would know to head for Rush. He decided it best to leave without delay.

A country doctor cleaned Ryan's wound as best he could and

dressed it but was unable to extract the musket ball. He didn't give Ryan much chance of surviving. Under the pale glow of a nearly full moon, Dowlin and the others placed Ryan on a litter and moved him back to the ship that same night. With heavy hearts, an uneasy crew weighed anchor and headed out to sea. The ship's French doctor, with better instruments, and more accustomed to the injuries men can inflict on one another, managed to remove the ball but the loss of blood was great.

Eight

Thoughts of Bloody Work in Dunkirk

After the *Prince* had crossed the open sea and reached Dunkirk safely, Torris had Ryan moved from the ship to his house when he heard about the shooting. For reasons known to only himself, Jumbaaliyia went along too, refusing to leave Ryan's side despite one or two insincere threats from Dowlin. Jumbaaliyia possessed some power Dowlin couldn't quite comprehend and he found it impossible to refuse the African. He also had a sense, constantly nagging at him, that he had known Jumbaaliyia from somewhere before. But before what, he had no clue.

When news of Ryan's injury reached his friend Sartine, Sartine sent his family's personal physician and one of Paris's best surgeons to Dunkirk to examine Ryan. The surgeon didn't like what he saw and reopened the wound to clean it more thoroughly and then arranged for a local doctor to visit Ryan once a day for several weeks to apply healing ointments and to replace his dressings. When the local doctor finally declared that Ryan would make a full recovery, with more time and rest, Ryan was moved back to his hotel room on Dunkirk's waterfront.

As time passed, Ryan's body slowly continued healing and he grew stronger by the day - but not his spirit. No. The wounds were still too deep.

The only feeling he had at first was numbness. Later the emptiness came and that was far worse. And whenever he felt a twinge of something good, some spark to let him know he was alive, he picked up the bottle to suppress it and lost himself to grief.

And as the leaves began to turn, as the days grew colder and lonelier, Ryan withdrew to an even darker place. He kept to himself, rarely venturing out from his hotel room, which itself was a dark and austere place. He didn't like clutter and owned few possessions. The room's one good attribute was a window overlooking the water and he often spent his time just sitting there, staring out at a vast and desolate sea. But beyond the horizon - just barely out of sight - he knew lay England, rich, mighty, loathsome England.

"What do you see out there in the mist and rain, Luke?" Dowlin asked after letting himself in. Dowlin stopped by each day to check on Ryan's progress and today he found Ryan as he usually found him, sitting at his chair looking out an open window. The room was ice cold.

Dowlin shook his head and sighed when Ryan ignored him. "I see. A foul mood to match the foul weather again is it? Ah, well, fine, just fine. Fine by me I says. Be quicker, more humane, if you just jumped out that fookin' window! Sweet *Jesus*, ya don't even have a fire goin' in here. Damn fool. You'll catch yer death in this damp chill. Damned if I know why I even bother anymore. Well, anyways, I brought you two presents to try and cheer you up. The first is this here English paper. Says *Ulysses* captured the *Black Prince* and all her crew! Won't old King Georgie be surprised when he learns that the *Prince* is still ravaging his lands and sinking his precious ships, hey? Also says here the *Hopewell* was recaptured off of Brest. I fear those prissy English newspaper folks got that part of the story right. So now we know the fate of our poor prize crew. Lads should have listened to you. I'll wager all I own they're sittin' in some stinkin' British gaol right now moanin' and wailin' and all sayin' the same thing: '*woe is me; boohoo, boohoo, we shoulda listened to Luke, we shoulda listened to Luke!*' Ah well, some lessons have to be learned the hard way."

Ryan offered no reply, refused to even acknowledge Dowlin's presence. He sat, indifferent, at the window, content to watch the sea.

"I'll just leave the paper here on yer bed," Dowlin said, unruffled by Ryan's aloofness. "I see that you're unimpressed. Well, you can look at it later p'haps. I can see yer rather busy now. Not to worry, bein' the good friend I am, I brought you a second gift, somethin' more pleasin' to the eye, and then I'll be on my merry way."

He went to open the door and waved a young girl in.

"Come on in here my love," Dowlin commanded.

She was dark and fair and sheepishly entered Ryan's room with her head bowed low.

"Luke, this wonder among women is Jacqueline."

Ryan didn't budge, didn't look up.

Dowlin picked up the girl's bag sitting outside the door and paused to give the young beauty an appreciative glance. "She's skilled in medicines and the healing arts. Local doctor says she's good, very good - or did he tell me that she's a witch who knows the black arts, knows how to mix potions and conjure up spells? Ah, bless me, I can't remember now whether he sang her praises or tried to warn me! No matter, she is a joy to the eye and she'll help you get around 'til yer all healed, ease yer discomfort too. Look'ee here inside this bag. My, my, she's brought dressings, ointments and all manner of medicines and herbs with her. Aye, I'd say she knows her trade well enough. I'll wager she could cure anythin' that ails a man with those lovely, healin' hands! Go on over to the man, love, and introduce yerself. He's, a bit, shy..."

The young woman did as she was told. She stood in front of Ryan and curtseyed.

Ryan looked up and saw that she was a rare beauty with long, dark hair and large, brown eyes. She gave him the hint of a smile and then bashfully lowered her head again.

"I taught her English myself," Dowlin said with a wink, "if you catch my meanin', sir."

Ryan shifted uncomfortably in his chair and resumed his silent vigil.

Dowlin took no offense. He set the girl's bag down on a table and then started a fire. Satisfied he could do no more, he gave the girl a friendly pat on the behind, she put a hand to her mouth and giggled, and then he left.

Dowlin knew that Ryan's body was on the mend but now worried whether his friend's heart, ravaged by hate and sorrow, would ever heal. When it came to Ryan, and only Ryan, Dowlin had mastered the virtue of patience. What Ryan needed now, he figured, was the healing power of a woman's charm. Not that he had any illusions that anyone could replace Shannon. But, perhaps, he hoped, the right woman could help Ryan find his way through the dark woods of his depression and repair his shattered heart.

Not for long can a man resist the urges that drive him, the natural yearnings that stir his blood to find affection. And, despite her youth, there was something special about Jacqueline. Dowlin was confident she was up to the task.

The day finally came when Ryan, with the use of a cane, started to walk again. He was fully recovered from the musket wound and the fractured bone in his ankle was healing nicely. He still kept mostly to his room, closing out the world, and only Dowlin, Kelly and Jumbaaliyia were allowed to visit him. Well, Jacqueline too, lovely girl with the glossy, dark hair who, with patience and understanding, had managed to win him over. She was always at his side. Ryan had not been easy on her but she proved to be, despite her tender years, a tenacious, strong-willed woman and had grown fond of the mariner.

Ryan was pacing around the room when Dowlin walked through the door. He managed a smile for Dowlin.

Dowlin braced himself for some snide remark. But then he could see that Ryan was sincere.

"Pat, I, I should like to thank you for all that you've done. I know how, well, I know difficult I've been for some time now."

Dowlin broke out into a wide grin. Ryan's good mood was as important a victory as any of the battles they had won at sea together.

"Difficult? You? Ha! More like a horse's ass... Anyway, no need to thank me. Someone's got to help you get through this miserable life Luke seein' how you can't possibly do it on yer own..."

Ryan's smile vanished as his thoughts unexpectedly turned to Shannon. She should be the one helping him now. His eyes turned watery and he turned away. But his eyes began to smolder as his heart filled itself with black hate.

"I want the men who did this Patrick. I... *want*... *them*. After that, our business in Ireland is finished. I'll not return there again - ever."

"Steady now. What do you plan to do thar, lad?"

"Set matters right. Avenge the wrong done to Shannon."

"How? We have suspicions but no real proof who was behind the ambush at the house."

"One man, I did not know him, had a long scar across his left eye and cheek from on old wound. A very distinctive scar. A man like that will not be hard to find."

"Luke," Dowlin replied sternly. "Listen to me, listen well. Take what I have to say to heart, I urge you."

Ryan hobbled over to his chair by the window and plopped down. Jumbaaliyia and Jacqueline retired to a small table in the corner to amuse themselves with a game of cards. Neither one ever seemed to leave Ryan's side.

Dowlin nodded to them, grabbed a bunch of grapes off a platter, a gift from Torris who sent fresh fruit, vegetables, breads and cheeses to Ryan's room daily, and walked over to the window to stand next to Ryan. He placed his hand on Ryan's shoulder and stared out at the cold, barren sea with him.

"Luke, with a sound ship under yer feet and good crew behind you, yer the most dangerous man I know. Truly you are. I'd sail anywhere with you. Fight any battle. The lads all feel the same. You know this. But this notion swirlin' around in yer head now, 'tis madness, fool-hardy nonsense. It would be suicide. I want these men too. But whoever set out to run Shannon off and bring O'Keeffe's little empire crashing down must be powerful indeed. No doubt, they had the Crown's blessin' behind 'em. And if they were after you and not Shannon, well, not much difference is there? Shannon's dead. How are you goin' to take 'em all on anyhow, hey?"

"One at a time I suppose."

Dowlin frowned. "Ah, Luke... Now thar's a smart-ass answer from an otherwise clever fellow. Yer not usin' yer wits man! That's what Shannon would say straight out to you now if she was standin' here. You lost a precious thing, Luke. She was exquisite. And she was like a hurricane too from what I seen of her. Never happened across a woman like her before. She possessed elegance and a raw power at the same time and was, I'd say, the fairest lass among our island people. Shrewd in matters of business too. But look at you. Yer not even fully healed up yet!

Go after these bastards like this and they'll cut you down like some mangy, back-alley dog. Mark my words they will. Me now, well I can hold my own in a fight with the best of 'em and that's no lie. I'm equally good with a knife, a sword or a rapier. *Gawd's* blessed me with a keen eye too. With a good musket and extra powder, I can hit just about anythin'. Guess I was born to it."

"I can hold my own..."

"Aye, Luke, that's true. I've seen you fight hand-to-hand. No question yer brave and a good fighter too, but yer not good enough to take on these rough men, not by yerself anyways. Remember the Spanish off Cádiz? You, me and big Chris fought them Dagos off side by side. But who saved yer arse more than once? Yer skills at single combat is not your strength. You'll get us both killed and for what? Shannon's gone. Nothin' we do is goin' to bring her sweet, shinin' face back."

Ryan felt a single tear roll down his cheek, used the back of his hand to wipe it away. "You needn't worry yourself, Patrick. This matter is my business, mine alone."

Ryan's callous remark offended Dowlin. "Needn't worry *myself* is it?" he asked indignantly. "You cut me to the quick! Shannon was my friend too. Do you truly suppose I'd let you go alone? Fine friend I'd be if I let you get yerself killed without so much as a by yer leave! Humph! Ruin my whole future it would!"

Ryan realized he had given offense, had wounded Dowlin's pride, and all unfairly, true. He suddenly felt ashamed.

"I am... I'm sorry Pat... I didn't mean to question your loyalty. No man could ask for a better friend than you. I call you brother. You know this. I only meant there's no reason for you to risk your neck."

Dowlin accepted the apology with a nod. "Well, it's my neck isn't it? Fine, fine. I know when yer mind is made up. You've always had a pig-headed obstinacy about you and you can be one ornery bastard at times. Well, if yer goin' out to find these men to set matters right, I'll be goin' with you and that's that. One day is just as good as the next for a killing, them or us."

"Pat, Shannon was with child."

Dowlin's face turned pale. "What?"

"Aye."

Dowlin squeezed Ryan's shoulder. "Oh... Well, for Shannon, for the child, there will be a reckoning, a blood reckoning, aye..."

Dowlin caught Jumbaaliyia and Jacqueline watching the exchange between them, saw the concern in both their faces, saw their thoughts too.

"No!" Dowlin sternly told them. "You two just go on with yer game thar. There'll be no rompin' around Ireland's green hills by the likes of either of you! I see what's in yer eyes. A Blackamoor and a young Frenchy girl walking hand-in-hand through the hills of Ireland! *Jesus* help me! Have you both lost yer senses? It an't goin' to happen so just put the thought out of yer minds... Auck! I'm goin' to go find me a quiet place to pickle my brain with liquor. The world's clearly gone quite mad here."

Macatter, traveling up and down France's coast from port to port looking for a second heavy cutter for the privateers, finally found a suitable vessel in Boulogne on his third visit there. She was an older ship, and not as fast as her consort, but she was the best Macatter could find with a world at war.

Torris financed the purchase by forming a new company and enticing a number of his French business friends to invest in the new venture in exchange for shares of stock. With Ryan's growing reputation, it was not a hard sell despite the risks. The founders divvied up the shares of the new company in proportion to each's investment, with Torris easily taking the lion's share, making him the majority owner. The founders awarded Ryan a 28 percent share to do with as he liked from which he gave Dowlin and Macatter eight percent shares each.

Nine

A Pair of Fighting Lions

As Winter began to stir from her long slumber, as the days turned more hostile, Ryan used the time to convalesce - and plot - while Dowlin and Macatter occupied themselves with the preparations of war, dreadful, destructive, profitable war. Marchant was paid his wages and discharged. Command of the *Prince* went to Dowlin - a dream fulfilled - while Macatter, who had learned the art of raiding well under the tutelage of the master, took command of the new privateer, the *Black Princess*.

The *Prince* and *Princess* sat peacefully side by side at their moorings in Dunkirk harbor, tied against the wharf in front of the Torris warehouse. The Irishmen needed only fair weather - and new commissions - before they sailed.

Torris reached out to his old friend Coffyn again for help with Franklin. He told Coffyn about the second raider and explained why Marchant had to be released. Coffyn understood and agreed to travel to Paris to meet with Franklin on Ryan's behalf, but warned Torris that persuading Franklin to issue commissions to the Irishman would not be easy.

Marchant hurried on to Paris ahead of Coffyn, hoping to expose and ruin Ryan. But matters did not quite play out the way he had intended.

Franklin invited Marchant into his home at Passy once more where Marchant proceeded to disclose everything to Franklin, beginning with Ryan's smuggling days to the breakout from the *Black Dog*, Poolbeg, and the escape of the Irish to France. Ryan was an outlaw Marchant explained, a felon on the run, and, together with his gang of thieves, they had used Marchant, an American captain with legitimate credentials, to dupe Franklin into granting them an American commission just so the Irishmen could avoid execution for piracy.

Franklin listened to Marchant's story with fascination. First Poreau, he thought, now Ryan. People seemed fond of using the poor Captain Marchant for their own ends, and at Marchant's own expense it seemed. Franklin felt a twinge of guilt because he was about to do the same.

Franklin pressed Marchant for more particulars about the *Prince's* escapades, though he had no intention of helping Marchant. It was the 25-year-old Irishman Ryan, the scoundrel, who now piqued Franklin's curiosity.

Marchant was a man who loved to talk and gladly recounted the details of the *Prince's* cruises for Franklin, pausing here and there to stuff his generous frame with food and drink. He spoke for several hours, describing every battle, and ended his tale with Ryan's nearly fatal wound and the killing of his woman in Ireland.

And when he had finished his story and said his farewells, he left Franklin's home certain that he had destroyed Ryan. But, unable to get another ship of his own, he returned to America a few months later and sold his story to the American newspapers, claiming all the glory for the *Prince's* success for himself and with no one in America the wiser.

Franklin grabbed his hat, his coat and his walking stick and took a stroll through the well-manicured gardens around Chaumont's estate as he mulled things over. He had become quite an expert over the years in sifting fact from fiction. He could hardly have survived Versailles without the skill. Oh yes, the doctor recognized that Marchant was not above embellishing a fact or two to inflate his own importance. Still, once he cut through all of Marchant's spin, Franklin knew, through multiple sources, through spies and agents, through the papers and even from the parlor chitchat of the rich and powerful in Paris, that most of what Marchant had told him about the *Black Prince* was true, even if the real mastermind behind it all was Ryan. Ryan's skill and cunning had made a great impression on Franklin.

"Grandfather, did you ever in your life hear such a wild tale?" Temple asked excitedly after Franklin returned from his walk.

Franklin peeked over his spectacles, gave his grandson a quizzical look. "Can't say that I have, my boy. You have notions of high adventure swimming around in that head of yours, do you now?"

"No, sir. My place, I know, is with you. Still, Grandfather, I should like to meet this Captain Ryan someday! But what will you do? Are you not furious, Grandfather? Will you have him arrested? Bring him up on charges? After all, this Irishman is a renegade, a common criminal. He manipulated and deceived you Grandfather!"

A broad smile, a wicked smile, lit up Franklin's face and his belly began to shake as he erupted with gut-wrenching laughter. The old doctor had to take a handkerchief to wipe away the tears.

"Bless me, Temple! Arrest Ryan? For what precisely? For this splendid bit of trickery that has served our cause so well? No. No. I wouldn't arrest such a wonderful rogue even if I could. He has duped us for his own purposes to be sure - but he has done so much for us in the bargain. Consider the Irishman's success. This is hardly the work of some common criminal. The Irishman fights with skill and daring! He fights with passion! If Captain Ryan doesn't make too much of a fuss about his nationality and the technical legality of all of this, neither shall I. As God is my witness, I'd engage the services of every fraud, every cheat and liar I could find if the results were as satisfactory as those of our audacious Captain Ryan! If only our country had a few more men like Ryan with his exceptional gifts, we might win this war! Of late, I sometimes have my doubts whether we will. Ryan, Captain Ryan, hm, that is not a name I shall soon forget. I should like to meet him too someday."

"What do you intend to do Grandfather?"

"Do? Ah, what to do indeed? Cut the man off at the knees and let the world know that the great Doctor Franklin can be so easily fooled? Or let him loose again to ravage English shipping? No doubt by his visit our intrepid Captain Marchant intended to see this Irishman undone. But how do we profit that way I wonder? We lose a brave and clever soldier it seems to me, and two ships. Let me have Coffyn's letter again, Temple. Coffyn was most persuasive in singing Ryan's praises, practically begged me to give the Irishman fair consideration, and Coffyn is no fool."

Temple quickly found Coffyn's letter and Franklin sat next the fire to warm himself and reread Coffyn's words. Coffyn had yet to steer him wrong.

Franklin carefully refolded the letter and handed it over to Temple to return it to its proper file. Franklin kept nearly all his papers and letters.

"Hm. This is what I think best: I believe our estimable Captain Ryan deserves our thanks and gratitude, not our rebuke. He has earned that much at least. I shall give him the commissions he craves so much. Let's see what he makes of them."

Franklin paused to remove his spectacles, folded them and absently ran them across his lips deep in thought. "Yes, that is precisely what I shall do. More, we shall honor this Captain Ryan. We cannot give him land or titles perhaps, but we can present him with some token of our gratitude. That watch and glass shop, Temple, the one owned by the Swiss fellow next to the German tinker's shop, do you remember it?"

"Yes."

"I will send you there in the morning. I know just the thing!"

Following Marchant's visit, Franklin decided he had better inform Congress about his authorizing the use of privateers before Congress learned about it from Marchant or from someone else. "We continue," he wrote in his dispatch, "to insult the Coasts of these Lords of the Ocean with our little Cruisers. A small Cutter which was fitted out as a Privateer at Dunkirk, called the Black Prince, Capt. Stephen Marchant, a native of Boston, has taken, ransomed, burnt and destroyed above 30 Sail of their Vessels within these 3 months."

A few weeks later Ryan received a package from Franklin with a letter, penned in Franklin's own hand, thanking the mariner for his contribution to the American cause and congratulating him on his recent string of victories. When Ryan opened the package, he found the two new commissions he so coveted and a beautifully carved wood case. Inside the case was a magnificent night glass, an unheard of luxury for most ship's captains. The night glass used specially crafted optics to enhance the ambient light at night to improve vision. Etched on one side of the telescope's brass casing was a likeness of the *Prince* and engraved on the obverse side were the words: *On Behalf of a Grateful Nation, this Glass is Presented to Captain Luke Ryan, Master of the Warship Black Prince, in Recognition of his Faithful Service to the United States of America - Benjamin Franklin this 3rd Day of October, 1779.*

Ryan wept when he read the inscription. For reasons he did not fully understand, or really care to know, pride filled his heart, an unconditional pride for America, a land that he had never even seen. And like some schoolboy eager to please his teacher after receiving some bit of praise, some acknowledgement of exceptional work, Ryan was eager to please Franklin by winning new victories on even grander scale.

Ryan promptly thanked Franklin for "... the Letter your Excellency did me the honnour to wright me, with the present of the Night Glass, Expressing your Satisfaction of my Conduct, in my Cruise with the Black Prince, fills me with Gratitude, and Secures for Ever my Subjection and attachments to the Government of the United States of America, and your Excellency...". He also advised Franklin that he would, because of his health, entrust Dowlin with one commission who was "...the best Calculated in Every Respect to re,implace me..." and give the other commission to Macatter.

Ryan closed his letter by informing Franklin of his plans to build a third cutter for himself too, from the keel up, and asked Franklin for "...a Rank in the Navy of our united States which I will all ways uphold As My Owne Natural Government, and Losse the last Drop of My blood to Gain honnour to the American flag."

And as his Irishmen well knew, Ryan was a man who would deliver on such a promise or die trying...

A week before Christmas, Dowlin and Macatter met Ryan, or the *Admiral* as the Irishmen liked to call him now, at a favorite tavern to discuss their next cruise. Ryan had learned from his friend, and benefactor, Sartine in Paris that a huge English merchant fleet - over 100 ships strong - was riding anchor off the Downs, waiting for better weather and the arrival of frigates to protect them before sailing.

"A hundred ships you say?" Dowlin asked and whistled.

"Aye, a hundred ships," Ryan replied, pouring drinks all around.

"All scrunched together in one place?"

"All scrunched together in one place. Remarkable, isn't it?"

"And you think Sartine's information is still good?"

"We're going to find out or, more precisely, you two are going to find out."

Macatter, quiet, deliberate, looked up from his plate and grunted. "We're goin' to need bigger boats..."

Dowlin drained his glass and smacked the empty on the table. "And bigger guns if you want us to tangle with frigates, Luke. Alrighty, let's have it then..."

"Have what?" Ryan asked.

Macatter chuckled.

Dowlin reached across the table, took Ryan's glass out of his hand and drained it. "The plan of course - damn well Ed and me both know you've been workin' that brain of yers. *Jesus*, Luke, all evenin' you've been a tease. Don't think I don't know it!"

Ryan smiled, poured both men another whiskey. "Well, I certainly don't have any bigger boats or bigger guns to give to either of you so I suppose we best not sail in with guns blazing."

"I figured that part out for myself, *Admiral*," said Dowlin. "I doubt the fleet sails as a whole. Ships will split up and head out in different directions most probably, some with frigate escorts and some without. I don't suppose Sartine has a clue who is sailin' where?"

"No."

Macatter, stroking his beard and deep in thought, cleared his throat. "We could stand off ten miles or so and never see a single ship sail. Move in any closer and we invite the curiosity of the British Navy."

"How true, how true," Ryan said coyly. "So what do you good captains think best?"

"It's all just a game of chance," Dowlin answered. "We pick a spot and stand off a good bit as we always do and see what comes our way. Odds favor us that something will sail by eventually."

Macatter nodded in agreement.

Ryan smiled. Dowlin had been right. He had given the matter much thought.

"Ah, gentlemen. You are bold and fearless men and bold men deserve a bold plan and I have just the thing for your consideration. To stand off a ways and wait is, as you say Pat, a game of chance. How to improve the odds I wonder? Hm..."

"Luke, I swear," Dowlin said through clenched teeth in phony anger.

"Oh, all right, all right. I've had my fun. This is what we do: we dress the ships up as English merchantmen and sail right into the fleet, drop anchor and wait. When a group sails without escorts to protect them, you mark their course and follow them, pick them off one-by-one well out of sight from the rest of the fleet. It is Christmas season. Hearts will be light and caution will be lacking. There is risk, certainly. But what havoc you both might wreak if you can pull it off!"

Dowlin and Macatter instantly warmed to Ryan's plan and exchanged smiles.

"To bold men," Macatter said and raised his glass.

"Hear, hear, to the boldest of men!" Ryan agreed and raised his glass too.

"Or to the boldest of fools if we're caught," Dowlin replied.

On the morning of December 21, 1779, with the feel of snow in the air, two *American* warships, manned by Irish, English, Portuguese and French sailors, quietly slipped out of Dunkirk's harbor and headed out to sea. To fool British spies lurking around Dunkirk's waterfront, the tiny fleet sailed due north first, as if heading for the German Ocean, and then, once well beyond the sight of land, Dowlin and Macatter made a wide left turn and headed for the Downs.

With a heavy heart, Ryan watched his ships sail off into a foaming sea from a desolate stretch of beach. He longed to be with his men but knew he needed more time to heal. He stayed at the water's edge until his ships disappeared into the mist. And when the surf started splashing up against his boots, the wet sand turning pink in the morning sky, he tried to picture her face. But her image would not come to him and so he walked back to his hotel, feeling neither happy nor sad.

For the next several weeks he kept himself busy sending out

solicitations to different shipyards to build his third ship. Torris had already raised enough capital for the project. He hired a shipwright in Boulogne to design and build a heavy brigantine, larger and more powerful than the *Prince*, and then, with Jumbaaliyia's help, he began to comb the taverns and inns along the waterfront to find willing men to sail her.

There was the *unfinished matter* too, which consumed his thoughts. He quietly put money out on the streets of Dublin for information about the shooting. Ryan knew very little about O'Keeffe's secret organization but knew two or three of O'Keeffe's former associates who he hoped might help him. He soon learned that Flanagan and his men had all been killed and that Shannon's books had mysteriously vanished. And then one of his inquiries paid off and he was given the names of several men who had participated in the raid that awful night, though they turned out to be nothing more than hired thugs.

Posing as a Dutch businessman, Ryan left Dunkirk after Christmas on a ship bound for Dover, crossed England by coach and took a packet ship from Holyhead to Dublin as a passenger - a ship he would have intercepted and burned as a privateer before - and from Dublin, he rode on to Kenmure to find Shannon's grave. She had been buried on her father's property on the hill that overlooked the stream, a spot she had treasured in life, a place she often took him with a basket of fruit and wine. He sat next to her gravestone and sobbed for some time, at a clumsy attempt to cleanse his sorrow. And when he had no more tears to give, he said his farewells trying, as best as he knew how, to set his heart free from the twisted wreckage of loss and pain. And then he left Ireland - vowing never to return.

Several days following Ryan's departure from Ireland, and not far from O'Keeffe's burned-out house, a farmer found the bodies of three men, luckless, petty thugs of no particular importance to anyone, hanging from a an enormous tree in the middle of his hay field, hanging from a magnificent, old oak with massive branches that had somehow, miraculously, escaped the ravages of time and men. One of the murdered men had a jagged scar, a most distinctive scar, from an old wound across his left eye and cheek. The men were rumored to be Whiteboys. No one, not even the authorities, gave the matter much thought and so the killings were little investigated and never solved.

Ten
Machinations

ot far distant from Dunkirk, nestled against Holland's windswept shores, lies the small Dutch seaport town of Oostend where the French Minister of Marine, Count Antoine Raymond Jean Gaulbert Gabriel de Sartine, agreed to meet secretly with the First Secretary of the British Admiralty, Philip Stephens, at a hotel there with a reputation for discretion. The two men knew each other well and had both profited handsomely over the years from the relationship.

Officially, the men met to discuss preserving certain trade arrangements beneficial to their respective governments - even though their countries were locked together in brutal war. They also had agreed to talk about prisoner exchanges and other mundane matters. After all official business had been concluded, the two men dismissed their aides and retired to a small, private dining room for supper and their discourse turned to small talk and fluff until their the meal was served and they were alone.

Stephens took a sip of wine and then put a napkin to his lips. "You had a happy Christmas?"

"I am pleased to say, without having to lie about it for once, that I did indeed enjoy the day. But the devil can take Midnight Christmas Mass! And you?"

"Of course, of course. I have a niece who bakes the most splendid fig puddings at Christmas. She remembers me without fail and so I look forward to her puddings each year. Your nephew, David, he is well, I trust?"

"*Oui, merci.* After his bit of bravado with *Toulon*, I had him reassigned to Paris and out of the range of British guns. He is a good boy, but inexperienced in the ways of the world. Well, except when it comes to fast horses and beautiful women, his two passions. On those subjects, his knowledge seems to know no bounds. Ah, but he is a

Frenchman after all and remarkably good looking."

Stephens smiled and gave a knowing nod. "Ah, yes. I recall the *Toulon* matter. Captain Hughes, the officer who captured her, is presently attached to my office. Antoine, *mon ami*, there is an issue I am compelled to address and thought it best to discuss this matter with you in private. It is a matter important to us both."

"The Dunkirk Irish, no?" Sartine asked, anticipating Stephens's thoughts in between a mouthful of food. A slight, almost imperceptible smile formed at the corners of the Frenchman's mouth. His files on the Irishmen, he had no doubt, were thicker than the British Admiralty's own. Friend or no, he took a perverse pleasure watching the Englishman squirm. The English were always so smug, too smug for his liking.

"Precisely," replied Stephens, his voice rising with disdain. "Specifically, this ship *Black Prince* and her crew of Irish brigands. These are not American patriots fighting for some foolish, silly cause. These Irish rogues are subjects of the English Crown and fugitives from English justice."

English justice? thought Sartine, looking up from his plate. He gave Stephens a blank stare. *My God, the man is serious.* He started to chuckle, but masked his laughter with a cough.

"They are," Stephens pressed on, "murderous thieves and kidnappers of the worst sort. They are pirates masquerading as sailors - all because of that damn Franklin and his commissions. Make no mistake, the good doctor is an odious man. Unscrupulous really."

Sartine set his fork down and rocked back in his chair. "I dare say my friend, you would find Paris takes an entirely different view of his Excellency. I have met him of course. The American is both engaging and charming. A most brilliant and gifted individual actually. A true son of the Enlightenment."

"Ahem. Yes, well Antoine, perhaps in the field of science the fellow is entitled to a bit of notoriety. What do I know or care of science? But in military affairs and diplomacy, subjects I do possess some experience in and expertise, he is a bungler, a meddler and an amateur - an altogether dangerous combination I am sure you would agree. I blame that man, that scientist, that *amateur*, for involving our two countries in this hideous war. England has every right to put down the rebellion of these despicable *Yankees*. The colonies after all are the property of the Crown. But where is there any profit for our two countries in warring against each other over American independence? And this Irish captain of Franklin's, this Luke Ryan, this puppet, God, he is a brazen rascal! He attacks British merchant ships - and ships of neutral countries too - with impunity. He and his Irish thugs, Antoine, have committed murder on the high seas. He has sunk unarmed vessels. He has pillaged villages along the coast in Wales and Scotland and threatened helpless women and even children! He is a most barbarous man..."

Stephens could hear himself talking too fast. He was allowing his anger get the better of him. He paused to take a breath, to calm himself down. "And this... this *young rascal*... has escaped every snare we have set for him."

Stephens picked at the fruit on his plate and waited for Sartine to speak.

Sartine nodded sympathetically and sipped his wine. *How embarrassing for you, Philip. The great English fleet, impotent against one irksome Irishman!* He took a moment to listen to the music from an adjacent room. The musician at the harpsichord, playing for their personal delight, was a particularly attractive young woman with an alluring smile and dressed boldly in bright yellow. No, she had not escaped Sartine's roving eye. *You are an old fool Antoine! Still, perhaps later introductions could be made...*

Sartine shook her lovely image from his mind. Business first. He dared not reveal that he knew Ryan, that his very own nephew had introduced them and that he had profited nicely from the Irishman when Ryan had sailed as a smuggler. No. No need to complicate things or to ruffle any feathers. The smuggling business had been before the war. There was no need for Stephens or his masters back in London to know of such things.

"Young rascal, Philip?" Sartine asked with indifference. "Perhaps so. Young lion some would say."

Stephens bowed his head. "As your grace prefers. This... *young lion...* has confounded my admirals and, under French protection, has been allowed to insult His Britannic Majesty's coasts at will. Citizens are frightened. Insurance costs for merchant shipping are increasing at an alarming rate, threatening economic chaos. Ryan and his men are common thugs, nothing more. He preys on the defenseless. He hits and runs like a coward, not like a man of honor who faces his opponent across the field of battle for king and country with honor. He has no cause. He fights for money only. And after he and his men have glutted themselves on pillaging, they run back to France and hide behind Franklin's skirt while your government turns a deaf ear to British complaints. There are rules in war, Antoine. He has caused much harm. And my sources inform me he intends to set out against England soon again with two ships! Perhaps they have sailed already."

Sartine resumed eating, said nothing. He already knew about Ryan's two ships. And he knew that they had sailed from Dunkirk already for English waters without Ryan, who was still convalescing from the wounds he suffered in an ambush near Dublin. But, again, there was no need to reveal to his English friend just how good the French secret police were.

"Antoine, please consider this as well: this man, left unchecked, may very well affect our private arrangements from which we have both profited handsomely, you and me, over the years. Do you understand, my grace? There are those in my government who would escalate the war between our two countries and send larger numbers of privateers out against France and her allies in retribution! Where would it all end for you and me, Antoine?"

Sartine looked up at Stephens. "*Oui*, but of course," he said still chewing on his food. "I understand full well. It is a delicate situation. Our countries are at war. This American pirate ship, with her Irish crew, is an ally of France. And this, *young rascal* as you say, this Irishman, has caused your prince some embarrassment. Your finer point, however, is not lost on me, Philip."

Stephens allowed himself the faintest of smiles. Sartine's last remark was the one he yearned to hear. Now he knew he could count on the

Frenchman's full support. Sartine would proceed carefully and act indifferently at first. That was Sartine's way, the French way. Stephens knew his man though. Sartine could be frustrating at times but he was, like himself, a shrewd and clever fellow. For the first time in weeks, Stephens allowed himself to relax. His trip to Holland would not be a wasted effort after all. He leaned back in his chair, with his wine glass resting on his knee.

"Our two countries are at war Antoine, true, but you and I are not."

"True enough, my lord. What to do? Hm? My English friend is here to ask me for my help, no?"

"Ah, Antoine, my *friend*, always so observant," Stephens said, smiling broadly. "You always cut to the chase of any matter with skill. I knew that I could count on you. Allow me to pour you another glass of this most excellent claret. What to do indeed? In England, the matter would be easily resolved. We English prefer the direct approach. When a man offends the Crown, he is arrested and then imprisoned or executed. The legality of it all can be sorted out later if necessary. In France, well, your people have their own ways, do they not? You French prefer to be discreet and are more skilled at subtlety and at the wily crafts. What to do? Confiscate his ship perhaps? Your king requires no pretext."

Sartine shrugged as he concentrated on a slice of rare beef, cold and bloody, and considered the Englishman's suggestion. *English justice. Ha! But was France really any better?*

"My king may require no pretext. But I am not the king. And this Irishman has friends at court beyond Franklin. On what grounds could I confiscate the Irishman's ship?"

Stephens watched Sartine eat for a moment, chewing with an open mouth. For a Frenchman, the man's manners were down right uncouth.

"Ryan," Sartine added, "has broken no French law that I am aware of."

"Revoke his commission then?"

"It is an American commission issued under Franklin's own hand. The American government is an ally of France and a sovereign country in the eyes of the French Court. I cannot. I have no such authority."

Stephens set his glass down, stood up from the table and paced around the small dining room, his impatience growing. He could feel his rage getting the better of him too. But he dared not lose his temper, not in front of Sartine.

The Frenchman was being difficult. Sartine could do far more than he was letting on. Stephens knew all too well that Franklin would find it impossible to refuse a request from the powerful French Minister of Marine to withdraw his commissions. A request from Sartine would be the same as a command. Sartine, Stephens understood, was playing some game with him for his own purposes.

Stephens grabbed his glass and drained it. Delicacy was not his strong suit, *patience*... "Ah, I have it then, Antoine. An *accident*."

Sartine cocked one eyebrow and snapped his head around. He gave the British Secretary a cold stare through a pair of heavy eyelids.

"*Pardon?* An accident did you say? You are not suggesting I have Ryan and his crew murdered, Philip? Surely you jest?"

Stephens stepped back, collected his thoughts. He knew he had gone too far. *Damn. Too much wine. Subtly is needed here, a measure of diplomacy.*

"*Murder?*" he chuckled nervously. "My word no, my grace, certainly not! I fear that you have misunderstood me. Though, I shall confess, Antoine, Ryan's death would not cause me to shed one tear. I was thinking more of an accident to his ship, a mysterious fire on board perhaps? Without a ship the Irishman poses no threat to me, ah, to England."

Sartine accepted that explanation, although he began wondering whether Stephens had any hand in the Dublin ambush. It annoyed him when he did not have the answers to such questions.

He gave Stephens an approving nod, turned his attention back to his food and resumed his attack with nervous energy. "I will think on it. It is my desire to help my English friend. In truth, Frenchmen are complaining also. The Irishman's successes have taken prize money away from French privateers and this deprives the French Crown of revenues. Ryan has also hired Frenchmen to sail with him to make up his own shortages in men. I am well aware your country has the same problem as we do in France. War chews up young men at an appalling rate. Able-bodied men needed to serve on the king's ships are becoming scarcer each passing day. Well I know! The French Admiralty thinks I am a magician. That I can just clap my hands - and poof! - make men appear out of thin air. What do admirals know of the burdens of administration? For every Frenchman that signs on board with Ryan there is one less sailor for our own ships. Of course, we are speaking only about small numbers but you ignore one ship and before you know it, other captains will do the same. The floodgates will open. But do not fret my friend. Yes, Philip, I shall help you. The Irish are bad for business. On this we are of one mind."

Stephens found the complaints from French privateers utterly absurd, even laughable. But he did not laugh. No need to insult his friend. French privateers posed no threat to England. Their captains lacked daring, their crews were uninspired and undisciplined - often made-up from unsavory Laskers, double-dealing Arabs and ignorant Africans - and their ships were often slow, leaky hulks that would flounder in the first ill wind. Because of this, French privateers rarely ventured very far from port. Stephens would rather face ten French raiders to Ryan's one.

"Ah, excellent!" Stephens exclaimed, clasping his hands and rubbing them with satisfaction. "I knew that I could count on you, on our long friendship. Ridding ourselves of this Irish scourge helps France as well as England. Trust me. You shall see the wisdom of it all - as your holdings in Scotland increase..."

Sartine held up his hand in warning. He would not be rushed. "I shall handle it Philip, in the French way!"

Stephens sighed. *The French way! Bah!* The French way was often a slow, tortuous path that could lead to disastrous consequences. But Stephens knew he had accomplished as much as he was going to that night and said no more on the subject. He had already authorized additional muscle off the northern coast of France and in the Irish Sea. The British navy had dispatched more frigates to patrol the waters favored by the Irishmen. England had caught many a bold privateer that way.

But Ryan had proved too clever so far, and elusive, and Stephens was beginning to doubt whether he could rid himself of Ryan without Sartine's help. That was his true purpose in traveling to Oostend.

Sartine understood Stephan's true intentions in coming to Oostend, but took no offense as his interests coincided with Stephens's own on the subject. Before the war, the Irish smugglers had put money in his pocket. Now they were taking money from him and he was looking forward to retirement soon. It was a matter of simple arithmetic, of profit and loss, nothing more or less...

Eleven
Intrepid Americans & Breakout at Old Mill

A heavy snow, like finely sifted powdered sugar, began falling across southern England, transforming a stark, gray world, with all its blemishes, into something pure and perfect once again. Winter, disgusted with her three mellow sisters, and never fond of men, had in mind a long, cold reign.

Captain Conyngham couldn't sleep and passed the time watching the falling snow through a crack in the door. He was too excited to sleep. The weather couldn't have been better. He had been patiently waiting for this day since the *Galatea*, a 20 gun, Six Rate post-ship, had captured his privateer, the *Revenge*, back in April.

Just before daybreak a handmade pickaxe broke through the soft earth, just beyond Old Mill's double stone walls. Forty American prisoners, led by Conyngham himself, crawled quickly, silently, through a muddy tunnel and made their way out into the cold, night air. The snow was coming down in thick, heavy flakes now. A foot had fallen already with no let-up in sight. A biting wind, coming off the sea, began shaping the snow into deep drifts. No guards stood along the walls, no alarm was sounded. Conyngham and his men were invisible.

Conyngham's nerves settled a bit. *By all the Saints above, this mass escape just might succeed! Don't jinx things now old man, keep the men moving...*

Once the last man had cleared the tunnel, the Americans moved off into the woods where Conyngham broke the escapees down into small groups of three or four men each. Every man had been issued false identity papers before entering the tunnel and had been given a sack of rations, enough to last one week. The Americans wished each other well, tightened their belts and fanned out in different directions through knee-high drifts until vanishing into the countryside.

Patterson, Simmons, and young seaman Amati, who Simmons had nursed back to health, decided to head for London. They traveled by night and rested by day, keeping off the roads whenever they could. On the second day the three men, cold and hungry, came across an abandoned stable and rested there. But no one could really sleep and for the rest of their journey they contented themselves with sleeping in the woods, covering themselves over with leaves and dead branches. They never lit a fire, they avoided any contact.

Their cautious ways paid off handsomely. Two weeks later the three Americans, filthy and exhausted but free, managed to safely reach London and went straight to the home of Thomas Diggs. Diggs gladly took the Americans in and provided them with clean clothing, food and money. He kept them in his house for two more weeks, until the search for Old Mill's escapees finally quieted down, and then helped them obtain passage on a ship bound for Oostend.

Unfortunately, not all their comrades fared as well. Good Fortune is never generous with every hope or dream.

Many were caught. Some fell to the bounty hunters and their dogs and British pressgangs snagged a few others. A handful died from the elements. The unlucky ones were returned to Old Mill and thrown into the black hole to reflect on their past transgressions. Conyngham's tunnel was filled in of course but that was of no consequence to Old Mill's enterprising Americans who soon began digging anew in a different place. All-in-all, Conyngham's mass breakout was a success as more men, including Conyngham, reached the shores of France than didn't.

Once in Oostend, Patterson and his small party managed to find a Frenchman named Coffyn and Coffyn provided the Americans with food and shelter and then put them on the road to Dunkirk with money in their pockets. He suggested they seek out a certain young Irishman there who might, he told them, have an idea or two on what they might do next.

Several days later the three Americans found themselves crowded around a small table in the Spartan-like hotel room. A dark-eyed beauty named Jacqueline began serving them generous portions of wholesome food, ale, and mellow wine. The Americans were hardly shy and heaped their plates high.

Ryan sipped his ale next to a roaring fire, listening intently to the

Americans tell their stories in turn. Their sacrifices sadden Ryan. Their selfless devotion to duty impressed him. None of them had any desire to go home. With grim resolve, the Americans seemed determined to find a ship to sail out again against the British as soon as they could find one.

"Well now, Captain Ryan, there you have it all," said Patterson, "our stories, told start to finish."

"You are all," replied Ryan, "to be congratulated on your bravery and cunning. Men like you are rare."

Patterson noticed an open wooden box sitting on the mantel with a brass telescope. "May I?"

"Please."

Patterson stood and carefully removed the telescope out of its velvet-lined case. "This is exquisite. A night glass?"

"Aye, there is an inscription on the side."

Patterson turned the narrow tube around and whistled softly as he read the inscription. "A gift from Franklin?"

"Aye, my men and I have had some luck against the British," Ryan answered. "I take it that you lads didn't come all this way to Dunkirk to admire my collection of nautical gear? What now is it I can do for you and your men exactly, Capt'n Patterson?"

Patterson carefully placed the night glass back into its case and returned to his chair. "Well, we heard from Mr. Coffyn that the British have Captain Jones bottled up in Texel pretty well. I understand there are a few small American ships at L'Orient, but that's a distance away and there's no telling if those ships will be still be in port by the time we get there. Mr. Coffyn suggested that we see you, that you might be able to use a few good men. I've not had the privilege of sailing with Mr. Simmons or Amati here. But I can attest to their stamina and to their courage. These are first-rate lads, men of quality, and I will personally vouch for them. If you cannot use us, then we will push on to Paris and ask for Franklin's help."

Ryan struggled to rise out of his chair. The damp air was causing the pain in his ankle to flare up again. Jumbaaliyia saw Ryan wince and emerged from the shadows to help him. Ryan waved him off. Jumbaaliyia and Jacqueline had both been spoiling him too much.

"As concerns both your stamina and your courage," replied Ryan and hobbled about the room, "I've no doubt, Capt'n Patterson, none whatsoever. As it happens gentlemen, I could use some good men, men of stout hearts and with a resolve to fight the British. I could use all three of you, truth be told. We presently have two heavily armed cutters, the *Black Prince* and the *Black Princess*. They're sleek, exceedingly fast and maneuver well. The *Prince*, I tell you on my oath it is true, is the fastest ship in the Atlantic and both vessels can come about in no more time than it takes a man to spit. They're at sea now under commissions from his Excellency, Doctor Franklin. Fine ships with fine crews. If you're looking to cause the British some woe, well, we haven't done too badly so far. We've caused old King George some grief all right. I'm about to commission a third ship. If all goes well, she'll be ready to sail by early March, certainly no later than April. I don't have much of a crew for her yet and there's the tricky part. The war has made good men hard to find. Gentlemen, I beg you to consider - why not stay here in Dunkirk? Sign on with me, help me find and train a crew? Capt'n Patterson, I regret I have no command to offer you. You'd need to step down in rank a peg or two. Mr. Simmons here strikes me as a fine petty officer and he could retain his rank. And young Mr. Amati, well, sir, I've been at sea long enough to size up a first rate seaman when I see one. I could sorely use you too. I can't promise any of you riches. But I can promise each of you a crack at the British. A chance to cause a ruckus. Why not think on it lads, hey?"

Ryan walked over to the fire, stoked the coals with an iron poker and suddenly felt very tired. He didn't think his pitch was very impressive and expected the Americans to politely turn his offer down. And then again, his thoughts turned to Anderson, the young Pennsylvanian with the strong farmer's hands, and the American's passion, his unyielding, unselfish, stubborn passion. These Americans were just like Anderson.

"No need for any of us to think on it, sir," offered Patterson cheerfully. "That's why we've come to see you. We've heard about your attacks against the British. Some fine work if I may say so, sir. We'd be much obliged to you if you'd take us on. When could we start?"

Ryan whirled around and looked at Patterson with a grin. A tingle sot up his spine. He knew at once he was going to like these Americans.

"Well, now, why not tomorrow? I'll arrange for your lodgings here in town and get you each a bit of money to tide you over. I'll send Mr. Jumbaaliyia there over to see you in the morning. Don't let him fool you. He's the biggest, scariest man I've ever laid eyes on but he has a kind heart. He'll see to your immediate needs."

Patterson looked over at the black giant and nodded. "Is he your man servant?"

Ryan laughed and looked over at Jumbaaliyia. The African had resumed his position in the corner of the room with his arms folded like some royal sentry.

"You mean slave? No, sir. He's a seaman, a first class gunner's mate and a free man. He stayed behind with me to raise a crew. Serving along with a Blackamoor doesn't create a problem I trust for any of you gentlemen?"

The three Americans exchanged glances.

"As he is a free man," explained Patterson, "not at all."

"Excellent. Capt'n Patterson, why don't we talk tomorrow and see where we might best use your talents, hey?"

Patterson returned Ryan's smile with one of his own. "You mean, sir, you intend to test my skills as an officer. I take no offense, Captain Ryan. I'd do the same if I were standing in your shoes. Until tomorrow then?"

Ryan laughed. The American was perceptive. "Splendid, gentlemen! Until tomorrow it is."

For the first time in a long while, Ryan felt something almost like happiness, a feeling like warm waves washing over his body, soothing out all the aches. He had endured pain on pain. His suffering had worn him down. The Americans had suffered too and they were coming to him for help. They were a curiosity. They gave no thought to money or rank. The only question the three Americans seemed to care about was: how soon can we go up against the British again? He was looking forward to the day they all sailed together.

As Jacqueline led the Americans downstairs to find rooms for them,

Ryan turned his attention to the fire. "Jumbaaliyia, when my Irish woman was dying in my arms I cursed God. She gave me a curious rebuke. She admonished me for cursing God as the world, she said, was made and ruled by men, not God. And men, being imperfect, created an imperfect world, bringing woe to us all. God, she claimed, is constantly calling us back home to His own perfect world. Her point, I believe, was that her dying had nothing to do with God as He never does any harm. I do not know why I speak of these things to you now except, as of late, her words have troubled me and you seem to me to be a man of good, clear sense, of foreign ways perhaps, but even so... Do you ever - wonder - about such things?"

The African, who, like Ryan, was well accustomed to having hardship as his companion, a man long in suffering, knew the burden of regret. He paused for a moment to consider Ryan's words and replied carefully. "Your woman, Captain, possessed a wisdom beyond this world."

"Aye. That she did. Do your people believe in God or gods?"

"Yes, my Captain - do not all men?"

"I don't know about all men. And I am hardly wise enough to know the answer myself. Did you ever hear of a fellow named Epicurus?"

"No, sir."

"Epicurus was a Greek philosopher who lived in ancient times and he proffered this riddle: God either wants to destroy bad things and cannot, or He can but does not want to, or He neither wishes to nor can, or He both wants to and can. Here is the dilemma according to Epicurus: If God wants to but cannot then He is weak and weakness is hardly a quality that applies to a god. If He can but does not want to, then He is a spiteful being - which is equally foreign to a god's nature. If He neither wants to nor can, then He is both weak and spiteful and so He is not a god and is not worthy of our exaltation. If He wants to and can, which is the only thing fitting for a god, then where do bad things come from and, more importantly, why does He not destroy evil? Ha! I recall the riddle well enough now but, bless me, I don't remember how Epicurus solved problem - or if he ever did."

"This Greek must have been very wise."

"Are you, Jumbaaliyia, Muslim?"

"*Muslim...*" Jumbaaliyia repeated the word thoughtfully and smiled. "My faith is whatever the Father who rules us all commands though my poor ears may not hear His words... If God is a Christian, I am Christian. If He is a Muslim, I am Muslim. If He is Hebrew, then I too am Hebrew."

Ryan smiled back. He liked that answer.

"I see."

"I am a true believer," Jumbaaliyia volunteered. "But, I am no wise man, no holy man. Once I was a prince among my people, a terror to behold, a lawless brute. I cannot undo what has been done. Now, I walk the earth alone, seeking my path that will lead me back to Allah, back to Yahweh, back to God Almighty. *Jumbaaliyia*, the name my people gave me when they delivered me to the slavers - the word means *misery*. It was meant as a curse. But I keep the name to remind me of who I once was. There is but one God and He is great and perfect beyond our imperfect understanding. If those words are true, then man's corruptions must be of his own making and an offense to God's eyes. Without God, there is only suffering and death on this barren island. What would be the purpose? With God, there is hope and life everlasting. It must be so. But who am I to say? I am no one. All will be revealed by Him at a time and place of His own choosing, and in His own fashion, according to His infinite wisdom."

Ryan shook his head. The African's eloquence had caught him off guard.

"You speak well. What would be the point indeed my good prince? I often wonder though, will the words and deeds of the prophets, no matter the religion, fade upon the memory of the world as time marches on? I think it must be so and this is what confounds me. Will men remember God a thousand years from now if He does not speak..."

Twelve
Wolves in Sheep's Clothing

ike a pair of black eels slithering across the water, fearsome predators and lightning fast, the *Prince* and her new sister zigzagged their way through heaving seas and icy winds. Stinging rains and sea spray bit into flesh and made bones ache. The watch had to be rotated every hour and sailors - men who loved their swift, trim ships and brave lads all - gathered around the galley fires to thaw numb fingers and frozen toes. Men stayed below for as long as they could.

For three days and nights the cutters plowed across the dismal sea until, on the dawn of the third day, the Irishmen found the English merchant fleet, over 100 ships strong, riding anchor at Spithead - just as Ryan had foretold. Flying English colors, and with guns hidden under cargo crates, Macatter and Dowlin slipped their ships into the middle of the fleet and dropped anchor. No one thought to challenge them. With North Wind wreaking havoc across the world, men hid themselves inside where life was warm and dry.

On Christmas morning tamer winds and calmer seas returned to England and the fleet commander, Sir George Brydges Rodney, signaled the fleet to make ready to weigh anchor. Rodney already had his orders in hand from the Admiralty. He was instructed to take the bulk of his fleet to Gibraltar, to re-supply the garrison there, as soon as the weather turned fair. And then he was to proceed due west, across the Atlantic, with supplies for the Leeward Islands. He had 22 ships-of-the-line to protect the great merchant ship flotilla. The rest of the fleet, merchant ships with cargo holds stuffed full of rich cargo and bound for different destinations within the British Isles, were to sail out alone.

After seeing Rodney's signal, the cagey Irishmen weighed anchor and were the first to head out. And like a pair of tawny lions on the prowl, lingering in the bush, lying in wait for unsuspecting victims, the Irishmen sailed out a ways into the Celtic Sea, turned their ships around and waited. They waited in the mist and rolling waves for unsuspecting, unprotected merchantmen to blunder into them.

The Irishmen did not wait long. The day after Christmas, off Lizard Point, the *Prince* took the very large brig *James & Thomas*. Dowlin removed her 16 crewmen and, feeling lucky, sent her off to Morlaix with a willing prize crew on board. After *James & Thomas*, the *Prince* caught the small *Betsy* and Dowlin decided to ransom the ship and parole her crew. Then *Princess* snagged her first prize, the schooner *Camden* loaded down with a cargo of lumber from Memel. As she was a valuable ship with a rich cargo, Macatter elected to take the risk, as Dowlin had, and sent her on to France with a prize crew on board.

And then something odd caught Dowlin's eye. A small, unarmed sloop with an unusually large number of men crowded along her rails, their gaunt faces white with cold, sailed past the privateers with barely a hundred yards of water between them. Curious, Dowlin brought the *Prince* around to have a closer look. He saw the sloop's poor condition, she had no value, and counted 21 men, too many men for a crew and too poorly dressed, too dirty, for passengers and so he and his men simply let the sloop sail on.

On board the sloop, 21 Americans stared back at the handsome warship, nervous and fidgety. To a man, they thought a Royal Navy battle cruiser had found them. Every man held his breath and prayed as the fearsome cutter closed in on them. Well they knew the waters they now traveled were infested with the king's warships. Their poor sloop carried no weapons and was too slow to flee. It would be a quick trip back to Pembroke Castle if they were intercepted. Hell on Earth. But standing on the quarterdeck of the cutter was a big man with flowing red hair who simply nodded to them and let them go their way. And then the warship's men unfurled more sail and sped off towards more promising prospects on the horizon.

"Queer that was, sir," offered a seaman with a heavy, Southern drawl. "You'd think she woulda at least hailed us, asked us who we was?"

The ship's thin master nodded. "Maybe they're on the run like us, Mr. Hitchcock. She flew no ensign. Suppose we'll never know."

So far, their luck was holding. It had almost been too easy. They still had a good three to five days of sailing ahead of them though and the sudden appearance of a British warship or a December gale would end their desperate gambit across the waves. One meant a slow death in jail, the other a quick death at sea.

"Mr. Collins, sir," said Hitchcock, "I must report there's no water. Nary a drop to be had on board, sir."

Midshipman Charles Collins, the senior ranking man, nodded, acknowledging the report. He really didn't care.

Hitchcock studied the midshipman's glum, dirty face. "An't no food to be found either, sir, not a morsel, not even a crumb for a ship's rat. Things could get a bit desperate in a day or two for us, sir."

"Where you from Hitchcock anyway? That accent of yours - it's a bit thick."

"Accent, sir?" Hitchcock asked with a cagey grin. "What accent would that be now, Mr. Collins? Where I come from folks don't have no accents."

"And where, pray, might that be?"

"Outside Charleston, sir. Charleston, South Carolina. Lovely place. Hot as blazes in the summer tho'."

"Well, Mr. Hitchcock," offered Collins with a raspy voice, "I've heard you boys from the South come from pretty sturdy stock. We'll see. We've got a sound ship under our feet and a fair wind at our backs. 'Tis a damn sight better circumstance, even without food or water, than Pembroke. If only the winds hold fair for a bit. I figure the coast of France is no more than five days sailing, six at the most. We'll make due with rain water. Have the lads tighten their belts. There's no goin' back. Do you understand me? *There's no goin' back.*"

Hitchcock abruptly came to attention, touched the brim of his hat. "Aye, sir. The boys are all with ya, sir. Rest assured of that!"

And then Hitchcock made his way forward to give the men, his fellow escapees, the bad news.

Like fat, senseless cows going to slaughter, for the next several days the merchant ships not sailing with Rodney on to Gibraltar, witlessly sailed straight into the jaws of the hungry lions. Dowlin and his men captured the brig *Owner's Adventure*, loaded down with peas, flour and iron, put a prize crew on board and sent her off to Morlaix. The *Prince* took the *Providence* next, a sloop with a cargo of wool, and the privateers sent her on to France behind the *Owner's Adventure*. Damn the risk Dowlin decided. He was feeling lucky. *Franklin will have his prisoners, Torris will have his money and Ryan will have his glory.*

Macatter, not to be outdone by his headstrong rival, took the brig *Prince William* along with the sloop *Peter & John*, two excellent prizes. He put prize crews on board both vessels and sent them scudding back across the sea to France. And then Macatter caught two smaller ships, the *Samuel* and the *John & Hereford* but, short-handed now, he was forced to ransom the vessels and parole their crews.

Seven English ships in all, each a rich trophy, were racing back to France with Irish crews. Each prize master chose a different route home to avoid the disaster that had befallen their brethren with the *Quebec*. The five smaller vessels set free had been ransomed off for a total of £3000 and between them, Dowlin and Macatter had taken 68 prisoners.

Ryan's bold plan had succeeded brilliantly. But his Irish lieutenants had no wish to tarry too long on the open sea so close to England and risk drawing the god of war's attention - how the whimsical god favors men of daring with daring plans but disdains the foolhardy, marking them for an early doom. And so Dowlin and Macatter, flushed with victory and not wishing to press their luck, turned their ships around and headed back for France.

But just as the Irishmen finished plotting a course for home and trimming sails, the *Prince's* lookout spotted ships emerging out of the haze a mile off or so.

"Sails broad off the port quarter; three masted... square sailed... English... full sail, wind abeam..." The lookout then hesitated, not sure at first, and cried out franticly: "*Frigates! Two frigates* I say thar below!"

The man's words sent a chill through every heart.

Dowlin grabbed his glass and scanned the horizon. "They be a brace of frigates all right!" he shouted over the waves to Macatter, a hint of apprehension in his voice. The British warships were uncomfortably close. "One looks like the *Achilles*, don't recognize the other..."

"I see 'em, Patrick," Macatter answered back calmly. "Too big for us to handle - I say we split up, go our separate ways and take our chances. You've got the faster ship, you head south. I'll take the shorter way and head due east with the better wind. We'll rendezvous in France by different routes. What say you, Pat?"

The sight of two powerful frigates was enough to quell the fighting spirit of even Ryan's two intrepid captains. No shame to the warrior who takes flight - *top speed* - and yields the field to the far stronger man when to press on would only seal his own doom. No glory is won that way.

Dowlin readily agreed to Macatter's desperate plan, wished Macatter good luck and waved him off, uncertain of whether he would ever see his friend again. Morgan pushed the tiller hard over and brought the ship around and the *Prince* struck out to the south, fighting against a nasty, head wind. Every stitch of canvas the wind could hold was hung out on her spars. Dowlin gave the order to set the stuns'ls too despite the fluky winds, which made using them a bit risky.

The *Princess* headed due east at full speed, shooting straight for the French coast.

Standing next to Morgan at the helm, Dowlin kept one eye on the British frigates and the other on the wind. He tapped Morgan on the shoulder. "I don't believe it," he said and pointed. "Look at that Morgan! Not our lucky day, good *Gawd!*"

Morgan looked over his shoulder. As the cutters parted ways the pair of British frigates turned, turned in unison, ignoring Macatter's ship, and both brutes came tearing after the *Prince*.

"Hey you bloody bastards!" Dowlin shouted at the British, too far away to be heard, and pointed his finger at the *Princess*. "What the fookin' hell is wrong with that ship over there? She'd make you a handsome prize and she's the slower ship! Stupid shits, you should be chasin' after her!"

He looked back again at Morgan with disgust in his eyes. "Jesus, Michael. Do you believe this? I'm cursed. Truly, I am."

Kelly made his way back to the ship's stern rail, casually removed a pipe from his mouth. "Looks like we're the grand prize," he offered nonchalantly, "the prize they fancy most, Capt'n."

Dowlin took a deep breath and sighed. "Appears so, Chris. Can't believe my eyes. Two frigates hot on our tail! What a triumph this cruise was until now. Those damn frigates are goin' to spoil it all. It woulda been fun to rub Luke's nose in our success a bit, hey?"

"Why so glum, Pat?" Kelly asked calmly and raised a finger at the British hunters. "We've outrun frigates before and we'll do it now. See thar Pat, they're just barely able to keep pace with us. Neither ships gainin' on us. Once we turn east, we'll have the wind abeam. Then, the good Lord willin', we'll fly across the waves and leave them jackals far behind, leave them wonderin' who those damn fine sailors are!"

Dowlin took a closer look at the frigates with his glass again. "All the same Chris, I don't like it. Damn Macatter is probably laughin' his fool head off right about now at our predicament."

"Aye," grinned Morgan, "I can just hear him say: *Patrick Dowlin, you old sea dog, don't you be cryin' in yer grog now; if you want to be runnin' around with the big dogs, you can't be pissin' in the wind!*"

Morgan slapped the rail and began laughing hysterically. He had done a pretty fair imitation of Macatter and was rather pleased with himself.

Kelly started chuckling too.

Dowlin, the weight of command resting heavily on his broad shoulders, was more sober. He collapsed his glass, slipped it inside his coat pocket and frowned.

"Well, lads," he said, "I hope we're all laughin' in a day or two. Mr. Kelly, double the watch, no need to have the guns run out. Not much sense in fightin' if they catch up with us I suppose, but we'll see about that if and when the time comes. Keep all her canvas stretched out. Double-check all the irons, buckles and braces and pray we don't lose a spar or sail now. Alrighty then, let's give these Englishmen a lesson in real sailin'. Better have the boats provisioned and ready to launch - just in case..."

"The boats, Capt'n?" asked Morgan, eyeing Dowlin suspiciously.

"Aye," answered Dowlin, a thin smile crossed his lips. "If they outrun us, I'll scuttle the *Prince* first before I let 'em bastards get their filthy hands on her. Wait a bloody moment. I just had an inspiration. Better yet, we'll snuggle up real close to one 'em and try to get tangled up with her, get the rigging all fouled, maybe cross the bowsprits, and then we'll torch the *Prince*. Aye, make ourselves a fireboat! Wouldn't that be somethin' now lads if we could sink a frigate! We'll set all the boats in the water and scatter just before we light her up. Some of us might even catch a friendly wind or current and escape if night closes in. And if that don't work, by *Gawd*, I'll swim to shore. No British jail for this Irishman."

Kelly and Morgan exchanged knowing glances, snapped to attention and saluted. Kelly's brother John, standing nearby, joined them as did young Tim, after his uncle gave him a nudge in the ribs. It was a show of respect and trust from crew to captain. It was the warrior's way, acknowledging their captain's difficult position and letting him know that they believed in him, win or lose, and with no regrets.

A tingle shot up Dowlin's spine, his heart overflowed with glowing pride. He and the Irish veterans, the Shadowmen, had given Ryan the same honor on more than one occasion. This was why, he realized, Ryan loved command so much. With a boyish grin - and newfound courage - he returned the salute. *By Gawd, we'll lose those frigates even if I have to get out and row! I'll not let these good lads down!*

The British frigates, small but swift, pursued the *Prince* relentlessly all through the day, never losing sight of their prey. No matter which way the Irishmen turned, no matter what sailor's trick they employed, the privateers couldn't shake the frigates off. But neither were the British able to close the distance with the Irishmen enough to pummel their cutter with heavy iron.

The chase continued through the night and well into the next day until the privateers came within sight of the Passage du Pour at Brest.

The Irishmen entered the channel and tried to nudge their cutter into the harbor. Safety was but a stone's throw away. But the currents and shore breezes were too strong and against the Irishmen. The *Prince* was pushed back out to sea.

The British seized their opportunity, were quick to close the distance as the cutter struggled in the channel. The gun crews on the nearest frigate even primed and loaded their 12 pounders. They were so very close...

Dowlin knew better than to make a second attempt at trying to enter Brest and so swung the *Prince* around and headed south again, tacking against contrary winds all the way. The Irishmen rounded France's great peninsula during the night, the massive finger of land known by all as Brittany, and raced east, catching a better wind in the morning, for the friendly shore batteries at L'Orient.

And after a harrowing three day chase, the *Prince* reached L'Orient first, just a cannon shot or two ahead of the two British frigates. The lead frigate fired off one salvo, a salute to Irish skill and gallantry, and then turned around and her commanded set a course for home. The *Prince* saluted the French fort as she passed it by and coasted into a harbor crowded with ships of every kind and description, ships crammed full with French soldiers and French weapons waiting to cross the Atlantic for America.

The Irishmen took in the enormous array of men and arms assembled and felt puny. And then again, they had proven themselves. The Irishmen were a potent weapon.

Two days earlier, Macatter and his men had safely reached Morlaix where they found five of the seven prizes anchored in the river. Macatter soon learned that British frigates had retaken two ships though. Twelve more of Ryan's men were in custody. Despite their losses, the Irishmen had just cause to celebrate. They had embarrassed the Royal Navy, had seized a fortune in ships and cargo and had captured a good number of prisoners to further Franklin's cause. The first joint cruise of the *Prince* and *Princess* had been a stunning success...

But Irish triumph was not the only excitement in Morlaix. A small group of Americans, 21 brave men, had made a daring escape from Pembroke Castle, had stolen a sloop and sailed into Morlaix just before the *Princess*. The Americans had sailed for days without food or water. They were the talk of the town, celebrities. The French hailed the Americans as heroes and billeted them at a nearby French army barracks, attending generously to their every need and care, until Franklin could decide what do to with them.

Macatter stepped out of a fine drizzle mixed with sleet, stopped at the doorway to stamp the mud off his boots and let the water trickle off the brim of his hat. The air inside the barracks was damp and cold and the furnishings were austere.

The Americans all turned their heads when the short, barrel-chested man with an impressive black beard entered. He had the bearing of an officer, a sailor, though he wore no uniform.

Macatter quickly looked around the room and took in its occupants. Some men were standing about talking while others tried to sleep. One man was stretched out in his hammock, reading. In the back two men were engaged in a friendly game of billiards, playing over a badly worn table.

"You sir, might you know where Mr. Collins is?" Macatter asked the nearest man in his unmistakable Irish brogue.

The American removed a piece of straw from his mouth and used it to point to a tall individual across the room.

Macatter walked across the room. "Are you, sir, the intrepid Mr. Collins of Pembroke Castle?" he asked and offered his hand.

Collins, a tall, lean fellow with long spindly legs and the face of a country farm boy, shook the Irishman's hand firmly. Macatter liked him straight off.

"Allow me, sir, to introduce myself," Macatter said loudly for all to hear. "I'm Edward Macatter, though some know me better as Captain Wilde, and I am master of the American privateer *Black Princess*. She's the sixteen gunner sittin' in the river just over the hill and down at the end of the road."

"Pleased to make your acquaintance, sir," replied Collins, giving Macatter a toothy grin. "You Irish?"

Macatter returned the American's grin in kind. "Well, now, some say that I am, lad. Had Irish parents to be sure. Tough for any man with any pride in him to deny his Irish roots. But I'm originally from Boston myself. Enough about me tho'. I've heard about yer escape from some of the locals in town. I'd be interested to hear yer story."

"Well, sir, not much to tell."

Macatter cracked a wide smile, which was not an easy thing to do for the serious-minded Irishman. "Nonsense lad, no false modesty now. The French have laws against it."

Men laughed.

"Out with it now," Macatter prodded.

"Well, sir, I was a midshipman with the Continental sloop *Resistance* mounting eighteen guns. Capt'n William Burke was her commander. We was captured by the British in '78, on the 9th day of September, off of New England. We was sailin' to rendezvous with Count D'Estaing's French fleet. Anyways, I was imprisoned in Rhode Island for a short spell and then taken to England in the *Culloden*. Me and some of the boys here landed at Milford Haven on December 15th last year and was sent nearby to Pembroke Castle prison. Well, sir, we didn't favor Pembroke very much. No sir, we didn't. Not with rotting victuals for our rations, and a plank for a bed and a stone for a pillow. And so we waited until lady luck showed us a way out. That happened about two weeks ago when we was able to overpower a guard and found an empty sloop sittin' in a nearby river. We waited for nightfall and sailed her here. That's pretty much all there is to tell, sir."

Macatter erupted into a hearty laugh and patted Collins firmly on the shoulders. "Well done, Mr. Collins! Well done indeed!" He turned and looked around the room. "To all of you lads, I say, well done! A fine piece of work! Aye, you should all be most proud of yerselves. Brave lads all!"

The Americans nodded or politely smiled back at the curious

Irishman.

Macatter wrapped his arm around Collins's shoulder and led him around the room in a circle for a bit. "What did you say your rank was lad?"

"Midshipman Charles Collins of the United States Continental Navy, at your service, sir."

"Midshipman Collins, is it?" Macatter asked with a gleam in his eye. "A week ago I was sailin' through the same waters as you. We damn near must have passed each off the Downs! My ship, and another privateer, the *Black Prince*, have just returned from a successful raid in those waters. We took twelve good prizes and their cargos. Plenty of prize money to share in. We brought in sixty-eight prisoners too for our good Benjamin Franklin who will use them in prisoner exchanges with the British to help free your brothers still held in English gaols. Very good haul, I'd say. Wouldn't you agree?"

"Indeed, sir. Most impressive. The *Black Prince* did you say?"

"Aye."

"Well, I'll be. We heard stories about her in prison. British say she's a pirate ship crewed by a band of Irish thugs and outlaws. She's done some mischief of late I take it from the talk that went around."

Macatter grinned approvingly and slapped the side of his generous belly. "Aye! That she has, my lad, that she has - and I'd wager you all I own that old King George's men will be talkin' even more about us once they learn about our last cruise! I know the *Prince's* crew well. I sailed on her myself as first officer before takin' command of the *Black Princess*. She's black and fast and crewed by Irish rogues sure enough, I can attest to that! Her captain is a man named Dowlin, Patrick Dowlin and we all serve a man - Captain Luke Ryan."

"We passed a ship like her along our way. Thought it was the English hunting us down but a big fellow waved at us and let us go."

"Long, red hair?"

"Why yes!"

"Ah, then you saw the *Prince*! And the man who waved at you was none other than the irascible Mr. Dowlin."

The Americans listened to what Macatter had to say with more interest now. His boastful talk had caught their attention and feeling more at ease with the brash but likeable Irishman, there were grins all around.

"What, if I may ask, sir, are your plans, Mr. Collins?"

"Don't know exactly, sir. I wrote to Ambassador Franklin seeking his good counsel. The French have put us up here until we sort things out. P'haps we could put in with Capt'n Jones. Some of the enlistments of some of the boys here are up; they might want to go home. Billy, the curly, blond fellow over there, he's from Boston. I know his time is up. Maybe you two crossed paths in Boston?"

Macatter smiled at the boy named Billy. He had never seen Boston or the boy before. He took in the barrack's shabby whitewashed walls, the few tables and chairs, and the billiard table. There was not much. The Americans had placed straw mats along the walls for bedding. Some clever soul had made two hammocks out of burlap and rope and strung them from the rafters next to the only fireplace.

Macatter thoughtfully stroked his beard and took in the small flames tickling the bottom of a black kettle set in the middle of the fireplace. He took the kettle's large spoon and stirred the hearty soup mixture inside, thick with vegetables and just beginning to simmer.

"Well, lads, this place doesn't look much different from a prison to me. As for Jones, well, he had himself a good showing in September with the British up in the German Ocean didn't he? Another handsome feather in his cap, I'd say. You could do worse than Capt'n Jones to be sure. But the British navy has his ships bottled up in Holland. Nothin' for you there. You could return home. Franklin will give each one of you the money for the passage. At least that is what I've heard he does for escaped American prisoners. For any man whose enlistment is up, yer free to go yer own way certainly. But think on this now, I've told you who I am. The *Black Prince* and *Black Princess* sail under the orders of his Excellency, Franklin. Life aboard a privateer, if you haven't heard already, is pretty fair. Better than navy life by a long country mile, lads. We all share in the prize money, all of it - no government takes a cut of it - and we've taken in a good number of prizes so far."

He paused to test the soup and winced. "Our victuals I dare say are much better than this sad concoction and discipline is easy as long as you pull yer weight. Yer at liberty to speak to my crew. They'll vouch for everythin' I've said here to you today. The truth of the matter is lads, for any of you who still has a fire in his belly, we could sorely use some help and I ask each of you to chew on that for a bit. Well, that's my pitch. I'll take my leave of you now. Again, congratulations on yer escape. I'll send my cook along later with something a bit tastier than this, something to put some meat back on yer bones. No matter yer decision, God speed to each of you."

With that, Macatter put on his hat, shook Collins's hand once more and left.

The following day, the first day of the New Year, a group of rag-tag Americans, 21 strong, appeared in a heavy downpour on the river bank across from the cruiser the *Black Princess*. All 21 souls signed up with the privateer for three month enlistments. Collins was promoted to lieutenant. And after the Americans swore the oath of allegiance, the whole crew went into town to celebrate - the Irish way.

With ships and men in fighting trim, Dowlin and Macatter set out again in early February to increase their fame and fortune. The *Prince*, sailing out of L'Orient, and the *Princess* from Morlaix, rendezvoused on the leeward side of the Isles of Bas where Macatter joined Dowlin on board the *Prince* for a hardy supper and to plan their next attack. Their appetites were large and they set off for the fertile waters around Lands End that very night.

Half way between Ushant and Land's End, they happened upon the luckless *Philip* first, a large brig from the West Indies with a valuable cargo of sugar, cotton and coffee. The Irishmen put a prize crew aboard to sail her into Morlaix, an easy day's sail away. And then near Land's End the dauntless raiders caught the even larger brig *Friendship* next, loaded down with salt, fruit and wine. She was another prize worth the risk of a prize crew and off she went towards Morlaix right behind the *Philip.*

A few days later, cruising across the dark blue waters of the Celtic Sea, Dowlin decided to have some fun. Why not take a British packet ship or two? True, Franklin had put the Dover to Calais packet ships off limits, but had said nothing about the packet ships plying the sixty miles of water between Wales and Ireland. His Majesty's post office operated the packets, ships ferrying mail and passengers between the two islands daily. The Crown employed some of the fastest vessels at sea for the task and the service took great pride in the fact that American rebels had failed to intercept any packets, not one, since the war's beginning.

That unblemished record did not sit well with the Irishmen and so the two raiders sailed north and waited off Dublin for the evening packet from Holyhead. And, right on time, the hapless *Hillsborough* sailed straight into their trap.

Once Hillsborough's master realized what was happening, he weighted down his mailbags and tossed them overboard before the Irishmen could board his ship. Those were his instructions in case trouble found him. Dowlin led the boarding party and had the passengers and crew form a single line along the deck. His men then went down the line and relieved each one of any money, jewelry or trinkets having any value.

When McCloud asked an older English woman for her purse, she protested loudly. She held her bag tightly to her bosom as if she were protecting a baby.

"Now, ma'am," said McCloud, "behave yerself and give us a look at yer purse."

"Certainly not, you uncouth *barbarian!*" replied the woman staunchly. She took a gloved hand and slapped the seaman's fingers.

Now McCloud was angry. "Don't be gettin' yer bowels in an uproar now, missy. Hand over yer bag, I say!"

Dowlin was inspecting the ship's papers when he heard the commotion. "What's the problem here?" he demanded.

"Capt'n, her royal countess here doesn't want to part with her purse. Fact of the matter is, sir, she's bein' a bit of a bitch."

The woman's jaw dropped at the seaman's use of coarse language.

The ship's master then stepped out from the line and started protesting the harsh treatment of his passengers.

Dowlin held up his arm and cut him off. "Ma'am, my name is Dowlin," he began softly with a reassuring smile, "Capt'n Patrick James Dowlin. That ship you see over yonder - why that would be the dreaded *Black Prince*. I'm sure you've heard of her. Her fame has spread far and wide across yer island, tho' some say she's been captured or burned, as you can plainly see ma'am that just an't so. There she sits. Now yer country and mine are at war..."

He paused to make sure he had everyone's full attention. His demeanor then changed abruptly, and not for the better. He brought his face nose-to-nose with the woman and clenched his teeth. He had no malice in his heart but wanted to make the right impression.

"And," he resumed in a sterner tone, "you'll *kindly* hand over yer purse to my man here or I won't be responsible for what happens next. King George's soldiers do far worse to Americans across the sea. You'll be set free shortly. Thank yer lucky star for that! Then you can petition yer king with all yer complaints and protests to yer heart's content. But thar will be no more trouble here, lest you and yer purse want to return to France with me. And I very much doubt, ma'am, that our accommodations on board the *Prince* will be much to yer likin'..."

The old woman gasped, had no more to say and reluctantly handed her purse over to McCloud. No one had ever spoken to her so rudely. Dowlin stood back, smiled politely and touched his cap.

All the fuss had been over nothing though. McCloud, all smiles, searched the purse, found nothing of value and handed it back the woman intact.

A moment later, another woman, young and exquisitely dressed, started chiding McCloud. She refused to surrender the key to her trunk after the Irishmen finished bringing all the passengers' baggage up on deck for inspection.

"Fine, keep yer bloody key," McCloud told her gruffly. "Now move yer tits back ma'am, wouldn't want to hurt 'em any."

He had no more patience for these proper English women and so removed a pistol from his belt, took aim and shot the lock on the trunk clean off. Inside the trunk he found clothing, several pieces of jewelry and a set of sterling silver utensils. He tossed the clothing over the rail and seized the rest.

After his men had taken everything of value, Dowlin decided to take the *Hillsborough* in tow. The privateers crossed the Celtic Sea that very night to Holyhead, bent on catching the morning packet there. They arrived just in time to find the *Hillsborough's* sister ship, the *Besborough*, getting under way, leaving punctually at seven, and snagged her right outside the bay, well in sight of land. Macatter boarded the *Besborough* and took paroles from every prisoner. And then, with paroles and ransom notes in hand, Dowlin and Macatter decided to free both ships, the privateers had delivered their message, had made their point, and then crossed the Celtic Sea again for Rush to take on supplies, to see friends and family, and, of course, to recruit new men. The *Hillsbourough* and *Besborough* dashed back into port.

Sometimes bad luck is truly good luck in disguise. Who can know the why of it?

Once the Irishmen reached the Irish coast, they thought their luck had turned. Foul weather, a freak storm, kept the privateers from dropping anchor and reaching shore. With provisions running low, the Irishmen could not afford to tarry long. They cursed their bad luck and set a course for France. But Good Fortune had been smiling on them, pouring out her generosity, when she kept the Irishmen from landing. Not long after Ryan's men pulled into Morlaix, the Irishmen learned that several companies of British regulars and militiamen, a force 300 strong, had been lying in wait for them along the shore.

One of *Hillsborough's* passengers had overheard one of Dowlin's men, a man with a careless tongue, say that Rush was their next destination. She was quick to tip-off the authorities in Holyhead and a British warship was dispatched immediately to get word to Dublin. British soldiers marched through the night, through whipping winds and hail, up to Rush to set an ambush for Ryan and his men. But Ryan wasn't with his men and the privateers never landed.

As the Irishmen regrouped in Morlaix, word of their fresh victories at sea was received across the Empire with renewed disgust and anger. Many of the king's subjects, particularly maritime trade investors, were losing patience, were losing money, and wanted the Irish outlaws captured or killed or both. Petitions flooded into the Admiralty demanding that the navy add swift cutters to the chase. The frigates had proven to be too slow. The petitions landed on the desk of the First Secretary of the Admiralty - and did nothing to improve his humor.

The French Minister of Marine had not attained his position of power by being careless. He was by nature a deliberate and cautious man, qualities enhanced by his 15 years of service as Paris's Lieutenant General of Police and commander of France's infamous secret police, a position he bought for 175,000 *livres* back in 1759.

And, while many considered him gifted intellectually, he had not achieved his position through brilliance. No, rather over time he had mastered the twins duplicity and deceit. These were his disciples, his trade and craft. He was also a man who valued subtlety. Why kill an enemy or rival and risk discovery and reprisal when you could lay him low with one well-placed lie, a scandal, something to harm his reputation, something to discredit his honor? Brutality was for butchers, men of limited intellectual means, unimaginative dolts. Sartine much preferred the indirect approach, the graceful political *coup de grace* and if a few *sou* could be made in the bargain - so much the better.

After reading reports describing the latest string of victories of the Irish privateers, he recalled one of his most trusted lieutenants from Italy. The work the Minister had in mind required he make use of one of his very best resources.

"Ah, Doumar, do come in. Sit down."

Sartine was not being polite. It was a command as Bertrand Doumar, a captain in the king's guard, but in reality a colonel in France's dreaded secret police, knew all too well. Doumar, physically an unremarkable man with a plain face and dressed in unremarkable, plain attire to match, took a seat.

Sartine laid his quill pen down and rose up from behind his desk, a rich African mahogany piece with intricate gold scrolls and flourishes carved into the legs and topped off in fine leather. He walked over to a matching credenza, poured out two generous measures of cognac, and hand one to Doumar.

Doumar accepted the liquor but said nothing. He knew he was not in the Minister's office to talk. He was there to listen and the Minister, always all business, loathed the usual pleasantries. Doumar's eyes darted about the room, a room he had been in many times before. Sartine's office was cold and dark but the Minister kept it fastidiously neat.

"I have some work for you, Doumar. Delicacy and secrecy will be required. Are we clear?"

"Of course, your grace," the man responded stiffly. He did not lie. He understood the meaning of the words *delicacy* and *secrecy* very well. No matter what he was asked to do, there could be no trace, no trail, leading back to Sartine. His life, perhaps even the lives of his family, depended on it. He would take no notes and commit all instructions to memory. And if he was caught and questioned, he would admit no association with Sartine even under the threat of death or torture. The financial rewards for success were well worth the risk.

"It is not a difficult task, Doumar, but I want you see to it personally. The matter requires your special talents. It requires, *finesse*. Understood?"

"Yes, your grace."

"These privateers of the American Franklin, you know of them?"

"But of course your grace, all France knows of their victories against the English. They capture and sink English ships in England's home waters at will it seems and, it is said, sometimes even within sight of the vaunted Grand Fleet. The *Black Prince* and *Black Princess* are the names of the vessels. I would enjoy seeing the faces of those pompous English Admiralty officers as they discuss their Irish problem."

Sartine sat back down behind his handsome desk. His eyes disappeared behind his heavy eyelids as he tapped out a drum roll with his fingers.

"Yes, how true. The *Irish problem*. I am certain the English are much annoyed. But these privateers have become something of an embarrassment to our King as well."

Doumar looked at Sartine perplexed. "Embarrassment my grace? To our King? How so?"

Sartine turned his head away to look at a wall. The drapes were pulled tight to keep any light from seeping in.

"Please, Doumar. Do you intend to disappoint me now after all these years of stellar service?"

Doumar had known better than to ask for any clarification and instantly regretted his question. It was - unprofessional. Men in his trade did not ask questions. They listened and then they obeyed. It was crucial that he retain his master's utmost confidence. Sartine's remark about the king's opinion, whether true or not, were entirely irrelevant. Still, how English losses could embarrass or even trouble the King of France was beyond his comprehension.

"No, my grace - I, I misspoke," Doumar quickly answered and dismissed any notion of asking Sartine to forgive the error. Sartine was not one to forgive, not anyone, not for any reason, not ever.

"*Good*. The ringleader of the privateers, this Luke Ryan, do you know him?"

"Not personally, my grace, no, I only know of him," the colonel offered evasively. He did not volunteer that he knew that the Irishman had made Sartine a pile of money before the war despite the temptation to impress Sartine with extent of his resourcefulness. Some things were simply better left unsaid. Information was power and Doumar, not unlike his master, had a gift for collecting information, vast amounts of information on interesting people. Doumar lost his train of thought for a moment as he let his mind wander, curious about what this Irishman could have done to earn Sartine's scorn. Such knowledge might prove valuable to him someday, should he ever have need to soften his master's displeasure.

"Well, his reign of terror against our British foe, for political reasons expedient to the Crown, must stop. Even in war, there are rules.

We will try a bit of *gentle* persuasion first. You are to leave for Morlaix immediately. I will provide you the necessary papers, giving you authority to act on my behalf. You shall instruct the local commissary there to send out his press gangs. He is to gather up all able-bodied men for immediate sea duty. The usual bribes are to be refused by him. You shall repeat this process with each commissary from Brest to Dunkirk. Morlaix first though. Additionally, any Frenchman found serving aboard any American privateer is to be removed. No exceptions, no excuses. If the captain of either privateer gives us any trouble, he is to be arrested and detained until I say otherwise. My sources tell me the privateers are short-handed and depriving them of French sailors should prevent them from going to sea. My sources also inform me that this resourceful Captain Ryan proposes to sail out of Dunkirk soon against the English with a third ship. That causes us a different problem. Even if we deprive these privateers of using French sailors, these Irishmen might think to continue their marauding ways by leaving one ship behind and consolidating crews."

Sartine paused to sample his cognac, smacked his lips with approval. "Do you follow me so far?"

"Yes, your grace."

"Excellent."

Sartine was confident Doumar understood his every word. While Doumar was exceptionally very strong, a dangerous man, Sartine rarely called upon him to use his physical strength in his work. His mind was what Sartine valued most. The man had a rare gift for cunning and subtlety.

"Captain Guilman of His Majesty's frigate *Calonne*, do you remember him?"

"But of course. *Calonne* is reputed to be one of our navy's fastest frigates."

"Yes. It better be. I was the one who commissioned her and I was the one who put this racehorse into Guilman's hands. You'll find Captain Guilman at Boulogne. He is waiting for my orders. He is to search out and find the *Black Prince* and he is to sink her - not threaten or wound her - but sink her, destroy her, and he is to make it appear as though it was the English who attacked her. He is at liberty to kill as many of her crew as he is able. The more, the better. For obvious reasons, under no circumstances, is he to take any prisoners."

"Whatever the purpose, no survivors would seem best," Doumar suggested.

"Quite right. I want the matter handled *discreetly* though. The man has always been dependable in the past, but he has not always had your gift for being shrewd. Ah! We make do with the tools at hand, no? As soon as I learn the whereabouts of *Black Prince*, I shall send the information along to Guilman by mounted courier. He is to be ready to deploy his frigate on a moment's notice and that means he is to keep his men out of the damn taverns and whorehouses, no liberty for his crew. Understood?"

"Again, yes, my grace. All is clear. And, if I may ask, what of Ryan's new ship?"

"Ah, the impatience of youth. One bird at a time, my friend. You may take your leave of me now. You have your orders, Colonel. See to them with care. The written authorizations I give you are forged. If, by bad luck, they were to fall into the wrong hands you shall of course confess to forging them yourself. And as always my dear Doumar, return to me with glad tidings - or do not return at all..."

Doumar subserviently bowed his head and made good his escape from his master's dark office quickly. He could feel Sartine's eyes on the back of his neck, following his every step, and prayed that Sartine would not someday find a reason to send out another to terminate his services.

Thirteen
A Third Raider Puts to Sea

own to the sea he marched to sooth his troubled soul. Jumbaaliyia, long-suffering and faithful friend, and Jacqueline too, the dark-eyed beauty with healing hands, followed behind at a respectful distance. Once they reached the shore, Jacqueline took up a position on the crest of a dune and watched the mariner as he stood at the water's edge, alone. And once she was certain Ryan could manage on his own, and that they had not been followed, she sent Jumbaaliyia back into town. The African reluctantly agreed. There was a price on Ryan's head after all and the French had warned him to be on his guard as Ryan, even under France's protection, was not beyond the long reach of English power.

Angry, gray clouds swirled overhead. Snowflakes, only a scattering at first, drifted down from the sky in soft, fragile pirouettes. Ryan had hoped the pounding surf might somehow cleanse his spirit, free it from the chains of pain and loneliness, if only for a bit. But this was not to be. The death of his Irish lass with the long, blonde hair, and of the child he never knew, haunted him still.

Ryan took in the deserted stretch of beach, a desolate, lonely place, and was pleased. He had chosen well. His eyes welled-up with tears. He had no power to stop the grief from coming, fell to his knees and sobbed. A wave of conflicting emotions engulfed him. Guilt, emptiness, weariness, disillusionment - all tried to claim him as their prize.

He wiped away his tears, struggled to see her face. "Please God, please," he cried out to the wind. "Let it pass, let it be all right again."

But even as he uttered the words, he was uncertain of what he was praying for. His heart, like the broken bits of seashell underneath his boots, had been shattered into a thousand pieces and, he was certain, beyond repair. His hurt was deep and cutting. He needed peace. But beyond this he dared not think, not today. His mood was much too fragile.

A few tears, too few, stained his rugged cheeks. He did not have, not yet, the strength to let the hurt go. He gritted his teeth, swallowed hard and struggled to his feet. Time again to bury the past, to give thought to the living.

He buttoned his coat up to the neck and wrapped a wool scarf across his face to ward off the Atlantic's cold and blustery winds. The scarf, thick and warm, was Jacqueline's handiwork, a luxurious gift from the heart.

Jacqueline, exquisite, patient girl, with a deep and abiding love for the Irishman, approached him from behind, silently wrapped her arms around him and held him close. She was a joy to the eye, a dark-eyed beauty.

He wanted to return her love in full, had tried hard to do so. But he wasn't sure how. At first, he tried to send her away, told her not to waste her youth on him, to go and find another. But she was a stubborn girl and refused to leave. And that, to his surprise, had not displeased him. He could feel the bonds between them growing - the natural way between a man and a woman, to desire one another, to long to become one. They shared quiet moments and tender exchanges together. She was loving and generous and a comfort to his heart. But he could not bring himself to love her completely, unconditionally. She was not Shannon.

For her sake, he made an effort here and there to reach out and taste the good things in life again. But the effort was too early and depression was his only reward.

He reached back with a rough hand to touch her soft skin and there he felt a tear against her cheek. To know that he had caused her pain hurt him even more. *So much anguish in this imperfect world - no escaping it - what's the point to any of it?*

Jacqueline had chosen to remain by his side even after his physical wounds had healed. The love inside her young heart was patient, was kind, and she hoped and prayed that his heart would mend for her in time. The inexperience of youth had not clouded her good judgment though. She knew his heart might never heal. No. She would love and cherish however much of him he allowed and she would be grateful for it. He was that good of a man in her eyes.

Ryan turned to face her, kissed her cheek, her eyes, her mouth, and then pulled her hood up over her head to keep her warm and dry and there - where the land meets the sea - the couple stood close together, holding one another in silence.

They started walking along the shore hand-in-hand for a while. And then Ryan pulled two letters from his pocket, one from Macatter and the other from Dowlin, and slowly began to read them. His two captains had sent him reports, Dowlin from writing him from L'Orient and Macatter from Morlaix, on their most recent cruises with details on ships and prisoners taken. He allowed himself a brief taste of joy. Dowlin and Macatter were doing well and his bold Christmas attack against the British merchant fleet had been a success, a stunning triumph.

He felt Jacqueline start to shiver against the cold. He slipped the letters back into his pocket and held her close to warm her. He kissed her on the cheek and she squeezed him, to let him know that all was well. And then the low rumble of thunder rolled across the skies. The snow turned thicker. The Irishman and his Frenchwoman turned around and headed back to the city, walking arm-in-arm.

When Spring returned, in all her radiant glory, Ryan found the strength to put aside his walking stick aside for good. He broke the wood over his knee and tossed the pieces in the fire. With Jumbaaliyia at his side, and the Kelly brothers too, on loan to him from Dowlin, he spent his days down at the dry-docks overseeing the refitting of a very fine merchantman he had found and purchased. Ryan had to abandon his plans to build a new raider from the keel up. The shipyards were too busy churning out new cruisers for the French king for his own war against the English. Still, his new ship, a barque-rigged vessel, was a real find. She was sturdy and larger and heavier than either the *Prince* or *Princess*.

After the shipwrights had finished their work, the merchantman, rebuilt for rugged war, was towed over to the wharf next to the Torris warehouse where teams of men stood by with wagons parked along the waterfront, wagons loaded down with the instruments of war. One-by-one the drivers pulled their wagons up next to the new ship to offload their freight. Heavy guns, swivels, crates of shot and barrels of gunpowder were hoisted on deck where Ryan's men were waiting.

Since naval guns were impossible to find, Ryan and his men had liberated army artillery pieces from a nearby militia depot, after paying-off the quartermaster's gambling debts. The ship's carpenter easily converted the cannons to naval guns by removing the barrels from their large field carriages and fitting them to naval trunk carriages he had built. Armed with ten six-pounders and eight nine-pounders, the new raider was more dangerous than her two sisters in muscle.

And then there was her name. To a landsman, choosing a ship's name might seem like a trivial matter. Not so for superstitious men of the sea. A ship's name must be selected with care. And so, when all the work was finished, when the ship was ready for her shakedown cruise, Ryan struggled to find a suitable name for his new barque. He toyed with warlike names like: *Vengeance* or *Vengeance Is Mine*, *Revenge*, *Black Revenge*, *Reprisal*, *Resilience*, *Independence* and *Freedom Fighter*, but none seemed quite right, none inspired him.

And then one night - when sleep was difficult before lovely Dawn, wrapped in glittering, saffron robes, could close his eyes with sweet ambrosia - Shannon came to him. She was a gift to the mariner from the mistress of the morning, a gift to ease his pain. *Surely, this is a dream* he thought. But then again, he could feel the mattress dip where she was sitting at the edge of his bed and he could feel the warmth of her soft skin against his own as she stroked the unruly lock of hair off his forehead. And then he could smell her perfume. This was no dream.

"My dear heart," she said softly to him, smiling, "'tis wrong to worry so. Why give yourself to grief? Foolish man. Good man too. You must live your life. All is well, I swear it. Sleep now my dearest. Sleep. I shall wait for you patiently, here, across the stream. Fear not my good mariner I am with you always. Fear not, fear not..."

He opened his eyes and quickly made a sweep of the room to look for her. But she was gone. A shiver ran down his spine - the vision had been so real.

During the day the words *fear not* kept buzzing around in his head. He could not shake them. And then it hit him - he had the ship's new name: *Fearnot*. He filed the ship's registry papers with the local authorities that day and swore an oath to himself: *I shall fear not - but fear, fear by the bloody barrel, is what I bring my enemies...*

After spending a long day checking and rechecking rigging, gear and equipment, inspecting everything on board, and satisfied the ship was ready to sail, Ryan made his way back to his hotel room through light snow flurries brought on by a late winter storm. Winter's last gasp. After supper, he would write to Franklin and formally request a third commission.

He unlocked the door to his room and was startled to find an intruder. Sitting comfortably near the fire was a French naval officer, an exquisitely handsome fellow with flawless, olive skin, a pencil thin mustache and coal black hair braided in a queue. Sitting next to the fire was his old friend, David Sartine.

"Luke!" Sartine called out and jumped to his fee to embrace Ryan. "Ah! You look splendid! It has been too long, much too long. You are well?"

"I'm fine, David! I had no idea you were coming to Dunkirk. I received no letter."

"No, there was no letter. This all happened rather suddenly. I have orders to report to Brest. I am to join a new-built ship-of-the-line there. Then it is off to America to rendezvous with our fleet in the West Indies. I am off to fight the British!"

"What?" Ryan asked confused. "You're going back to sea?"

"Yes, yes. Exciting, no? I have been attached to Admiral Lucurbain de Guichen's fleet. Guichen is a decent sort or so I've heard. Why this look of surprise?"

"But I thought you preferred the good earth under your feet? The sea is not in your blood. And your position with your uncle..."

The young French captain reached inside his cloak and produced a bottle of wine. The two friends took seats near the fire.

Sartine took a long drink, then passed the bottle to Ryan. "I am only here for this afternoon. My coach leaves at four. I was saddened to learn of your loss. Shannon? Shannon was her name, was it not?"

"Aye," Ryan replied sadly and took a drink. He turned to look at the fire and for a moment lost himself in its flames. "Shannon was indeed her name."

"Yes," Sartine offered softly and reached over to touch Ryan's arm. "To capture your heart as she did, well, she must have been beyond compare, someone very special. I regret we shall never meet. I am sorry for your loss, Luke." He paused for an awkward moment to watch the fire with Ryan and then asked, in an upbeat tone, "there was a young woman here earlier, a rare beauty herself, Jacqueline I believe is her name?"

Ryan nodded.

"Well, you have exceptionally good taste in women my friend. I sent her and that Nubian giant of yours off to run an errand for the afternoon, to allow us some privacy. I trust you take no offense?"

"You are welcome in my home, always, David. I call you brother."

"And, in all honesty, you are mine. I understand you recently returned to Ireland briefly? To... settle... some old business accounts?"

A smile, nothing friendly, touched Ryan's lips. Sartine saw the dark shadow pass across Ryan's face.

"As always, David, you are well-informed, my friend."

"Yes, well, we shall speak of it no more. How do your wounds heal? You look fit enough to me!"

"I'm well, thank you. And I am grateful for your Parisian physician and all his special medicines, most kind of you. I'm certain he cost a pretty penny."

"This was nothing. Now, as time is short, and we yet have some drinking to do, I must be brief and explain to you my purpose here. First, of course, I wish to say *au revoir* to my dear friend! It may be sometime before we meet again. More importantly, I bring urgent news.

As I say, I return to sea. Not my favorite duty. No winsome, enchanting women to warm my bed. No absurdly extravagant balls or sumptuous feasts requiring me presence. Bad food - worse bad wine! Poor hygiene, obnoxious smells - and, good God, obnoxious commanding officers! And, of course, there are the ubiquitous hazards to contend with on board any warship. Ah, the list of hardships one must endure in the navy goes on and on. Alas, the sea is an altogether boring place!"

"Too bad you could not sail with me," offered Ryan. "Our voyages are short and, I dare say, exciting. The money is good too and in between cruises the men have found France to be a most hospitable place."

"Ah, you *pirates* do seem enjoy the good life!" Sartine replied laughing. But then his expression turned serious. "But now, Luke, you must be on your guard. Times have changed. I leave my position in Paris because I will serve my uncle no longer."

"Your uncle, the Minister of Marine?"

"*Oui.* The same. When you and your men were smugglers, and France was not at war, my uncle eagerly sanctioned your work. He looked the other way. No one interfered with your enterprise because of the handsome profits you made for me, the lion's share of which my uncle took - and fairly so. He is the patriarch. I have learned though he is your friend no more. There is no profit in it for him. I am no great patriot, but I have my honor, my scruples, and will serve that man no longer."

"I am not sure I follow, David."

Sartine, as was his habit, took his fingers and smoothed down the tips of his thin, black mustache at the corners of his mouth. "I have come to warn you, Luke."

"Warn me?"

"*Oui.* Your raids against English shipping have been brilliant! And you have done it with such *élan*, with such *panache*! From the moment we first met on board *Toulon*, you recall that fortuitous day, I had you pegged as an exceptional man. If the French Admiralty had any sense, had just one admiral with any brains, they would have offered you a command of a French frigate - or better - make you a commodore of a whole fleet! Your escapades are talked about in the best salons in Paris. The ladies are always quite impressed when I tell them that I am the friend of the famous Captain Ryan! Why the Queen herself inquires about you! You have certainly brought honor to your new country. Perhaps, you have done your work too well?"

"How so, David?"

"Luke, *mon ami*, you have attracted the attention of many powerful people both in England and in France. Even in war, England and France maintain certain, shall we say, trade arrangements beneficial to them both. Profitable business does not stop because of the inconvenience of war. *Comprendvoius?* As Minister of Marine, my uncle is privy to such arrangements and I have no doubt he personally profits from them all. Your fierce attacks on British shipping have caused financial damage not only to many in England, but to some in France as well. To my uncle, you are an asset no longer. You are, in fact, a liability. And my uncle is not, how shall I say? He is not an enlightened individual. Do you understand my meaning?"

"Aye, I believe I do. But America and France are allies in a war against a common enemy. Franklin has issued us legitimate American commissions. I am an American subject now. Sworn to defend my country with the last drop of my blood. We break no laws of France. How is your uncle a threat to me?"

Sartine shook his head, turned to face the fire again. "This, I do not know, Luke. You and I are truly brothers. The bonds that bind us are as strong as any blood. Frankly, I truly have never understood the chemistry. We are so different! My uncle knows that we are friends and so has not confided such things to me. His opinion of me is, well, shortsighted. He sees me as a philanderer, a man with no ambition who enjoys the company of women, enjoys good food and good wine. And so I am! No secret there. But he fails to look beyond the veneer. Alas, he has told me nothing. Still, there is always idle talk in the salons. One picks up bits and pieces of information here and there. I know he met with a man named Stephens, of the British Admiralty, not too long ago, in Oostend. They have been on friendly terms for many years. Both are snakes. Who knows what matters they discussed, what foul schemes they concocted together? I beg you, Luke, do not underestimate my uncle."

"I appreciate your words, your advice, David. I owe you much."

Sartine slapped the armrest of his chair. "Ha! Perhaps for once you do! Before I depart, I have one last gift for you. I know you now have a third raider ready to put to sea. I can arrange a French commission for you. A third share of all prize money would go to the king and a fee, I am certain, would need to be paid to my uncle - discreetly, of course. But I think this would be a safer path for you to travel. I urge you to consider this option, Luke. Well, the time has passed more quickly than I anticipated and I must take my leave of you now. We shall save the drinking for a better day. God go with you always, Luke Ryan. And pray that I do not get myself killed in the Americas... I have too much living in this world yet to do!"

Ryan smiled. "I shall pray for you David, for all the good it will do you! The Almighty, as Pat would tell you if he were here, always seems to take pleasure in listening to an Irishman's prayers - but rarely finds cause to answer them because, they say, He's afraid of the mischief we might cause the world with all that whiskey!"

"Ha! Ha! How true. Well, all will go well for you and we shall meet again. I know it."

"Likewise, David, All will be well for you. I know it."

Sartine stood and put on his cloak. "*Allons*, Luke!"

Ryan chuckled. There was never very much Sartine didn't know. *Allons* was the command Ryan always gave his crew before setting out on a new voyage.

"*Allons*, David!" Ryan replied. He grabbed his coat and walked Sartine through Dunkirk's quiet streets, covered in thick snow now, to the coach that would carry Sartine on to Brest.

The friends embraced one last time and wished each other luck. Ryan hurried back to his hotel room.

He sat at a small table near the fire, dipped his quill in the ink, and began to pen his letter to Franklin. "I persuade myself Your Excellency," he wrote, after first explaining to Franklin that he had been offered a French commission but had declined, "will approve of my refusal and Inclination... and will grant me forthwith the Commission from

Congress I Do Sollicit for the Cutter privateer the fearnot under My Command... I am bold to assure your Excellency that my Cutter manned as she is, may do as much harm to the Enemy as one of Double her force."

Sartine's extraordinary visit touched Ryan. Sartine had traveled a long way. But his friend's warning meant nothing and, as for a French commission, Ryan was indifferent. The French were fighting to enrich a king's glory, the Americans fought to rid themselves from a king's yoke.

He sprinkled sand over the wet ink to help dry it and then sealed the letter with wax. He sent the letter on to Paris by special courier, hoping for a quick response. He was not disappointed.

Several days later, the same courier returned to Dunkirk with Franklin's reply: "I received yours of the 29th, past, am glad to hear that your Health is reestablished and that you got a Vessel that you desire, to which I make no doubt you will do honour by your Bravery and good Conduct... I wish you a prosperous Cruise and safe return with much Profit and Honour." Enclosed with the letter, Ryan found his new commission for the *Fearnot*.

In late March, with the perishables stowed on board and a motley crew of 96 officers and men assembled to sail her, America's newest raider, *Fearnot*, eased her way out of Dunkirk's harbor and into the boundless sea. Only half her crew was Irish. French, Italian, Spanish, Portuguese, Americans, and one African, made up the rest. British intelligence agents, always snooping along the waterfront, watched the new raider sail into the English Channel and sent word of her departure to the Lord Lieutenant of Ireland, warning him "...that Luke Ryan, the former captain of the Black Prince privateer, was to sail from Dunkirk as Captain of another privateer, mounting 18 six and nine-pounders, to cruise, as it is supposed, on the coast of this kingdom."

But Ryan was not headed for Ireland. He had other plans.

Long months had passed since he had been on the rolling waves, had stood on a deck sanded smooth with pride by men who loved their swift, trim ships. And as the barque sliced through the blue waters, the magic returned. Exhilaration and new hope filled him, soothed his troubled soul. The crew could sense their captain's good humor, his enthusiasm for the adventure that lay ahead, and set about their work cheerfully and with high spirits. His crew, one and all, could feel the energy. They were going to strike at the mighty British and with Ryan at the helm, they were going to win and win in grand style!

As land slowly faded from view, Ryan had his officers gather on the quarterdeck. He produced a bottle of rum and glasses and started passing out new promotions all around. He made the Irish giant Kelly his first officer. Kelly had earned the right. Patterson was given the rank of first lieutenant, making him the ship's new second officer. John Kelly was promoted to second lieutenant and shared the position of third officer with a new man named John Trevett, an American Yankee from Rhode Island, who had signed on board just moments before the ship departed, after having served with the famous Captain John Paul Jones.

Kelly drained his glass and turned to face Jumbaaliyia. He had trained the African well.

Like a huge piece of polished, black granite, Jumbaaliyia, his skin glistening in the warm sunlight, stood proudly at the helm with his huge hands wrapped firmly around the wheel. Unlike Morgan, Jumbaaliyia couldn't talk to ships. But he had Morgan's gift for coaxing the most out of them and *Fearnot* glided effortlessly through the arbitrary waters of the storm-tossed sea.

"Look at the man," Kelly said to the other officers. "Like Moses, I swear, if he commanded the waters to part right now, the waves would obey him."

"The Negro does have a certain way about him," Patterson remarked.

"Say thar, Jumbo," Christopher Kelly called out. "Have you seen that big Spaniard, Pepe?"

Jumbaaliyia looked over at Kelly and nodded.

"Some of the lads are puttin' together a wager on who's the strongest man on board. Thar's talk of settin' up a wrestlin' match and a prize purse for the winner. You interested? The winner would have the pleasure of takin' me on next. Whatcha say? Winner takes all?"

Jumbaaliyia thought on Kelly's words for a moment. "Aye, Mr. Kelly, you would be a challenge."

"Ha! Ha! Ha!" Kelly roared. "Spoken like an Irishman! You've got grit lad! I like that, but first you've got to get through the Spaniard. You seen his arms? As thick and as hard as a ship's spar."

Jumbaaliyia smiled thoughtfully, tended to his work and said no more.

Ryan set a course to take them north. Short ventures into the Irish Sea no longer interested him. He had in mind something more daring, something on a scale to match his mood - and his mood for once was grand.

"Mind tellin' us where we're goin', Luke?" Kelly asked.

"Gentlemen, I'm taking *Fearnot* into the German Ocean where Captain Jones did so well several months ago. I intend to sail around the whole of England, Scotland and Wales and capture or sink every ship we cross."

John Kelly whistled. "*Jesus*, Luke, you get bolder and bolder every time we put out. I swear one of these days you'll have us sailin' up the Thames to storm the Tower of London!"

"Now there's a thought," Ryan said and smiled. "Better spread the word down the line. This ship is sailing well and I intend a long cruise."

"You don't want me to assemble the lads, Luke?" Kelly asked.

Ryan shook his head. His tough Irish veterans and the grizzled American patriots didn't need a rousing speech and the rest, the *foreigners* as the Irishmen liked to call them, would only grumble. It galled Ryan that he had to worry about the loyalty of any man on board his ship. He no longer had the luxury of a completely trustworthy crew and knew he would need to keep a wary eye out.

"Unless you're desperate to hear one, no speech, Chris."

Kelly grinned. "I suspect not, sir. The German Ocean it is..."

Rising out of the depths of the German Ocean, midway between Orkney and Shetland, is a small spec of rock barely large enough to have earned the title island. Known as Fair Isle, from the old Norse *Frjóey*, little is fair at that northern latitude. But this is where the men of the *Fearnot* sighted fair game, where they took their first prize. Ryan ordered English colors hoisted and *Fearnot* easily overtook and pounced on the large brig *Noble Anne*, making her way from Greenland and bound for the River Tyne. Ryan removed her English crew and sent the brig on to Bergen in nearby neutral Denmark, a province of Norway, with a prize crew on board.

But after taking the *Anne* the Irishmen sailed on for long days without spotting one sail. Frustrated, Ryan finally gave the order to turn south and took his ship and crew through the Hebrides in search of fresh victims along Ireland's northern coast. But the Irishmen found those waters just as barren as the German Ocean.

When boredom set in, Kelly organized a bit of entertainment and the crew was treated to a glimpse of an age long past, where men were larger, stronger and far more fearsome. They were given a glimpse of a time when the weakest warrior could lift and hurtle a huge boulder across a field that the strongest man today, as weak as men are now, could hardly budge.

The crew gathered straw and blankets and laid them across the main hatch grating. Then they tossed a tarp over the blankets to fashion a crude wrestling mat and formed a circle, made wagers and cheered their champions on. Two towering behemoths, stripped to the waist and bare-foot, stepped into the ring. John Kelly blew a whistle and the match was on.

Massive arms, rippling in thick muscle, grappled and locked together. Both men turned in a circle, the wrestler's dance, each man looking for the other's weakness, probing, waiting for the moment to throw the other down with a crushing body blow. Long minutes passed as the two combatants grunted, pressed and squeezed. The spectators cheered on.

The African, taller, leaner, his ebony skin slick with sweat, locked eyes on his opponent and never blinked - eyes of pure determination. The Spaniard, called the *Bear* by his shipmates, had a stocky build and was much heavier. Thick brown hair covered his chest, his neck and arms.

The Spaniard snorted loudly through a large nose, crooked at the bridge, a trophy from some previous fight, and summoned up all his brute strength to try and lift the African off his feet but failed. Jumbaaliyia matched the Spaniard strength for strength.

And then, a few more twists and turns, and Jumbaaliyia saw his opportunity and made his move. He managed to free one leg and tripped the Spaniard. Down the Spaniard tumbled. Jumbaaliyia fell on top of the Bear to try and pin him but the Spaniard wasn't finished yet, pushed his arms up hard into the African's chest, flipping him, and Jumbaaliyia went sailing over the Spaniard's head.

And then the Spaniard, feeling cocky and ignoring the African now behind him - a fool's mistake - struggled to get back up on his feet. The Bear should have turned around first to see where his opponent had landed.

With god-like speed, Jumbaaliyia sprang to his feet. Like some panther poised to spring, he coiled his body into a low crouch and lunged at the Spaniard from behind. He brought his huge arms up through the Spaniard's armpits, wrapping them around his thick neck, and slowly forced the Bear down to his knees. The spectators gasped at the African's display of raw power. The more the Spaniard struggled the tighter the African's grip. Exhausted and gasping for air, the Spaniard finally nodded and yielded. Winners cheered and losers grumbled.

Kelly helped the dazed Spaniard up, beaming. "A fine effort thar, Pepe," he said, slapping the Bear on the back. "A great match - you'll get him next time."

Then Kelly looked over at Jumbaaliyia and winked. "Well now, Jumbo. Truly an extraordinary example of how the sport should be played. When yer up to it lad, we'll see how you fair against an *Irishman*."

Jumbaaliyia smiled, with just a hint of arrogance.

But then the crew froze. Everyone looked up at the lookout high in the masthead.

"*Sail ho!*" Amati cried out.

"Where away, lad?" Kelly shouted.

"Portside, dead amidships. Large sloop. She's sailin' straight for us."

On board the English letter of marque, *Friends*, Captain John Sinclair, paced back and forth along the quarterdeck, debating what to do. He was about to take his ship across the Atlantic for Quebec when his lookout spotted a large barque flying the Union Jack on the horizon, a ship neither he nor any of his men recognized.

Sinclair had a long sail ahead of him and was tempted to ignore the barque. But he could see that she was French-built, which he thought queer, and he was well acquainted with the reports of American privateers operating in English waters. And while no privateer had been seen so far north, he knew his duty and he had the firepower to handle anything smaller than a frigate.

The two ships closed fast and when they were within hailing distance, Ryan brashly ordered the English captain to shorten sail, to standby to be boarded. Sinclair refused and instead demanded to know what ship the barque was and ordered Ryan to shorten sail so that he could inspect the barque's papers.

Ryan smiled at the Englishman and shook his head no.

Sinclair, no slouch, quickly barked out orders to his men to sheer off, to swing there vessel around. And then he gave the order for battle and his men cleared the deck for action, readied their heavy guns. If there was to be a fight, he wanted to put some distance between his ship and the barque to give himself time to think things through. His ship was fast and well-armed and he had a full platoon of Royal Marines on board being transported west to fight in the Colonies, but the barque looked formidable. She was no smuggler's coaster.

On board *Fearnot*, men scrambled to clear the deck for action too. Ryan ordered a single warning shot fired across the bow of the English ship as she began to pull away.

But Sinclair was a seasoned veteran - he had never lost a fight - and his Englishmen were no strangers to the bloody grind of war. Sinclair ignored the warning shot, regarded the gesture as no more than empty bluster.

The privateers could hear the beating of a drum as the English scrambled to put their ship in fighting trim. Then Royal Marines, looking sharp in their red jackets and white cross-belts, poured out on deck - a whole platoon! And when the drummer rested, the sound of cannon cracked the sky.

BOOM! BA-BA-BOOM!

Friends was first to open fire with a full broadside.

The sage tactician, churning out plots and plans, ignored the English barb, not one shot struck home. Ryan calmly issued his battle orders, his cocky privateers were all too glad to treat the English to a brawl. Ryan hauled down the Union Jack himself and ran up the stars and stripes while his men stood anxiously by their big guns, waiting for their orders. And when the order came, the Irishmen more than paid the English back in kind.

"*FIRE!*" Patterson shouted.

BA-BA-BA-BOOOOOOOOOOOOM!

If the English had any notions of an easy fight, of taking a quick prize, the boom - the precision - of the privateer's heavy cannon quickly dispelled any such overweening arrogance. Half of *Fearnot's* first salvo struck some part of the English sloop. The English crew chalked the enemy's marksmanship up to dumb luck and fired off a second broadside. But again not one ball struck home. With supplies of shot and gunpowder rationed for the war, English gunners were out of practice. The barque's men, moving even quicker, followed suit and did the same. They fired off a second, well-placed volley and again half their iron struck wood. That was when the English first began wishing they had just let the barque sail on.

Ryan could feel the excitement, the awesome power inside him rising. His whole body tingled with anticipation. His talent was for war and he knew it. It was his gift, the skill he excelled at above all others.

He reached for his spyglass and carefully studied his opponent. The heavy sloop-of-war was impressive, her crew disciplined and she had an unusual number of marines on board. Ryan considered the strength of the enemy, the size and number of his guns, the effectiveness his gun crews and watched how well the sloop's captain handled his ship rolling atop the heaving seas. The Englishman knew his business but his gunners were slow and poor marksmen. Ryan made some quick calculations for current, wind and speed, and then checked his watch. Four o'clock. Plenty of time to do what had to be done and with no land in sight, no ships on the horizon to interfere with their lethal contest.

The two prizefighters were bound together in a death match with nowhere to run, nowhere to hide. That was good. *Very good indeed*, Ryan thought to himself because, before the sun laid down its golden crown, it would be the English aching to see a friendly sail, wishing a friendly port were close by...

Kelly went forward to take charge of *Fearnot's* guns. Patterson was good but he was better. He bellowed out his orders down the line like some raging bull. "Easy thar. Steady. Watch yer linstocks. Wait. Wait. On the swell... Make ready! *FIRE!*"

BOOM! BOOM! BA-BA-BOOM! BOOM! BOOM!

Tongues of red flame reached out over the waves. Hot gases cracked the sky. Heavy iron punched through the air. Clouds of white smoke rolled over the deck obscuring, for a brief moment, the English sloop.

With eyes full of fire, Kelly strutted up and down the line of booming cannon and urged men on, stopping here and there to lend a helping hand where needed. He shared his captain's burning desire to take a British warship. If sheer force of will could have done the trick, there would have been no need for battle. But more than strong will is needed for mortals to move mountains.

For the first hour the two ships stood off a ways and exchanged broadside after broadside, their captains both content to simply slug away at each other. Ryan had his Irish and American veterans at the guns - American steel honed with a fine Irish edge - and their ferocity knew no bounds. They worked their nine and six-pounders like demons, striking fearful blow after blow against the sloop, relentless, no mercy. Ryan used his foreigners, under the watchful eye of John Kelly, up in the rigging as topmen. The Kelly brothers had trained them hard and the foreigners worked the sails and braces with a fearlessness that impressed even Ryan. The topmen, trimming sails and repairing lines, seemed oblivious to English shots whizzing by.

The English fought stubbornly and bravely for their king. But *Fearnot's* hull proved too thick for English iron. English balls by the score bounced off her side. Sinclair proved himself a worthy opponent, maneuvering his ship skillfully, but Ryan's gunners far outclassed his own and worked their heavy guns with grisly efficiency. One Englishman fell wounded, and then another and another...

And then CRACK! That hideous sound that brings no joy to the heart of any sailor - the sound of splintering wood - was heard by all. The sloop's foremast suddenly split in two and a good length of wood tumbled into the sea, taking the topgallant sail and spar along with it. The sloop staggered from the blow. Her trim lacked balance and she began losing precious speed.

Ryan, with no mercy in his heart with enemy guns still blazing, still belching out deadly iron, saw his chance for glory. He used the wind and *Fearnot's* speed to maximum advantage. *Fearnot* pulled ahead of her hobbled opponent, then turned in to cut across the sloop's bow. Kelly and his gunners stood ready and at close range raked the sloop's weak spot with brutal iron. Both ship and crew took an appalling pounding. One well-placed ball broke the Friend's bowsprit. Two more balls punched holes through her hull below the waterline. Cold seawater began pouring in, more water than the sloop's pumps could handle, and that took all the fight out of her crew.

Sinclair slipped below deck to determine the extent of the damage. Once he saw the volume of water gushing in, he knew they were in real trouble. He made some quick calculations and concluded his ship was doomed if they continued to fight on, down to the bottom she would go. It was a matter of simple mathematics, of physics, of the law of buoyancy and displaced fluid as first espoused by Archimedes of Syracuse. A ship's density must be less than the water it displaces or else it will sink as any child knows.

Sinclair returned to the deck with a dour face. He had done all that honor and duty required. His men, obedient to his will, still serviced their guns, still desperately trying to inflict some mortal blow on the American vessel as she came around again. But this day was not theirs for glory. The English captain took in the dirty, sweaty faces of his men and then considered the rest of the damage to his ship. The topgallant sail was gone, shot away. The bowsprit had splinted and the jib sail sat on the deck in a crumpled heap, splattered with the blood and gore of wounded men resting against it. Miraculously, no one, so far, had been killed.

He removed his pocket watch, a gift from a loving wife waiting for him in Plymouth, and popped open its gilded cover. Six o'clock. Darkness was near but not near enough and his ship in any case was now too slow to slither away. He scanned the horizon with his spyglass next, trying desperately to find a friendly sail but saw only empty water.

He cursed his foul luck and gave his first officer a nod. His first officer understood his captain's grim gesture and gave the order - the unfair, wretched order - to cease fire. A peaceful calm instantly settled over the English ship.

Ryan watched in stunned silence as Englishmen stepped away from their guns, as the English warship struck her colors. He gave the order to cease fire as the English raised a white flag off the stern halyard.

Finally, finally he had captured a British warship! *Fearnot's* men cheered wildly. His Irishmen and their American brothers saw triumph and glory. His foreigners saw only money. But either way the English warship, a handsome prize, was theirs...

"*Lieutenant Kelly!*" Ryan cried out excitedly, unable to hide his jubilation.

Kelly was readying his guns for another round just in case the enemy was inclined to pull some dirty trick. He turned to look at Ryan, saw the sparkle in Ryan's eyes.

"My compliments to you and your lads! As good a piece of work as I've ever seen, Chris. Joyous day! Well done!"

Kelly cracked a wide grin and touched the brim of his hat. Like a proud father, he was happy to see Ryan have this day. No man deserved it more.

"Looks like we've finally humbled these English dogs, sir. A great day indeed, Capt'n!"

"Aye, a great day. Have John lower a boat away. If thar's any trouble - you know what to do."

Kelly gave a nod. He knew what to do all right. He would pummel the sloop, shatter her to pieces and send her to the bottom.

"You'll be leadin' the party, sir?" asked Kelly with hesitation, but already knew the answer even before Ryan nodded back.

Kelly didn't care much for Ryan boarding an enemy battle cruiser with only a handful of Irishmen at his side, even with the sloop's men pulling in their guns and closing the port lids shut as a good faith gesture, he had doubts. But he knew it would be useless to try and stop him. This was Ryan's shining moment. Still, he sent his brother John along to watch over the man who was like a son.

Though he tried to conceal his joy, lest it be mistaken for gloating, Ryan stepped aboard his new prize beaming. True, she was not a great warship, not a ship of the line or even a Sixth Rate frigate that a king might miss. But she was a dangerous warship nonetheless and she had been taken by one of Franklin's raiders. There was glory enough to relish that...

Sinclair greeted Ryan with a cordial smile, without any bitterness in his heart. The American had the better ship and crew and simply outfought him. The two captains exchanged salutes.

"Welcome aboard, sir. My name is John Sinclair and I command His Britannic Majesty's Ship *Friends*. If I may be blunt, this vessel is in imminent danger of sinking. It would seem pointless for us to continue this little scrap of ours today. We will need to be quick about it if we are to try and save her. This day is yours Captain - you have the better gunners, the better ship. My compliments to you and your crew, sir. A fine display of seamanship. If you are in a position to offer the customary terms - we best not dawdle."

"Agreed. Customary terms."

"Very well then. The ship is yours. Would you do me the honor sir of giving me your name and title?"

Ryan slipped into his refined English accent. "I am Luke Ryan, master of the American corsair *Fearnot* under the commission of his

Excellency Benjamin Franklin, at your service, sir..."

Sinclair gave Ryan a suspicious look. "Ryan? *Ryan*... I've heard that name before. Aye, of course! How foolish of me. I've read about your exploits in the Irish Sea. But enlighten me, sir, is not your ship the *Black Prince?*"

"Aye. Just so. But the *Prince* is now under the command of one of my subordinates. No doubt the *Prince* is stirring up some mischief for your king somewhere in the Irish Sea just about now along with her escort, the *Black Princess*. If I may inquire, what is the extent of damage to your ship?"

"Of course. I am your most humble servant, sir. I think it best if I take you below, so you can judge matters for yourself. But first, sir, protocol requires it: my sword..."

Sinclair undid the buckle to his belt and offered Ryan his sword and scabbard.

But Ryan refused the trophy. "No, sir. I must respectfully decline. You and your men have served your king and country with honor and gallantry on this fine day. You keep your sword. I'm certain you have earned it and you shall no doubt have need of it again, for another day, for some other battle."

Sinclair bowed his head in thanks. His lieutenant leaned close to his ear and whispered, "This Irish brigand not only has talents to match our best, sir, but knows chivalry. He conducts himself like some refined English lord."

"Beg pardon, what was that, Lieutenant?" Ryan asked, unable to hear what the man was whispering to Sinclair.

Sinclair offered a reassuring smile. "A compliment to your gallantry only. Shall we?"

As Ryan followed Sinclair around his ship, his Irishmen began disarming English sailors. Ryan could feel the deck begin to list. He saw the wounded sitting against the bulwarks with bloody dressings too.

"Your guns are well-served, Captain Ryan," observed Sinclair as he pointed out the damage here and there to his ship. "My compliments again. Why one would think you and your men were veterans of the

British Royal Navy."

Ryan offered the Englishman only the thinnest of smiles.

"Something must be done with the topgallant," Sinclair continued. And some rigging shall need replacing as you can plainly see. Of more urgency are the two holes below her waterline. She's heavy in the well I'm afraid with about two or three feet of water already. Would you happen to have a good carpenter and spare planks on board your ship?"

"Indeed we do. Mr. Kelly, instruct the carpenter to come over at once, better remind the man to bring his tools. And have the surgeon brought over as well to lend a hand with the wounded here."

"Aye, aye, sir!"

"Your crew suffered no casualties?" Sinclair asked.

"No, we were most fortunate."

Sinclair raised an eyebrow. "Indeed."

Fearnot's carpenter hurried over to *Friends* and wasted no time patching up the holes as best he could. Just before midnight he declared the sloop seaworthy. But Ryan, back on board the *Fearnot* and entertaining Sinclair, having seen the steel blue-gray clouds gathering on the horizon earlier just before sunset, was not so sure. The smell of rain was in the air and the winds, coming out of the north, were freshening, turning blustery. Any prudent sailor would have waited until morning before setting out to determine *Friends's* true condition. But Ryan had no desire to remain stationary, to tarry too long in the same waters, and discussed sinking the sloop with his officers.

Several French crewmen overheard him - they had been away from home long enough. Roaming the open seas for a week or two to capture unarmed merchantmen was one thing, sailing for an extended cruise and taking on British warships was something else again. They had signed aboard with Ryan for easy money and had no desire to die for the freedom of a land inhabited by backward pioneers some 3,000 miles away. The sloop-of-war presented them with an opportunity. They concocted a plan amongst themselves, a plan to get home early, and with money in their pockets.

A small contingent of three Frenchmen approached Ryan, told him that they spoke for all 21 French sailors on board, that they had enough, and rudely demanded Ryan spare the sloop. They insisted that he agree to release them, allow them to sail the sloop back to France.

Ryan listened politely as Kelly, standing next to him, caressed a pistol hidden inside his jacket, ready for any trouble. The giant could have put a musket ball between the eyes of the ringleader and slept peacefully that night. But Ryan, after the French ignored his warnings about the incoming hostile weather, relented, glad to be rid of these discontented men.

And so 21 Frenchmen rowed over to the sloop just as a light rain began to fall. The French set sails, manned the pumps, and headed due east on, taking the shortest route for France.

Sinclair had listened to the exchange between Ryan and his French sailors with interest. Ryan's cool handling of a potentially ugly situation impressed the Englishman. He moved over to the rail, stood next to Ryan and watched his sloop sail off.

"Even with her holes patched up, she's still got near six feet of water in her wells by now Captain Ryan - or so I overheard your carpenter say," Sinclair offered.

"You are correct, Captain."

"And see over there, on the horizon?" Sinclair asked, pointing towards a line of advancing clouds with silent lightening. "That angry looking mass to the west? Even in the dark, you can still make out the downpour of heavy rains from here. I'll wager that we are looking at a squall line blowing hard this way."

Ryan nodded.

"Those Frogs of yours," Sinclair chuckled, "unless they seek shelter somewhere along Scotland's coast, will never make it back to France."

"For their sake, I pray you are wrong, Captain Sinclair. I can, however, sir, find no fault with anything you say. I did try to reason with them."

Sinclair shook his head, disgusted. *Save me from all Frenchmen and their ignorance.* While the loss of French sailors was of no particular concern to him, he felt sorrow for any pointless waste of life.

"Damn hot-headed Gauls," Sinclair muttered to himself, but loud enough for Ryan to hear him. "Always acting on impulse, always letting their hearts do their thinking for them."

"They are." replied Ryan. "A curious people but, in truth, aren't we all?"

"A fair point," Sinclair chuckled as the doomed ship with her doomed crew fade into the blackness.

An hour after midnight a squall of frightening raw power, unstoppable, broke over the *Fearnot*. How that cold bitch North Wind, her heart forever filled with overflowing contempt, disdains all mortals. None - but one of the ancient gods perhaps - can ever hope to outrace her cruel fury. No, never. Sheets of blinding rain slashed at the frail ship made of wood and canvas and icy winds howled with an anger to put fear into the bravest heart. But the men of the *Fearnot*, no strangers to hardship, and brothers in desperation, spent a restless night keeping their vessel intact. And in the morning, North Wind, grudgingly, allowed the Irishmen to pass - in tribute to their skill and bravery. The good ship *Friends* and her crew, however, were less fortunate. Neither the ship nor her 21 Frenchmen were ever seen again.

After several days of cruising off Barra Head in calmer seas, *Fearnot* caught her third prize. She was the *Jean* from Liverpool bound for Lubeck with a cargo of salt. She was a rich prize, but Ryan was down to 69 men with English prisoners from *Friends* to worry about and could spare no man for a prize crew. So Ryan brought the *Jean's* master into his cabin to settle on the terms of ransom.

Ryan treated the man cordially, offered him what he considered a fair price but *Jean's* old master was a cantankerous sort and his mind could not be turned. He refused to agree on any amount. Sinclair quietly sipped his wine, amused by watching the two men spar.

"No, sir, Mr. Ryan," said the *Jean's* master with a scowl on his face. "I'll not pay five thousand guineas for *Jean*. You've served me here with mellow wine and tasty food and when yer lips move I hears such polite words come out of yer mouth - but no matter how you cut it, yer still just a common, stinkin' thief. Sink the poor old *Jean* if that's yer pleasure. I'd rather see her on the bottom of the ocean than see you get yer dirty hands on her. That's me final word on the matter."

"As you wish, sir. You'll soon bear witness that I am not a man given to idle bluffing. I'll set the torch to your ship within the hour if we cannot come to terms, and see you and your men in a French jail. But I fail to see how either one of us profits that way. Oh well. Please, finish your meal first and then we'll go on deck and entertain ourselves by watching her burn. Whether I ransom her or light her up, my purposes are served either way..."

Now it was Sinclair who saw an opportunity. "Ahem. Pardon me, gentlemen. Captain Ryan, if I may, you have treated me graciously these past few days. Our countries are at war, yes, and you, with the better ship and crew, outfought my own. A few months back I had the good fortune of intercepting an American brig and I took her as a prize. The glory was all mine that day. Ah well, that was then and this in now. Such are the shifting fortunes of war. And here I sit - a prisoner. I hold no grudge. As I listen to you gentlemen debate back and forth, I am struck by an idea though. Perhaps I can be of some service to you both, offer a solution to this impasse."

Ryan looked over at the English master and smiled. Ryan had liked the Sinclair from the very first, from when Sinclair had first fired on his ship, doing his best to fight the better-armed privateer off. More, the cocky Englishman had dared to try and win.

Ryan narrowed his eyes. He tried to appear all business, all serious but, inside, he was feeling giddy. It was all so much fun.

"By all means Captain, do tell us of your plan. You have seemed to me these past few days to be a man of good, clear sense. You must have a wee bit of Irish blood in you. I take it we'll be doing a bit of haggling here?"

Sinclair smiled. "Five thousand guineas seems a trifle much for the *Jean* to me, but, I concede, it is by no means an outrageous sum. I doubt very much the good master here will pay any price you offer. His decision appears final and I take the man for his word: that he will not be persuaded otherwise. I shall not be a bore, try to haggle over price. Would you consider allowing me, Captain Ryan, to purchase *Jean*? I believe as of this moment the *Jean*'s master has forfeited all rights to his ship. Seems a shame, as you have said, to burn such a handsome vessel.

I'll sign your ransom note and pay it too once I'm back in England. On my oath, I will. Parole me a crew and I'll do my utmost to see to it that they honor their obligations as well."

Ryan would not have thought it possible. The scowl on the old man's face turned even more ugly.

Jean's master blew his nose on his shirtsleeve and cleared his throat. "What the devil are you talkin' about Sinclair!" he blurted out angrily across the table, the veins in his neck bulging. "That's my ship you're tryin' to buy from this rogue pirate capt'n who didn't come by her proper. He stole it. It an't his to sell damn you! I'd keep my mouth shut if I was you. Yer bein' the capt'n of one of the king's royal navy ships don't give you no authority to buy my ship. Buy yer own damn ship back if you have a mind to waste yer money..."

Ryan and Sinclair exchanged glances and both men ignored the *Jean's* difficult master.

"I beg to differ with you, sir," Sinclair replied without troubling himself to face the man. "Rules of the sea and all that. It would appear to me that you have abandoned your ship and that gives the finder certain salvage rights. Captain Ryan, do you accept my offer? Shall we shake on it?"

Ryan thought Sinclair's offer over for a bit. Sinclair was a schemer, a man after his own heart. But the man appeared to have a sense of honor too. Ryan couldn't help but like the Englishman, or his plan for freedom.

"Done, Captain Sinclair!" declared Ryan happily. "But I'll require a signed written parole from each English sailor and marine - and I shall expect every man to live up to the terms of his parole."

"Agreed," Sinclair answered warmly. "With pleasure, Captain Ryan, I shall sign the first parole myself and you shall have my word, as an officer of the king's Royal Navy, and as a gentleman, that I shall honor it!"

Taking paroles at sea was contrary to Franklin's instructions, as Ryan well knew. Franklin wanted live, warm bodies as the British continued to refuse to recognize even written paroles. It troubled Ryan to go against Franklin's wishes. But the old man simply did not understand the logistics of Ryan's own precarious situation. The privateers simply could not provide for so many prisoners so far away from friendly shores and so Ryan decided to parole all his prisoners at once to make room for more.

After Ryan and Sinclair shook hands, Sinclair quickly disappeared to gather his men. Before going over the side, Sinclair snapped to attention and saluted.

"I do believe, sir," he said to Ryan with a smile, "that our English papers have treated you unfairly. I have found you to be a brave and gallant opponent and a courteous jailer to boot. It has been my privilege to make your acquaintance and, though I cannot wish you good luck in your future endeavors against my country, I do wish *you* well, Captain Ryan. Godspeed to you, sir."

"Thank you, Captain Sinclair," Ryan replied with his own smile. "I trust," he continued, pausing long enough to wink, "that you'll keep your kind remarks about my character to yourself. Such news of my courteous ways would be contrary to my goals."

"Ha! Quite so! Your reputation is safe with me. Should anyone ask me, you're a most despicable villain! *Au revoir...*"

Sinclair and his men were ferried over to the *Jean* and the Englishmen wasted no time getting their new ship underway and headed south-east, heading home for England. Ryan and his men then turned south, hoping to find and rendezvous with Dowlin and Macatter. The three privateers sailing out together would make an imposing force!

Along the way *Fearnot* intercepted another merchant ship, the *Fortitude*, in blustery winds off the island of Canna. She was a modest vessel on her way to Hull from Workington and loaded down with iron ore. Ryan ransomed the ship and cargo, took one sailor as a hostage and paroled all the rest.

Once the *Jean* and *Fortitude* made port, the bitter news about a third American privateer being on the loose, and cruising the northern waters of the Empire, traveled fast. No one could remember a time when maritime trade was more dangerous. Insurance rates were skyrocketing and some ships' masters were even refusing to put to sea until something was done. To many in London, and in towns along the coast, it seemed the vaunted Royal Navy was inept. There was rising frustration, even panic.

As the English debated what to do, Ryan, having had no luck finding and rendezvousing with Dowlin or Macatter, decided to return back to France to take on more provisions and more men. *Fearnot* sailed triumphantly into Dunkirk Road in early May and fluttering in the breeze off her stern line halyard, just below the American stars and stripes, was a distinctive, green pennant with a single, diagonal white stripe. A red, three leaf clover adorned the top corner of the pennant and embroidered on the bottom was the French *fleur de lys* in white. The pennant was Ryan's own design and had been stitched together for him by Shannon. It was his victory flag - to proudly announce to all the world that his privateers had taken on and beaten a British warship...

Fourteen
Treachery

hile Ryan was exploring the German Ocean with his new battle cruiser, and winning new glory, Macatter and Dowlin were having great fun in the Irish Sea, plundering enemy ships and snagging sorry Englishmen. They took many prizes and prisoners by the score. But they were forced to end their lucrative cruise early and sailed back to Morlaix. The poor *Princess* was taking on too much water. She was a broken ship, too old and worn to put to sea again for combat. Macatter sent word on to Torris in Dunkirk that he needed a new raider.

A few hours after docking their vessels, a short, potbellied man in rumpled, civilian clothes, but strutting around the wharf with an air of authority - and with 20 armed militiamen at his back - boarded the *Black Prince* at midnight. It was his duty as the town's commissary officer to comb the land with royal press gangs from time to time, looking to fill the royal levies for the navy. For a reasonable fee, however, the Commissary of Morlaix had always warned his better patrons of his coming in advance and the Irish were among his very best. But now Morlaix's commissary was acting on strict orders directly from Paris and gave no such warning this time.

The sound of boots scuffing against the deck roused Dowlin from a sound and peaceful sleep. A copy of the London *Chronicle* slid off his chest as he sat upright in his bunk. Before dozing off he had been reading a report from Truro in Cornwall claiming that "...the Black Prince privateer, which has made such havoc, and caused such fears in the coasting trade, is this morning brought into Falmouth by the Aurora frigate." The story had brought a smile to his lips, though he hoped Ryan hadn't seen the paper yet lest Ryan worry the news was true. Oh how the English liked lie!

Dowlin rubbed the sleep from his eyes and quickly dressed. He grabbed two pistols off a shelf over his bunk and a cutlass hanging from a hook on the door and made his way topside where he found Morgan, who had the night watch, talking to a Frenchman with an armed escort.

"Mr. Dowlin, good evenin', sir," Morgan offered carefully. "I was just about to fetch you. This here gentleman says he's *Monsieur* de Champlain. Says he's the Commissary of Morlaix. I was tryin' to explain to *Monsieur* Champlain that this is an American ship and that he can't be bringin' armed men aboard without permission."

Dowlin nodded. *Gawd*, he thought to himself, how he hated dealing with French *bureaucrats*. He immediately recognized the commissary. He had paid the man and had paid him well in the past for one favor or another. He tried to manage a friendly grin. *The next time I fight some bloody war, I pray it's against the bloody French.*

"Yer Excellency," Dowlin began cheerfully, addressing the man as politely as he knew how. He eyed the militiamen, dressed in black shakos and dark blue jackets with red piping and white cross belts, standing behind the commissary.

A young sublieutenant formed his men into two rows, and then had them unsling their muskets and stand at rest. Dowlin didn't like what he was seeing.

"*Monsieur* Dowlin, good evening to you, sir," Champlain answered without his usual humor.

"What brings you here out into the chilly, night air and away from yer wife's warm bed, hey?" Dowlin asked. "And with armed men at yer back too? We've done business together before. Have we ever given you any offense? None at all, I'd say. No need for armed men now. We're all friends here and allies after all."

"*Monsieur* Dowlin, I do regret boarding your ship in this way. But I have orders and my orders are very clear, quite precise. Among your crew, I am to remove all French citizens and they are forthwith discharged from any obligation to you. Now, please assemble any Frenchmen in your service on deck and instruct them to follow me at once."

"Sir," Dowlin began to protest, "these men have been recruited legally and I must -"

"Enough!" Champlain erupted nervously. "The matter has already been settled by powers beyond us. I have my king's orders. Please, Dowlin, for your own sake, do it, do it now."

Champlain stepped closer to Dowlin. "My hands are tied my friend." he whispered into Dowlin's ear. "Make no trouble, I beg you. The men with me tonight are not my own. The young sublieutenant there would gladly shoot you down. He's indifferent. To say anything more in present company could be dangerous for us both."

Champlain stepped back and resumed his defiant manner. "There will be no further discussion," he said gruffly. "If you have complaints, you may petition the French Admiralty in the morning for relief if that's your pleasure. Now, sir, you shall do as I have instructed. I have the legal authority and you have no choice."

Champlain's last words rang true and so Dowlin sighed and gave the order. Morgan went below to gather all French hands. And as Dowlin's Frenchmen, still half-asleep, stumbled on deck they saw the French press gang waiting. The sight brought no man any joy. They stared down at their feet, dejected. Champlain lined the unhappy French sailors up in single file and marched them down the gangplank, then quickly disappeared into the darkness like a thief in the night with his loot.

Dowlin was left with a compliment of only 53 officers and men. Not enough for a warship of *Prince's* size to go out raiding and so in the morning he sent word of his predicament off to Torris.

After receiving Macatter's letter first, Torris sent one of his agents, a man named de Chautereyne, off to Cherbourg to purchase a suitable replacement for the *Princess*. Chautereyne quickly found a beauty and Macatter marched his men across the peninsula from Morlaix to Cherbourg to go and claim her. She was a well-constructed vessel and carried eighteen six-pounders, two nine pounders and thirty swivels. With handsome profits rolling in, Torris had spared no expense this time around. Macatter christened his new ship with his old ship's name, the *Black Princess*, allowing him to sail under the same commission from Franklin.

With Macatter and his men in Cherbourg, readying their new battle cruiser for action, Dowlin, unable to replace his French losses in

Morlaix, headed out to sea for Dunkirk, hoping to recruit new men there. Dunkirk was a far larger port than Morlaix with a friendlier commissary.

Skirting around the windward side of the Channel Islands, just north of Normandy, the *Prince's* men sighted a very fine brig. The Irishmen hadn't expected to do any hunting during their short ferry cruise up the French coast, but they couldn't resist taking another prize. The nimble *Prince* ran the fat merchantman down with ease. Dowlin boarded the brig himself to inspect her papers. She was the *Flora* from Holland and that made her a neutral. But according to her papers, which her master, Henry Rodenberg did not dispute, her cargo of grain, drugs and spices were destined for merchants in Dublin and that, Dowlin reasoned, made her cargo fair game. So he decided to seize the *Flora*, put a prize crew on board and sent her off to nearby Cherbourg.

But Dowlin, superb soldier and master tactician, true, was ignorant in matters of foreign diplomacy. Little did he know the *Flora* would set off an international crisis that would bring the privateers nothing good.

Not long after taking the *Flora*, the *Prince's* lookout spotted yet another fine looking merchantman. She was close to shore off the Picardy coast and sailing lazily in a westerly direction. Dowlin couldn't believe their good luck! He looked up at the sky and thanked his lucky star - but he had misread the signs...

The privateers put their cutter in battle trim and smartly maneuvered towards the brig. But as they drew closer to their prey and furled sail, *Prince's* lookout reported seeing a second ship. She had been sitting behind a spit of land at the mouth of the River Somme, near Le Hourdel, and hidden from view - until she lumbered forward out into the English Channel under full sail.

"She's a frigate by the cut of her sail, Mr. Dowlin. And she's wearin' around. Masts all in line. She looks French. Wait... Oh shit, Capt'n! She's hoistin' *English colors!*"

Dowlin, never slow to act, snapped his head and barked out new orders to spin his ship around. The Irishmen hung out all their canvas, every stitch, and started sailing north to find shelter in a friendly French port. But the fearsome English frigate's crew had a jump on the Irishmen, had already set their ship's sails, and came tearing after the privateers at a disheartening rate of speed.

At the helm stood the feisty brawler Mulvany. That stout veteran needed no lessons on how to coax the last bit of speed out of their sleek, black cutter.

Mulvany caught the anxious look in Dowlin's eyes, gave him a confident smile. "No worries Capt'n. We're flyin'. That brig musta been a decoy."

Dowlin chewed on his lip, turning Mulvany's words over in his head for a bit. Mulvany might be right about the brig.

"Aye. Aye, Mulvany - I believe yer right! That brig was cruisin' a bit queer out here, as if she wanted us to catch her. P'haps... just p'haps, she was bait! But how'd the English know we'd be here, now? Nah. Couldn't be. And what English captain would risk sailing into the Somme? Seems a stupid thing to do. Doesn't make a wit of sense..."

Dowlin shook his head. There was something to all of this that did not sit right with him. He sighed and put the uneasy feeling aside for now.

Another race was on and this frigate was fast - and tenacious. The British always were.

The English 36 gunner pursued the privateer relentlessly all through the afternoon and on into the evening. After supper, Dowlin assembled all his officers.

"Lads, no lights, no fire. No tobacco either. No talkin' except in whispers. I want no light, smells or noises comin' from this ship. Let the British mark well our course to the south-west. After dark we'll alter course, swing around to the north-east and in the mornin' make a run for Dunkirk. Pass the word to all hands..."

His officers quietly nodded, carried out their master's orders and not one man, despite their predicament, showed any fear or offered the slightest grumble. They had evaded frigates before and they would do so again. And when night fell, they applied all of their resolve and energy, employed every trick, to try and lose their pursuer. Confidence filled every heart. But as Ageless Dawn, matchless in her beauty, stretched her fingers across an azure sky to embrace her lover once more, the mariners rubbed the sleep from their eyes and looked across the waves, astonished. The British frigate was still there, close off their stern and just barely out of range of the heavy guns. Despite all their valiant efforts, the British had failed to take the bait. It was if the British knew where the Irishmen were headed.

Even so, the *Prince* hugged the French shore through the morning and the frigate could gain no ground. By noon, the *Prince* came within sight of the small towns of Berck and Estaples, just south of Boulogne, and the Irishmen raised a cheer. They were nearly home-free and spirits soared. And then, for no good earthly reason, Good Fortune up and left their side. The shore breezes suddenly, inexplicably, dwindled to almost nothing. The cutter's sails went slack.

The frigate, standing farther out at sea, and with a driving sea-wind to fill her canvas, began to close on the privateers at an alarming rate of speed. Her captain was clever too. Instead of turning in at his quarry straight off - where his ship would encounter the same calmer shore breezes - he pulled his ship *away* from *Prince* at first, headed further out to sea, and then, only after his frigate had pulled ahead of the cutter did he make his turn, did he make his move to kill.

Dowlin saw the Englishman's plan clearly and grimaced. It was a good one. The *Prince* sluggishly pressed on up along the coast as fast as she was able. There was nothing more for any man to do except pray.

The Irishmen watched, helpless, as the frigate completed her wide arc and then charged straight at them. Stomachs churned, men felt queasy, dread filled every heart. Even Dowlin, for the first time he could remember, felt Panic's cold fingers resting on his shoulders. He paced nervously up and down the deck debating what to do. His stout Irishmen could plainly see it all and braced themselves for trouble. Some began eyeing shore, wondering how bad the currents might be, thinking a risky swim to land was better than jail or worse, the noose.

"Winds aren't failin' her," reported young Tim, hanging from the ratlines with a spyglass to his eye. "She's closin' fast, sir!"

Dowlin found no need to respond to the obvious. Like some

cornered fox, eyes darting back and forth, looking for some way out from the hounds dashing towards it, Dowlin desperately looked around the ship, searching for some trick or ploy to play. Then his thoughts turned to Ryan. *That man would never panic! No, never!* He could picture Ryan standing rock steady near the helm, his hands linked behind his back, his mind calculating, turning out plan after plan until he found a plan to save them all.

Ryan liked to say that no trap was foolproof. Stay calm and never succumb to fear Ryan had told him, or then all will be lost for certain. Whenever a man keeps his wits about him there is always a fighting chance. Dowlin shook his head. *Fine words! Think man, think!*

To their starboard shoals and sand bars prevented any escape in to shore and even, if by some miracle, they successfully negotiated those hazards, Dowlin could see the killer white breakers smashing up against a rugged, rocky coast. There was no safe place to beach their handsome cutter there. To port stood the open ocean with rolling, blue-green waves - and one English sea monster, skulking, relentless, barring any escape that way.

Morgan strolled up next to Dowlin as he kept pacing back and forth, saw the anxiety in his captain's face. "We'll get out of this jam yet, Pat. You'll see."

Dowlin scanned the horizon, as if looking for something. "I'm not so sure, Michael. By *Christ*, we've got ourselves caught between the Scylla and the Charybdis."

"Between who and what? What the devil are ya talkin' about, Pat?"

"Between death and destruction. You know, Scylla. She was the six-headed sea monster who ate any sailor passing too close, snatched them right off the deck, and Charybdis was the other hideous creature, ugly and enormous, who gulped down seawater and belched three times a day, making great whirlpools big enough to suck down whole ships."

"Oh, aye, like between the devil and the deep, blue sea," Morgan answered thoughtfully and gave Dowlin a curious look. "So we are. Yer startin' to sound like Luke."

Dowlin nodded, took Morgan's words as a compliment. Now, he told himself, it was time to start acting like Ryan too.

"Spread the word to the lads. No one's goin' to end up in a British gaol. Not on my watch. We'll find a way to beach this lovely bitch of ours first and swim to shore if we must."

Morgan grinned and raced down the deck to spread the *word*.

And then the English captain made his first mistake. He had miscalculated the distance between his frigate and the cutter, had misjudged the currents too. He had begun his turn in towards land too soon, a sign of impatience - hardly an *English* trait - and the *Prince* began to pull ahead.

Like an eagle swooping down out of the sky on its prey, but missing on the first pass, the eagle climbs again for altitude and circles around for a second dive, the frigate came about, swung herself away from the *Prince* and headed back out to sea again to catch a better wind. But precious time had been lost giving the Irishmen new hope.

Dowlin again weighed each possibility over carefully. They could continue their present course up the coast and trust the wind's return to speed their cutter safely home. Or they could maneuver in towards shore, less rugged, less hostile now, and head for shallow water - the frigate, requiring far more water under her keel, would never follow. Even so, Dowlin had doubts about their chances as he watched the breakers splash white foam up against the craggy rocks. Running aground was every captain's nightmare.

But there was, Dowlin knew, a third option. They could turn their ship in towards the frigate and head for open sea. The maneuver would expose the cutter to the frigate's heavy guns for a time but, if the *Prince* could steal the wind from the frigate's sails to fill her own, the Irishmen could pull fast away and might yet escape. But that plan brought Dowlin no joy. One lucky shot from a twelve-pound ball could break their cutter's keel, splinter a mast or shatter her rudder. Down to the bottom they would all go then. Still, Dowlin had to smile. He knew that was the bold move, the unexpected course, the choice Ryan would have taken.

Dowlin looked to his left and to his right and then to his left again, alternating his attention between the British frigate and the French coast - agonizing over what to do. The frigate was in her second turn now, heading towards them again and closing fast.

Then, with the distance between them melting, the English frigate's men opened fire with her starboard bow chaser, a long barrel nine-pounder, and lobbed the first ball at the *Prince*. And then another and another...

Dowlin's fidgety crew watched the frigate close, watched the deadly missiles flying overhead and waited for their orders. Despair set in. It had all been so much fun until now but this, they knew, was the end.

And then, from the masthead, the boy with the angelic face cried out. "*Forts ho!*" Tim yelled down cheerfully. "I see forts! Fine on the starboard bow!"

"Aye! Aye!" Dowlin boomed with excitement. "Berck I do believe has shore batteries! We an't done for yet lads! Damn miracle! Mr. Morgan, put a good man in the bowsprit with the lead. Send two lookouts with him to watch for rocks and shoals. Don't want to snag one now! I'm takin' her closer in lads, bring us under the long reach of those lovely French guns."

He looked up at the vaulting sky and prayed. "Please Lord, hear my prayer - I'll not utter another contrary word about any Frenchman if 'em soldiers in that fort do their duty now and save us from this trouble..."

Dowlin looked to see who was at the helm, saw it was Smith. Not the best man with the tiller.

"Helmsman! Look alive thar, lad! Be ready to shift her around to either port or starboard in a snap! Be no time for the lads at the braces to help you much. You've got rocks to yer left and to yer right! Now turn her two points starboard. Let's ease her over to those Frenchy cannon! Steady now, careful. Ease yer helm, man!"

Panic could no longer hold Dowlin down, not that man, in looks and build a match for any of the deathless gods of old. He straightened back his shoulders and grinned. The world was pleasing to his eye once more.

"Ha! Ha! Ha!" he laughed. "We'll give this English dog nothin' but empty sea to claim as a prize!"

He looked for his first officer, the American, Collins, whom he had borrowed from Macatter after Ryan had stripped him of the Kelly giants, and found Collins standing idle at the rail, gawking at the frigate.

"Mr. Collins, if you please. Lieutenant! Get Morgan. I want him on the helm now! No offense Smith - but yer a bit of a ham fisted yokel at the tiller. Morgan has the touch. I swear ships obey him like a mistress!"

Collins regained his composure and rushed off to do his master's bidding.

The privateers hoisted a large American flag off the stern line and fired off a distress signal at the fort nearest to Berck. French soldiers heard the plea for help and saw the English frigate chasing down an American vessel. They quickly manned their fortress guns and soon heavy French cannon, belching smoke and fire, shattered the peaceful morning. The townsfolk of Berck, men, women, children, heard the deadly manmade thunder and dropped whatever they were doing to hurry down to shore. People flocked in droves to the beaches under a clear, bright sky just in time to see a small American ship carefully picking her way through the shoals and rocks, struggling in the light winds, trying to flee from a larger British frigate firing at her. People gasped. Brave American allies were in trouble!

The spectators could see the English frigate's crew rolling out their main guns. French fortress batteries fired a second salvo. People gasped and jumped. Fountains of white water shot up all around the English frigate and the French spectators cheered wildly as trouble found the English ship! *Triumph!* A French *victory!*

"We've made it, Capt'n!" Morgan, standing at the helm, cried out excitedly. "By God, you've done it, sir!"

Dowlin, never more proud, beamed.

Ah, but how the god of war, that master of cruel heartbreak, loves to play and torment! And since the beginning, throughout all their heady days at sea, the sisters Rout and Panic had failed to impress the Irishmen. The Irishmen were oblivious to the twins. So down a jealous god of war sent his faithful double-headed henchmen, Death and Destruction, to do his twisted bidding. For too long Good Fortune had been allowed to run amuck, for too long she had been free to protect her favorite mariners.

"Look thar!" cried out Collins, "frigate's lowerin' her colors!"

"What?" Dowlin asked incredulously. The English couldn't be

surrendering. *Impossible!*

The fort's guns fired again - and again overshot their target, sending up harmless jets of spray.

Dowlin shook his head in disgust. "Damn French gunners," he muttered softly. "Horrible, fooking marksmanship, always."

And then suddenly, inexplicably, the battle ended. The frigate's guns fell silent. Her crew hauled down the British Union Jack and replaced it with the French *fleur de lys*. The fort's commander took a closer look at the frigate and recognized her. She was French. He ordered his men to stand down. The frigate whirled about and headed out for open sea. All was well once more - or so things seemed.

The privateers, bewildered by the frigate's bizarre actions, raised a victory cheer nonetheless, loud and long. But then, at the moment of their triumph - a horrible screeching noise drowned out their celebration. The proud *Prince* shuddered violently, her nose shot straight up out of the water. Men lost their balance and tumbled backwards. Those who couldn't grab on to something rolled down the deck, breaking legs and arms or jamming fingers. Topmen in the rigging were jarred loose and tossed into the sea like dolls. Morgan lost his grip on the tiller and was catapulted over the stern rail. Dowlin went down too, hitting his forehead hard against the edge of something sharp. Blood trickled down his handsome face.

The *Prince* had struck a jagged rock, hidden just below the murky waters and impossible for the leadsman or his lookouts to see. Then the cutter's bow, with a great splash, settled back down on the waves and she came to rest. Cold seawater began pouring into her through a long gash, an ugly wound, in her side and quickly filled up her wells. Her back was all but broken too. Nothing could save her. The noble *Prince* was doomed.

Dowlin wiped the blood from his eyes, wrapped a neckerchief aound his forehead and helped Morgan back on deck. Such and inglorious end Dowlin thought to himself, for a ship that had served the Irishmen so well. *Fool, you haave no time to dwell on that now! Get the lads off safely!*

The ship was floundering, true, but the Irishmen were only 100 yards or so away from shore. Men struggled to their feet and fished their mates out of the churning sea. Amazingly, not one man was lost or seriously injured.

Dowlin next gave the order to abandon ship and men carefully slipped the long boat and the launch in the water and began to move off smartly.

Dowlin remained on board to gather the ship's papers, charts and all their nautical instruments. He wrapped his loot in oilskin, carefully stuffed it all into a canvas bag, and then braced himself for a cold swim to shore. The boats were already half way over. But then, to his astonishment, he suddenly realized that the *Prince* was stable. She was no longer sinking. He grabbed a lantern and went below to inspect the damage. The *Prince* had settled nicely on the rocks, refused to die, but once Dowlin saw her cracked keel, he knew the *Prince* was finished. Still, there was time, and so he rushed back up to the deck and called out to his men on shore. He had a team row back to the ship with rope and tackle and then they strung out lines from ship to shore. For the next 24 hours the crew labored tirelessly, off-loading all the *Prince's* guns, equipment and supplies, anything that could be salvaged - an amazing feat.

And then Dowlin sent his men on to Berck for food and shelter but, stalwart warrior and a loyal friend, he remained behind, just for a little while. He picked a spot on a rock and sat, surrounded by all the ship's stores, her guns and gear piled high along the beach, and opened a bottle of whiskey. He thought it only fit and proper that someone keep vigil, until the greedy sea pulled their poor ship off the rocks and claimed her.

And when the end did come, Dowlin watched in silence and wiped away a tear. The tide came in and pulled the good *Prince* down. Graceful to the last, first her stern slipped slowly under the waves and then her bow, with bubbles all around, until she disappeared forever. But after settling softly on the sandy bottom, the tops of her two great masts still jutted above the water's black surface to mark her shallow grave.

again. "Aye. That's no lie. It fills a ... *void...*"

Ryan nodded, watching Dowlin as he drained his tankard in one swallow. He had known the same void.

"Luke, the captain of the frigate who forced us on the rocks is here. He's here right in Dunkirk! *Gawd*, if I didn't have any bad luck, I wouldn't have any luck at all."

Ryan looked at Dowlin, puzzled. "A British officer? Here in Dunkirk?"

"No. *French.*"

"French?"

"Aye..."

"You've managed to confuse me, Pat. I don't understand."

"The lads and me stayed in Berck for a few days to handle what we had salvaged off the *Prince* and heard a lot of curious talk. Nearly two thousand people flocked to the shore to watch the battle that day and many recognized the frigate - she's French navy, the *Calonne*, a thirty-six gunner under the command of a man named Guilman, Capt'n Francois Claudius Guilman. Everyone was asking the same question: why would a French warship mascaraed as English so close to the French coast and then attack an American warship? When I got back here to Dunkirk, I went to see Torris. He made some inquires. It was not hard to learn that Guilman was indeed a captain in the French navy and keeps a home right here in Dunkirk!"

Ryan slowly began to understand. He reached out and squeezed Dowlin's shoulder. His heart filled itself with kindness for his friend.

"There's no blame to you, Pat," Ryan told him and chose his next words carefully, hoping to offer comfort. "You did all you could to save your ship. I could have done no better. I might have tried making a run for open sea as you say, but then again, I might now be dead for my efforts too. You saved the lives of your men and saved all your ship's guns, provisions and her gear too - that's impressive, that's the important thing. Fine work under difficult conditions. Now listen, David came to see me in March before I took *Fearnot* out into the German Sea."

"Sartine?"

"Aye. He tried to warn me. His uncle, the Minister of Marine, is a friend to us no longer. Can't say that I understand all the forces at work here, Pat. But I'm sure at the bottom of all this stink we'll find a trail of money."

Dowlin nodded. "And a rat."

"Aye, and a rat. There's some sort of treachery afoot no doubt. I should have taken more serious heed of David's warnings. I had no idea it might come to this. The fault, the blame, if there is any, is mine old friend - not yours."

"Well," Dowlin began in a more thoughtful voice and considered his empty tankard. "Irish vengeance is horrible to behold. Some boot-licker is gonna pay mark my words - and pay dear for what they've done..."

Several days later, Dowlin learned that the villainous Captain Guilman was back in Dunkirk and enjoying his supper at a nearby tavern favored by French officers. He had a good description of the Frenchman and found the tavern easily with Ryan and Kelly at his side, unaware of what he was about to do. Dowlin went in first and spotted his quarry straight off, sitting at a corner table, eating and laughing with fellow officers. Rage, unstoppable rage seized him.

He rushed towards Guilman's table, knocking over chairs and a nearby table, and lunged at Guilman, grabbed him by the collar and yanked him from his chair. Dowlin would have killed the Frenchman with his bare hands, snapped his neck right then and there - before scores of witnesses - had Ryan and Kelly not pulled him off Guilman.

The Frenchman, with bulging eyes, stared at the maniac in horror. He took several steps backwards, hobbling along on a gimp leg, until his back hit the wall. He couldn't place the big man's face, his flowing red hair, and frantically searched his memory, trying desperately to understand. *A jealous, irate husband perhaps? An unhappy gambling companion? Who?*

Ryan wrapped his arms around Dowlin's upper arms, held him fast as best he could until Kelly, a step behind, added his strength to restrain Dowlin. Lucky thing too that Kelly was there - because no ordinary pair of men could have held Dowlin's brute force in check that night.

"Your friend is a madman or a drunkard!" Guilman exclaimed, shaking. "Get him out of here and away from me now before I have you all arrested!"

Guilman's three friends stood, each man with a hand on the hilt of his sword, ready to draw.

"*Swine!*" Dowlin shouted back, spit flying from his mouth. "You fired on my ship, forced her on the rocks!"

"*Monsieur* is a liar and too drunk to know what is true and what is not!" Guilman shot back, but, then again, he now realized who Dowlin was.

Dowlin clenched his teeth. "*You deny it?*"

The Frenchman's flat denial amazed him. He had expected at least some weak and useless explanation.

Having regained his composure, Guilman stared back at Dowlin with sheer disdain. "But of course I deny it! I have never seen you in all my life. Irish *merde!* I am an officer in the king's royal navy - get out of here before I run you through with my blade. No one will complain if I gut you here and now..."

The big Irishman, three heads taller than the Frenchman, stopped struggling against Kelly's iron grip. He looked around the room. All eyes were on him. He paused to collect his thoughts.

He lowered his voice, spoke slowly so everyone could hear. "There were two thousand people lined-up along the shore at Berck who can bear witness to your foul deed. You and yer ship *Calonne* are well known in these parts. Who's the liar now, hey?"

A few heads in the tavern nodded in agreement. The French captain's hands began to tremble as he realized that he had been caught in his own, obvious lie. He quickly corrected himself.

"Berck? Why, yes. Yes, very well, I was there. But your ship flew English colors! What was I to do? I know my duty!"

Dowlin lunged at the Frenchman again, but Kelly held him fast. "Ha! Once again - a damn lie you sorry sack of shit! We flew American colors that day and fired a recognition signal to the harbor fort at Berck for help. *You* ignored our signal and came at us hell-bent on our destruction. 'Twas yer ship that flew the English Union Jack! Why else would the garrison at Berck train their guns and fire on yer ship and not my own? Everyone saw it... I demand satisfaction you bastard! Better yet - I'll spare yer miserable life, you dog, if you tell me who yer master is!"

The French captain froze, was speechless. Death was staring him in the face. He anxiously searched for allies in the room, could see that no one believed him.

Ryan could see Guilman's companions, standing at his side and armed, were ready for a brawl. Ryan jerked his head back, motioning to Kelly to pull Dowlin away.

"Come now, Pat," Ryan whispered into Dowlin's ear, "This is no good. We're outnumbered here. Keep your powder dry. They're better ways to settle-up with this Frenchman than gettin' yourself killed. Give me some time to find out what intrigue has happened here. We'll set matters right at a time and place that favors us, on our own terms. I swear it."

"P'haps, Capt'n," Dowlin answered calmly, keeping his eyes fixed on Guilman. He freed one arm from Kelly's grip and wiped away the spit from his mouth. "But whatever we do later, it won't be nearly as satisfin' as snuffin' this bugger's life out right here and now."

Kelly released Dowlin, ready to restrain him again if needed. Dowlin took a step forward, unimpressed by the number of Frenchmen arrayed against him.

"Patrick!" Ryan shouted - with a warning in his tone. "Enough I say! You'll only get yourself killed man, or get yourself thrown into the shithole of a French prison! We leave this place - now. That's an order!"

Dowlin's good senses did not desert him. He had thought the matter through, knew that Ryan was right. He could have gladly accepted death that night, following Guilman's own, but he didn't want to get Ryan and Kelly killed too. That he could not bear. His lips curled into an evil smile. His dark, smoldering eyes - impossible to look away from or all too easy to avoid depending on the grit of the other - locked hard onto the nervous Frenchman. One last trick to play. Perhaps he could bait the Frenchman into a duel and, if not, he would heed Ryan's advice, wait for a better time to set matters right.

"Our paths will cross again my good Capt'n - that much I promise you. Until then, *au revoir*. One last parting word before I leave you though - I curse the whore bitch who brought such a bastard runt like you into this world. No mother would claim you as her own, no father would keep you. I will piss on yer grave when yer gone..."

But Guilman did not take the bait, kept his tongue still. The man had prudence even if he had no pride, no honor. To taunts and jeers from the tavern crowd, every one of them a Frenchman, the three Irishmen slowly began stepping backwards and retreated into the street.

Fifteen
Scotland's Ripe for the Plucking Lads!

While Ryan and his Irishmen prepared *Fearnot* for war once more, and went about raising a new crew, the French Minister of Marine was busy too and dispatched new orders, this time to the Commissary of Dunkirk, and told the man to marshal his hoodlums. The Minister was demanding a large harvest. Dunkirk's commissary sent his Royal press gangs out immediately and they did their work uncommonly well, taking over 700 men into custody in one fell swoop, including all of Ryan's French sailors, nearly one-third of his crew.

But Ryan's situation was not as bad as most. He had Dowlin and his Shadowmen back and that gave *Fearnot* a compliment of eighty fighting lions, mostly Irishmen and Americans and they had taken to one another like brothers.

Like many blessed with a sensitive soul, Ryan had the gift of intuition. He understood that their privateering days were near an end, that their days of glory were all but over. The destruction of *Black Prince* was no accident, of that much he was certain. And the curious timing of the Royal press gangs, robbing him of able-bodied seamen each time any of his ships was about to sail, was no coincidence. In Cherbourg, Morlaix and Dunkirk, the press gangs had pounced each time the Irish privateers made port. And then there were the threats to imprison Macatter and the impounding of the *Black Princess* to consider. These could not be mere random acts. There was intelligent thought guiding all of it - a plan. And Ryan sensed that whatever was afoot, in the end, their benefactor, Franklin, would be powerless to help them.

Even the prizes Ryan and his men had captured brought controversy. The taking of the Dutch brig *Flora* was boiling over into an international incident. Holland was a neutral country and filed angry protests with Versailles, in turn causing a serious strain between France and America. Under pressure from Versailles, Franklin agreed to release the brig. But, at the same time, he also showed loyalty to his privateers and declared *Flora's* cargo fair game, enemy property, and properly seized by Dowlin. He informed the Judges of the Admiralty in Cherbourg of his decision:

> "TO THE JUDGES OF THE ADMIRALTY AT CHERBOURG.
>
> *Passy, 16 May, 1780.*
>
> GENTLEMEN,
>
> *I have received the proces verbaux, and other papers you did me the honor to send me, agreeable to the eleventh article of the regulation of the 27th of September, 1778. These pieces relate to the taking of the ship Flora, whereof was captain Henry Roodenberg, bound from Rotterdam to Dublin, and arrived at Cherbourg, in France, being taken the 7th day of April, by Captain Dowlin, commander of the American privateer the Black Prince.*
>
> *It appears to me, from the abovementioned papers, that the said ship Flora is not a good prize, the same belonging to the subjects of a neutral nation; but that the cargo is really the property of the subjects of the King of England, though attempted to be masked as neutral. I do therefore request, that, after the cargo shall be landed, you would cause the said ship Flora to be immediately restored to her captain, and that you would oblige the captors to pay him his full freight according to his bills of lading, and also to make good all the damages he may have sustained by plunder or otherwise; and I further request, that, as the cargo is perishable, you would cause it to be sold immediately, and retain the produce deposited in your hands, to the end, that if any of the freighters, being subjects of their High Mightinesses the States-Generals, will declare upon oath, that certain parts of the said cargo were bona fide shipped on their own account and risk, and not on the account and risk of any British or Irish subjects, the value of such parts may be restored; or that, if*

the freighters, or any of them, should think fit to appeal from this judgment to the Congress, the produce so deposited may be disposed of according to their final determination. I have the honor to be, &c.
B. FRANKLIN."

Ryan now took Sartine's warning to heart and decided to leave Dunkirk immediately while he still could - determined to cause some real damage on what he knew might be his last cruise. He could not afford to wait for Macatter and the *Princess* to join him, there would be no joint cruise with *Fearnot*. And so, in early July, the privateers looked west once again, seeking high adventure.

Men cast off the warps and then went up into the rigging. They spread out across the yardarms, standing in the foot stirrups, shook out the reef points and the sails, one-by-one, fell out with a loud flap. With wind filling her sails, the American battle cruiser slowly lurched forward, towards a hostile sea.

Ryan stood quietly next to Dowlin at the rail. The two mariners watched Earth's good sister - full and radiant - climb into the evening sky. Eternal splendor. And when the Moon caught the two Irishmen admiring her beauty, she blushed, a stray cloud passed across her face. She gave the seafarers a parting gift, something to warm their hearts and to speed them safely along their way. She illuminated the harbor's black waters with a path bright and broad enough for any stalwart seaman to follow. And then Earth decided to favor the gallant Irishmen too. From bogs and marshes, she unloosed a thin mist, engulfing the land with wisps of rolling fog to shroud the warship from prying eyes on shore. Ryan smiled - it was a perfect warrior's night.

And once the Irishmen had cleared Dunkirk Road, the mighty hunter appeared overhead, his bow in hand stretched taught. Magnificent Orion, dazzling to behold, took his place in front of the celestial giants and led them in their great wheeling turn across a coal black sky, a spectacle of majestic, regal beauty - God's own signature written across the heavens for all to see.

With Orion pointing the way north Ryan tapped Dowlin on the shoulder. "Mr. Dowlin, if you please, it's time. Let's take her due north and pour on some speed..."

"With pleasure, Capt'n!" Dowlin replied enthusiastically and saluted. "What a grand evenin' to set out."

"Aye, a marvelous night. Must be some of the Lord's handiwork."

Dowlin nodded and relayed Ryan's orders to the crew who, always eager to please their captain, coaxed the maximum speed out of their good ship. Had any ship been dispatched to follow them, the Irishmen were already too far away. The helmsman pointed her nose towards the German Ocean where they all hoped to find fat victims to plunder. *Fearnot* sliced her way through the sea's rolling waves with ease.

After a week of sailing the privateers found nothing but empty water so Dowlin, never fond of sitting idle, kept the men busy putting the ship into fighting trim. Guns were cleaned and polished, gear properly stowed away and ropes were rolled into neat coils. The deck was sanded down smooth and then re-sanded and under Dowlin's watchful eye, every line of rigging and all the spars and cast-iron fixtures were inspected each day and any part showing the least bit of wear was promptly replaced.

Still more days passed and the Irishmen did not sight one vessel.

Ryan found Dowlin at the bow sipping coffee, watching the first light of a new day peek over the horizon, and handed him hot bread and a chunk of cheese from the galley. "Pat, I know you must still be smarting over the *Prince*, but I must say, 'tis so good have you back, old friend. The only man I've ever known who even comes close to matching your skills at sea is Macatter. I must say, the ship has never looked finer and the morale of the lads is high despite our poor fishing so far, all because of you. Thank you."

"Aye. With all 'em schemes swirlin' around in that thar head of yers you never did have time for lookin' after the minor details of runnin' a ship. She's a rare beauty. *Fearnot* is every bit as fine as the *Prince*, a tad slower p'haps but she makes up for it in muscle. What is it you plan to do once we reach the German Sea anyway?"

Ryan took a sip of coffee and winced. "Whoa, this is a strong brew;

the cook must be in an ornery mood this morning. I thought we'd drop in on Scotland and give those hearty folks our warm regards. Remind them there's a war going on."

Dowlin stamped his foot and laughed. "Ha! Lismore all over again! Ah, yer chasin' after Jones's glory. I shoulda known. You can't fool me, Luke Ryan. You won't be satisfied until yer as famous as the good Capt'n."

Kelly and his brother John overheard Dowlin and joined Ryan and Dowlin at the bow.

"Chris, John, good mornin'," Ryan offered cheerfully. "Pat has made an interesting observation. If only we had Jones's man-of-war and all his men, good God wouldn't we do some damage then! Jones did some fine work up in these waters. No question about that. But I never would have allowed myself to get bottled up at Texel!"

Dowlin nodded quietly in agreement. He had no doubts, none whatsoever, that what Ryan said was true. The master tactician, his friend, always had some scheme, some ready plan to warm the hearts of his men, to cause their enemies some woe.

"If only we had more time too," Ryan added and sighed. He tossed his coffee over the rail. "Lads, I fear our days of privateering are nearly over."

Dowlin dropped his smile and looked away. "From everythin' you've told me, I think yer right, Luke. A blind man could spot it straight off from a distance. *Gawd*, but it was fun. And didn't we ride the *Wave* for a good, long spell?"

"That we did. We did indeed."

The two giants nodded silently in agreement.

"What do we do then, Luke?" asked Dowlin. "A French commission? That might turn my stomach."

Ryan shook his head. "Honestly, lads, I don't know. Around Christmas, I asked his Excellency Franklin for a lieutenant's commission in the regular navy of the United States. I don't know how or even if he'll respond to that. I'll make the same request for each of you if you so desire it. One thing's for certain though - I'm not finished with the English, not by a long shot. The ledger's not been balanced yet - I still owe the English a pain or two."

"Me and John," offered Kelly, "are with you, sir. Whatever you decide."

John Kelly nodded. "Wouldn't want to sail with no other, sir."

Dowlin removed a long-stem pipe from his jacket and chewed on the tip. He didn't smoke it much anymore but he still found comfort in having a pipe in his mouth.

He put the bowl to his nose and savored the rich smell of tobacco. "Through thick or thin, Luke, through thick or thin..."

Ryan had been tempted to return to the Irish Sea after hearing about Macatter's extraordinary good fortune there. But he was also leery of Macatter's nearly disastrous run-in with three British warships - all speedy interceptors. The British navy was making a serious effort to hunt the privateers down. So he decided to cruise around Scotland's rugged coast instead. For three weeks, they plied the waters there without coming across one sail. Frustrated, Ryan swung *Fearnot* around the north tip of Scotland and sailed her into the Outer Hebrides, but the Irishmen found no better hunting there.

After almost a month at sea, with not one prize taken and provisions running low, Ryan's mood turned foul. He summoned all of his officers into the ship's galley for a council of war where everyone - except Dowlin - expected him to call it quits and issue the order to head for home. But that was not to be.

Ryan sent for the ship's youngest crewman, Jean. The Irishmen had always kept the boy safely hidden away from the king's greedy press gangs. He was one of them now. He was *Irish* through-and-through despite his French accent. Jean rushed to the galley after being summoned, his once scrawny legs and arms now wrapped in thick muscle. Ryan had him fetch several bottles of Madeira and glasses and Jean dashed off obediently with an easy smile, a smile he had learned from Dowlin.

"Lads, I know you're disappointed, as am I. A whole month at sea wasted and the sand is running out of the glass. Lost time. Precious time. But we're not returning to Dunkirk, not empty-handed. No. I propose we find a suitable Scottish town to land at and take whatever fresh provisions we require. Scotland's ripe for the plucking. Then we'll put to sea again and continue with our hunting for as long as we can."

His plan did not startle his Irishmen any. They had not forgotten their bit of fun at Lismore. But Patterson, no coward, fidgeted uncomfortably in his chair. Ryan had pegged the American as brave and competent but thought he lacked imagination. Simmons, the ship's senior ranking petty officer now and as Irish as the Irishmen, smiled. He had found himself a home.

"You buyin' the first round, Luke?" Dowlin asked with a cagey smile.

"Aye, first round's on me. That is, I believe our custom."

Ryan unrolled a chart across the table and pointed to the town of Stornoway on the Island of Lewis, where the mysterious Stones of Clanais stood. Stornoway was his target. And on 24th day of July, nearly 500 years after the Viking King Haakon, lord of the Magnus, had lost the island to King Alexander of the Scots in the Treaty of Perth, the fearless Irishmen launched their own invasion to claim the land their own - if only for a day. The privateers announced themselves with style, announced themselves with the boom from a single nine-pounder.

The people of Stornoway went down to the sandy beach to see what mischief was brewing and found a strange warship sitting peacefully in their harbor. They watched silently as a boat with armed men pulled up to their wharf. A handsome, well-dressed man with sad blue eyes was the first to step ashore, followed by 12 rough looking men, all bearing arms. With crisp military precision, the 12 foreigners formed themselves up into two neat lines behind their captain.

Ryan took a moment to take in the lay of the land. Stornoway was a lonely outpost on the outer fringes of the Empire. The town appeared clean and well cared for. The surrounding hills, much like the men and women who inhabited them, were rugged and austere. Some fool of an ancient king had burned almost all the trees down, but Ryan found the stark beauty to his liking.

He could feel his boyish sense of fun returning. "My good people. This is Stornoway is it not?"

Several faces in the crowd nodded.

An older man gave Ryan a cagey grin. "Are ye lost, lad?"

"Why, not in the least good, sir!" Ryan laughed and placed his hands on his hips. "I know exactly where I am. Allow me to introduce myself. I'm Captain Luke Ryan of the *American* privateer *Fearnot* and I like your town. In the name of the government of the United States of America, I hereby demand your surrender."

The Scots exchanged puzzled looks with each other. *Surely, the man was joking?*

Rocking back and forth on his heels, Ryan tried to look serious. But inside he was grinning, he couldn't help himself, and was enjoying himself immensely.

"Well, what say you all?" Ryan demand, wishing to give the Scots an appropriate sense of impatience and arrogance. "I haven't got all bloody day to stand here watching the likes of you folks dawdle. To the north and south I have other towns to sack and burn."

A plump, but handsome woman with rosy cheeks stepped forward from the crowd. She was unafraid. "Sack and burn? Fancy yerself a sacker of cities do ya? I gave birth to three fine boys. All three serve in the King's Black Watch Guard. I fancy they'll soon put an end to yer boastfulness with one quick thrust of a bayonet straight through yer bowels. No pretty words will come spillin' out of yer mouth then. There's nothin' but trouble waitin' for you and yer lads in Scotland. Word to the wise: go on and be off with you now before you do somethin' you'll soon regret."

Ryan laughed out loud, a good, hearty laugh. "Ah, madam. You must be Stornoway's very own champion! Such bravado, such bold speech! Well now, I'll send your sons your love when I see them. But that is for another day. Let us discuss today's affairs today. My terms are these: I require a large ransom to spare your town from the torch. I'll let you name a price seeing how you know the value of your precious homes better than me. If I like the offer, I'll spare your town. If not, well... You have 'til the sun sets to decide. I have a ship to the north of you and one to the south as well. My patrols are out. There will be no soldiers coming to save your town, not in time anyway. Oh, and I'll be sending a few of my men over later to gather some provisions for my ships. I trust you'll be generous hosts to we, your weary guests. 'Til sunset then?"

Ryan of course had no ships or patrols out, but the people of Stornoway didn't know that and from his smuggling days he knew the king kept no troops stationed nearby. Stornoway stood all alone and far away from the protection of London.

The Scots exchanged anxious looks as Ryan took his men and rowed back to the ship. Nothing like this had ever happened before in Stornoway - not at least since the Viking raids centuries ago. The elders of Stornoway gathered at the miller's house, as the miller always kept a respectable store of chilled ale on hand, and held an emergency town meeting to discuss their dire situation.

Dowlin made good use of the afternoon. He formed two small foraging parties and went back into town to gather provisions for the ship. Ryan went with them, but remained on the wharf and had himself a nap against a piling while Dowlin and his men combed the town, taking only what supplies they needed and nothing more. Those were Ryan's orders.

Ryan was sleeping soundly when a rough hand shook him. He looked up to see a small group of the town's elders standing over him.

"Are ye awake? We're here, Captain Ryan, to accept yer terms."

Ryan pushed his hat back off his face. "Accept my terms? Excellent news! And the price to be paid to spare your fine town?"

"We've settled on a sum of five thousand guineas - but we cannot make that payment all at once. We'll need time to assemble such a hefty sum as this."

Ryan stood up and smoothed the wrinkles out of his clothes. "I see. Five thousand guineas you say? Hm. Some might say you're a trifle light. But I say - 'tis not a bad offer from a Scot, your folk being renowned throughout the world for being frugal. How much time did you say you needed?"

"Oh, just a wee bit, about a month or two, maybes three. After we sheers the sheep and takes the wool over to market in Glasgow, then we'll have enough."

"Glasgow's a might far isn't it friend?"

"Maybes for a foreigner. Ships cross the Minch right over there and sail into Ullapool all the time. From Ullapool the wool is taken overland by wagons to factories in Glasgow."

Ryan looked over at the patch of sea the Scotsman was pointing at. "Of course, my good fellow, I meant no insult," he replied with a smile. "Well, five thousand guineas sounds like a reasonable sum to me. I never have had much of an appetite for quibbling on any day so fine as this. Let me tell you how it's done, just so we are clear. We capture a ship you see, just as we've captured your town. The ship's master and I sit down and have a drink or two and then we do a bit of haggling until we come to an understanding, an agreement, on price, a ransom price, in order to set the vessel free - or - if no agreement is reached, why then my lads simply burn the ship and all her cargo and we take her whole crew prisoner. Now, if we reach an accord, the master signs a note, a ransom bill, promising to pay the agreed amount. Payment is guaranteed by the taking of a hostage. That hostage goes with me. He'll be treated with decency aboard my ship and released when the note is paid in full. Our two countries are at war after all. But I'm not a barbarian. I do try to keep this sordid business of ours *civil*."

The lead Scotsman scratched at the gray stubble on his chin. "Aye. I see how it's done. Very tidy. Yer a strange one for a pirate lad. We're much obliged to ya for yer courteous ways. Yer men helped themselves to some our stores earlier, but they left enough behind for our own purposes. And they were most respectful. Disciplined lot you have there. We'll sign yer note and give you a hostage and pay the note as soon as we are able. We'll be sendin' letters of protest to the Crown too mind ye. Rest assured of that my good man. Let the king pay yer sum, if he has a mind to. He leaves us here unprotected so far from London. Sorry to say it lad, you seem well-intentioned to me, but I suspect we'll be readin' about yer hangin' in the papers soon enough."

Ryan smiled broadly at the Scotsman. "Hanging? Ah, I trust you'll be sorely disappointed there my friend!"

The good people of Stornoway, save one, the hostage, watched the *Fearnot* set sail and disappear into night. Everyone agreed the pirates had been most courteous and oddly fair in their plundering. But even so, the town sent a ship that very night unto Ullapool with news of what had happened.

Later that evening *Fearnot* happened upon a set of lanterns dancing on the water, with music and laughter too. The privateers sailed towards the dancing lights and came upon an unarmed sloop carrying a group of well-dressed men who all seemed to be enjoying themselves. Dowlin brought the *Fearnot* in close and shouted over to her master to shorten sail and to prepare to be boarded.

After taking in the strange vessel's heavy guns, the sloop's master, a man of good, clear sense, gave the order. His men furled sail and the sloop coasted to a stop on the sea's smooth waves.

Three musicians, sitting at the stern, abruptly stopped playing their instruments when Ryan stepped aboard. And when Ryan saw the sloop was carrying gentlemen, each man with a drink in hand and clearly feeling mellow, Ryan waved Dowlin up from the longboat but had the rest of his men stay put. The sloop's passengers posed no threat. The sloop was a pleasure craft.

In the middle of the deck stood a long table, draped in white linen, with platters of food and two gaudy, sterling silver candelabrums. These men had money.

A stocky, little fellow dressed in a kilt and bonnet greeted Ryan and Dowlin. "Good evening, my dear fellows. Name's MacGregor, Alexander MacGregor and this is my ship, *Dionysus*. Who might you be and how may we be of service to you here out in the middle of nowhere?"

Dowlin eyed a large sterling silver badge, embossed with a coat-of-arms, pinned to a wool sash across the man's chest and smiled at the ceremonial dagger tucked inside the Scotsman's stocking. The Scotsman made a splendid sight.

"Well, now, sir," Ryan began, employing his best in English manners. "We appear to have lost our way. I will tell you gladly who we are but first tell me, sir, what are such fine gentlemen as yourselves doing out in the middle of nowhere at this late hour? Dear me - I pray you haven't lost your way as well!"

"Oh, heavens no, but 'tis an honest question you ask my good man," the Scotsman answered cautiously. "And I'll give you an honest answer. My estate is little more than an hour's sail away, north of here near Stornoway. P'haps you've heard of it?"

"Stornoway? Bless me, we're that close to Stornoway?" Ryan asked with a smile. "See Pat, I told you we sailed too far north! Aye, we've heard of Stornoway. Rugged, lovely country up that way or so I've heard."

The Scotsman returned Ryan's smile with one of his own and a set of bad teeth, but he had a kindly face. "Aye. God's own country to be sure. Now you know where you are. These gentlemen, my guests and friends, are from Londonderry mostly. During the day, we did a bit of hunting, some shooting and fishing. Soon we'll be on our way to my home to enjoy some parlor games and a good night's rest."

"Excellent, such a coincidence!" Ryan exclaimed playfully. "Why I enjoy a bit of hunting from time to time myself. Alas, pressing business in Dublin restricts me from engaging in such outings much these days. But as it so happens my friends and I were on our way to do the very same."

The sloop's master, who had been standing off to the side and eyeing Ryan suspiciously, moved up next to the Scotsman. "I couldn't help but notice those guns on board yer ship, sir. Mighty big ones too. Just what game is it you intend to hunt in these waters?"

Ryan tossed his head back and let loose with a hearty laugh. "Big guns indeed! My ship is a pleasure craft with a *sting* to be sure! I've been robbed by pirates before. In these very same waters, I might add. A gentleman cannot be too careful in guarding his possessions. Next rogue who tries to part me from my purse is in for a rude surprise!"

MacGregor started laughing too. He liked the *Englishman* straight off and Ryan's fashionable clothes, refined speech and good manners had not escaped the sage Scotsman's eye.

"Wonderful, sir! You strike me as a gentleman yerself, English I take it from your speech, London I'll wager, yes?"

Ryan nodded.

"Of course! But how rude I've been to you and your man here. Please accept a glass of wine, pressed from the grapes of my own vineyard. I trust you'll agree it is an excellent, hearty vintage. Why not stay with us for a bit; enjoy the good things life has to offer. I promise you'll not be disappointed."

The Scotsman looked around, taking in all of his guests. "Come, gentlemen. 'Tis such a lovely evening. Libations all around! Let us celebrate life! You there, musicians, play us a tune. Something lively now."

The Scotsman's servant handed Ryan and Dowlin each a glass of wine from a silver tray.

Ryan raised his glass and tipped it towards the Scotsman. "To good company, to good hunting and to better days to come," he offered gamely.

"Here, here!" replied the sloop's elegant passengers with one voice. Each man stood and raised his glass and drank. The musicians took up their instruments and resumed playing. The men from mostly Londonderry returned to their games and chitchat.

Dowlin, a bit more relaxed, was beginning to enjoy himself. He looked over the faces of the Scotsman's guests. He was certain he could out-shoot, out-drink and out-gamble any man on board. If only he had the time - he could make some real money gambling this fine evening!

The Scotsman refilled Ryan's glass. "I'm a fair judge of character. You strike me as a good fellow. Why not join us for the evening? It's too dark now for shooting or fishing. We'll take those sports up again in the morning. A drink or two and then a game of chance perhaps back at my home? For modest wagers only, of course - all in good fun. What do you say? Please accept my invitation. Be good to have someone other than these stodgy old cronies of mine to converse with for a change."

Dowlin watched with amusement as Ryan shook his head no, declining the offer. The fun was about to end so he drained his glass and helped himself to one more. The Scotsman had not lied. The wine was delicious.

"Your offer tempts me sorely, Mr. MacGregor. But alas my good man, with sincere regret I must decline your kind invitation, sir. I have pressing business to attend to."

The Scotsman frowned, genuinely disappointed. "How unfortunate. May I inquire what business you are off to on this fine evenin'? I thought you said you had a mind do so some hunting? And I didn't catch yer names."

"Ah, of course, how rude of me not to introduce myself and my good Lieutenant here," replied the raider of ships, the sacker of cities. He looked around the ship and raised his voice for all to hear. "Gentlemen. My men and I are indeed out here to do a bit of hunting too. But we neither hunt for fish nor fowl. We hunt Englishmen on English ships which, I am sorry to say, this is."

Whether too drunk or too brave to care, the Scotsman didn't flinch a muscle. But his guests fell silent and the musicians stopped playing.

"My *Lord!*" MacGregor finally blurted out. "A *pirate*? In these waters? Heaven forbid! I've never heard of such a thing this far north! You hardly appear a barbarian to me, sir."

"No pirate, my good Scotsman," Ryan answered courteously and bowed his head. "Allow me to finally introduce myself. I am Captain Luke Ryan, of the American privateer *Fearnot*. In the name of the United States of America, I declare your ship an enemy vessel and claim it as a prize and all aboard her are my prisoners. I thank you for the wine. Most delightful. But now it's down to business."

Ryan explained, for all to hear, their options and when he had finished there was grumbling. But all-in-all, MacGregor's Irish and Scottish guests took their new circumstances in good stride. MacGregor excused himself for a moment to have a word with his guests and soon returned with an answer.

"Captain Ryan, we have discussed the matter through and through. We are men of some means. That must seem plain enough to you. On board, pooling our resources together, I am assured we can meet any reasonable demand. No need for any hostages. We're all gentlemen here, men of our word. But if you deem a hostage absolutely necessary, then, these are my guests, let them be and take me if you must for yer security on payment."

Ryan looked at Dowlin. "One good gesture should be rewarded in kind I have always thought. Isn't that so, Mr. Dowlin?"

Dowlin shrugged and grinned. "If you say so, Capt'n."

"I do. I do indeed!" Ryan said and turned to face the Scotsman. "Well my fine Highlander, you have been a most gracious host despite my rude intrusion on your pleasuring this lovely summer evening. I'll agree to a ransom price of, shall we say, one thousand pounds sterling?"

The Scotsman turned to his guests and they all nodded their approval. "We can pay that amount this night."

"Wonderful! No need for hostages then. And no need to fear for your estate either. My crew is a *desperate* lot, but I'll not let them at your properties. You have my word on that. Please accept my sincere apologies for tonight. Regrettably, our countries are at war. An altogether unpleasant, distasteful business."

"Aye," replied MacGregor with a wry smile, "a nasty business indeed! But you wage it with such flair! You have, may I say, sir, style! I can imagine a fate far worse in war than your brief intrusion."

Sterling pound notes and gold coins were collected in a canvas bag and handed over to Dowlin. Ryan didn't bother counting it, touched the brim of his hat and bid all a good night before he disappeared over the rail.

As they rowed back to the ship, Ryan saw the faraway look in Dowlin's eyes. "Out with it Pat. Why the sour look, hey?"

Whatever look Ryan thought he saw in Dowlin's face vanished in an instant.

Dowlin smiled, slapped his knee and burst out laughing. "Why I'm hardly glum! Not at all - although I do take exception to bein' called part of a *desperate* lot - I was just thinkin', that's all. Always a dangerous thing for me to do to be sure. But by *Gawd*, Luke, yer a corker! I was just reflectin' on all our years together. We've enjoyed some pretty fair times together and we've shared some bad times too. We've made some money and we've lost some money along the way. Leastwise I think we've made some money. That old glutton Torris hasn't shared much of it with us so far. I swear tho', this one encounter with 'em gentlemen back thar has made this whole damn business worth the while! We could've taken more. We coulda raided that Scotsman's lands. I'll wager he's worth a pretty penny. But you did the right thing. A lesser man woulda taken everythin' on board and then sunk that boat just for spite. Not you. Not yer style. You never would have burned that village back thar either. I do believe yer becomin' a modern Robin Hood. Aye! A Robin Hood of the high seas so to speak and we're yer merry men! Ha! Ha! Better yet: *Ryan's Raiders*... Aye, that title suits me better. You sure put on a damn good show. You actually had 'em gentlemen smilin' as you took their money. Anyways, I wouldn't trade a moment of any of it for all the whiskey in Ireland. Win, lose or draw, it has been a grand ride with you, Luke."

Ryan was touched by Dowlin's words and grateful for his friendship. "It hasn't been a bad life all-in-all for us has it my friend?"

But as soon as said those words, his thoughts turned to Shannon and he fell silent. A tear touched his eye.

Even in the dark Dowlin could see the shadow pass across Ryan's face. He looked away and said no more.

The next day, flying the stars and stripes, *Fearnot* sailed into the harbor of Portree on the Skye. The privateers announced themselves with a single cannon shot as was their custom and the town's inhabitants responded by coming out in droves. They lined themselves up along the water's edge. Ryan was in the mood for a bit of showmanship and took his sleek barque into Portree's small harbor with too much sail and too much speed. The barque glided across the smooth waters, passed neatly between two sloops riding anchor. People gasped. The Scots thought the master of the vessel was some lunatic - they thought the reckless fool was about to beach his ship! But no lunatic commanded this vessel and Ryan, at the last moment, gave the order to let go the anchor. The cable roared through the hawsehole and men scrambled to furl all sail. When the anchor snagged the harbor's rocky bottom, the cutter came to an abrupt stop with barely a groan - and with plenty of water to spare.

The citizens of Portree debated among themselves what the strange American vessel in their harbor meant and agonized over what Fate might have in store for their poor, defenseless town. But they needn't have worried. The two sloops were fair game and Ryan ransomed both vessels. But the scared looks in the faces of the people back in Stornoway troubled him still. He had no stomach for frightening innocent women and children and so sent his Irish giant Kelly ashore to *purchase* more provisions for the ship. The townsmen eagerly delivered several lambs and one good heifers down to the water's edge. The animals were slaughtered on the beach and the meat was salted and packed into barrels. And to show their gratitude, the good citizens of Portree even threw in a cask of single malt scotch for good measure.

And then, with his commission nearly at an end, and feeling uncharacteristically weary, Ryan gave the order to return to France. He was tempted to go south and cut through the Irish Sea to try their luck there one last time but his instincts warned him not to. And so he headed north, where the privateers retraced their steps back through Raarsay Sound, and passed through the Kyle until they reached the German Ocean again.

But before the brazen privateers left waters of Scotland, Ryan decided to make one last stop. One of Ryan's English sailors had heard rumors that the king kept a good bit of treasure stored in the town of Kintail twelve miles up Loch Alsh. Dowlin led a raiding party into Kintail to seize the public storehouse. Dowlin and his men took it easily but for their troubles they found only eighteen guineas.

But on their voyage home Ryan's luck improved dramatically. The privateers took eight good prizes. Five vessels were ransomed and three, their masters being ornery and unreasonable men, were burned. Thirty-eight days after leaving, *Fearnot* sailed triumphantly back into Dunkirk with 14 prisoners with several dozen paroles for more and ransom bills for eight ships - and one town – with £1000 in sterling and gold. The privateers could rightfully boast that their cruise was a huge success.

After learning about Ryan's latest exploits in the German Ocean and Scotland from one of his own agents, Franklin penned a letter to Torris congratulating him "...on the success I hear Capt. Ryan has lately had, and wish you a continuance of Good Fortune."

Before Dowlin had taken the *Flora*, Count Vergennes had paid scant attention to Franklin's tiny fleet of privateers. But France could not afford a hostile Holland on her flank while waging war against England and Vergennes wanted to know how such a silly dispute over one inconsequential bundle of wood could risk a political catastrophe. He sent word to the Minister of Marine and demanded the Minister look into the whole messy business immediately. Sartine did so gladly and sent Vergennes his own files on Franklin's privateers, along with a strong recommendation that the king put an end to Franklin's lawlessness at sea. France derived no benefit from American privateers Sartine argued. But, by allowing Franklin's privateers to operate out of French ports, without control or oversight, exposed France by risking France's allegiances with friends. The *Flora*, Sartine said, offered clear proof of that.

Vergennes agreed with Sartine's assessment and urged Franklin to revoke all commissions for any American privateers operating out of French ports before any real damage harmed Franco-American relations. Franklin could not ignore Vergennes and, with a heavy heart, he instructed Torris to recall both the *Black Princess* and the *Fearnot* and suggested the Irishmen pursue French commissions if they still had any burning desire to fight the British.

And then, to make certain that Franklin never again dabbled in privateering, King Louis issued a Royal edict prohibiting any American from acting as a French judge of the admiralty in the future. Henceforth, any prizes taken by any American privateers operating from France would be subject to the jurisdiction of the French Council for Prizes. Not only did this give the French government control over American privateers - it also meant that one third of any prize money flowed into French royal coffers.

And so Franklin's private navy, and his private war against the British over prisoners, came to an abrupt end with little fanfare. Franklin had mixed feelings. On the one hand, he no longer needed to concern himself with judging the validity of war prizes, a thankless, bureaucratic task that had required long and tedious hours of his precious time. He detested reviewing lengthy legal documents. On the other hand, his privateers had inspired the imagination and had caused real damage. They had achieved a string of stunning successes against incredible odds. And Franklin was very proud of the accomplishments of his tiny navy.

Ryan gathered his officers at Torris's warehouse to discuss their situation. With no more American commissions to be had and no money - Torris claimed he still hadn't collected on the ransom bills or judgments from the prizes brought back to France and had no money to pay the privateers - the meeting accomplished little. Disillusioned, all but a handful of Americans elected to return home. Macatter and a number of Irishmen decided to go their own way too. But for Ryan and his veterans, his Shadowmen, which now included several Americans, patriotism inspiring some, an unquenchable hatred for the British consuming others, the war was hardly over. And so, in the fall of 1780, Ryan, with little enthusiasm, but with no good options, filed an application for a French commission with the French Admiralty.

Sixteen

A Young Soldier Calls Upon an Old Diplomat

emple found Franklin sitting in his study, attending to his letters. "*Grandfather!*" Temple called out excitedly as he led the Irishman inside. Temple saw the frown on the old man's face and knew his grandfather was annoyed by the intrusion.

Peering over his wire-rimmed glasses, Franklin stared up at Temple and saw a young man with wavy black hair and a handsome face standing at Temple's side. He didn't recognize the face. Franklin hated surprise visits and Temple knew better than to allow a stranger in without first seeking his approval. He was already behind in his work and pressed for time and began searching for some excuse to rid himself of this unexpected visitor without appearing too rude.

But then again, Franklin had lived long enough to size others up fairly quickly and this intruder had a certain way about him, some quality that intrigued him. The visitor was well dressed in French clothes but didn't look French. And then there was the stiffness, a certain regal bearing, in his stance. The man's eyes were keen, full of intelligence and yet, a trifle sad too. This was a person of authority. *Nobility* Franklin wondered? *No. An officer perhaps?*

Temple was beaming, delighted he had caught his grandfather off-guard.

"Grandfather. May I introduce *Monsieur* Luke Ryan to you, Captain of the American privateer *Fearnot.*"

The old man cracked a smile. *So this is the Irishman Luke Ryan! I should have known.* He studied Ryan more carefully. *And what I've read about you is true; you do indeed like to dress well.*

"My word... Our famous Captain Ryan! Or should I say the infamous Captain Ryan? Here in my house! You honor us, sir. Do come in. Better yet, shall we retire to the parlor? Much more comfortable there. Temple, be a good lad and see what treats we have to offer our good Captain. No doubt, he has traveled far. The Ambassador of Spain sent over some wine the other day. Perhaps we can sample some of that?"

"Most gracious, your Excellency," Ryan replied and bowed his head.

Franklin rose from his chair and offered Ryan his hand. Ryan was surprised by the old man's firm grip.

"Captain Ryan, this is such an unexpected surprise and it is truly an honor to finally make your acquaintance," Franklin said as he led Ryan into a larger, warmer room with a generous fire. "That is a compliment I use sparingly and I offer it now with all sincerity."

"The honor is mine, your Excellency. I promise not to keep you long from your important work. I intend to be quick."

"Rubbish, I'm delighted you are here," Franklin replied truthfully. Still, he braced himself for an argument, worried that Ryan might try to waste his time asking him to reconsider his decision revoking Ryan's commission. The old man was not about to change his mind on the subject, no matter how persuasive the intriguing Irishman might be. Versailles simply would not permit it.

"Please, do sit down, Captain. My grandson will bring us some refreshments."

"Don't wish to trouble you none, sir."

Franklin thought for a moment he smelled a set-up - his eyes, clear and alert, narrowed. "Why 'tis no trouble at all."

Ryan scrutinized the old man carefully as he removed his cloak, unbuttoned his coat and took a chair across from Franklin. He smiled. The old man was just as he had imagined: spectacles, rumpled clothing and strands of long, gray hair resting, uncombed, around his round shoulders. Franklin looked like an ordinary shopkeeper. But these traits hardly defined the man. Franklin used his appearance for affect, to make a statement, not unlike himself.

"Doctor Franklin, thank you for seeing me. I shall, as I said, not impose on your hospitality for too long."

"Oh, please, no more apologies. I have time for heroes, sir. But tell me, what can I do for you, Captain?"

"Why nothing, sir, nothing at all," Ryan replied reassuringly.

Temple entered the room with a decanter of wine and two glasses. Ryan gladly accepted the wine, tilted the glass Franklin's way and took a sip.

"Ah, an excellent beverage. My thanks to you young Master Franklin. Your Excellency, rest easy - I am not here to ask anything from you. My only purpose in Passy today is to express my gratitude, my sincerest gratitude, to you for all you've done."

Franklin began laughing and slapped his hand against his chair's armrest. "Is that so, Captain Ryan? Do you hear that, Temple? The good Captain has traveled all this way from Dunkirk to thank us for what we have done for him! By God, sir, you are a rare bird! Over the past year, I have read and heard so many stories about you and your fighting men and splendid ships. I must say, you are a remarkable young man. You and your men have shown great skill and courage that matches America's best. Why you are even talked about with admiration at Court, jealous admiration perhaps, but admiration nonetheless. It is I, on behalf of our fledgling nation, who is most indebted to you."

"You are too kind, your Excellency."

"I think not. In any event, I offer my sincerest thanks and gratitude to you and to your men. As I utter these words, they hardly seem adequate to express how very much your work has meant to America. Why you insulted His Majesty King George in violating his home shores and a good many Americans have been freed from the horrors of imprisonment because of you. Your accomplishments stagger the imagination! And I dare say - though I wouldn't care to have him hear this - I hold you in the same high esteem as I do our indomitable Captain Jones. Ah, I only wish we had time to do more good. I am sorry, sincerely so, that it became necessary to withdraw your commissions. Politics my lad, it's all politics - one of man's most odious creations, but, I suppose, a necessary one."

Ryan raised his hand. "No need to apologize, your Excellency. I have read the articles in the French *Monituer*, and in the English papers too. I have some poor understanding of the troubles we must have caused you."

"Mere inconveniences that shall pass with time. Trifling matters really when compared to the sufferings our soldiers and sailors have had to endure at the hands of their British jailers. Any troubles to me personally are far outweighed by your victories at sea, by your audacity against the enemy in the face of overwhelming numbers."

Realizing that the Irishman had no intention of harassing him for money or a new commission, Franklin began feeling more at ease. He sipped his wine, let the liquid work its magic, and settled back in his chair.

"I have often thought it good policy for young men to listen as old men talk. There are exceptions of course. Tell me, Captain, if you have the time, tell me of your exploits. I would be fascinated to hear the story directly from the author..."

Ryan grinned, flattered by the request, and gladly told Franklin his tale from start to finish. Temple pulled up chair to listen too. Lair soon joined them.

To the old man's delight, Ryan had a gift for storytelling and recounted his adventures without boastfulness or embellishment. That was not Ryan's way and, besides, there was hardly any need to embellish or boast.

Temple and Lair sat spellbound and Franklin listened carefully as Ryan spun his story, a story well-bred and true. When Ryan finished Franklin gingerly rose from his chair. With the help of his cane, he walked over to the fire to massage his stiff legs. He found himself liking the brash, young Irishman.

"Remarkable. Truly a remarkable tale my good Captain. Tell me, what will you and your Irish lads do now? You cannot go back to Ireland I take it?"

"No. Ireland is no longer my home or country. Not while the British rule over it. Perhaps I will travel to America someday. But for now, the British have not yet seen the last of me. I have applied for a French commission and shall endeavor to prosecute our war that way."

"A dangerous proposition if you're caught, Captain Ryan."

"Aye," Ryan answered with a smile, reverting back to his native Irish brogue. He Temple and Lair a wink. "We'll be needin' a bit of the old, Irish luck, hey?"

"Grandfather has often said," Temple interjected, "that the wise man is the man who knows how much to leave to chance, or luck, and how much not to. Isn't that so, Grandfather?"

"Ha! Ha! Well said, lad! If you say so, Temple. A nice, homespun proverb. And I'll be all too glad to take the credit for it if you fail to do so!"

Ryan tipped his wine glass at Temple and stood. "I'll try to keep such sage advice in mind, young Mr. Franklin! Well, the hour is late and I've intruded on your time your Excellency long enough. God bless you, sir. And, of course, I look forward to the day that America wins the last battle over the English, the day she wins her liberty. I only wish we could have accomplished more with the time we had to help America in her just and noble cause."

The old man stretched out his hand and smiled. "I am flattered, Captain Ryan, that you came all this way to call upon an old man. Truly, sir, it has been a pleasure making your acquaintance. This has been a most memorable evening."

Ryan shook Franklin's hand, was again surprised by the firmness of the old man's grip. "Thank you, your Excellency. Oh, beg pardon, sir, I almost forgot. I fear I misspelled your name in my correspondence to you. I take it I spelled your name in the *English* style. My humble apologies. My education is somewhat lacking."

"Mine too, mine too," Franklin replied with a wry smile. "At least as for any formal schooling. There are different forms of education though, wouldn't you agree?"

"I would indeed."

"I thought you might. I tried to introduce a phonetic alphabet once in the Colonies to simplify the English language. Never took. Ah well, I have heard it said: 'tis a damn poor man who can't spell a word more than one way!"

Ryan chuckled as Franklin walked him to the door.

The doctor looked Ryan in the eye and patted his shoulder. "Captain Ryan, please do take care. Plenty of sharks in the water. Though I am old and you are young, I pray I live long enough for our paths to cross again someday. Thank you again for all that you have done for our cause and Godspeed to you."

"I'll be on my guard your Excellency," Ryan promised confidently.

The two men shook hands one last time. Then Ryan stepped into the darkness and caught the next coach back to Dunkirk, riding to a future he could not see.

Seventeen
Flying French Colors

he six foot high windows to his office had been opened wide to allow in fresh air. There wasn't much. Shafts of intense sunlight cut their way past the heavy blue drapes, rotted with mildew at the bottom fringes, and settled on the Minister of Marine's fine African mahogany desk. The grain in the exquisite wood sparkled in the strong light, as if wood had been set on fire.

Despite the onslaught of fall, a hot, humid bubble of air had settled over Paris. The toxic mix of oppressive humidity and harsh morning glare was giving Sartine a headache and neither the cleansing power of the sun nor the fresh air could kill the musty odor forever permeating his office. He removed his powdered wig, carefully laying it on the corner of his desk - the damn thing was simply too hot to wear - and took a lace handkerchief tucked inside his ruffled cuff to blot away the beads of perspiration forming on his brow.

Doumar arrived punctually at ten. The man was habitually precise in all things, including time. Sartine liked that. Punctuality showed a proper measure of respect and dependability. Not easy qualities to always find.

Sartine motioned to Doumar to take a seat while he handed him a sheet of paper.

"Read this," he ordered, not wasting time on pleasantries. After Doumar had finished, Sartine asked him to repeat what he had just read and Doumar recited his instructions back verbatim. The Minister nodded his approval. Sartine would not tolerate any mishaps like the colossal blunder of Captain Guilman. Thankfully, he could assess no blame to Doumar for Gilman's botched effort.

"Do you understand your assignment?"

"Quite, your grace. I am the clean-up man."

"Yes, that is precisely what you are - the clean-up man. Well, better said: you are my clean-up man. Any questions?"

"None."

"Good."

Satisfied that Doumar understood what was required of him, Sartine took the paper back and tossed a red velvet purse filled with gold coins at Doumar, to cover the costs of bribes and expenses. And then he dismissed Doumar with a wave of his hand and Doumar left at once for Dunkirk to do his master's bidding.

After Doumar left his office, Sartine touched the corner of the paper he had given Doumar to read to a candle and let the incriminating evidence burn.

Sartine's thoughts turned back to April and Guilman's bungled attack on the *Black Prince*. He couldn't believe Guilman's stupidity. Yes, Guilman had run the privateer down - but in plain view of several thousand witnesses and with not one Irishman dead! *God Almighty! France has more than its fair share of incompetent fools.*

Sartine had rewarded Guilman with forced early retirement at half pay, though the disgraceful amateur deserved far worse. And then Sartine had sent Doumar on to Dunkirk a few weeks later to fix Guilman's mistake. But when the international flap with the *Flora* fell into his lap, all the former Minister's problems with the Irish privateers seemed miraculously solved and he had recalled Doumar.

Ryan and his men had been under Franklin's protection for the last year and a half. But not so now. The Irishmen were fair game and still a menace.

The Minister picked up a folder on Ryan and his privateers and glanced over Ryan's application for a French commission. The Irishman's arrogance had astounded him. Ryan's lawlessness had cost him a tidy sum of money and he wasn't about to let Ryan run loose again like some fox in the hen house, even under a French commission, and so he had rejected Ryan's first application outright.

But the matter wouldn't die. While the Minister had rejected Ryan's application, he had approved several others and soon learned from one of his agents in Dunkirk that a French privateer, under a Captain Piccardi, was making preparations to sail with a largely Irish crew. Sartine thought that suspicious, checked his files and soon realized that he had indeed issued a commission to a Captain Piccardi. Investigating things further, he discovered, to his dismay, that Piccardi's ship, *Le Cologne*, was actually the *Fearnot* rechristened under a new name! Ryan had duped him just as he had duped Franklin before - *à la* Marchant.

The Irishman's impertinence stunned Sartine again and he considered having Ryan arrested. But the charge was thin and didn't carry much of a sentence. Then he stumbled on a better idea. A plan took root in his mind, an inspiration really, to rid himself permanently of this pest.

A fresh ocean breeze, cool and dry to please the senses, blew in through the window as he sat in his hotel room, reviewing the ship's crew list. Ryan looked up and could see his powerful cruiser sitting, useless, in Dunkirk's harbor. But now, at last, everything was in place for her to put to sea again.

It had not been easy or cheap. The French Minister of Marine had rejected his first application for a French privateer commission, filed in his own name, so he had been forced to find himself a French captain as a front man. And then he forged a new set of ship's papers, changing the *Fearnot* into *Le Cologne*. Under any name she was still the same vessel and in prime condition. Dowlin had seen to that.

Macatter had taken his family and left Dunkirk. Patterson caught a ship back to America. But Dowlin, the Kelly clan, and all Ryan's Irish veterans choose to remain with him, as did the Americans Simmons and Amati too. And there on the list was Jumbaaliyia's name. For reasons known only to the African, Jumbaaliyia decided to remain and refused any money for a passage home.

Ryan provisioned the ship using the last of his own funds. No more help came from Torris. The man still claimed he had no money, but curiously, he always put Ryan off whenever Ryan asked to inspect the company's books and records. Ryan didn't much care. He was a man possessed. He would wage war against the British on his own if necessary.

When evening came, as was their custom on the eve of any voyage, the Irishmen gathered at their favorite tavern and reached out one last time for the good things in life. Ryan was unusually pensive and stood in a dark corner by himself, leaning against a wall and sipping his ale. In the past, he had always been excited, even jubilant, before setting off on a new cruise and would mingle with the men. But not this time. *Odd mood*, he thought to himself.

He quietly watched his men amuse themselves. Dowlin, the Kellys and a handful of the lads were sitting at a table drinking and playing cards. The tavern was alive with music, dancing and laughter and the Irishmen were having fun.

Dowlin looked up from the table and caught Ryan watching them. He smiled at him, waved hello and returned to his drinking. Dowlin recognized the mood, knew to give Ryan his space.

Then the most peculiar thought struck Ryan. He realized that his image of Dowlin smiling at him at that moment, like some portrait, would be indelibly etched into his memory for the rest of his life. And then, without warning, an ugly premonition hit him. It occurred to him that he might never see Dowlin, or any of his men, again. He shook the evil tremor off and blamed the ale. He quietly scolded himself - he knew better than to drink when he was in the grip of one of his darker moods. Then again, he had experienced premonitions before and they always had come true...

Ryan left his men to their games and drinking and returned to his room. Jacqueline, dressed in a nightgown and mending some piece of clothing for him with needle and thread, was sitting near the fire, waiting for him. Her eyes sparkled as he walked into the room and she gave him a loving smile.

"Oh Luke, I am happy you have returned early. You are well?" she asked cautiously in her broken English, unable to hide her concern. Like Dowlin, she had come to know Ryan's moods well.

Ryan leaned over her shoulder and kissed her cheek. "Fit as a fiddle. Weather is holding. We sail in the morning with the tide."

She placed her work in her lap, slipped her hand into his and pulled it to her cheek. She always took pleasure in feeling his rough skin against her own. "Yes," she said softly.

Ryan stared absently into the fire, absorbed in thought.

Jacqueline saw the faraway look in his eyes, as if he was a world away. "Luke. I was pleased to see you off on all your voyages before. I know how much you love the sea, how important your work, your crusade, is to you. Always, always before I waited for you to return, anxious, yes, but in my heart I was confident you would return. Luke - I beg you - do not go this time. Let Patrick take *Fearnot* out. He is strong and able."

Ryan looked down at her with curiosity. She had Shannon's gift of knowing when and how to hold him, but she did not share Shannon's gift of knowing when to let go. He saw her beautiful, dark eyes turn to liquid pools, saw the tears roll down her cheek.

"My dear, lovely Jacqueline. Why the tears? What is this all about now? Hm?" He took his thumb to wipe away her tears, leaned down to kiss her eyes. "I do not understand. Tell me, Jacqueline."

She tried to smile. "I cannot explain it, Luke. I am just a silly, young girl. I know this. But I've always had a good sense of, hm, how do I say in English...?"

"Intuition?"

"*Oui!* Intuition, *mon amour*. Something is not right. I feel it, inside, I feel it."

Numb with fear, she pulled his hand to her breast and pressed it firmly against her heart. How much she wanted Ryan to stay. But she knew his mind was firm...

"Luke, I love you so much. Stay, just this one time, stay with me. I beg you - do not go. Doom, Luke, doom hovers over your shoulder like a shadow. I see it plainly. Do not sail out under a French flag."

Ryan moved around in front of her and dropped to his knees. He took her hands into his own, looked into her eyes and smiled.

She was a joy to his heart and her love for him had always been patient and kind. She had been a treasure. His smile was warm, loving and reassuring.

He reached up and held her chin in the palm of his hand. "So now you can predict the future woman? Pat always tried to warn me that you were a sorceress with all those magic potions of yours!"

"No, no sorceress. Just a fool perhaps."

He kissed her forehead. "You're no fool, my love. But, I *must* go. Listen now, I've been fighting the British for a long while now. Not one scratch on me by their hand. My ship is faster and my crew is better than anything they have. And, I dare say, I have a few modest skills myself! All shall be fine, I promise you. It is my duty to go. The lads expect it. Do you understand?"

His promise was a lie. He had felt the undercurrents too. An uneasiness permeated the air, a foreboding filled his heart. But he was powerless to undo those things that had already been set in motion - by a force far greater than himself.

"But I..." she started to say.

He put a finger to her lips. "Hush now, dear girl. It is beyond the power of men to stay the hand of Fate - no matter how hard we might try. I do not fear destiny. When Dawn's light comes, what shall be, shall be. The hour is late dear woman, let us talk of this no more. Come now to bed. I will show you the love inside my heart for you. I will make you moan with pleasure and bring a smile to your lips..."

She smiled bravely at him and obeyed. But in her heart, she was afraid, afraid that she would never see her mariner again.

In his dream, he was all alone on a small ship. The ship was floundering in heavy seas and her hull kept smashing against the rocks, over and over again. He bolted upright in the bed, bathed in sweat, and heard a fist pounding against the door.

"Capt'n, it's John, sir. I must speak with you. *Now*, sir."

Ryan quickly slipped on his trousers and went to unlock the door. Jacqueline wrapped a shawl around herself and followed him, stood behind him as he opened the door, clutching his arm with both hands.

Kelly was alone. Beads of sweat covered his forehead.

"Well get yourself in here man," Ryan commanded and with a hint of annoyance. "You're lettin' in a draft." But he knew Kelly would never come to him like this without good cause.

The big man slipped inside the room, removed his knitted, wool cap. "Sorry Capt'n. Miss Jacqueline, good evening ma'am, sorry to wake you both. I know the hour is late, sir, but this won't wait."

"Go on with you, John."

"Aye, well, sir, it's like this. Dowlin, Chris, Tim, Morgan and some of the lads were down stairs drinkin' and playin' dice when one of king's press gangs burst into the tavern and took away every seaman in sight. I was out back takin' a piss and managed to slip away. Oh, beg pardon, ma'am."

"*Christ!*" Ryan clenched his teeth and said.

Jacqueline squeezed his arm. Apprehension clouded her thoughts, her heart was filled with fear.

"Whatcha want to do, sir?"

"I'll fetch my clothes. We'll go down to see the commissary and straighten this matter out right now. There's been a simple mistake. That's all there is to it."

He looked at Jacqueline, exquisite girl with the soft, brown eyes and glossy dark hair, but fragile too, and patted the small white hand clinging to his arm. "Not to worry now, love. I'll be back to you shortly. Go back to bed and keep it warm for me."

Ryan quickly dressed and the two Irishmen hurried down to the Admiralty office a few blocks away. The office was a cramped, shabby place lit by a single oil lamp. The duty officer, a petty sub-lieutenant, sat behind a cheap desk and listened sympathetically to Ryan's protests.

"I do understand your dilemma, *mon Capitaine* Ryan. And you sail with the morning tide? A pity. But these things do from time to time happen. It is regrettable, but easily corrected."

"Excellent, *Monsieur*," Ryan replied hopefully. "Where can I collect my men?"

"Oh, but I am afraid that is quite impossible for the moment."

"Beg pardon?"

"Your men are not here. And besides there is paperwork involved. Ha! Always there is paperwork! It will be a matter of some days, I would imagine, before your men can be released. Perhaps longer. But I assure you, they will be released to you if what you say, and I doubt you not,

Monsieur, is true. With so many foreign sailors roaming about in our French ports mistakes like this are not all that uncommon."

Ryan massaged his temples. He could feel the repulsive beast, always lurking somewhere inside of him, wrapping its strong tentacles around his brain, squeezing harder. The terrible pounding would soon begin. No stopping it now. Excruciating pain. And it would not release him until it had laid him low, not until its victim prayed for death to take him.

"This," Ryan said, raising his voice, "is intolerable. Nothing like it has ever happened before. These men are being illegally detained. For pity's sake where are my men?"

The French officer rifled through some papers on his desk, found one sheet in particular that caught his interest and reviewed it under his desk lamp. "Ah, yes, here it is, *mon Capitaine*. Why they are being transported to Brest. Yes, Brest is their destination."

"Bloody hell!" cursed Kelly. "Why were they moved out of Dunkirk in the middle of the night and taken to Brest?"

The French lieutenant ignored him.

Kelly looked over at Ryan with a scowl on his face. He was sorely tempted to reach across the desk and ring the scrawny Frenchman's neck. "Somethin' an't right here Capt'n. This stinks, stinks bad. Thar's an ill-wind blowin' this night."

The French officer shrugged. "Gentlemen, it is late. I bid you good night. There is no more I can do for you. File your petitions for the release of your men with the Admiralty in Brest. Must I remind *Monsieur* you are on French soil and subject to French law? There are proper procedures for these matters which must be strictly observed..."

"Let's go, Mr. Kelly, looks like we've been outmaneuvered here."

When morning came, Ryan gathered the remnants of his crew. The press gang had snatched Dowlin and Kelly and eight good men. Someone with power seemed interested in foiling his plans. He had assumed with a French commission and a French captain in his pocket he would have no more problems with the French authorities. But he was wrong.

The mariner stood on deck, watching his crew bring the last of the perishable goods on board. All through the morning drizzle he had felt nervous and on edge. Worse, his thinking was muddled, sluggish. Always a bad sign.

At least Captain Piccardi had the good sense to arrive punctually. Ryan had found him to be a congenial fellow so far who had no interest actually *commanding* the privateer. Piccardi seemed quite content to be paid to do nothing. And when Ryan informed him of what had happened to his crew the night before, the resourceful Frenchman disappeared into town and returned an hour later with 20 French sailors, all volunteers and able seamen, or so he assured Ryan, to bolster Ryan's numbers.

After men rolled the last barrel up the gangplank, John Kelly, the ship's new first officer, reported the ship ready to sail. Ryan hesitated and stared out across the blue Atlantic with a vacant look in his eyes. Sail or stay? He had a ship and crew to fight with and he had provisions for an extended cruise. And he knew that his Irish and American veterans, all fiercely loyal, would keep the *foreigners* in line. But then there was that *voice* nagging at him, begging him not to sail. *I am thinking like a silly child,* he told himself and shook it off and blamed his mood on too much coffee.

"*Monsieur* Ryan?" Piccardi asked, confused by Ryan's hesitation. "All is ready. The crew awaits your orders."

Ryan looked up at the masts and rigging, still unsure. He hesitated.

"Your orders?" Piccardi repeated forcefully, barely able to conceal his impatience.

Ryan turned to face Piccardi, is desire for hot action had finally won him over. "Aye, Captain Piccardi. Mr. Kelly, ease her out of the harbor and into the bay with the tops'ls set. *Allons...*"

But through the morning, his first officer had shared his captain's premonition. Uncertainty and doubt had been gnawing away at John Kelly too and now he hesitated.

"Beg pardon, sir. Might be a better wind for us tomorrow? Just a thought, sir."

But Ryan had given the order and had no intention of looking weak or indecisive in front of Piccardi or his men. "Today, Mr. Kelly. We sail today."

Kelly closed his eyes and took a deep breath. Ryan's mind was firm. He swallowed hard, strutted down the deck and barked out orders. Bare-chested and bare-footed Frenchmen, wearing nothing but dirty trousers, climbed up into the rigging under a hot, October sky. The sun was just beginning to burn her way through the clouds. The Frenchmen unfurled sail while their mates below strained against the capstan to raise the 1000-pound anchor. The ship's dark canvas caught a light breeze and pushed the battle cruiser slowly out towards the open sea while seagulls, squawking and circling overhead, took turns swooping down to try and snatch some morsel of food discarded by the cook.

Once the warship cleared the harbor, Kelly had all her canvas stretched out to catch the freshening Channel wind. The handsome barque responded well, picked up terrific speed and skimmed across the waves like some magnificent black eagle on a rush of air.

And it was not long until the master mariner was smiling broadly once again. The privateers were hardly an hour out from Dunkirk Road when they ran down their first prize. Ryan's decision to sail had been the right one after all. After putting a small prize crew aboard their first catch, and sending her into Dunkirk, he went to his cabin to take a quick nap. He had barely closed his eyes when the lookout cried out a new warning.

"Sails on the horizon! Two large luggers... off the quarter port... red sails... I see Laskers and Ethiopians aboard."

Ryan raced up the companionway and went directly to the helm, took his spyglass and scanned the waves for sails. "What do you make of those vessels, sir?" he asked Piccardi, handing his glass over to the Frenchman.

"I see the silhouettes of dark square sails," Piccardi offered in broken English. "They're French, *Monsieur*. Privateers out of Boulogne no doubt."

Ryan nodded. "Possibly. Mr. Kelly, if you please. I'll have the deck cleared for action."

"Aye, aye, Captain! Mr. Simmons..."

Simmons cracked one of his rare grins as he charged down the deck. Only Dowlin exceeded the American's enthusiasm for hot action.

"You thar boatswain - pipe us to general quarters!" Simmons roared. "And you lads over there, yep, I'm talkin' to you! Move your asses, look lively now and get them braces in line!"

But Piccardi began fidgeting. "*Monsieur* Ryan, why do you ready your ship for battle?"

"Simply as a precaution, sir. We do not know what ships approach us nor do we know their intentions, thus the precaution."

"But *I* have already told *you*."

"I beg to differ, sir. You've told me who you *think* they are."

Piccardi muttered something under his breath and put Ryan's spyglass to his eye again to study the two vessels more closely.

"Ah, yes, one ship is the *St. Vincent*," he offered with a testy voice. "I am certain of it. I know her master well. And the other I see now is the *Lyon*. Both these ships are French privateers as I have said. They mean us no harm. Perhaps they wish to join us in the hunt? They are fast and well-armed cruisers. We would do well to sail with them."

Kelly returned to Ryan's side, reported the ship was cleared for action.

"Very well, Mr. Kelly! No need to run out the guns just yet."

Kelly touched his cap and made his way back to the guns to wait for Ryan's orders. The French ships were coming up fast. The French had the wind and *Fearnot* was not yet fully under way after her crew had furled all sail to board their first prize.

And then - a puff of smoke, followed by the dull report of one cannon. *BOOM!*

The small explosion sent an iron ball flying over *Fearnot's* bow and her crew watched it splash harmlessly into an empty sea several hundred yards away.

Ryan gave Kelly a nod and Kelly ordered the port lids opened and had the guns run out. The gun crews moved smartly and the deck rumbled under the weight of rolling cannon. The swivels were brought up too and mounted on the rails. *Fearnot* began to stir as topmen shook out the sails.

Piccardi took a step closer to Ryan. "*Monsieur* Ryan, I do not understand this hostile act. This is a mistake. Be warned, sir. Neither my men nor I will fire on a French ship! I urge you to reconsider, bring your helm hard over and shorten sail! We all fight for the same cause."

Ryan wavered. 'My men' did Piccardi say?

Ryan considered matters. There were over 30 French and Spanish seamen serving on board *Fearnot*, nearly a third of his crew. Without the *foreigners*, he did not have enough men to maneuver his ship in battle and service all his ship's heavy guns against two ships at once - if French intentions were hostile.

"Mr. Kelly! Mr. Simmons! A word if you please!"

Kelly and Simmons rushed back to the stern. The two French cruisers, with hundreds of Laskers and Ethiopians crowded in their rigging, were nearly within range of *Fearnot's* big guns.

"Gentlemen, our good Captain Piccardi here will not fire on his own countrymen. And neither will *his* men or so he has informed me. Understandable enough. That leaves us with about fifty men?"

Kelly, smelling a rat and seething, turned to Piccardi, gave him an evil look. He was sorely tempted to take his sword and run the Frenchman through right then and there. With one simple lunge at Piccardi's worthless heart, he could end the Frenchman's miserable life quickly and with little pain. No man was more loyal to Ryan than John Kelly. But Kelly knew that Ryan should have heeded his advice and not sailed. *I shoulda knocked Luke out flat in Dunkirk and let the tide leave without us. No sense mullin' such things over now, best keep focused, see a way through this jam...*

"Aye sir, forty-six lads and four officers includin' you, me and Simmons. That puts us in a bit of a fine fix, sir. I don't like it Capt'n - I don't like it one wee bit."

"Why not bring her about now, sir," prodded Simmons. "Make a run for it back to Dunkirk? We have the men to do that at least."

"It's too late, Jeremiah. Those luggers have the weather-gage on us. We can't turnabout and sail east. No. We can fight and make ourselves enemies of France - or we can wait and see what these French fellows want. P'haps it's all quite harmless..."

"Thar's nothin' harmless about French privateers," offered Kelly in a low voice laced with contempt.

Ryan considered their options. To run would be difficult. The French were nearly on top of them and besides, where would they run to? To fight seemed futile. He thought of the French frigate *Calonne* chasing down the *Black Prince*. Today was somehow connected to that. He was certain of it. But it mattered not at all now.

"Mr. Simmons, belay the order to sail. I'll have the sails shortened if you please. John, I'm sorry, but I see no other good way around this."

Ryan spun around and looked hard into Piccardi's eyes, searching for some bit of honesty there but found none. "Besides, as our good Captain Piccardi has just observed, we're all on the same side after all."

"Shorten sail, aye, but I still don't like it," Kelly replied gruffly. He took in the beauty of the azure blue sky and then looked back at Piccardi. "'Tis a pretty day to live, just as good a day to die..."

The two French luggers came to rest on a rolling green sea barely 50 yards away from the *Fearnot*. The *St. Vincent* lowered two boats in the water and within minutes, 20 Frenchmen with muskets and cutlasses were climbing over *Fearnot's* rail and fanning out along her deck. The sight turned Ryan's stomach. No ship under his command had ever been boarded before.

A small man, holding a pistol in one hand and a sword in the other and dressed in a soiled, white suit, was the last to board. He gave Ryan a harsh and threatening stare and a nod to Piccardi.

Ryan considered the Frenchman. He was someone's lackey. He appeared more comical than threatening.

"Your papers!" the Frenchman demanded coarsely without introducing himself. He took the scarf wrapped around his neck, a red silk scarf with a curious blue crescent moon embroidered on the tip, and used it to wipe away the sweat in his eyes.

With a nod from Ryan, McCloud went down to Ryan's great cabin to retrieve the *Fearnot's* papers. For an awkward minute, Ryan's men and the French boarding party stared uneasily at each other in silence, listening to the waves slap against the hull, to the pintles grinding in their gudgeons as the rigging blocks clattered in the breeze.

McCloud soon returned with a bundle of papers and gave them to Ryan. Ryan flipped through them quickly before handing them over to the Frenchman.

The Frenchman took time to examine each document carefully.

"So *Monsieur*, you are the great Luke Ryan?" the Frenchman finally asked with an air of contempt.

"No. I am simply Luke Ryan, *Monsieur*. Nothing more. May I have the pleasure of knowing your name and rank?"

The Frenchman spat on the deck. "Save your polite gentleman's talk, Captain. It is wasted on me."

"This vessel is the American privateer *Fearnot*, no?"

"No. She is the French privateer *Le Cologne*."

"Oh? She was the American *Fearnot* last I saw of her. We shall see. You and your first officer, Dowlin, you will both come with me, immediately."

"What did you say?" Ryan asked indignantly. "Who the devil do you think you are coming aboard my ship with armed men at your back to give me orders?"

"Ha! Who do I have to be?"

"A better man than you are..."

"Enough of this. I have the power. Now where is Dowlin?"

"Dowlin? Ahem, you seem well informed, *Monsieur Capitaine* - of the *St. Vincent* I presume? In any event, Lieutenant Dowlin is not here. A French press gang took him by mistake last night in Dunkirk. But we are getting ahead of ourselves, sir. Why should I go anywhere with you? This ship flies the same royal *fleur de lys* as does yours - as you can plainly see. You have inspected the ship's papers and they are in order. Now, *kindly* remove yourself from my deck and allow us to go about our business."

A crooked smile touched the Frenchman's lips. He let the *Fearnot's* papers slip from his hand, let the breeze catch them and scatter them across the deck.

"Ah, see there! Your papers are no longer in order. Now then, you and your first officer, whoever he might be, will come with me. This ship will return to Dunkirk under escort and you will accompany me to Brest."

"Va te faire foutre, trouduc," Kelly whispered under his breath and moved next to Ryan's side. He kept a hand resting on the hilt of a sword tucked inside his belt. Jumbaaliyia moved up behind Kelly, fondling two loaded pistols tucked inside his belt against the small of his back.

"Capt'n," Kelly whispered, "I'd just as soon send this little French *merde* down into the bowels of hell than go with him. P'haps we should not have sailed today. After what happened last night - we shoulda known thar was trouble ahead. Well, what's done is done. Give the word Capt'n and we'll clear the deck of this scum. See McCloud down thar by the swivel? It's loaded with grape shot and McCloud has his orders, sir. One nod from me and poof! Twenty dead Frogs splattered across the deck, guts and all. I'll clean the mess up myself after we're through."

"The little man with black eyes," Jumbaaliyia whispered into Ryan's ear, "speaks falsely to you, my Capt'n. Trust not his words. Kill him and the rest will scatter like chaff in the wind..."

There were murmurs among the crew. Every Irishmen was armed and ready to draw his weapon.

The *St. Vincent's* captain looked around anxiously. He and his men were surrounded and outnumbered.

Tension saturated the air. Men struggled to breath.

The urge to fight seized Ryan. He could hear the music, the sound of fife and drum - a *call-to-arms!* - it set his blood on fire. He wanted to bellow out Dowlin's shrill war cry with all his might and call on his Irishmen to slaughter the intruders on board his ship! His men were up to the grim task. Easy work for his hardscrabble veterans. Clearly, the captain of the *St. Vincent* was no soldier, exposing himself and his men as he had, with his ships not even on alert. But after spilling French blood, the Irishmen would face two ships, only luggers, true, but still bristling with heavy bronze cannon. And both ships carried large crews. How many good men would fall before the Irishmen could make good their escape? Too many Ryan decided. He had no desire to be remembered by his crew as the man who allowed them to be butchered. He loved them too much.

And so, his decision made, he would go quietly with the *St. Vincent's* captain who, Ryan was certain, meant him no good. It was the only choice an unselfish could make.

Ryan turned to Kelly, and then to Jumbaaliyia, and offered both men a faint smile, a smile that said: *thank you.*

Kelly's lower lip began to quiver; his eyes turned misty. His earlier exasperation with Ryan, mild as it was, all but vanished now. He had no bitterness, no regrets. He looked hard into Ryan's eyes, dark blue like the sea, and saw the sadness there, saw the intelligence in them too. *Queer,* he thought, he had never noticed the sadness in Ryan's eyes before.

Ryan snapped his head around, looked into the sweaty faces of his men. Such loyalty he knew was rare. They stood shoulder-to-shoulder ready, to a man, to fight and die for *him* if he chose to give the order. It was a proud moment worthy of remembrance. He swore he would never forget it.

He felt oddly at peace, even relieved, as if some heavy burden had been lifted from his shoulders. And then he suddenly recognized the truth: ever since the Black Dog he had known this day would steal upon them all. And now it was here, staring him in the face.

The game was at an end. If only Dowlin and Christopher Kelly were here with him now - with all his Irish and American veterans behind him - he would be the one dictating terms to this stooge! But he would go with the Frenchman and was certain they would not be returning him to France. There was a price on his head after all and French privateers were mercenaries before all else with a lust for money. No patriotic fever burned in their hearts. That meant England. The British would hang him for certain. But, somehow, that prospect did not trouble him.

Different images took shape in his head. Shannon's lovely face came to him first. He would have slipped the hangman's noose around his own neck for just one more precious night with her. And then there was Jacqueline too, an exquisite, dark-eyed beauty and a patient girl. He loved her very much in his way.

And then he thought back to the day when he had boarded the *Toulon* to accept Sartine's surrender. How he had pitied the young Sartine then. He remembered thinking that he could never handle such humiliation, not as gracefully as Sartine had done. He smiled to himself. *Not such a difficult task after all.*

He caught himself, daydreaming and thinking like a fool. *Mustn't think on such things now,* he chided himself; *there shall be time enough later to dwell on these matters, plenty of time...*

"Avast there!" he bellowed out to his men and turned to Kelly. "Mr. Kelly," he said in a soft, level voice. "We're heavily outmatched here I'm afraid. I alone am to blame..."

Then he raised his voice so that the men of the *St. Vincent* could hear him. "And besides, these Frenchmen are our friends and allies. Our papers are in order. We've nothing to be concerned about. Mr. Kelly, have the lads stand down and set a course for Dunkirk. Wouldn't want to lose this good wind... *Monsieur Capitaine*, I shall gladly accompany you back to *France* where we can satisfy any irregularities."

"A wise choice, Ryan. Your first officer too, those are my instructions."

"John, truly I am sorry for not listening to you earlier. Would you be so good as to accompany me?"

Kelly took a step forward and defiantly tossed his sword down. Jumbaaliyia moved forward too but Ryan held him back, told him he must stay. The giant African cocked his head to one side, as if to say he did not understand Ryan's last order. Then he nodded and stepped back.

Ryan removed his French cocked hat, raised it above his head to shield his eyes from the sun's blinding glare. He wanted to take in the beauty of the sky as a free man one last time. He bit his lip and looked back at his men. He wanted to speak to them as their captain one last time too.

"Lads!" he said in an Irish brogue, "I'll see you all back in Dunkirk in a day or two! Every man here has faithfully served me, this ship, and your country well. You've covered yourselves with glory. For all you have accomplished against a dangerous, zealous enemy, and for your steadfast loyalty to me, each of you has my respect, my eternal gratitude. If what men later record about this great struggle is true, future generations will know of your part in it, of your skill and bravery, and speak of it with reverence. Would to God I could sail with you all again someday. It has been my privilege and honor to serve with each of you. A captain could ask for no finer crew, for no better men to call his friends and brothers."

About seeing them soon, he knew he had lied - his first lie ever to his own men. He hoped they would understand over time.

The Irishmen showed their discontent. Like distant thunder, low rumblings rolled down the deck. His men were itching for a fight, English or French - it made no difference to them who they put to the sword.

St. Vincent's captain saw Gorgon raise her ugly head, saw it plainly in the faces of the Irishmen. Gorgon, that monstrosity, born of unholy Devastation and sign of storming Zeus - what a sheer horror to behold - with power to fill some men with madness to kill, others with madness to live. He shifted uncomfortably on his feet, looked around anxiously, and realized his life might soon end. He debated what to do. *I was a fool to expose myself like this.*

Ryan could see in his men the lust for blood rising to a fever pitch. The moment had turned explosive. He smiled reassuringly at them all and chose his next words carefully. The Furies would be disappointed this day.

"*Men of the Black Prince!*" he cried out in his command voice. His Irish veterans, as he knew they would, snapped to attention at those winning words. His Americans did the same.

His voice cracked as he choked back tears. "My *Lords of the Ocean Realm*; to you men... to you men who have risked so much for so little, to you warriors who have dared to pull the lion's tail, I... *salute*... you! God bless and keep you all..."

He raised his hand and saluted. His veterans saluted back. There would be no bloodshed.

Then young Jean ran up to him, his cheeks stained with tears, he reached into his shirt and pulled out a neatly folded piece of green cloth and handed it up to Ryan. It was Shannon's victory pennant, the same pennant they had flown after capturing the English warship *Friends*. Ryan had given it to Jean for safekeeping until they had cause to raise it again someday. Ryan smiled down at the boy, rubbed his fingers through the boy's thick hair - the way Dowlin always did. He accepted the flag from Jean and carefully tucked the green cloth away in his breast pocket.

"The day will come," Jean said with a cocky smile, looking and sounding for all the world like Dowlin, "when we will sail again together, sir. I swear it..."

Such brave, but foolish words from one so young thought Ryan. But then again, by some power beyond his imagining, he could plainly see that Jean's words were true. He grinned at the boy, a victory smile, then walked towards the rail and the waiting French.

The *Lyon* escorted *Fearnot* with a prize crew on board back to Dunkirk where she was impounded and her crew detained. Ryan and Kelly were clapped in irons, brought on board the *St. Vincent* and taken to Brest - not England as Ryan had supposed - where they were tossed into a jail at the Sourdéac Bastion and charged with the felony crimes of falsifying official documents and fraud.

Eighteen
Grim Resolve at the Game's End

⚓

Spring 1781

The newly appointed Minister of Marine took in his surroundings, made a mental note to himself to have his office's heavy, blue drapes, rotting with mildew at the edges, replaced along with the offices faded and dreary wallpaper. Charles Eugène Gabriel de La Croix de Castries, the marquis de Castries, stared at the batch of military communiqués, reports, dispatches and orders covering his ornate desk and winced. The forces arrayed against him seemed daunting.

With the king's blessing - and a gift of 175,000 *livres*, plus a pension of 75,000 *livres* paid annually for the rest of his life - Count de Sartine had retired from public service the previous October. Or, more accurately, as the new Minister of Marine well knew, the king, displeased, had allowed Sartine to quietly retire to avoid the embarrassment of dismissal.

Despite being months away, summer promised to be brutal. Castries stepped away from his desk and pulled back the sad looking drapes hanging over his office's windows to allow the morning light in and then opened the windows wide to let in some fresh air. The days had turned hot and humid again, unusually so for April. Castries could feel the first pangs of a headache coming on and he was facing a full day of tedious, bureaucratic work. Administrative functions bored him although, in truth, he knew he had a talent for it.

Unlike his predecessor, Castries was a professional soldier, through-and-through, and less a politician. He was an old army man, as tough as nails, with an illustrious record spanning decades. He began his career in 1739 as a young lieutenant serving with the crack *régiment du Roi-Infanterie*. Later he fought with distinction in the Seven Years' War and was promoted to *Mestre de camp* of the *régiment du Roi-Cavalerie* and was then again promoted to *maréchal de camp* and *commandant général* of the cavalry. He was wounded twice in the Battle of Rossbach 1757 and was thereafter promoted to lieutenant *général maître de camp général* of the cavalry. And then, at the Battle of Kloster Kamp in 1760, against superior British and German forces, Castries's skill and bravery on the field saved the day and propelled him to the rank of national hero.

Castries returned to his desk and undid the ribbon to the first folder that caught his eye marked, simply, "Franklin," and removed a subfolder with the words "Franklin's Privateers" scribbled across the jacket. While a novice in naval matters, Castries was nonetheless an astute and exceptionally gifted military man, a veteran of many battles, and did not understand Sartine's bitterness towards the Irishman, Luke Ryan. Ryan was a fighter.

Colonel Doumar had briefed Castries on a number of matters he had been handling for his former master of course, including the foolishness of Captain Guilman who, in command of the *Calonne*, had run the *Black Princess* down in front of several thousand witnesses the prior April. Castries was aware that Sartine, for reasons he did not entirely grasp, had ordered the unsavory deed and then rewarded Guilman with forced early retirement at half pay, though the disgraceful amateur, in Castries's opinion, deserved far worse. And then Sartine revoked Ryan's French commission, had the *Fearnot* impounded and charged Ryan - a hero - with petty crimes against the Crown! One of Castries's first acts as Minister of Marine was to have the charges against Ryan quietly dismissed and the court records on the matter expunged.

Castries thought it all very curious. He had in mind to reach out to the Irishman and make amends. France needed gifted, audacious military leaders like Ryan. The outcome of the war against England, in truth, was still very much in doubt. England seemed determined to hold on to her American colonies at almost any cost.

The Minister considered the file on Franklin's privateers in front of him for a time. And then, after thoughtful reflection, he stumbled upon the perfect solution and summoned Ryan to Paris.

"Ah, Captain Ryan, I am delighted, honored, to finally meet you," Castries said warmly and stood to offer Ryan his hand. The Irishman was a handsome man who liked to dress well and, while Castries knew Ryan was no more than 26 or 27 years of age, Castries was nevertheless struck by the Irishman's fresh face, by his boyish youthfulness. He tried to remember the time when he had looked that young and handsome.

Ryan shook Castries's hand and took in the Minister's office, surprised by its somewhat rundown appearance. "I am honored, my lord Minister."

"Please, sit. I am grateful you accepted my invitation."

"I am humbled - and perplexed."

"Ah, well, all shall be made clear. Please be at ease, you are among friends here. I do apologize for your brief stay at the Sourdéac. That was an unfortunate misunderstanding."

"I'm no worse for wear because of it."

"Good, good. As you might imagine, my office maintains detailed files on all naval operations, including those of our friends the Americans. But even without such files, your adventures under Doctor Franklin's authority are well known throughout France, in high and low society! Even before my appointment to Minister of Marine, I read about your bold attacks against the English with fascination. Your victories are well documented. You and your men have shown great bravery and resolve against a very dangerous foe."

"You are most gracious."

"Nonsense. May I offer you tea? Coffee? Something more potent perhaps?"

"I will follow your lead, my lord."

"Ah! Excellent! It is not too early to imbibe I think."

Castries grabbed a decanter sitting on the corner of his desk. He poured out two measures of whiskey, handed Ryan a glass.

"To your health and continued good fortune!" Castries offered.

"And to yours, sir! Ahhhh, that is good."

"Irish whiskey, I think," Castries said and smiled. "Captain Ryan, let me begin by saying that the Crown holds you in high esteem. The King and Queen both favor you. I am aware of your recent trials and tribulations. The *Flora* was one of those insignificant incidents that mushroomed into an unforeseeable international crisis. Most unfortunate. No blame to you but Franklin, I am sorry to say, shall not be running any privateers out of France again anytime soon. And I am aware that my predecessor was not, how shall I say? He was not well disposed towards you or your men. But, that is neither here nor there. That is in the past. I am interested in the future."

"Things were done, things to cause me harm. Sartine is an immoral man. He has no honor. But I bare no hard feelings against France or the King. I never made any protest."

"I know."

"I only wish my captains and I could have done more with the good doctor's commissions. We could have caused so much more damage to English shipping."

"Yes. Spoken like a true patriot. I suspected as much and that is why you are here."

"Oh?"

"I am a soldier. You are soldier. There is an invisible bond, a fraternal order if you will, between soldiers, between us. We must look out for one another where and when we can. You have a particular set of skills. These skills are rare and hard to come by. I know talent when I see it and France has need of such talent. Are you at all interested?"

"You have my full attention, sir."

"Excellent. I know you presently have no command, no ship, and that most of your men have moved on to other prospects. So, then, I would like to offer you command of a newly commissioned privateer with a ready crew - in part because I trust you will use her to full advantage and, in part, as reparations for your losses, to redress old wrongs."

"What ship?"

Castries couldn't resist a bit of playfulness with the young Irishman. "Ah, but you know her."

"The *Fearnot?*"

"Ahem, alas, no. I had something else in mind. Something with more punch. I had in mind a frigate."

"A frigate?" Ryan asked, hardly able to contain his glee.

"*Oui*, a frigate. More precisely, *Le Calonne.*"

"*Calonne?* The same vessel -"

"Yes, the same," Castries interrupted with a smile. "Seems only fit and proper to me. There is a certain, um - elegant justice - to it all don't you think? The King has given his blessing already."

"Forgive me my lord Minster but, well, I am not accustomed to such generosity. What is the catch?

"Pardon? The catch?"

"What is expected from me? What price must be paid to the piper? I tell you plainly, sir, I have no money, no resources of my own."

"Ah yes, I know of your troubles with *Monsieur* John Torris and his peculiar circle of investment bankers. I disdain bankers. Perhaps it is because of my own ignorance in financial matters - or more likely it is because they deserve our disdain. Greed is the only thing that seems to motivate such men."

"It is my experience that greed motivates most men."

"How true, how true. Well, I am new to this post and am not altogether yet certain of the full extent of my powers and authority. I may not be in a position to offer you much assistance in collecting what is owed to you or to your men."

"Then, what?"

"Ah, the *quid pro quo*. What I expect from you, Captain Ryan, is success, victory at sea against the hated British. Nothing more, nothing less."

Spring, enchanting, lovely, a shameless flirt, returned to breathe her warm breath across the land, stirring new life into all living things. And with her gentle kiss the Earth turned green and fertile once again. Spring quieted, at least for a season or two, Winter's cold bite, dispelled her angry storms. It is in the midst of such magic that new hope is rekindled in the hearts and minds of men.

Ryan sat at a small table in his hotel room, reviewing the ship's crew list. He recognized only a handful of names. Dowlin and Kelly, and most his Shadowmen, had all taken jobs on other ships to make some money or had traveled back to Ireland to visit family. Jacqueline had left for Lyon to visit her mother. Most of his crew, a compliment of over 250 strong, were men he had never sailed with. They were French, Spanish and Portuguese, rejects from the navy or on the run from some wicked thing. Only a handful were seasoned sailors. Ryan was far more accustomed to serving with men who had worked the sea since boyhood, who understood and cherished the fraternal bonds between comrades-in-arms, who understood obedience and loyalty. His only Irish veteran now was John Kelly.

In Dunkirk's harbor sat a fine frigate, a 600 ton, two-decker armed with 36 heavy guns and registered under the name of *Le Calonne*. Formerly in service with the French navy, she had been recently decommissioned and sold to unnamed, private investors even though she was only several years old. Ryan had inspected the frigate earlier and found her fit in every way.

And yet, he could muster little enthusiasm for the cruise ahead. Castries had been exceedingly good to him so far, providing him with a sound frigate, a crew and provisions. But Castries wasn't Franklin and fighting under French colors was not the same as fighting under the stars and stripes.

John Kelly assembled all hands on deck. On the quarterdeck stood Ryan, looking down upon his crew. He tried to connect with a face or two in the crowd but failed.

"Men, I am Captain Luke Ryan," Ryan said flatly in French and waited for his words to be translated into other languages. "I intend to cruise up the Channel and into the German Ocean. We sail with the tide and shall return I know not when. Lieutenant Kelly here has explained the rules to you already I know and has told you how any prize money is divvied up. This ship sails under royal commission, approved by the King. Any questions? No? Very well. Mr. Kelly, sir, please have all petty officers and officers report to the wardroom in one hour where I will lay out my plans in more detail."

"One hour it is, sir!"

"You may dismiss the men, Mr. Kelly, and make ready to get us under way."

"Aye, sir! Division commanders, dismiss your men and then report to me on the quarterdeck!"

Ryan retired to his great cabin, embarrassed by his own lackluster speech and indifference to the imminent expedition. Worse, a foreboding, not unlike the uneasiness he had experienced on the eve of his last cruise, blurred his thoughts.

Captain Philip Patton was thoroughly enjoying himself. Lamb and roasted carrots, his favorite, had been served for supper along with fresh bread. His steward started clearing away dinner plates to make room for dessert. And following after-dinner cordials, an easy mood settled over the table as his junior officers traded stories about their adventures at sea and savored the last of the wine. The sun, well over the horizon, her power diffused by thin, wispy clouds, peeked in through the great cabin's portside windows. Patton turned to catch a glimpse of sunlight and saw, just barely visible, the silhouette of the mighty 74 gun *Berwick*, an Elizabeth class, Third Rate ship of the line under the command of his best friend, Captain John Ferguson.

Patton's orders were to take his new frigate, *Belle Poule*, and accompany the *Berwick* to Leith Road in Edinburgh. Both *Berwick* and *Belle Poule* had been in service with the Channel Fleet in Torbay but were now reassigned to the North Sea fleet under the command of Rear-Admiral Sir Hyde Parker. The *Poule*, a 36 gun double-decker, was French built, a 650 ton frigate of the *Dédaigneuse* class, but had been captured by the *Nonsuch* the previous July. After being inspected and refitted, the Admiralty had commissioned *Poule* for British military service and had her readied for sea duty barely two months earlier in February. The *Poule* was Patton's first command.

With light breezes and calm seas, the sail from Torbay north to Edinburgh had been a pleasant affair so far. A young midshipman, coming down from the quarterdeck, interrupted dessert to report they had just passed St. Abb's Head and that all was well.

Patton thanked the boy, playfully tossed a hunk of bread his way, and sent him off. He intended to enjoy what he knew might be their last peaceful evening for some time as rumor had it that Admiral Parker intended to sail out against the Dutch immediately. Patton decided he could afford to relax just a little while longer before checking on the watch and rejoined his officers in their idle banter.

Six days out from Dunkirk Road, trolling the waters around the Firth of Forth and looking for merchant ships coming in and out of Edinburgh, the French privateer had failed to take one prize, not even a poor fishing trawler. But then, in the late afternoon of the sixth day, their luck changed and Ryan was smiling again. His decision to sail had been the right one after all.

Off the waters of St. Abb's Head the privateers caught a good prize sailing a bit too close to shore which made her easy prey. She was the Scottish brig *Nancy* from Aberdeen and headed for Newcastle. Her master, a Scot named John Ramsay, was rowed over to the French privateer to negotiate the terms of ransom.

Ryan treated Ramsay to supper first and, with after-dinner cordials in hand, the two captains began to haggle over price. Following some back and forth, Ryan and Ramsay finally settled on a sum of 200 guineas for *Nancy*'s cargo of tea and 100 guineas for the brig herself. Ramsay agreed to remain on board *Calonne* as a hostage without complaint, thanked Ryan for his civility, and signed a ransom bill.

But then, just as the two men were concluding their business and ready to shake hands, they heard the ship's lookout.

"Sails on the horizon, off the port bow - square rigged..." the lookout called down from the masthead, followed seconds later by the sharp *ping-ping-ping!* from the ship's bell.

Ryan raced up the companionway and went directly to the helm. He took his spyglass and searched the waves for sails. Dusk and haze had settled on the ocean like a shadow and visibility was poor.

"What do you make of that vessel, sir?" he asked the officer of the watch, a serious-minded, young Frenchman named Laurent Gossieaux who had shown some promise as a ship's junior lieutenant over the past few days.

"Difficult to know in this poor light, sir," Gossieaux replied thoughtfully. "She's quite a large two-decker though. That much is clear."

Ramsay, having followed Ryan up to the quarterdeck moved next to Ryan. "May I?" he asked.

Ryan handed Ramsay his spyglass and the Scot took a quick look. "Aye, I know her. We passed her by earlier today, though she had three others with her then, and traded words with her crew. She's a Greenland whaler. She's with a whaling fleet headed for the Arctic. She's very large indeed. A far plumper prize than *Nancy!*"

"Possibly," Ryan answered with uncertainty and took his spyglass back from Ramsay for a second look.

John Kelly and another Dunkirk Irishman, a new man named Thomas Coppinger, who had signed onboard *Calonne* as the ship's master just before the privateers set sail, joined Ryan at the helm.

"Watcha thinkin', Luke?" asked John Kelly.

Ryan handed his spyglass over. "Have a look-see for yourself John - what do you think?"

"My she's big. Must be 1500 tons or more. Didn't think they made whalers that big."

"Aye. Mr. Ramsay here says he passed her earlier today. She's a whaler from Greenland headed for the Arctic."

"Oh? Then what's she still doin' out here? No whales in these waters."

"No."

"I'm no expert on whalers, Luke. But she appears to have a lot of port lids for a whaler. Leastwise they look like port lids. Hard to tell in this light. She wears no gun port bands tho', yellow, white or otherwise. Here, Mr. Coppinger, take a look. What say you?"

The new man took the spyglass from the Irish giant. "Whoa... She's huge! She's got to be worth a fortune."

"Thank you, Mr. Coppinger," Ryan snapped, annoyed, and took his spyglass back. "Mr. Kelly asked you," he continued in a testy voice, "about port lids, not for your opinion on the ship's value. Not everything out here on the high sea, sir, is always as it seems..."

Several French sailors, working on the quarterdeck and having overheard both Ramsay's and Coppinger's remarks, spread the word. Soon the whole ship was abuzz with talk, careless talk, that they were about to snag a truly worthy prize, enough to make them all rich. Curiosity brought men topside and ears strained to hear what the captain was planning from the quarterdeck. The main deck was soon crowded with men.

"Your orders, sir," inquired Gossieaux. "We are losing the light. Should we give chase, run out the guns?"

Ryan did a 360-degree sweep of the ocean with his glass, saw no other sails. "Mr. Kelly?"

"Well, sir, since you've asked for my opinion - I'd vote no."

"No?" asked Coppinger indignantly. "I vote yes! Where's the harm in moving in and getting a closer look? 'Tis nearly night and we can turn about and run if we don't like what we see."

"I must agree with Mr. Coppinger," Gossieaux chimed in.

"Mr. Coppinger, Mr. Gossieaux, gentlemen," Ryan began in carefully measured tones. "I don't recall asking either of you for your opinion or of asking for a vote. I thank you for your thoughts, but this is not a democracy."

"Then you do not," asked Gossieaux, "intend to pursue?"

Ryan took one last look at the whaler. "No, I think not. If we find her nearby in the morning, then we shall reconsider."

"But she'll be gone by then!" Coppinger protested forcefully.

"Mr. Coppinger!" Kelly said, his tone rising with anger. "You forget you yourself, sir!"

A voice from the crowd below, an anonymous face, cried out, "Coward!"

"What man just spoke?" Gossieaux demanded. "Step forward I say and show yourself!"

But the crew, now of one mind, answered back with grumbling only.

"Petty officers!" cried out John Kelly. "Form your divisions, now! Those on duty will return to their stations and those not on duty are dismissed and are ordered to go below! I want this deck cleared of any rabble. See to it!"

But no man moved.

"I best go and find the master-at-arms, sir," Kelly said next and clenched his teeth. He was not a happy man.

Kelly's words did not sit well with the assembly on deck, looking more and more like a mob than a crew. Men began to stir and whisper.

"Lieutenant Gossieaux," another faceless voice in the crowd cried out. "Are you with us or against us?"

"That is mutiny!" Ryan shouted, now fuming, and pointed at the rating. "Arrest that man!" But Ryan already knew his order would be ignored. And he instantly realized that he had violated a cardinal rule of command: never issue an order that won't be obeyed - unconditional obedience disintegrates soon after.

"Stand aside, Capt'n, if you're too squeamish," a third man yelled up to the quarterdeck. Dozens of his mates echoed their agreement. "We take that whaler and then can go home - rich men!"

Ryan took in the faces of the men arrayed against him, stared down at them with contempt. "Am I to assume, then, that you all stand as one?"

Gossieaux tapped Ryan on the shoulder. "Capt'n, the tide has turned against us. I beg you, sir, give the order to pursue or, with regret, I will be forced to do it for you."

"*Petite merde*," Kelly muttered scornfully under his breath.

"I'm of a like mind with Mr. Gossieaux, Capt'n," interjected Coppinger.

Kelly grunted and looked at Coppinger with disgust. "Now thar's a revelation..."

"Very well," Ryan said, in a voice loud enough for all to hear. He knew that he could either issue the command himself - or be locked away instead and then Gossieaux or Coppinger would do it for him . "Mr. Kelly, if you please. I'll have the deck cleared for action. Mr. Gossieaux, take us in close and choose *your* boarding party..."

Men then nodded their approval. There were smiles all around and they dispersed, eager to take the whaler as a prize.

"Aye, aye, Capt'n," Kelly answered loudly, but then whispered into Ryan's ear: "I'd like to take some action all right, clear this deck of Frenchmen! This is a sad, black day, Luke..."

"It is indeed, John. I am sorry you had to witness it. But what else can we do?"

"Nothin', except get us back to Dunkirk quick so we can toss these shits in the water and raise a loyal crew..."

The gun crews scrambled to their positions, opened port lids and rolled their heavy guns out while scores of their mates climbed up into the rigging with muskets in hand. Gossieaux maneuvered *Calonne* close in, until they were within hailing distance of the whaler.

"What ship are you?" Coppinger called out from the rail, but there was no response. "Shorten sail, prepare to be boarded or we will fire on you!" But still no one from the whaler answered him.

He looked over at Gossieaux, ignoring Ryan. "A warning shot I think will loosen these Greenlanders' tongues."

Gossieaux nodded and gave the order and BOOM! One shot went flying over the whaler's bow - and then her men moved out smartly to shorten sail.

The whaler came to rest on the glassy sea. Coppinger repeated his question. But again, there was no answer. The Greenlanders lined up along the rails to watch *Calonne* in action, but seemed otherwise clueless what to do.

Coppinger and Gossieaux, bound together in a silent pact to share command, exchanged whispers. Both men nodded.

"Lower away the longboat!" Coppinger bellowed to the coxswain.

Within minutes, Coppinger and forty armed Frenchmen were in the water, rowing towards the whaler - until all hell broke loose...

"She's opening her port lids - she's got guns!" *Calonne's* lookout cried out in panic.

Gossieaux and Ryan rushed to the rail, whipped out their spyglasses and took a look at the whaler - they saw the heavy guns being rolled out on two gun decks. And the whaler's topmen started to work the sails to turn their big ship around. The whaler was still sitting at a right angle to *Calonne* and could not yet bring all her guns to bear...

"Gunners," Gossieaux cried out, prepare to fire a broadside. At my command - FIRE!"

BABABABABOOM! BOOM! BOOM! BOOM!

Balls of ugly iron struck the whaler's hull square on.

And then the mystery ship raised the Union Jack.

"Reload," Gossieaux cried out.

"*Capt'n*," Ryan called out facetiously.

"What?" Gossieaux asked confused and spun around.

"Lieutenant Gossieaux, clearly that ship is no whaler - you've got a third rater on your hands, lad. I'd shake out the reef points and get us out of here quick if I were you, before she brings all her heavy guns to bear. She'll make short work of us when she does..."

"But the longboat, our men..."

"Leave them! You have no time..."

Gossieaux, young and greedy but no fool, knew at once that Ryan was right and quickly gave the order. Topmen shook out sails and worked the braces to get *Calonne* underway.

The British battleship had turned just enough to let loose a partial broadside.

BOOM! BABABABABABABABABABABABOOM! BOOM! BOOM! BOOM!

Large 18 and 32 pound projectiles - an even mix of ruthless, killing iron - crashed into *Calonne*, wreaking havoc at such close range. Lines snapped, wood cracked and splintered and a dozen men fell groaning, victims of painful, ugly wounds.

Gossieaux, no veteran of hard, cruel war, turned to Ryan in panic. He grabbed Ryan by the arm. "Please," he pleaded, horrified by the destruction all around them. "Please help me."

Ryan nodded, wondering to himself, had he just been the victim of history's shortest mutiny? "You take the guns. John, go with Mr. Gossieaux and keep the gunners at it. They don't appear all that well trained to me. Just do your best while I work the helm."

Calonne fired back with her 12-pounders, a full broadside, and did some damage. She began lurching forward as her canvas caught the wind.

British seamen scrambled to get their ship underway too. But the third rater was heavy and cumbersome and slow to move. Her blunt bow could only punch through the water.

As French topmen dropped and trimmed sails, *Calonne* picked up more speed and the smaller, more agile frigate quickly started pulling away from the big bruiser.

Ryan took the ship's wheel himself, brought the frigate a full 180 degrees about and headed south to pick up a stronger breeze. He did his best to give the British as small a target as possible too. Still, British gunners managed to fire off a few of their forward main guns along with a matching pair of nine pounders positioned at the forecastle. A half dozen balls smashed in and around *Calonne's* stern, blowing out windows and decimating Ryan's great cabin. But soon, despite her crew's best efforts, the ominous battleship, never once a whaler, fell further and further behind until her guns were out of range.

Calonne's men breathed a sigh of relief, secured their guns and thanked their lucky stars. Too bad about their forty mates all agreed. Such is life, *c'est la vie*, men said and shrugged.

But as men congratulated each other and thoughts turned to celebration, and home, the lookout raised a new warning.

"Sail ho! Two points off the stern, portside!" the man called down to the deck below, jolting all his mates.

John Kelly and Gossieaux rushed back to the quarterdeck.

"It appears, gentlemen," Ryan said dryly and handed his spyglass over to John Kelly, "we have a second ship to worry about. A British frigate. She's sleek and fast and it appears her captain would like to meet us - observe..."

Gossieaux and the Irish giant raised their spyglasses to view the new threat.

"Where the devil did she come from, Luke?" John Kelly asked.

"She must have been sitting beyond the third rater, out of sight, when poor Mr. Coppinger set off on his little adventure. Even so, how our eagle-eyed lookout could have missed her from the masthead is something of a mystery. Hardly a surprise the battleship brought an escort with her to the party tho'."

"No," replied John Kelly softly as he looked up at the masts and sails. "No surprise there. And she's got the wind over us."

"Aye. Perhaps more troublesome, she's between us and the open sea and she'll soon have us pinned against the shore. No place to maneuver. We'll need to slug our way out of this jam I fear - if we can. Gentlemen, see to your guns..."

It did not take the British frigate, a swift 30 gunner of the French *Dédaigneuse* class, long to pull up alongside *Calonne* and open fire with half of her armament, thirteen 12-pounders and two 6-pounders. The two frigates traded broadside after broadside. Some of Ryan's Frenchmen recognized the frigate and sent word up to the quarterdeck that they were facing the *Belle Poule*, a French ship - until her capture by the British the year before. The name meant nothing to Ryan.

The two frigates, evenly matched and sailing leisurely south, exchanged heavy shot with neither ship able to inflict a mortal blow. The British seemed content to keep their prey boxed-in against the shore, to keep her from reaching the open sea, and did not try to move in.

The duel went on for an hour or so until night closed in around them and then French spirits rebounded. The darkness would save them all. Privateers excelled at slipping away from trouble in the dark. But then, on the near horizon, off their starboard bow, muzzle flashes lit up the night sky - a second ship had sailed ahead and cut them off! Truly the privateers were cursed this day!

Slower than a frigate, but catching a better wind further out at sea, the British battleship had finally managed to close with the pair of fighting cruisers.

Calonne's thick planks had warded-off *Belle Poule's* punishing 12-pound blows well-enough, but now *Berwick's* 18 and 32 pound balls came raining down around them. Huge geysers of water shot up in the air, dashing any hopes of escape.

Trapped against the shore by two deadly warships - the British outgunned the privateers by more than three-to-one in heavy cannon and men - and with no room to maneuver, Ryan knew the game was up. He had no tricks left to play.

He gave the ugly order to shorten sail, to strike their colors, before the *Berwick* could fire-off another broadside that might send them to the bottom. No man raised a contrary word...

Patton, his first command, his very first time out as captain, marveled as he watched the privateers shorten sail and haul down their flag. He had taken a French frigate! He could barely contain his glee and tried to work off his exuberance by strutting around the quarterdeck.

Patton sent his first officer in the ship's launch over to the French frigate. He was to fetch the frigate's captain and all her officers. Patton had in mind to be magnanimous in victory, to treat his prisoners cordially and as honored guests. Privateers or not, these men had fought bravely, skillfully, and with honor after all.

And there on the quarterdeck, standing tall, Patton watched his boarding party pull at their oars, heading towards his prize. His men soon returned with a dozen privateers in custody. Patton started pacing up and down the deck again with nervous energy as the crew went about securing guns, lighting the ship's lanterns and making repairs.

As the Frenchmen stepped aboard his ship, Patton greeted each one in turn with a warm handshake. But then, just as he was about to lead them all down to his great cabin for drinks and polite conversation, *Berwick* raised a string of lanterns and signal flags. Patton excused himself and called for his signal book, assuming his best friend was sending him his hardy congratulations.

But Captain Ferguson sent no congratulations, not yet. Ferguson signaled Patton instead that he had just captured the infamous Irish pirate and murderer, Luke Ryan! After the *Berwick's* men had fished Coppinger and his boarding party out of the sea, Coppinger had gladly spilled his guts to Ferguson, hoping to save his own neck.

Patton handed the signal book to the officer of the watch and called for his master-at-arms. There would be no drinks, no polite chitchat after all. He had the privateers clapped in irons instead.

"Which one of you is Luke Ryan?" he asked as marines shackled each prisoner.

There was no reason to deny who he was. Someone had talked and so Ryan took one step forward.

"That would be me, Captain."

"Well, well," Patton said with no charity in his tone and staring coldly into Ryan's face. "Your days of lawlessness are done my friend and the day of your reckoning is at hand. You can expect a quick trial for high treason my dear fellow, followed by your prompt execution to atone for your sins. Smyth, take the prisoners below. No food, no water until we put in at Leith Road."

The master-at-arms made a knuckle and led Ryan and his men, and none too gently, below in chains.

After two years of unchecked terror, after two years of frustration, failure and humiliation, the British Navy finally had their man.

Ryan brooded as he sat in the dark, chained inside the ship's rope locker. He had only space enough to sit. The locker was damp and suffocating in the heat and stank of bilge water. He closed his eyes and thought of Shannon. He would see her sooner than he had imagined. There was comfort in that at least.

And then again, the long enduring mariner, soldier of cunning, wanderer on the open seas, suddenly felt very much alone and empty. To claim he had no regrets would be a lie. He was a man with no family, no home, no country, no land to call his own. A man's life should not be forfeit this way he told himself and, if nothing else, he deserved a better end.

Their adventure into smuggling had started out as something fun - a way to make some money. But down life's road there are often many unexpected twists and turns and through circumstances beyond their reckoning, the adventure of the Irishmen took a turn, a turn no one had expected. Fate, chance, destiny, the hand of a higher power - call it what you will - Ryan and his men were swept up by the wind, winds of ruthless change, and found themselves pursuing far more than just silver and gold. Fate had led them to share in something rare and fine - a struggle for a noble cause, a fight to the death to establish a new nation, a nation of free men in a world that had known little more than iron-fisted tyranny.

Ryan was grateful he had been a part of that. In his mind, he was an American, in his heart he was, a patriot...

The mariner stared through the iron bars of great Edinburgh Castle to catch a glimpse of the world outside. Magnificent Orion, mighty hunter with bow in hand and a favorite of the gods - dazzling to behold - led the celestial giants in their great wheeling turn across the vast, imponderable heavens. The mid-night air settling over the city below the castle was chilly. The world was silent and at peace with itself.

He could see her bright, angelic face and found comfort in that at least. Ryan wondered whether he might really ever see her again. *Yes*, he decided and smiled. He was certain he would see his Shannon again in the next life and held tightly on to that warm thought. Once they had broken and hanged his body, his soul would be free, free to fly from England and a miserable world poisoned with pain and sorrow, free to fly to Shannon's side. The English had no power to keep him, not forever. How he longed to hold her in his arms again, to kiss her shining face.

He shook his head, wiped away a lone tear. *A man could go mad dwelling on such things* he muttered to himself in a low voice. But then he scolded himself. He needed to be strong for the difficult road that lay ahead.

He turned away from the window and took in the stark, stone walls of his prison cell. This life, he knew, was finished. He had failed miserably. He had squandered all of God's great gifts, had let life's precious treasures slip through his fingers like so many flakes of gold dust. His life had been a fraud, a sham.

If only, he mused, a man could live his life again, have a fresh start. If only he could be allowed to tarry in this world, just a while longer, to set things right, to make amends. All men deserve a crack at redemption Ryan told himself. All men, born flawed and in a world steeped in imperfection, deserve to learn from their mistakes. Every man, prince or pauper, deserves a second chance...

Epilogue
The Last of an Old Sailor's Tale

s the first shafts of light of a new day peeked through the tavern's small windows, North Wind ceased her mindless rage. The nor'easter had spent its strength and quit its siege against the small town of Newport. The young reporter set his quill pen down and looked at his fingers, smudged with black ink and aching from the long hours of writing. He began massaging them and stared at the large stack of disorganized papers in front of him with his notes scribbled on the front and back of each page. Crook then stretched his arms. The old man had talked straight through the night with barely a pause.

"Remarkable. Truly a remarkable story, Mr. Trevett. Do you remember the last time you saw Luke Ryan?"

The old man's lips curled into a sly smile. "Aye."

"And? My sense of it is that you didn't see him after *Cologne* was taken."

"Oh no, sir, that an't right, not right at all. Let me sees now, the last I ever seen of Ryan? Hm, that would have been around the summer of '95 I suspect."

Crook raised an eyebrow at that and gave Trevett a hard look. This was the first obvious error Trevett had made and raised concerns for Crook.

"1795, you say?"

Trevett removed his cap and ran his fingers through his long, flowing stands of silver hair.

"Aye, that's what I said. That's what I meant, laddie."

"But Mr. Trevett, that can't possibly be correct," Crook protested. "Even you said that Ryan died in debtor's jail, in the King's Bench Prison in London in 1789. His death was reported in all the London papers."

"Aye, so I did," replied Trevett smiling. "So I did, indeed. That is what the papers said true enough. I was sailin' on small lugger back in 'em days, the *Eleanor Ann & Me*, earnin' money to make me way back home. The *Eleanor Ann* was a packet ship makin' smooth and easy runs between Dublin and Liverpool. One of the passengers, a gentleman, just before we disembarked, came up behind me and tapped me on the shoulder with his cane. I don't recall now whether we were on the Dublin side or in Liverpool. Don't matter. I turned to see who had touched me. The man smiled at me and winked. Odd that was. I didn't recognize him at first mind you. He was dressed real fine, in gentleman's clothes, like yerself. He had a beard. Black and gray it was. The beard, that's what threw me off. The man's eyes though... Ah, ha. They was intelligent and deep blue like the sea, a trifle sad too. And his smile, well, it was the kind of smile a man makes when he's young and cocky, when he thinks he's got the world by the tail. I knew 'em eyes and I knew that smile! No mistaken that face I tell you plainly, beard or no. I stared at him for a bit and he just kept grinning at me. He knew I had finally come to recognize him and he put a finger to his lips. He squeezed my arm firm in friendship and then turned and walked away, went down the gangplank and out of sight, waving his hand as he did so. Last I ever seen of him. It was Luke Ryan sure enough."

"Are you certain of that, Mr. Trevett? The mind can play tricks. What I mean to say, sir, is you could have been mistaken about who this gentleman was, or, if it was indeed Ryan you saw perhaps you are mistaken about the year. Yes. Perhaps you have the year wrong. The newspapers..."

"I wouldn't give ya a witch's cold tit in December for what is in the papers, laddie! Exceptin' of course when they wrote stories about *Black Prince*. *Gawd*, how we loved to read about ourselves in 'em papers! What a hoot. Anyways, I know what I saw. And I know what year it was. Thar's no mistake. I an't feeble-minded and I an't the only one who seen him after '89 either. You believe what you will. You had to have known Luke Ryan. I heard he spent some time in France durin' their revolution, doin' what I do not know. It would be just like him to be gettin' himself involved in someone else's *noble cause*. Anyhows, that man was too clever by half to rot away in some stinkin' British prison. He would have found a way out. Always kept some ready plan tucked away inside his hip pocket just in case he needed to get himself or his mates out of a spot of trouble. Whatever corpse the jailer buried in '89 wasn't Ryan's."

"I see," said Crook, still unsure.

"Oh, dear me - I forgot to mention the ring, didn't I?"

"Ring, what ring?"

"The man I saw that day wore a gold ring on his small finger, a very unique ring, a Claddah Ring and one of a kind; the very one Shannon had given to Luke Ryan..."

Crook sat back in his chair and let out a deep sigh. "You are certain?"

"I have no cause to lie to you Mr. Crook. I knew that ring."

"Amazing, truly an amazing story."

"Glad you think so, young fella. They was amazin' times to be sure. And I wouldn't trade you one good memory of those days for all the whiskey in Ireland..."

"Indeed. Well then, perhaps I need to redouble my research efforts and try to dig deeper, see if I can pick up Ryan's trail after '95 if indeed, as you say, he was alive back then."

"You do that, Mr. Crook. I'm certain you won't be disappointed."

"May I call upon you again if needed, to tie up any loose ends?"

"If you can find me - and if yer buyin' - most certainly, aye..."

Separating Fact from Fiction

This book is a weave of both fact and fiction. Because we have been left with only a thin historical record, the author has taken artistic license to 'fill-in-the-gaps,' to romanticize true events to both entertain and educate.

So what do we really know about Benjamin Franklin's audacious Irish mariners? Well, precious little (Franklin's letters, reproduced in a number of books, offer some color and for pure history there is William Bell Clark's book *Ben Franklin's Privateers* (Baton Rouge: Louisiana State University Press, 1956) and for a pure historical account about Old Mill and Forton prisons see Sheldon Samuel Cohen's excellent book: *Yankee Prisoners in British Gaols: Prisoners of War at Forton and Mill, 1777 - 1783* (University of Delaware Press 1995)).

We all know who the great Ben Franklin was. Ryan and his two captains, Dowlin and Macatter, were real people. Marchant was indeed an unemployed American captain used by Ryan to dupe Franklin. The descriptions of Ryan's Irishmen are fictional accounts of mostly real people.

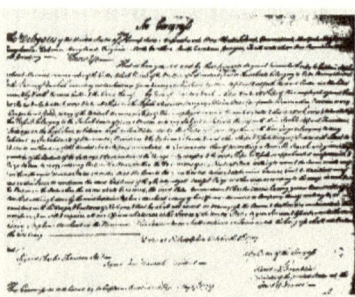

Franklin's 1779 Commission for the *Black Prince*

The O'Keeffes are fictional characters although certainly Ryan must have had good business contacts in Ireland and good political connections in France to run his smuggling operation. David Sartine is also fictional (Count de Sartine was real, as was the Marquis de Castries - both men served King Louis as Minister of Marine, Castries replacing Sartine after the king forced Sartine into early retirement). Crook, Dupery, Roberts, Perkins, Joyce, Bragg, Smarly, Harding, Conroy, O'Henry, Gossieaux, Jean, Piccardi, Jacqueline and Doumar are all fictional characters and, while black sailors were not uncommon during this period, Jumbaaliyia is fictional too.

Poreau, Coffyn and Guilman were all real people. Coffyn was indeed Franklin's trusted agent and he did all that he could to help Ryan. And Guilman was indeed the *Calonne's* mischievous captain who inexplicably ran the *Black Prince* down in front of some 2,000 witness from Berck who came down to the shore to watch the battle.

John Trevett was a real person and served as a lieutenant in the Continental Navy. As it happens, Trevett is the one man we know of who served with both John Paul Jones and Luke Ryan. When asked to compare the two men, Trevett said plainly that he had sailed with many brave men but "...none of them are equal to this Captain Luke Ryan for skill and bravery." High praise indeed from an expert in naval warfare who was an eye witness.

Cowdry and Conyngham were also real people. The escape from Old Mill by forty Americans is a true historical event as was the daring escape of 21 Americans from Pembroke Castle in a stolen sloop led by Midshipman Charles Collins. Thomas Coppinger sailed with Ryan on the *Calonne* and stood trial for piracy with him.

Captain Gustavus Conyngham
Continental Navy Engraving contemporary to the American
Revolution
The inscription reads: "The Original Sketch which was taken by an
Artist of Eminence, and stuck up in the English Coffee House at
Dunkirk."

As for the ships depicted in the book, *Le Toulon, St. Vincent, Lyon, Night Angel, Eleanor Ann & Me* and the slaver, from which Jumbaaliyia was liberated, are figments of the author's imagination. All other ships described in the book are authentic. For example, the incident between Ryan and the Scot, who indeed was entertaining guests on his yacht, was reported in the London Chronicle (September 5/7, 1780). The Chronicle quoted the laird as saying that he had been treated "...in the most agreeable and genteelest manner I could expect from an enemy." The other materials quoted from English and French papers are accurate as well. Ryan's victories over the British warships *Spry, Townsend* and *Friends* were real - a remarkable feat of arms by any measure.

The *Belle Poule*, the frigate that captured *Calonne*, was originally a French frigate of the *Dédaigneuse* class, designed and built by Léon-Michel Guignace in 1767 in Bordeaux and, as a point of interest, is the ship that returned Franklin back to America in 1778.

Belle Poule in a duel with the *HMS Arethusa* (June 18, 1778)
Artist: unknown

During the night of July 15, 1780, the 64-gun ship of the line *HMS Nonsuch* engaged *Belle Poule* off Île d'Yeu. The two ships fought for several hours until *Belle Poule's* commanding officer, Chevalier Kergariou, was killed and his crew surrendered. The British navy then commissioned *Belle Poule* (keeping the same name) in February 1781 - just weeks before she fought *Calonne*.

Warships were classified or rated by size and by the number of guns. The British navy used six classifications, from First Rate to Sixth Rate.

First Rate ships were the largest ships of the fleet. These were the super, three-decker battleships armed with over 100 heavy guns (mostly 32 and 24 pounders) and typically served as flagships fighting in the center of the line-of-battle. First Rate ships had crews of about 850 men and measured over 2000 tons in Builder's Measure (a formula for calculating the capacity of the ship, not the displacement of the ship as is the practice nowadays).

Second Rate ships of the line were also large three-deckers but were smaller, cheaper versions of the First Rates. They mounted between 90 and 98 heavy guns (32 and 18 pounders) and had crews of about 750 men and also measured around 2000 tons (BM). Second Rate vessels had a reputation for poor handling and slow sailing.

Third Rate ships of the line were the mainstay of the battle fleet. These were two-deckers armed with between 64 to 80 heavy guns (32 and 18 pounders) with crews of between 600 to 650 men and measured about 1650 tons (BM).

Fourth Rate ships were also two-deckers but carried only about 50 to 60 guns (mostly 18 pounders) with crews of about 350 men and measured around 1000 tons (BM).

Fifth Rate ships were the frigates, the Navy's glamour ships, with their main armament on a single gun deck. These were the fast scouts of the battle fleet. Fifth Rates typically carried about 32 guns (12 or 18 pounders) but some were armed with up to 38 guns with crews of between 250 to 300 men and measured between 700 to 1450 tons (BM).

Sixth Rate ships were small, lightly armed frigates carrying between 22 and 28 guns (nine pounders) with a crew of about 150 men and measured 450 to 550 tons (BM).

Unrated vessels included sloops, brigs, bomb vessels, gunboats and cutters and were commanded by more junior officers (commanders, lieutenants). A rated ship was always a captain's command. Sloops-of-war or brigs were 380 tons or less and typically armed with 10 to 18 guns with a crew of about 120 men. Bomb vessels (usually two-masted ketches) were armed with mortars for shore bombardment and first used by the French in the late 17th century. Gunboats were small, two-masted vessels and used for anti-invasion patrol. Cutters were typically single or two masted vessels built for speed and employed as patrol boats and dispatch carriers.

The accounts of how Ryan was captured vary somewhat. The British account seems the most accurate, that Ryan was in command of the French frigate *Calonne* and captured by the *Belle Poule* and *Berwick* sailing together near Edinburgh. The Edinburgh Courant reported the incident on the following day as follows:

> "*Yesterday morning, about two o'clock, the Berwick man-of-war fell in with Le Calonne, privateer of Dunkirk, the noted Luke Ryan commander, four miles off St Abb's Head. The Calonne struck at half-past eight. Ryan is now in irons. His crew are a mixture of French, Yankies, Scotch, Irish and a solitary Dutchman, who was pilot.*"

It is, however, hard to imagine how a man like Ryan could have mistaken a monster Royal Navy Third Rate ship of the line - a 74-gun two-decker with bright yellow gun bands - for a whaler and thus the author's concoction of French intrigue and a mutinous crew. Consider too that *Berwick* and *Belle Poule* were sailing to Edinburgh to join the North Sea fleet, not out looking for privateers, and just happened upon *Calonne*, so it seems improbable that the British would have been enough time to disguise either ship to try and fool Ryan. (As an interesting aside, Ryan supposedly was in command of a French privateer named *Tartar* prior to *Calonne* and managed to capture an unnamed British frigate sometime in late 1780 (as reported in the January 6, 1781 edition of *Finn's Leinster Journal* published in Kilkenny, Ireland).)

There is at least a whiff of evidence that French treachery may have been at least partially involved in Ryan's capture. We will perhaps never know the whole truth of it. There is no question though that the French government wanted to put an end to Franklin's private navy and certainly Guilman's attack on the *Prince*, an allied ship, in view of several thousand witnesses near Berck, was bizarre to say the least.

Whatever the truth, we do know that Ryan (as we will learn in *Napoleon's Gold*) was extradited to England and taken to London where he stood trial for piracy before the High Court of the Admiralty in the Old Bailey on March 30, 1782 where he was convicted by a jury for "Felony and Piracy on the High Seas." The trial was long and much publicized. Thomas Coppinger appears to have cut a deal with the prosecutor as he testified against Ryan and was acquitted. The court sentenced Ryan to hang at Execution Dock on May 14, 1782 (according to another account Ryan was initially sentenced to be 'caged' - a particularly gruesome end for a prisoner where he (or she) is partially strangled, taken in chains to a cage suspended above the Thames River and allowed to slowly drown as high tide rolled in).

King George commuted Ryan's death sentence to imprisonment (presumably for an indefinite term) after receiving a personal plea from Queen Antoinette to spare Ryan's life. After the war was lost, Lord North's government fell and a more tolerant Parliament pardoned all American prisoners, including Ryan. Ryan was thereafter released from Newgate Castle on February 9, 1784.

Charles Eugène Gabriel de La Croix de Castries, marquis de Castries -
appointed French Minister of Marine on October 13, 1780 following
Count de Sartine's (forced) retirement
Artist: Joseph Boze (1746 - 1826)

Finally, John Torris was also a real person. Apparently, he and/or his associates pocketed all the money the privateers had made. After Ryan's release from prison, he returned to France and petitioned the French courts seeking restitution from Torris for the money Torris owed Ryan and his men but it was too late. The Flemish businessman was bankrupt by then and was tossed into debtor's prison.

I have ascribed (or embellished on) certain uncharitable characteristics to some of the real people described in this book for fun for which there is either little evidence or is fiction. There was no intent to disparage the memory of anyone.

According to British accounts, Ryan returned to England and ended up in the King's Bench Prison in London (for failing to pay a doctor for inoculating his children from small pox) where he died on June 18, 1789 from septicemia. Others say that Ryan never returned England but remained in France, where he became a French citizen, and accepted a commission as a *capitaine de navires par le roi*.

Little is known about the fate of Dowlin (a/k/a "Dowling") or Macatter (a/k/a McCarty or Captain Wilde). We do know that Macatter was captured six months after Ryan and also tried, convicted and released. After Ryan was caught, Dowlin accepted a lieutenant's commission in the French navy but was soon cashiered for his horrendous drinking and womanizing. In September 1781, Dowlin took command of the French privateer *Fantasie* and seized a number of prizes, including the Belfast brig *Bell*, which appears to be one of the last ships taken during the war.

Even less is known about the fate of Ryan's men. We do know that John Kelly was given command of the French privateer *Dreadnought* and had some success operating out of Dunkirk for a time.

After Ryan relieved him of command, Marchant returned to Martha's Vineyard on February 16, 1780 (after no one in France would employ him) and he was not shy about telling the Boston papers about his accomplishments as captain of the *Black Prince*. Arnold, Marchant's inept first officer, escaped from Old Mill Prison to France and was eventually given command of a French privateer. His conduct was so abysmal that no investor "...was willing to confide a vessel to him after this experience."

Some historians have downplayed the significance of the privateers on the impact of the war. But, if we could ask the grand old doctor his opinion, Franklin would probably very much disagree. He considered the contribution of his "Dunkirk privateers" to America's final victory very significant indeed and boasted after the war, with no lack of pride, that *his* privateers were "...manned by old smugglers, who knew every creek on the coast of England, and, running all round the island, distressed the British coasting trade exceedingly."

The results speak for themselves. When the war began, America had no navy. In 1777, the Continental Navy had only 34 cruisers in service and by 1782, the fleet had dwindled to a mere seven ships. Privateers were used to augment this meager force and before the war's end, tens of thousands of men in hundreds of privateers ventured into hazardous waters against the most powerful navy in the world and sank or captured 16 British warships and well over 2,000 British merchant ships.

Of that total, Franklin's privateers were responsible for taking a total of 114 enemy vessels (the *Black Prince* took 35 enemy ships, the

Black Princess 43 enemy ships (the *Prince* and the *Princess* sailing together took 20 enemy vessels) and *Fearnot* took another 16 enemy ships). A number of other British ships were damaged and an unknown number of British seamen were killed or wounded. These statistics are impressive by any measure.

But even these numbers, as incredible as they are, do not tell the whole story. The Royal Navy sent out as many as 40 frigates at various times to hunt Ryan down, diverting precious naval resources from other theaters of war. And, as any businessman knows, skyrocketing insurance rates can rob profits faster than the fiercest competitor and bring financial disaster. Maritime insurance rates in England nearly tripled during Ryan's reign of terror, partially paralyzing British trade - the very blood of the Empire - and wreaked havoc on London's financial markets. (According to the British House of Lords during a debate in February 1778, American privateers had captured or destroyed 733 British prizes with cargoes valued in excess of £2 million and by 1783, the Admiralty informed the House of Lords that American privateers had cost the British merchant navy more than an estimated £8 million in damages.)

The total price tag to the British military in men and ships deployed to guard the coasts or used to hunt the privateers down is unknown but it was significant and the drain on the Empire's morale to prosecute the war should not be underestimated. Ryan took the war home to the British and caused panic throughout the kingdom.

Evidence of the panic Ryan and his men caused throughout the British Isles still survive. The following minutes, were taken on February 10, 1780 at meeting of the Concillors of Capbeltown on the Kintrye peninsula in Scotland:

> "Having taken under consideration that at present the Town of Campbeltown is in a defenceless situation should any of the French or American Privateers that so frequently cruise in the neighbouring creeks and channells make any attempt to plunder or impose contributions upon the town and that from the local situation of the Burrow it is very liable to be insulted by

those Privateers and therefore the more necessary to make application for a proper Military Force to defend such dangerous designs should they be attempted, it is therefore the unanimous resolution of the Magistrates and Council to Represent this matter to his Grace the Duke of Argyll and Request that he may be pleased to apply to Government for a sufficient Military Force and Liberty to erect Batterys sufficient for the protection of the Burrow as well as a sufficient number of Cannon and quantity of ammunition for those Batterys. For this purpose the Magistrates are hereby appointed a Committee with power to them to inform his Grace that the Burrow shall be at the Expense of building the necessary Batterys for such Guns as shall be sent them which they hereby bind and oblige themselves in the name of the Community to defray the said Committee being also full authorised to Explain to his Grace every other particular relative to this application and the Force necessary to protect the Burrow."

The request was favorably received and on 8th May 1780 it was reported:

"The Magistrates and Councillors having presented to this meeting of Councill a letter from his Grace the Duke of Argyle reporting that the Board of Ordnance have agreed at his Graces request to allow Six Twelve or Eighteen Pounders for the Defence of Campbeltown and that the Conditions upon which Guns and Stores have been hitherto sent by His Majesty's Orders for the Defence of Places on the Sea Coast are that the Inhabitants shall erect Batterys or Platforms upon which the Guns are to be placed, Provide the Houses for the safekeeping of the Stores which are sent with the Guns and furnish a proper proportion of Powder all at their own expense and the Board observe another customary stipulation which is that the Guns and Stores cannot be sent till information is given that these conditions are complied with and the Battery and Platforms are ready to receive the Guns.

"The Magistrates and Council of Campbeltown actuated by a lively feeling of His Graces Extensive Pattronage of the Community beg leave to present to His Grace their most grateful return of thanks for his benevolent attention through the various negociations of procuring aid from Government for the safety and protection of the town....In pursuance of these considerations and in order to relieve his Grace of his engagements for the town and to convey information to the Ordnance Board of their readiness to submit to the above conditions prescribed to them the Magistrates and Councill have unanimously agreed for themselves and in behalf of the community to erect and make fit for receiving six twelve or eighteen pounders Batterys or platforms sufficient for the Temporary Defence of the Town and Harbour against the predatory insults of the Enemy's Privateers."

One battery, known as the South Battery, was placed above the Red Quarry. The other was placed at the foot of Limecraigs Avenue. Ryan and his men never raided Capbeltown.

And so the contributions of American privateers during the war are worth more than a historical footnote and Franklin's Irish privateers were the most successful of these raiders. For over 18 months Franklin's small navy seriously disrupted British trade with the rest of the world. And these daring feats were accomplished at no cost to the United States in money or in manpower. No one, arguably not even John Paul Jones, caused more harm to English maritime interests than Franklin's privateers.

But more important to Franklin than the sea battles were the hundreds of British prisoners Ryan and his men took, giving Franklin the leverage he needed to force the British government into prisoner exchanges. The sufferings of Franklin's "unfortunate countrymen" held in British gaols weighed heavily on him throughout the war.

Benjamin Franklin (in 1778)
Artist: Joseph Siffred Duplessis (1725 - 1802)

And the principal architect of all this chaos? Well, now, that would be a certain cunning young lion with nerves of steel, a man who had never been to America, but found reason enough to fight for her liberty at the risk of his own and who, somehow, managed to inspire hundreds of others to fight with him for little more than a taste of glory. That man would be Luke Ryan, Irish swashbuckler and smuggler, fugitive from British justice, privateer extraordinaire and a true, selfless hero of the American Revolution...

www.ingramcontent.com/pod-product-compliance
Lightning Source LLC
Chambersburg PA
CBHW051315250626
47155CB00007B/2329